MW01234668

REVENGE

FACTOR

J.D. STARK

Copyright © 2011 by James D. Stark
All rights reserved.

ISBN: 1-4663-3737-0
ISBN-13: 978-1-4663-3737-4
LCCN: 2011916773
CreateSpace, North Charleston, SC

ACKNOWLEDGMENTS

Thank you first of all to my wife and sons for their ongoing inspiration and support, and to my brother and artist John, niece Jennifer, and Brett Coleman for their outstanding artistic work designing and developing the book cover depicting very appropriately what *Revenge Factor* is about.

Revenge Factor, although based on a historical event, is a fictional interpretation of events taking place during and after. I have drawn on and am especially indebted to the work of the following on Japanese culture and characteristics: *Viking Fund Publications in Anthropology*, edited by Robert J. Smith and Richard K. Beardsley in 1962, *Japan Patterns of Continuity* by Fosco Maraini, 1971, and *Day One – Before Hiroshima and After* by Peter Wyden, 1984.

Any views expressed in this novel are mine, not theirs, and to remind the reader that it has been over sixty years since the first use of an atomic bomb during a war. Many suffered immensely from that day in our world history. I could never imagine what it was like for anyone to experience the happenings surrounding a major, catastrophic event like this one. As such, I hope and pray no one will ever have to experience anything of this magnitude again.

REVENGE FACTOR

By J. D. Stark

A young boy of eleven, living near Hiroshima, Japan, in 1945, has no idea what is about to befall him, his family, or his country in just a few days. Living life to its fullest as a young boy is what Asao Ankawa looks forward to every day. A personally beneficial twist of fate takes him away from home just in time, but he will soon lose his mother, father, sister Yuan Mei, little brother Massey, his best friend Hiroshi, his grandparents, future wife Miki Okuno, and thousands of his countrymen to a devastating weapon of mass destruction. The horrific fate befalling all of them is more than he can come to grips with in mind and soul. As he struggles to handle the guilt of not being where he was supposed to be when it all happened, he will make uncompromising decisions dramatically affecting his life and futuristically the life of many others. Years later, he is determined to push ahead in his quest to punish those he holds responsible. And as he plans his revenge, execution of that plan throws his current family into total disarray, with the possibility of destroying it as well. A counterplot by Robert and Kirk Carrigan he may not see in time to stop, from those he thought he could trust, could totally circumvent everything he is trying to accomplish. As four young heroes step into his direct line of fire, their lives are suddenly and irreversibly altered. Jason and Josh Cade, Danielle (Danny) Wilson, and Mark Anderson (later discovered to be the son of Ankawa) are quickly thrown in front of this very large, fast-moving plan to destroy their country. Innocent as they were before their lives were changed, their innocence has been completely violated and lost in life-and-death matters of extreme national importance. As these four find they are alone against all odds, they will quickly see that even someone in their midst may not be totally reliable. What quietly transpires within one man's desire for revenge during the fifty–year period between 1945 and 1995 will most likely be the result of another major world catastrophe. The revenge factor embedded in one man's life will intensely transform any ordinary existence to one of extreme suffering with potentially long-term horrific consequences.

CHAPTER 1

AUGUST 3, 1945
HIROSHIMA, JAPAN

Three days before "Little Boy," eleven-year-old Asao begins the journey of his life. As he and his uncle ride away on the motorbike, the moment carries great significance for both, decidedly more so for Asao. He will never again talk with big sister Yuan Mei...never again hear the childish taunting from little brother Massey...never again share a make-believe world he and best friend Hiroshi visit almost daily. Their battles against formidable, though overmatched American fighter squadrons, will be a part of life he now, unknowingly leaves behind forever.

Slowly disappearing behind an increasing density of dust stirred and pushed into the warm morning air by the motor-bike's tires, the only home he has ever known becomes a final picture forever etched in his young mind. As he glances over his shoulder one last time, the small farmhouse fades from view as the bike carrying the two descends the crest of the final hill. Succumbing to their increasing speed and gaining momentum, they glance at the farmhouse as it appears to sink into the horizon, much like a normal Japanese sunset at the end of a day. His home, family, friends—as the distance grows between them—all will be gone from his life forever.

Any sensibility he is about to experience, as innocent as it may now seem, will haunt him for all remaining days of his life. Years from now, this boy's emotions will act as the impetus in driving a grown man's desire for substantial, undeniable retribution...a most exact revenge. Asao's happy, carefree life, taken for granted by one so young, will soon be lost in a proud country's struggle for survival in the face of destruction. Unabated, he will be driven...driven by a recurring nightmare, a nightmare surprisingly charged with guilt. Intrinsically he will assume the position as standard-bearer for his former compatriots; silently, patiently, he will one day carry the shield as their, and most importantly, his, family's avenger.

Planning a devastating retaliation against the country he holds solely responsible for his great loss, Asao will spend years under a self-induced, guilt-driven psychological torture. Fifty-some years into the future, one man's life will find dedication to that complete and just revenge. Millions will once again be endangered. As will thousands of Japanese children soon suffer, die, experience hell's inferno, so will children of a future America...so will they one day know the pain of a devastating loss, a horrendous suffering. There can be no other way. There can be no revenge more sweet or appropriate. There can be nothing less than this in his plan to gain the satisfaction he will seek. His plan will be successful. The "revenge factor" will take over and consume his existence...become that integral force in his life no other will be able to control. In a matter of days, this "all boy," child of eleven, will be forced into a darker, more sinister world unknown to him now.

Good-byes behind, the two are mere seconds into their journey. Asao's visit, a visit planned for one week's duration, has the young boy in a state of brisk anticipation.

However, those feelings are about to give way to an immediate pain, a pain emanating from within his small stomach...pain he may years later believe came to him as a warning, a warning of significance he failed to heed. For now, the young boy's self-diagnosis determines it to be nothing more than hunger, something with which he quite readily knows how to cope.

Stomach pain persisting, he reaches for a small cloth pouch strapped to the side of his uncle's bike, just in front of his right knee. It takes only seconds to find the treasure he seeks. Of certain medicinal value, the small juicy berries he now holds in his hand as it emerges from the bag, find their way, one by one, two by two into his small mouth. Promptly deciding to test his mouth's capacity with all that remain in his hand, he soon proves his diagnosis correct. Pain gone, the flavor of ripe berries inspire and stimulate thoughts of yesterday.

Unable to avoid an enormous hole in the road, the bike unexpectedly plunges downward, then lurches to the left, nearly throwing both Asao and his uncle to the ground. The bike's sudden deviation from its course on the road surprises the boy, forcing him to grab for his uncle's waist. Shaken from his thoughts momentarily, Asao secures himself.

Settled once again, he closes his eyes, allowing completion of his mental transfer to the previous day, a day that began for him at breakfast.

THE PREVIOUS DAY AS ASAO LOOKS BACK.

The Ankawa children's father has decided to deliver some very good news this morning.

"Children, your uncle Tomoko has sent word he will be arriving tomorrow."

This early morning announcement, this news in itself will be enough to bring great excitement to three children's day. Their uncle Tomoko is indeed a favorite of all.

A former warrior of immense superiority and status within the emperor's army, Tomoko is a hero to Asao. At least that is how Asao has portrayed him to his friends around Hiroshima. His best friend Hiroshi knows more than anyone how important a man he is. Asao's made quite sure of that. He had to, especially in light of many stories Hiroshi brings with him almost daily it seems, stories of his own uncle in battle against Americans. Stories Asao feels he must equal, though stretching the truth considerably to do so.

Today, however, Father is not finished. Today, there is additional news, and it is very good news for one.

"Asao, tomorrow you will begin your young life's first adventure. You will travel back to Okayama in the morning with Uncle Tomoko." *Asao's father pauses a moment to consider his son's reaction…he will also carefully survey the reaction of Yuan Mei, his eldest child and only daughter. Asao will now make the journey that has, in years past, been reserved for her. Their father understands this moment delivers happiness and excitement to one, sadness and disappointment to another.*

"I understand your sadness, daughter. While you have made many of these journeys before, it is now most appropriate for your brother to take your place in this, his eleventh year. This is as it was for you, and this is how it should now be for him."

As it seems, Asao's eleventh will now be a year of good, personal fortune. Unknowingly, his father's decision allowing his oldest son's first journey to Okayama tomorrow, has extended one life...sentencing the remaining Ankawa children to early deaths.

Concluding his address to the small informal assemblage, he resumes completion of his breakfast.

Each year, for as long as Asao can remember, Yuan Mei has made the very journey he will soon embark upon. He can remember anticipating her return from each visit; the enjoyment and images created in his mind while listening to each retelling of events experienced and people she met during those visits. The stories of the beach, the city of Okayama, the children...all were told with such great detail, he felt as though he had made the trip and visitations himself, that he actually knew the children living around his uncle's home. Yuan Mei, always competing with Grandfather as a storyteller in the family, spends most of her free moments writing of those and many other experiences. Asao knows that, and that's why he will always stop what he is doing when his sister is about to tell one of many temporarily locked inside her mind. And she thoroughly enjoys every opportunity to tell one to anyone who will listen, including Asao and Massey. They are as good an audience as anyone could hope for.

Asao had always dreamed of going there someday. He could remember standing in the road, watching Yuan Mei and Uncle Tomoko ride away on the motorbike. The motorbike!

"Will Uncle bring his motorbike, Father?" Asao asks, feeling a sudden, additional tremor of excitement as he remembers one of his uncle's greatest attributes. All of the Ankawa children relish his arrival in their own way, Asao's being the obvious excitement generated by thoughts and memories of the motorbike.

"I can only assume that will be so, my son."

Barely able to contain himself, his excitement quite evident to all at the small table, Asao quickly glances at his brother, then Yuan Mei. She will miss being able to make the journey she has made for the last six years, and initially she is very saddened by this most recent news. However, the love she feels for her younger brother and the excitement she sees in his eyes, will soon overpower any disappointment she is feeling at the moment. She manages a smile, nodding her approval. She is proud for Asao, pleased he will now experience what she has previously, and her expression pleases him greatly. At fifteen, she is wise beyond her years, which is a must for any young girl within the framework of Japanese society. Within months, she will wed her intended, away at the moment involved in one of many great battles against America. At five-one, diminutive in size, she holds great stature in Asao's eyes. Coal-black hair, her body developing adequately ahead of many her age, she is looking ahead to her impending marriage, although with a great degree of apprehension. No choice in the matter, as elders in her family will tell her quite often, her betrothed is quite handsome. She guesses she should feel herself lucky in that circumstance.

Being the firstborn, she is her father's favorite. Each time he looks at her, he can see her mother, his wife...deep within her eyes and facial features. She's as beautiful at her age as her mother was many years ago upon their marriage; as beautiful as she still is.

Little Massey does not share his sister's maturity and obvious understanding. He is still a child at the age of five, quite small from nearly dying at birth, a birth made difficult, as it came in winter. His arrival was such an important event at the time, his battle for survival a success of great magnitude, while his mother experienced health difficulties of her own. His first few years in this world have been spent under the watchful, loving eyes of Mother and Grandmother, protected from any outside influences possibly proving harmful. His health and physical stature improving immensely these last three years, he still lags behind most his age, although as Asao would now agree, no one would ever know of his past problems to look at him, or his near brush with death.

Massey can only remember how badly he wanted to go with Yuan Mei last year, how sad he felt as he watched her and Uncle as they rode away. How happy he was when she finally came home. No, it will be even more difficult this time. At his age, he knows just enough to realize he wants to be included in all of big brother's activities, particularly this one. Today, however, Massey will be forced to settle for less, much less; and for now, it appears his disappointment will be of little concern to Asao.

What a great day, Asao thinks to himself, for a few seconds forsaking all thoughts of the feelings of others. At four-ten, slim build and all, he can consume enough food for any army his grandmother will tell him almost daily. Short black hair, like his sister, he spends his days as most his age would be expected to, in the throes of battle and war against the Americans, entering an exciting, though imaginary world at will. Generally, a child too preoccupied with those events swirling about him to worry about anyone else, Asao would most likely say no more, appearing quite content in his great fortune this morning.

His next question however, surprises everyone, including himself.

"Father, what of Yuan Mei...and Massey? Will they not be able to go as well?"

The two seem very appreciative of their brother's unexpected, unselfish gesture.

"No. This is the time for your visit. Yuan-Mei has made the journey many times before, and now it is your turn. Little Massey will one day be allowed to travel in your place as you now travel in your sister's." His

father pauses, momentarily appearing to reconsider his last comment. "No, there will only be room for one on your uncle's motorbike." He looks at his daughter, then Massey. "You will both be needed here, as we prepare for market."

Asao listens to his father's words; readily, quite selfishly accepting what he has told them. He is glad he will be the only one making the journey. Before, during his uncle's previous visits, he was allowed to ride his bike, though sharing those rides with his brother. This time will be quite different. Although he will miss the trip to market, a favorite place of his to visit each month, he wants to go to Okayama more than anything.

Everything considered; today promises to be a very happy, as well as a very busy one. Asao's father informs him he must climb the hill, climb it to the spot where mulberries grow in abundance. There, he will retrieve enough juicy, ripe ones to not only supply the family's personal needs, but enough to sell or barter at market as well. Of the still few but growing number of responsibilities, gathering mulberries is one, and it has become a task he quite thoroughly enjoys.

Breakfast almost at an end, Asao's imagination gains control of his innermost thoughts; transporting him beyond real life, beyond those boundaries, into a world he enters often...a world where children can accomplish those feats generally reserved for adults...a world within which Asao finds no one capable of matching his skills.

His plane awaits and it will soon carry him into battle against a very powerful American armada. As he makes his way toward his awaiting ship, a crowd of well-wishers surrounds him, cheering every step. At the foot of his plane, he turns to acknowledge his admirers, noticing just a few feet away, to the front of the crowd; a very pretty girl stands, smiling. He answers hers with one of his own, as he has in previous dream encounters, then turns to begin the climb toward his cockpit.

The crowd grows silent as the emperor steps forward, apparently readying to speak. Asao stops for the moment, stepping down from his plane's ladder to listen.

"Asao, you are Japan's final hope...our only hope. If we are to survive as a nation, your mission must be successful. Defeating our enemies will not only save this land we all love, it will also strengthen your status as one of Japan's undisputed national heroes."

The crowd cheers loudly in agreement with the emperor's words. He raises his arms in a gesture meant to silence everyone.

"Upon your safe and triumphant return, you may have anything that is within my grasp and power to give, including my daughter's hand in marriage."

Asao hopes to see the pretty dark-haired girl emerge as the emperor's daughter. To his relief, she does. Having seen her before, Asao knows now she is much more than just a girl in the crowd. Her near-perfect features, dark hair, fair complexion...make her a prize worth the risk of any man's life.

She smiles again; immediately lowering her eyes as though shyness has suddenly invaded her senses, overcoming her. Asao wishes she would look up at him again. The same girl he sees in every dream, at night and during his daily departures from reality...he still knows little about her. Carrying her vision beyond his imagination, back and forth across the boundaries between what is real and what is not, generates a sentiment that confuses him, at times overwhelming him.

Immersed in a trance, his eyes apparently fixed on the diminutive girl; he initially fails to notice a rumbling making its way through the crowd. Suddenly, without warning, the ground beneath him shakes. The crowd immediately disperses, running, yelling "earthquake" at the top of their voices. The large gathering scatters in all directions, attempting to escape with their lives. Asao's status quickly downgraded to nothing more than an obstacle in their paths to safety; he is completely caught off guard. With little time to react, he is knocked to the ground, nearly trampled by the mass of people fleeing death at the hands of another earthquake.

An attempt to pull himself together is momentarily thwarted. Knocked to the ground again, he soon feels a firm hand on his shoulder, then another, pulling at his arm. He looks up in astonishment to see the emperor's daughter as she tries to help him. This is the closest his mind has ever allowed them to come. Within inches of one another, any potential threat to him or his life is all but forgotten.

The voice he hears initially is that of a young girl speaking his name. He watches her lips closely, surprised at the deepening, masculine tone spilling from her mouth...her voice now sounding more than ever like his father's voice.

"Asao! You must stop this daydreaming!" he tells him sternly.

Unfortunately, forced to abandon his son's frequently visited world many years before, his father's own memories of those youthful years are now gone. This is the way it is in Japan. The eldest son, a family's firstborn male, must mature quickly, for he is destined to a life of adulthood responsibilities at a very early age. And as will one day happen to his son, Asao's father has long forgotten the path to childhood fantasy. True to tradition and life, his youthful spirit appears buried deep within the veneration of his elevated position as head of the Ankawa family, never to arise again. Because of this, his inability to understand his son's propensity for dreaming has become a reoccurring point of contention between the two.

"Why must you always dwell in fantasy? You should save that for sleep. What is there that continues to pull you away from life? Why must

you continue to spend such great amounts of time indulging in this frivolous activity?" his father asks out of frustration with his son.

"But, Father, I am not daydreaming." Asao's misrepresentation of the truth to protect himself from further reprimand does not fool his father even slightly.

Because he knows the truth, his father will continue.

"Preoccupation with the other world is childish, completely unworthy of your time! You will soon understand all I am saying."

Attempting to further defend himself, "Father, I am thinking about those things I must do today. And I am thinking of my journey. I am sorry if you thought I was dreaming." If he is lucky, Asao's father will buy this explanation and apology; ending the possibility he will be forced to endure further lecturing.

Before his father can begin anew, Asao moves quickly from the table, and ultimately, the next confrontation.

"And just where do you think you are going now?" his father stops him.

"To the hill, Father, to complete the task you have assigned me." Today, Asao and his best friend, Hiroshi, will be forced to abandon their plans to battle the enemy. This, the highlight of every day for two would-be warriors, must be pushed aside for a task of much greater significance and importance.

Hiroshi and Asao will meet in front of the farmhouse as they always do. However, today, Hiroshi will fly away by himself, battling the Americans alone.

Asao's mother awaits him at the door, handing him his lunch. Once he reaches the mulberries, it will be too far to return for that. She pats him on the head, expressing her love in one of few ways she is allowed by her son. A warrior so brave cannot be seen by his friends being hugged or kissed by his mother. He will only allow that at night, behind the cover of farmhouse walls. And, although doing this is not a practice that she would normally condone, she will indulge her son this time. Not to do so, will be a violation of his personal code of conduct; a threat to his reputation.

Smiling, he exits the house through the only door to the outside. His mother can readily see his imagination beginning to pull him into his private world. His mission today, save the emperor's daughter; rescue her from the mountain fortress where she is being held prisoner by the Americans. He looks across the rice fields, in the direction of the hill, which through the eyes and mind of an eleven-year-old, has been transformed to a mountain of very treacherous proportions; a mountain he must soon scale to save the young, dark-haired beauty. The spot where mulberry bushes flourish and abound, instantly representing the heavily guarded citadel he must approach and ultimately conquer.

The bushes! The berries! Almost to the road, he whirls around, retracing his steps to the front door where his grandmother awaits his return, a return she knew he would be making. Standing in the doorway, a smile on her aged yet nearly wrinkle-free face, she holds the secret to her grandson's ability to scale the walls of the impenetrable fortress. Baskets in hand, she holds them out to him. As he reaches for them, Grandmother grabs him, playfully hugging and kissing him as she always does. Obviously she does not subscribe to her daughter's tendencies to indulge his whims, and she will not do so today. No, her grandson will have to endure his grandmother's open display of love and affection.

This could be quite embarrassing, he thinks. Glancing about, to make sure no one has witnessed this unfortunate event; he is quickly convinced of that and turns toward the hill.

In minutes he reaches the edge of the rice fields, where he stops, taking time to slip out of his sandals. Placing them in one of the baskets, he will carry them, as he takes a shortened path across the muddy, irrigated fields before him. Taking great caution not to get them wet or soiled will surely save him from yet another of his father's stern lectures at the end of the day.

As he steps into water, its warmth is immediate. The hot summer days and nights, along with its shallow depth appear to be ambient factors keeping it at a warm and very comfortable temperature. As simple a pleasure as this cannot be equaled. It is indeed worth the extra seconds it took to remove them. Soft mud forced between his toes with every step feels wonderful! Ah the pleasures of a child.

As luck would have it and because he enjoys it so, it takes him much longer to cross than it would have had he gone the more distant, drier route. But his thoughts on this summer day are much like those of all children across Japan, and for that matter, across the entire world. Carefree and unencumbered by the war between countries, Asao's innocence has not yet been tainted by the intolerances of humanity. Disgust and objection at the difference of others are a matter best left in the hand of elders. Children should not be made a part of this nor the untimely, hideous catastrophe about to take place. Indeed, they soon will, and innocently enough their suffering will come at a level no children before have ever been made to endure.

Asao arrives at the base of the hill, slips his sandals back on after rinsing his feet clean of the mud now caked between his toes, then looks to the sky before beginning his climb, searching for any indication of an advancing threat of rain. At breakfast, Grandmother had said she would not be surprised if it rained today; something about her body's aches and pains telling her that.

He begins his climb toward the spot where an abundance of berries awaits his arrival. Imagination again swelling within, he sees the hill before him as the tallest of all mountains…one of most treacherous proportions to climb. Scaling this one will take a great deal of courage on his part. Today, he is up to the challenge! The mulberries he seeks have become an integral component of the Allied base of operations. The emperor's daughter has been captured and will most likely be tortured, possibly killed, if he does not reach her in time. By saving her, he will command a vast fortune as he gains her hand in marriage…uh, well, maybe not marriage.

His imagination, overly active by most standards, is quite indicative of his people's way of life. The Japanese embrace life to the fullest, like no other culture in these days and times. They are a people passionately committed to, and enthusiastically rushing after life's awaiting successes and power. Both in work and relaxation, they are a people enjoying the mere thought of living their lives to the fullest.

Asao and the Ankawa's are no different. In the spirit of "Shinto," Asao's grandfather will tell him, "Work is good, wealth is good, sex is good, even war is good, providing you win!"

The youngster knows about most of what his grandfather says; he is just not sure about the "sex" part. When asking, his questions bring very different and confusing responses, depending on whom he asks. His mother or grandmother will smile and tell him to ask his father. When he does, Father provides his son the same answer he usually gives.

"You will learn of these things soon enough. For now, you must not concern yourself with such matters."

Hiroshi usually hears the same from his family, leaving few notes for the two good friends to compare. And Massey, he knows too little of anything.

Asao finally arrives at the location where bushes are thickest. He can indeed see they are quite full and in need of harvesting. Before beginning, he turns to look out over his family's land. From this vantage point, he can see his father and grandfather at work in the fields a great distance from him...his mother and grandmother at their sides, as is Yuan-Mei. Pretending to be emperor of all land at his feet and before him, he gazes out over his vast holdings, watching his servants at work.

Daily tasks of weeding, plowing, irrigating, and harvesting their crops from this fertile soil, are necessary tasks his family must perform to maintain ownership. A grant given his great-grandfather by the emperor's father for meritorious service in combat, in defense of his country is his family's proudest of all possessions. One, Asao's father and grandfather are more than willing to work very hard to keep as they pass ownership from one generation to the next.

Escaping his inner mind's world for a moment, Asao reverts to his childhood. Yelling and waving his arms to gain their attention, his actions undetected by all, they appear very small from where he now views them, as he tries in vain to attract their notice.

As it is getting later by the minute, Asao decides he must begin his work or most certainly risk the wrath of his father for not finishing the task assigned. But as usual, he will again lose control of his imagination.

After picking enough berries to barely cover the bottom of one of the two straw baskets, he hears the sound of aircraft overhead. It could be the enemy! Straining to look skyward, the group of planes he can now see appears to be an elite allied fighter squadron, accompanying a small group of bombers. The planes fly in near perfect formation as they approach his location. These must be reinforcements, called in due to his arrival and conquest of the strategically placed fortress. Sitting on the runway, out in the open as is, his plane will surely be an easy target...a target easily destroyed.

His immediate concern translates into immediate actions. He must move quickly, and take off before enemy bombers can destroy the runway and his plane with it. Arriving at the base of his plane unharmed, he climbs into its cockpit and quickly taxis to takeoff position, where he awaits the control tower's instructions. Overhead, bombers break formation, dropping to within a few feet of the ground on their approach from the south. Asao glances over his shoulder, visually confirming their advancement from his rear. The control tower is hit early in the attack and quickly destroyed by escort fighters. The tower engulfed in flames, Asao can no longer await further instructions. He realizes he is now on his own. Sitting at the end of the runway, he glances over his shoulder one last time. Bombers' closing quickly and almost on top of his position, Asao throttles up his engine, releases the brake, and rolls to the north, gaining speed quickly. About to overtake him, the bombers continue dropping their payload on the once smooth stretch of runway he leaves behind. Each bomb's impact and resulting detonation create vast holes in the ground, his plane trembling as each occurring shock-wave races to overcome him.

Almost to the end of what was once a smooth runway, Asao pulls back hard on the stick between his legs. His plane lifts into the air, barely avoiding a collision with the lead bomber, which continues throttled to full airspeed. The smaller support fighters break from their direct attack of the crippled airfield to engage the lone Japanese plane in battle before it can escape. Asao knows he must use every trick in his repertoire if he is to survive this next skirmish. As he expected, the ensuing battle is a tough one.

Suffering only minor damage in the conflict, thanks to his tremendous skills as a pilot, he is able to inflict ruin upon the enemy, one by one eliminating every plane. He looks to the sky in all directions, realizing he has single-handedly made a shambles of the once proud, but overmatched Americans. He will be a national hero. The skies over Japan are safe once again. There appear to be no enemy planes left anywhere. Besides, most of them have now landed for lunch, and the little black-winged bandits have, for the moment, regained control of the fruit-laden bushes.

Asao's heroics are legendary across the country he loves. The emperor awards his ace Japan's highest honor. In his acceptance speech, he thanks "Kami" for watching over and protecting him during his most recent battle.

Worn from the difficult fight, the young boy falls asleep. In sleep, time passes quickly. Sometime later, he is awakened by the voice of an angel.

"What are you doing? You have not even begun to complete your work, have you?"

This is obviously no voice from any angel. Asao braces for the imminent lecture. She will not understand the significance of any aerial battle just completed, and won, nor will she know how exhausted he is because of it. How could he have mistaken her voice for that of an angel? Then, without saying another word, Yuan Mei picks up one of the baskets, looks inside and shakes her head in pity and frustration at what she sees. She begins what she feels she must do, hurrying completion of what Asao should have done by now.

She will not, however, be able to let the moment pass without delivering a small lecture of sorts.

"Someday your imagination will surely get the best of you. Now, get busy! I can help for only a brief moment. I too have work I must finish. If you do not fill these baskets as instructed by Father, you will most certainly gain his wrath, and you will have to answer for your actions. You know fully how he can be."

Unfortunately he did, all too well.

Yuan Mei has ascended the hill in search of her dying childhood. She has journeyed back one last time, in an attempt to experience all those thoughts and feelings she did at a younger age, before she lost this particular task as one of her more appreciated responsibilities. Wrapped up in developing his own childhood memories, Asao is quite unaware of the battle raging inside his sister's heart and mind.

Already mid-afternoon, the two work diligently. Under his sister's direction and timely assistance, both baskets are nearly full in minutes. She stops, straightens her slender frame, wipes the small beads of perspiration gathering on her forehead, then looks out over the land the two know as home. Before Asao became old enough to take on his current responsibility, she was the one assigned this duty. It is here where she learned the value of solitude. It is here where she visited the world her young brother continues to and now ventures. It is here where she has some memories of her childhood, most lying nearly dormant within her growing maturity.

"I must go now. You should be able to finish your work completely and on time. I have just enough time left to complete what I must do."

With that, she leaves; running, skipping down the hill, acting like someone half her fifteen years, slipping back in time, possibly revisiting her childhood. Asao calls out, thanking her for her help. It was indeed an angel who had awakened him and come to his rescue. Her good heart and love for her brother had probably just saved him from further trouble, trouble he most likely would have deserved.

He continues, completing his work slightly in advance of day's end. He sets the baskets in the shade, under one of the larger bushes. There the fruit will be protected from the sun's rays and the drying affect those rays would surely have on their contents. Placing the berries there will also keep them from those persistent little blackbirds in search of another easy meal. He glances at the scarecrow in residence, constructed by his mother and grandmother, readily able to see why it would not scare away even the smallest of creatures. Amused at its sight, he laughs.

Knowing he still has some time left, Asao makes the decision to venture farther, toward the "mountain's peak." Opportunities such as these do not present themselves often. Once there, he can see for miles in all directions, marveling at the beauty of the surrounding countryside and most prominently, astounding views off into the distance on the other side. As a child, he is most unusual in this way...always has been. He is quite sure there is no other land more beautiful. But of course, he has never seen any other in his short life. Soaking in the view, he basks in its ultimate beauty.

Spending a great deal of additional time, he indulges himself in the finality of a most beautiful sunset before him. The growing darkness approaches, changing the surrounding landscape, forcing him to finally realize dusk and the impending nightfall are upon him. He begins his descent toward the bottom; rolling, tumbling, as did his sister earlier before, enjoying a great time. As day begins transformation into night, fireflies flicker, performing their evening dance to the melody of crickets.

Realizing it will be dark before his arrival home, Asao quickens his pace. In his haste, he has forgotten the loosely fitting sandals on his feet. Hitting the rice fields at a dead run, his sandaled feet pierce mud, stopping him abruptly, his momentum forcing him face-first into the muddy water. As quickly as he lands, he is pushing himself up and out, gasping for air, coughing, spitting mud and water from his mouth and nostrils.

With filth splattered about his clothing and face, he arrives home, nearly unrecognizable as the eleven-year-old warrior from this morning.

His uncle's motorbike stands in view, propped against the house...the mere sight exciting and reminding him of tomorrow's journey, the journey that will carry him to an unplanned safety. His excitement, however, is short-lived.

"Asao! Where have you been?" his mother asks, greeting him at the door. Stepping into light from the open doorway, Asao's mother now sees him more plainly. She does not see anyone resembling her middle child. "What have you done?"

He is about to explain, but before he can, she continues, "Dinner is over. You will have to eat alone, but not until you have bathed." His mother shakes her head in disgust, although she is somewhat amused at the sight. "What am I to do with you? Your father is very angry."

Asao quickly cleans and dresses himself, missing several areas of filth due to his hasty interpretation of a cleansing bath. Entering the room where the men have gathered, he acknowledges their presence respectfully...first and foremost his father, then his grandfather, and finally his uncle. After each bow, he straightens, encountering three distinctly different responses. His grandfather nods, puffing on his pipe, a half smile his only emotion; his uncle smiles, Asao his favorite; his father glares, the only facial expression exhibited, strong enough to get his message across.

"Well, young man, it appears to be a very gracious act for you to make room in your busy day to join us. What do you have to say for yourself this time?"

"Nothing, Father," Asao answers stoically, wisely deciding to say nothing more.

Finishing his dinner, he settles for an evening with the men, looking for what he hopes will be a time of stories and entertaining conversation.

He enjoys being allowed to share these times with them.

Soon his uncle will jolt him with one of his first comments. "I understand you spent the day gathering those juicy berries from the hill. I must say, I am truly looking forward to their sweet, juicy taste at sunrise."

Smiling and acknowledging what he just heard, the words and their meaning finally hit him like the muddy water of the irrigated rice fields earlier this evening. Suddenly at a loss as to whether he even carried those baskets with him back across the fields tonight, his look must have indicated illness. No, as hard as he tries, he cannot remember carrying them home, if he had, he would surely have dumped them into the water as he fell.

His imagination snaps to a most vivid picture of himself in his plane, going down in flames. Hit by enemy fire; his cockpit window is jammed and will not open; his tremendous skills as a pilot of no use to him this time. With no way out, he is doomed to ride his burning ship to an untimely death.

From across the room, Yuan Mei has stopped what she is doing and stares at her brother. She can see the increasingly sickened look on his face, surmising very easily and quickly exactly what he has done.

Allowing several minutes to pass in an attempt to obscure the obvious, Asao excuses himself, saying he is very tired from the long day, and in need of a good night's rest before beginning the trip to Okayama tomorrow. Bidding good night, and pretending to go to bed, he departs everyone's company. On his way out, he can see it in his sister's eyes…she must know.

His plan to imitate sleep fails when he actually succumbs. Later in the night, he is awakened by a firm shaking.

"Asao, wake up," Yuan Mei whispers. She shakes him again, a few seconds more passing before he comes to his senses and realizes what has happened.

Quickly sitting up, "How long have I been asleep?"

"Too long," she continues in a whisper. "You left the berries on the hill."

Her statement of fact rather than question, tells Asao what he already knows. He had indeed left the baskets of mulberries on the hill, on the other side of the rice fields. A centerpiece of the Ankawa farm, the hill still holds hostage those most fertile mulberry bushes and his family's favorite fruit.

"Yes," his reply is soft and sheepish.

"If Uncle is to have them for breakfast, you must go and retrieve them. You do not, Father will surely punish you, maybe not allow your trip to Okayama tomorrow."

The very thought of not being able to make his trip in the morning threatens to further distress him. However, making the trip to the hill at this time of night frightens and unsettles him. Maybe the punishment would not seem as bad an alternative to the potential of a late-night venture.

Sensing this, she comes to his aid once again. "I will go with you, but we must hurry...now"

Outside, two are in preparation for a late-night experience. Asao valiantly hides the extreme happiness he is feeling that his sister will accompany him on this next journey. Off in the distance, a summer storm churns in early development. Lightning illuminates the distant skies, otherwise darkened by nightfall. Thunder, muffled slightly by distance, warns of the impending change in weather.

"Grandmother was right this morning," Asao tells his sister as they begin their journey. "There is the storm she predicted. Lucky for us, it is very far away. Maybe it will not come this way tonight."

"Grandmother is usually right about these things," Yuan Mei replies. "We must hurry. I do not want to be on the hill as it arrives. Grandfather

has told us many times how lightning is attracted to humans, especially when on high ground, as we will soon be. We must be quick about it, and we must be careful."

As he knows she is right, Asao sees this journey becoming a dangerous mission, taking on a completely new dimension through his youthful imagination. "I must be brave for her." he thinks to himself. "Kami will protect us."

Sandals on, the two inaugurate their pilgrimage in the direction of their destination…in the same direction as the oncoming, yet somewhat distant storm.

"I will race you!" Yuan Mei playfully challenges her brother. Feeling his uneasiness at the task before them, she decides to make this task easier for him by making a game of it.

As the two disappear into the darkness, a lone figure steps from the shadows, into the doorway of their home. Exhibiting a father's concern, he will make sure they arrive home safely before returning to bed.

Playfully jostling each other as they run toward the rice fields, laughing, and in full stride, Yuan Mei slips ahead due to greater strides provided by her longer legs. They quickly reach the foot of the hill, tumbling to the ground, out of breath. A few seconds later, Yuan Mei sits up, noticing the storm advancing at a much more rapid pace. As they catch their breath, she silently counts the time between each illumination of lightning and the subsequent sound of thunder—the first, a second, finally a third.

"We must hurry!" she yells to Asao.

They rise to their feet to begin their climb. He and his sister remain side by side most of the way, Asao in a little better shape for this portion of their competition due to his daily activities with Hiroshi around the farm. Within minutes, they have reached their final destination.

"Where did you leave them?"

As hard as he tries, he cannot remember. He has never been here at night before now, darkness altering his favorite hill, dramatically changing its appearance.

"I do not remember," he tells her.

"You must! You have to, or we must leave! Think hard!" Increasing concern flies through her words as the storm moves quickly upon them. Winds increasing in intensity; swirling, and beating the trees and bushes about with an escalating savagery, heaves an obstacle at them of tremendous proportions. The storm shows its force as the lightning's energy and the sound of thunder engulf the two in a blinding, deafening display of frightening power.

Yuan Mei knows they must leave immediately. There are few things in life important enough to risk death. Their frantic search for the prized fruit continues for the moment, with more fervor than at any time previously. Within seconds, a mammoth lightning bolt charges the air with electricity, striking the top of the hill.

"We must go! Now! Leave the berries! They are no longer important!" But Asao can no longer hear his sister above the shouting of Mother Nature.

He closes his eyes to force the doors of his mind and imagination open, entering a familiar and protected world. In that world, he asks, Kami to come to his rescue and guide him to the hidden baskets. As his eyes open, the brightest electrical illumination of the storm streaks across the sky, transforming their night into day.

"I see them! I see them!"

Asao runs to grab the baskets, pulling them from beneath the bush. He places one in the outstretched hand of his sister as the two begin their journey home. Feeling secure and fully engulfed in Kami's protective womb, Asao stops to gaze out over his family's farm. Mother Nature continues her colossal output of sights and sounds, delivering one of the greatest fireworks spectacles of all time. The reflections off the standing water in the irrigated fields now filling with rain mirror the brilliance and excellence of her show in the heavens. The view he enjoys is astounding!

Several feet down the hill, Yuan Mei realizes her brother is no longer with her. She quickly turns to retrace her steps, making the climb she had just completed with him minutes before. With each new flash of lightning illuminating the surrounding area, she can see her brother standing motionless as he watches the storm in awe and utter amazement.

Another bolt departs the heavens, speeding toward its targeted destination. A split-second warning alerts them both to its sudden arrival. It may not be enough warning for one. Hair bristles from the electrical current filtering through the dampened air around them, as the evening storm's most dangerous and deadly weapon nears the end of its very short life.

Yuan Mei yells out her brother's name one last time. The lightning bolt arrives, crashing to the ground with the force of many bombs! It creates an explosion like neither has ever experienced previously; before her eyes, her brother disappears.

A tree standing but a few feet from where he once stood crackles as yet another bolt finds its mark, splitting its trunk in two!

"Asao!" she yells. "Oh my God!" Tears flow from her eyes, only to be washed from her cheeks by the driving rain, as she continues the climb toward her brother. Reaching his last approximate position, she finds him lying on the ground. Expecting the worst, she drops to her knees for the second time tonight, landing directly at his side. After moments of time appearing to be quite lengthy to Yuan Mei, Asao raises his head slowly.

"Get down! They're shooting at us! You'll be hit!"

Relieved, she cannot help laughing. She hugs him, makes sure he is not hurt, and then pulls him to his feet.

Bending down to scoop berries from the saturated ground figuring they have been through too much tonight to leave them behind, the storm continues raging about them. With many of the berries back in the baskets, she grabs Asao's hand, this time making sure he is with her.

Finally at the bottom, they both realize their problems are not yet over. Looking out across the irrigated fields, they see lightning striking randomly and rapidly, drawn by standing water.

Yuan Mei sees a potentially deadly, nearly impossible situation ahead. Her first thought is to take the longer way home, around the fields, bypassing the standing water. Asao has already summoned his imagination once again, this time to help him gain the courage he will need to lead his sister across the fields to safety. Surveying the battlefield before them, he can see fierce fighting in all corners. Guns firing from every flank, he knows what he must do.

"Do not be afraid. Stay close to me and Kami will protect us both."

"Asao, we cannot..."

"You have to believe!" he interrupts. "You must believe!"

Looking down at her much shorter sibling, she sees his stature growing with every passing second. For the first time in a long time, she really wants to believe again. She has never doubted the power of Kami, but she is older. She has lost touch with her inner feelings of imaginative resourcefulness. However, unlike her father, it has not been as long since her childhood. Throwing caution to the wind, she takes the first step into a journey she has not made in some time, a step across the boundary between what is real, and what she had believed she was losing forever.

Together, the two step forward into the irrigated field, expecting the warmth of water surrounding their feet. That which is expected, never occurs. Hands intertwined his right to her left; Asao tightens his grip as they begin their final adventure together. Neither will ever again experience anything of this magnitude as brother and sister.

During their crossing, nature unleashes a relentless barrage of deadly assaults. She and Kami lock in battle over the youngsters...two appearing undeniably insignificant in the total scheme of things.

Tonight, Yuan Mei experiences the supernatural or a miracle, and it takes her breath away.

Tomorrow, it will all seem as though it were a dream. A return to her childhood fantasies, or a miracle from Kami, she will not be able to understand, nor will she be able to explain what happened...and there will not be enough time left in her life to figure it all out.

A corridor through the fields opens. Materializing before their eyes, it totally engulfs them. Inside, dry and unharmed from all outside influences, Yuan Mei will look to the heavens. As lightning bolt after lightning bolt appears repelled from the invisible shield, she does not, cannot understand what is happening. She only knows, whatever the outcome, she is no longer afraid.

AUGUST 3, 1945
THE ANKAWA FARM

STILL IN THE THROES OF ASAO'S MEMORY...

Because of their late-night adventure, neither Yuan Mei nor Asao is able to rise early this morning. Exhausted from an extraordinary night of incredible occurrences, Asao is finally stirred by his mother. He quickly awakens when she tells him it will soon be time for him and his uncle to leave. With that reminder, he is up and out of bed immediately, dressing quickly as he walks from his home for the last time. Grandmother meets him, handing him a small cloth bag that she has bound and tied with a string. Inside rests the food he and his uncle will need for their long journey ahead. He foregoes any concerns of embarrassment this morning, hugging and kissing his mother and grandmother. He waves to his father and grandfather, already making their way to the fields. For them, today is just another like any other.

His eyes search in earnest for his sister, but he cannot find her. Massey stands beside Uncle Tomoko's bike, wiping tears from his eyes, unhappy he will not be allowed to go; most saddened his big brother is leaving.

Asao, readying to mount the back of the bike, delays that act when Yuan Mei finally appears in the doorway of the family's farmhouse. Her smile as bright as the morning sun; she looks at her brother much differently today. She approaches him, a small, shiny object dangling from her hand. As she comes closer, a lump enters Asao's throat, causing him great difficulty in swallowing. She reaches out, placing one of her most prized possessions around his neck then hugs him for what seems to him a very long time.

"You protected me last night, when I thought I would be the one protecting you," she says softly, so no one else can hear, except Massey, who has not yet left his brother's side. "I do not know how, but when we arrived home last night, neither wet from rain, or muddy from the fields, I knew we had experienced something very special together. You guided me back to a place I had almost forgotten existed. A place, I will never again abandon. That experience has changed my life forever, and I will remember and treasure it for as long as I live."

She touches the necklace now hanging about his neck, looking at him lovingly. He knows she is about to say something more; he hopes nothing as serious as what she has already said.

"This is all I have to give you. It has been in the family for many, many years. For what you have given me, I will never be able to give you anything more valuable. The jade stone will give you the strength to face all you encounter. As you convinced me last night, you too must believe what I am now telling you. If you are ever in danger, the stone's sharp edges will protect you. When you are sad and lonely, you have only to touch it, and it will bring your thoughts closer to home and those who love you. As long as you keep it in your possession, we will be there for you...always."

Asao hugs his sister. He will miss her more than anyone, and right now he isn't so sure he wants to begin this trip, but Uncle is ready, climbing on the motorbike, telling Asao to do the same. Hiroshi stands in the distance, watching his best friend in preparation for his departure, envious of Asao's upcoming journey. He waves. Asao waves back.

"See you in a few days," Asao yells.

"See you then," his friend replies.

As he and his uncle pull onto the roadway, Asao waves to his family. Massey's tears, the look on his face, his family waving...all of these things will haunt Asao for the remainder of his life.

Increasing the bike's speed, his uncle expedites the beginning of their journey. A short time later, the two approach the final hill before disappearing from sight of the Ankawa home. Asao turns to look one last time. He cannot explain the way he feels at this moment. Maybe in some strange way, he knows he will never see it again.

Turning around, he tightens the hold on his uncle's waist, reassuring himself of his return home a week from now.

Their ride across the countryside is very enjoyable today. The previous night's storm has left it cool, refreshed, with a renewed smell. His uncle's conversation about *Okayama,* and what he can expect, holds his interest for a while. Asao's favorite topic, the war, is what keeps him alert and awake most of the way. Although never a warrior, as Asao had painted for his friends, his uncle seems well versed on the many battles waging between the Japanese and Americans, including great detail of the Japanese victories. These stories make Asao most proud to live in Japan.

In just a few hours, the trip is nearly over. Almost there, Tomoko decides he'll pull to the side of the road. Thinking his nephew may already be a little homesick; he will try to make him feel as though Hiroshima is still very, very close.

"Come with me, Asao."

Uncle Tomoko walks to the edge of a cliff surveying a portion of the land over which they have just traveled. Asao climbs from the bike and joins his uncle moments later.

"If you look hard and long enough, you can almost see Hiroshima," his uncle tells him. "At night, you can most assuredly see the glow from the city's lights."

Asao stands at the edge, squinting, turning his head from side to side, straining to see what his uncle says he can, what he obviously cannot. Desiring not to hurt his uncle Tomoko's feelings so early in his visit, he will try pleasing him.

"Yes, Uncle, I can see it! I can see Hiroshima. And my house— it is as though we are standing on the hill. I can see little Massy and Hiroshi fighting the Americans."

Tomoko smiles, "Your father is right. You do have a very strong imagination. That is good. There are many things in this life too serious for a boy your age to engage in. No, you should not abandon your childhood too soon. These years should be some of your most enjoyable, if not your very best."

Asao does not realize it at this time, but his uncle...always the rebel, does not subscribe to the old ways of Japan, or his brother's indifference to the feelings of youth. Asao will one day find that, and many other things to love about his uncle Tomoko.

Climbing back on the bike, they resume their journey, progressing toward its completion. A few minutes later, they approach the home of his aunt and uncle. Asao sees his aunt Yuan Mei, his sister's namesake kneeling and working diligently in the garden near their home. At first glance, it looks much like his home, but it is not.

The two road warriors ride up to the gate of the fence surrounding the immaculate, neatly kept home. His aunt stands to greet them. Sensing an imminent hug, Asao has already made the decision to allow this initial one...the warmth of her greeting reminding him of home once again, but of course, it is not.

His first evening here will be uneventful at best. There being no best friend to help engage the enemy in battle, no little brother to tease or fight with. And with no sister to talk to, his evening will pass very slowly. Hoping to hear additional stories from his uncle about the war, he is soon disappointed, as Tomoko prepares for the workday ahead. Announcing early retirement for the evening, Uncle tells his nephew he will see him tomorrow, adding to the probability he will be spending the day alone or with his aunt. First night boredom consuming him, Asao retires at an uncharacteristically early hour.

Because of all that has happened the last two days, he has very little trouble falling asleep. He does so, holding the gift from his sister tightly in his hand.

Checking on him before she retires, his aunt notices it dangling from his clinched fist and pries it away, placing it on the floor beside him. He awakens immediately, grabbing it back, relaxing into a deep slumber once again. He can almost feel his sister's presence in the room...almost.

CHAPTER 2

Asao awakens to the smell of food. Slightly disoriented, he will quickly gain some sense of bearing by making his way toward that. Walking into the main room of the small home, he expects to see his mother and grandmother cooking, cleaning; performing whatever task there is to be done this morning. Instead, he sees only his aunt, who appears to be very busy. The sight of her quickly brings him back to the reality of the moment.

As she notices her little nephew entering the room, she greets him lovingly. "Good morning, Asao."

"Good morning, Aunt Yuan Mei."

"You were greatly fatigued from your trip."

"Yes, ma'am. Where is Uncle?"

"Oh, it is late. He left for work hours ago."

"I am sorry for sleeping so long. I did not plan for that to happen."

"You were tired from your journey. Neither your uncle nor I wanted to wake you. Now, would you like something to eat? I saved a little breakfast for you."

"Yes, ma'am. That would be good," he responds, feeling a little of the same pain he did when leaving home yesterday.

"Some of the children from the neighborhood have already visited this morning, expecting to meet this legend your uncle has apparently stirred so much interest in. It seems you are a very popular young man already."

She had no sooner made the statement, when a knock at the door interrupts their late-morning visit.

His aunt, finishing preparing him something to eat, asks his assistance. "Asao, would you please see who that might be."

"Yes, I will be most happy to," he tells her, walking to the door. Opening it, he comes face to face with a young girl about his age. Initially he is disappointed upon seeing it is a girl. However, she is quite pretty. Her short black hair, her nice smile...he believes he has seen her before somewhere...but where?

"You must be Asao. I have heard many things about you."

That's good. She knows who he is, but he has no clue as to her identity, and more importantly, how could she possibly know him. He is about to reply, when his aunt calls from within the house.

"Asao, invite your new friend in for tea."

Tea! Why would I want to invite her in for tea? What would Hiroshi think, drinking tea with a girl?

"Would you like to come in?" His words show politeness; his thoughts pray for a rejection to his offer.

"Of course, I would love to."

His aunt enters the room, and introduces them. "Asao, I would like you to meet Miki Okuno. She lives just down the road. You both have so much in common; I thought it would be nice to introduce you this morning. I have also asked her to take you out into the neighborhood and acquaint you with all the other children your age."

Asao makes a supreme attempt at being pleasant, but he is not at all pleased with this arrangement. Number one, she's a girl. Number two...she's...a girl. Number three...he didn't need a number three. Miki follows his aunt into the next room.

A second knock at the door comes before he can follow as well. *This may be the answer to my prayers*, he thinks as he hurries to answer it, this time needing no prompting from his aunt to do so. Opening the door, one thing is certain; Kami has indeed answered his prayers. A few boys, most appearing to be his age, stand ready to rescue him from this uncomfortable and very dire situation. Asao is quite happy to see them.

The larger boy, Asao assuming their leader, speaks first.

"You the boy from Hiroshima?"

Sensing the tone of his questioning to be a little less than friendly, Asao ignores that for the moment, presented with the possible sanctity of being with other boys.

"Yes, I am from Hiroshima."

"You wanna play 'war'?"

"Yeah. Sure. That would be great!"

Asao turns, planning to inform his aunt of the change in plans, but deciding she might not understand he stops abruptly. He'll make a break for it, figuring this to be his best chance of escaping the "countess" and the "wicked" aunt preparing tea with poison that surely awaits him at the bottom of the cup.

The group, now complete at six with the addition of Asao, makes its way down the road in the direction of the sea. This is the closest thing he's done to what his life would be like back on the farm since being here. Hiroshi would approve. His new friends ask many questions, which he answers honestly. He in turn, asks them many of the same things.

Soon, the tone of the conversation begins to change. The leader, going by the name Yami, lays ground rules for the consideration of Asao's induction into their group. As a test of his new loyalty, he must play the role of the enemy...an American pilot.

Appalled at such a request, he prepares to refuse. How can they ask such a thing of one as dedicated to the emperor and Japan as he, one so greatly honored and decorated? No one with his combat experience, his degree of success against the allies, would ever consider such a demand. About to tell them as such, he hears a slightly annoying, high-pitched voice as a girl approaches from behind.

"Wait for me! Wait for me!"

The group turns to see Miki running for all she's worth to catch up to them.

In fortuitous unison they respond, "Oh no."

"It's your little girlfriend," Yami tells Asao, disgusted with the prospects of any girl thinking she will be able to join his gang on this day, or any other for that matter.

"She's not my girlfriend!"

"Prove it!" Yami commands him. "Tell her she's not welcome."

I will, he thinks to himself. *I'll do just that. When I'm through with her, they will all know. There will be little doubt as to where my allegiance lies.*

Watching her approach, waiting for the right moment, he realizes he will not be able to do as commanded. This moment reminds him too much of home...little Massey, running to catch up with him and Hiroshi, pleading to let him play with them today, wishing now he had given in to his little brother's simple requests.

"No! I cannot do that!" ...under his breath, "I will not do that!"

The gang turns abruptly after Asao's announcement of outward defiance. All eyes viewing Yami snap back to Asao as though synchronized, awaiting their leader's reply. All are in tune with each other, wondering what his next reaction will be. No one has dared defy the boy they all must follow, at least not since he began his reign less than a year ago. Out of respect as well as out of fear for his sheer size, no one has had the audacity to do what Asao had just done.

"Then I will! Get out of my way!" Brusqueness one of his trademarks, he pushes Asao aside, his massive body stepping toward Miki as she stops within a few feet of the group.

"Get out of here! Leave us alone!" he barks, pointing a finger at the small girl.

Asao can tell the order frightens her and more probably the tone with which Yami delivered it. She looks at Yami, his gang, then to Asao, her eyes begging her new friend for help she is sure will soon arrive.

Asao breaks from the uninvited eye contact, quickly turning away. The entire gang, including Asao then turns to walk away from the dejected little girl.

Persistence and tenacity, both distinguishing trademarks of her own character, she will not give up as easily as they might think. Full of spunk and daring, she follows closely behind the roaming gang, looking for one chance...that one chance to persuade them to take a brave girl into their elite club. Asao can see her out of the corner of his eye, motioning behind his back with the use of hand gestures, telling her to go away. Very wise for one so young, he knows the situation could soon turn ugly should the highly spirited girl continue her aggressiveness.

Finally, it does as Yami stops to address this situation once and for all. The gang mimicking his move turns to face the tagalong. He moves in the direction to confront her, placing himself within inches...in her face with his.

"I told you to leave us alone! Are you so dumb you do not understand my words? That's it, she's dumb. Of course, she is a girl. That would explain it."

"And stupid...!" a couple of the other boys yell.

"Well, what do you have to say?" He pauses for some reply from her mouth, as though giving her one last opportunity to make a statement on her own behalf before imposing sentence. "Are you not stupid? Do you not understand what I am saying? One thing you really are: You are ugly...ugly beyond words."

Asao obviously does not see the same thing as Yami. He had determined in their earlier meeting she is definitely not ugly.

Although no words come from her mouth, she stands defiantly in the road, as though she is asking for continued trouble, asking for his next actions. Yami steps into her, pushing Miki to the ground. As she falls, she throws her arms behind to cushion her landing. Her left hand finds a sharp, jagged rock, slashing her skin, drawing blood immediately. Feeling pain from the injury, then seeing blood, she cries. Sensing easy victory within his grasp, Yami steps in for the kill, standing over the fallen girl, his clinched fists warning her, he stands ready should she even consider any form of retaliation.

"Ohhhhhhh, look at the little crybaby," Yami whines in a mocking fashion. He looks over at Asao, who is now feeling ashamed for doing nothing. "Well, what do you think of your little crybaby girlfriend now? No baby will ever be a member of my club, specially a girl."

"That's just fine with me," Asao remarks, continuing his appeal to the gang for acceptance, attempting to appear loyal to their cause, though his loyalty is beginning to subside with each passing second.

"She's no friend of mine. I don't even know her." He couldn't believe he said that.

With the realization she has no one willing to defend her, Miki decides she must take matters into her own hands. Like a cobra striking out at its prey, she lifts her right leg with as much force as she can possibly muster from her prone position. She guides her foot toward the groin of her assailant, connecting directly on target. Yami straightens up, as though feeling nothing. He begins chuckling at his opponent's ineffective defense tactic; then momentarily delayed, the pain hits. His eyes roll into the top of his head...the result of Miki's quick strike causes Yami to double over in excruciating pain, nearly vomiting.

Asao smiles slyly under the guise of concern, saying nothing.

Unfortunately for Miki, Yami is able to regain his composure quickly, overcoming the pain as quickly as it overcame him. Reaching out before she can strike a second time, he grabs her leg beginning his own approach toward a certain retaliation.

The look in his eyes tells the girl she has miscalculated her opponent's resolve, making a huge mistake in judgment. The need for revenge has taken over any sense of decency, driving his desire to inflict additional pain and suffering upon the smaller opponent, no matter the level now. Himself, having suffered great pain, yet more so the humiliation in front of his followers, he will stop at nothing, twisting her leg close to the point of fracture.

Miki's pain, obvious to everyone standing there, brings great satisfaction to Yami. All, with the exception of Asao, cheer his behavior.

"Owwwwwwwww! He's breaking my leg! Owwwwwwww! Somebody please help! He's breaking my leg!"

Asao remains motionless momentarily, suddenly at a major crossroads in his young life. To Miki, the seconds of his indecision seem like hours. Finally, he gains the courage to answer Yami's misdeeds. His answer however, will not come in words.

Asao quickly moves between the two engaged in battle. After breaking Yami's grip through the element of surprise, he reaches for Miki's hand, pulling her from the ground into a standing position behind him. He turns to Yami. "You have shown little courage by treating her as you have. All you have proven to me is that you...you are not a gang I wish to become a part of; on this day, or any other."

This sudden reversal of attitude surprises everyone, including himself. Feeling more confident than ever, for no reason whatsoever, he makes his next statement much like his last, without benefit of thought.

"Maybe you would like to test me as a Japanese warrior. No true Japanese leader would harm a defenseless little girl as you have. And I wIll not play the enemy as you expect. I am better than any fighter any of you could ever be."

The words escaping his mouth before he can stop them, he cannot believe what he has just said. Yami, obviously much larger and more experienced in these matters, will surely make him wish he had never pushed his luck. As the gang's leader, Yami cannot possibly allow some strange new boy from Hiroshima to gain the upper hand in a situation like this, especially someone as small and insignificant as Asao, not in front of his faithful followers. Unwilling to risk the loss of their respect, and quite probably his role as their leader, he will take immediate action. He feels now he has little choice. He has worked too hard to let go of that.

To no one's surprise, Yami grabs Asao's shirt, tearing it as he pulls him closer. Asao has never been in a situation like this before, at least not in real life. The many encounters with the enemy, defending the empire, those were all battles of the imagination, all well within his control. This battle will be outside that parameter and protected environment, and Asao believes this could quite probably be the end of his short life.

Then it happens! Asao's imagination engages, almost involuntarily coming to his rescue, instantly thrusting him into a familiar role as a courageous and fierce warrior. He glances at the crowd surrounding them, seeing nothing but well-wishers, all cheering him on. He can see the smiling girl in the crowd, this time recognizing her. It is Miki, the girl he is about to risk his life to defend!

Under Kami's protective care, Asao begins moving in well-coordinated gyrations of the body, arms, and legs, astonishing everyone standing along the Okayama roadside. As Asao catches his enemy off guard, the overweight gang leader is no longer able to continue his tight hold of Asao's shirt.

Within seconds, Asao has circled Yami twice; completing his final rotation before the larger one can react to his surprising movements. Fronting him, Asao steps away, and with the quickness and unpredictability of a streaking lightning bolt crashing to earth, he jumps into the air, extending his right leg, propelling his foot and body toward the oversized, protruding belly of his opponent. Slowed by his size, Yami cannot match Asao's quickness. Facing the boy from Hiroshima, he cannot stop Asao's momentum as he delivers a crushing blow to the midsection. Yami doubles over in pain once again.

Emerging from his trancelike state, Asao hears Yami's next command, though punctuated with the raspy sound of exasperation induced by sudden pain.

"Get 'em!"

Asao's response is immediate, reactionary. He knows he and Miki will surely pay if they do not escape with their lives now. He grabs her hand, pulling her behind him, back toward his uncle's house and the expected safety awaiting their arrival. A very short distance down the road, the gang is close behind and gaining.

Pulling Miki after him, Asao makes the turn through the gate of his uncle's fence...two of the fleet-footed gang members in close pursuit, almost catching them at that turn. Reaching out, one comes very close to grabbing Miki. Before it can happen, Asao slings the wooden gate behind him with all his might and strength within body and arms, catching both boys and knocking them to the ground. Unfortunately, neither the gate, nor the fence will stop the power and body of Yami. He enters the yard as though owning it, stepping over his fallen comrades, closing in to face this new rival from another city, a city miles from here.

Asao and Miki arrive at the doorsteps of the house, out of breath, and unfortunately out of time. Yami reaches out, grabbing Asao. With the enemy in his grasp, Yami prepares to land a final blow. Unknown to any of them, Asao's uncle has arrived home early from work and suddenly appears in the doorway. His surprise appearance halts the big one's aggressions immediately. He and his gang slowly, cautiously back away...retreat their only recourse with this new development. Yami and Asao's eyes meet one last time. Despite his contempt for Asao, Yami has reached a certain level of respect for his new adversary. But he still must attempt to save face before backing away.

"One thing is certain, we will meet again soon. You will not be as lucky then."

Asao looks up at his uncle, emitting a sigh of relief.

"What was that about?" his uncle inquires.

Asao does not answer, quietly looking to Miki.

"You were wonderful," she tells him, seeing more than just a playmate, more than just another boy in her neighborhood. With little warning, she throws her arms around him, catching him totally off guard...kissing, hugging, creating great feelings of distress with the young visitor from Hiroshima...this episode has pushed the young boy beyond the limits of any experienced thus far on this visit.

In a near state of shock, totally embarrassed, he can only look to his uncle for help, but Uncle will offer no relief for his nephew at this point. Asao believes he would rather have had Yami catch him on the road than to endure what Miki had just presented him.

"Looks to me as though one young man has had a very busy day. You must come inside and tell me about it. Tea is nearly ready. Miki, would you care to join us? We should clean that wound on your arm."

Through all the commotion and swift turn of events, Miki had almost forgotten her injury. "I must ask your forgiveness, but I cannot. I must return home now. I will be fine."

"Will you be able to make it home safely?" Asao's uncle asks.

"Yes, sir! I am not afraid of those bullies. Not any longer. Not with Asao living here now."

"I do not live here!" Asao interjects. "I am only visiting."

"Good-bye, Asao. I will see you again tomorrow."

AUGUST 5, 1945
THE EVE OF THE FINAL DAY

Weather continues warm and sultry. Asao awakens late again, as he did yesterday. Walking through the house this morning, he sees no one. When he stops to look through the open door to the outside, he finds his aunt working in her garden, Miki sitting on the grass beside her.

"Good morning Aunt Yuan Mei." He likes saying her name, rubbing the stone hanging about his neck. Saying her name, feeling the stone provide a much-needed comforting effect on his desire for home.

"Good morning, Asao," the two answer in near unison.

"Your breakfast is inside. When you are finished, your uncle's fishing poles are over there, against the house," she says as she points to their location.

Asao may have looked slightly confused, reflecting identical feelings he has inside at his aunt's statements.

"You're uncle decided he would leave work early today, so that we may spend time together. Your short visit will be over soon and we would like to show you a little of our world around Okayama. A day at the beach will be fun for you and Miki. Take the cane fishing poles. When your uncle comes home, we will join you at water's edge, where we may all eat fish you two have caught. You may go now and we will follow later."

Asao finishes his breakfast of rice and fruit; venturing outside quickly in hopes of slipping past his designated companion for the day. He grabs the gear Aunt Yuan Mei had mentioned earlier, walking briskly toward the road. The small dark-haired girl from Okayama is, nonetheless, at his heels before he can escape the picket fence surrounding his temporary home. The two are on their way, initially beginning their journey at a slowing pace. His short stride quickens substantially after Miki pushes one of her hands into his, extending her feelings from the day before, sending a message that he initially cannot begin to comprehend. His immediate thought is to pull away, except he really does like her. As Miki quickens her pace to keep up with his, he decides he will allow her hand to remain in his for the moment. She is probably doing this out of fear, he reasons, maybe thinking Yami and his gang could be lurking anywhere.

Miki, merely ten, is old enough to know of those boundaries within Japanese tradition. At her young age, she is promised to another, as she believes Asao must be. She cannot help what she is feeling though. In her new friend, she sees more than a budding childhood friendship, much more than possibly allowable within their country's traditions.

Yesterday was very meaningful to her, dealing with the many childhood emotions. Supporting a great deal of imaginative prowess herself, she sees Asao as her brave, courageous defender. Because of this, and despite tradition, she has made the determination to become his intended.

"Are you promised to someone as I am?" she asks.

"Yes, of course I am."

Her grip loosens. Although she knew what his answer would be, it still gave great pause for disappointment. She will soon regain her composure.

"Then she is very lucky. Any girl should be most proud to be your intended and have her hand promised to you. I...I know I would."

Asao cannot believe what she is saying. To say these things is most inappropriate. He believes she should not be speaking in this manner. Tradition and customs will not allow it. Feeling very uncomfortable with the conversation and the direction it appears to be going, he begins running, possibly his only mode of self-defense at this point. Although promised to another at a very young age, he has never met—much less seen—the girl his mother and father have agreed should be his bride. They have raised him to accept tradition, to accept those things as laid before him a few years back and throughout his learning's.

"Asao!" Miki yells after him. "Wait for me!"

Her new friend is quickly out of sight, offering no reply to her questions or comments, no indication as to why he suddenly bolted from her. She will run and catch him, too persistent for her own good, too young to know better...completely undeterred at this juncture.

ALLIED AIR FORCE BASE
TINIAN ISLAND

As he slips into the bomb bay, the man's internal heat protection system kicks in, triggering profuse sweating. He will sit snugly inside this extremely tight section of the plane for what seems to him to be an eternity; in reality, will be only a couple of hours. "Little Boy" sits before him in all its glory. Just to look at it, it emerges as an object of minute stature among life's many intricacies; in reality, it is one with extreme, devastating capabilities.

He begins his work. One of few men granted access to this plane less than twenty-four hours before beginning its mission; he is on a mission himself. His work in the next hour or two may determine the entire fate of his family, his countrymen, his entire homeland; and most eminently, the crew of men scheduled to board their planes early tomorrow morning.

His hands, directed by intensive training, practical experience, and what he had learned just days before, work to disconnect, reconnect, then disconnect the wiring attached to the large metal "death device." Over and over, he repeats this very intricate process, making damn sure he can do those things with Little Boy he must also do alone tomorrow.

Asao reaches the beach ahead of Miki, hesitating momentarily, allowing her time to catch him. After a lengthy search, they choose the ideal location for the planned evening picnic, where they will share time with his aunt and uncle later in the day. The decision Asao's, by his status in a male-dominated society, his strategic military thought processes aid his selection of the location with the greatest advantage should he need to defend his and Miki's lives at any time today.

The weather remains undeniably beautiful. The sky...clear and deep blue, the water...mirroring its sister's depth and darkness of color.

From their selected vantage point, the two can see in all directions for what seems to be miles. To hide from anyone on the beach, they need only lie down. Their location secure and complete, the two young ones...young in body and spirit, maturing rapidly in heart...kick off their sandals, run down the sandy bank toward the water, kicking and splashing through the very calming miniature waves slowly rolling onto the beach.

They never quite get around to fishing as planned, which means there will be no meat for dinner once Asao's aunt and uncle arrive. This has happened many times before, his imagination overpowering his ability to face responsibilities. He and Miki are enjoying the water and sand too much to let such burdens slip in their way. Although he will never admit it, he is beginning to enjoy her company with each passing moment. Well, maybe a little anyway.

The more he is around her, the more she reminds him of his sister, at least her forthright, outspoken trait. There is no resisting tradition. In a few days, he will return to Hiroshima...to the small farmhouse just outside the city, where he is promised to another, and where he will most likely soon forget the girl from Okayama.

As they walk along the beach, Asao thinks of home, rubbing between two fingers the stone hanging about his neck. Yuan Mei was right; it does make him feel better...considerably better.

A short time later, Asao decides they must begin their trek back toward their picnic spot, and they reach the chosen location before his aunt and uncle arrive. He also remembers his assignment and the fact he has not yet accomplished what his aunt asked him to do. There will be no Yuan Mei to help him today, no "angel of mercy." Suddenly, he stops dead in his tracks.

"What is it? What's wrong?" Miki asks before making out what Asao has just seen down the shoreline, a relatively short distance from where they now stand.

Before either can say another word, they hear the orders being given by the largest of the group now approaching at a much faster pace. Although somewhat faint by distance, his words are very clear.

"Look! There's the little 'creep' and his 'crybaby girlfriend'! Let's get 'em!"

The sand is like mush, instantly projecting qualities of "quicksand" for the two, who need no additional troubles now. There will be no uncle, no older sister coming to their rescue this time.

Asao and Miki quickly turn, making their escape in the opposite direction. As they continue to experience great difficulty gaining any kind of decided momentum, Miki falls, Asao stopping to help her to her feet.

"We have to make it to our fortress! We will be safe there!" Asao says, trying his best to reassure both of them.

The two run as fast as their legs will carry them, as fast as the slippery yet sinking footing in the sand will allow. Asao glances behind him, realizing Yami and his gang may be having the same degree of difficulty as they, now falling behind with each loss of footing. Light footed and considerably quicker, the two are able to place additional distance between themselves and the enemy. Miki and Asao round the bend in the shoreline, passing the huge rock formations jutting from the sand. Those rocks momentarily block them from sight of their adversaries, giving them the opportunity to ascend the steep incline without notice. Quickly reaching their fortress, the two drop to the ground just as the gang rounds the same bend.

Passing the formations, every member of the gang realizes Miki and Asao have completely vanished from sight. The most intelligent of the group, Yami, suspects they could not have just disappeared into thin air.

Asao's head bobs up and down every few seconds, giving him the opportunity to check on the gang's whereabouts in relation to their position. At one point, it appears one of the gang has detected him. That boy starts up the embankment toward their hiding place, forcing Asao to quickly drop back down out of sight.

"They've found us!" he whispers excitedly, out of breath from a certain anxiety in the moment.

"What are we going to do?" Miki whispers back in near panic, beginning to cry.

Asao could have easily chastised her for being such a baby, as Yami had done the day before, but instead, his experience in imaginative battle tells him to quickly review his options.

With Yami's level of respect for Asao probably much greater today due to his ability to defend himself yesterday, Asao figures he will not be getting by with what he did then. He also realizes he cannot avoid this confrontation.

"Do not cry. Kami and I will protect you," he boasts, this time allowing the passion of youth to intercede with common sense, that passion overtaking any prior doubts as to his ability to handle this next adversity.

"I am here to protect you for the rest of your life!"

Looking at Miki one last time, he identifies a look of horror in her eyes. Something, someone has stepped up behind him. The size of the shadow cast over them can only mean one person. Asao's inanimate posture exists mere seconds. He knows what he must do; he must react quickly and decidedly. With eyes closed by nature of the fear within, he whirls around, his doubled fist connecting firmly with a soft, slightly protruding stomach. He opens his eyes at the sound of a groan discharged from the one he has just attacked. This particular groan does not sound anything like Yami.

"What are you doing, Asao?" Uncle Tomoko winces, slightly doubled over from the solid blow his young nephew has just delivered.

"Miki, it appears you are well protected when under Asao's care. Young man, do you think you might calm yourself long enough to help me catch our dinner, since it appears you have made little attempt to do so yourself."

Startled at his uncle's sudden appearance, he quickly stands, checking on the gang's location. He can see them in the distance, quite away down the beach now. They must have seen the fortress and his defenses as too formidable to even consider a further attack. Once again, he has risen to the occasion.

"Yes, Uncle. I am ready. We are both very hungry," he says, looking at Miki, who smiles at her hero, shaking her head in quick agreement.

The sun has almost completed its fall from a beautiful Japanese sky, setting on another day; bringing the young boy yet closer to the time he will be able to journey home, to once again be with his family and friends. The distance between all of them, and the time elapsed, has revealed to Asao how important they all are to him, how much he has taken them for granted. He has decided he will never do so again.

While Asao and his uncle stand at the water's edge, poles in hand, Miki and Aunt Yuan Mei gather wood erratically strewn about the beach by waves, and then start a fire to cook the bountiful catch their men will surely provide. And as well they do, their dinner this evening is exceptional, Asao thinks. The fresh air and his mounting hunger, make it all taste so wonderfully delicious. Afterward, the four sit around the fire, visiting, telling tales of realism—some spiced with imagination—and enjoying the cooling breeze blowing inland over the water. Asao shares exciting episodes he, Yuan Mei, Massey, and his best friend, Hiroshi, share back in Hiroshima on his family's farm. And as this episode in his visit comes so very close to reminding him of those times in Hiroshima, he shares his remembrance of times when he and the other men in his immediate family sit to share stories at the end of the day. He is beginning to feel a certain attraction to this place, his extended family, and yes, even the little girl continuing to move ever closer to him as they sit in darkness of the day. Soon it will be time to depart the beach, leave the cooling air and serenity surrounding their evening existence, something Asao will be most disappointed about, nearly forgetful of his homesick feelings. Before the final ember begins its journey toward insignificance and their fire is out, Tomoko speaks.

"We must go. Miki's mother and father do not want her out late on this night. Tomorrow they plan a journey to your city, Asao. We promised to have her home early, as she must be ready for a very early start in the morning."

Asao hears what his uncle has said, and he is quite jealous of this young girl now sharing the evening with him. Envious of her situation, he would like to ask his uncle's permission to travel with Miki and her family, a few days earlier than his planned return. But he dare not speak his thoughts for fear he may appear weak to all around him. Fate, it seems, is keeping a watchful eye on the young one.

The walk home tonight will seem short. Before leaving the beach, Asao and Miki thank the adults for the evening. Asao then runs ahead, chasing fireflies, placing distance between him and his new friend for the moment. Only a few steps behind, she soon catches him, slipping her small hand into his once again. He almost pulls away, but again, reacting as he did earlier, he does not. Assured his aunt and uncle are much too far behind to see, he tightens his grip. He is looking forward to tomorrow. It will bring him one day closer to the time when he will be able to make the same journey to Hiroshima as Miki; his final journey home.

Innocence of youth cannot prepare him for the oncoming events of tomorrow. As he has no idea what this day's end signifies in his life, the dawn of the oncoming day approaches. And as it does, there are those many miles away, preparing to launch a mission of hope and desperation on behalf of their loved ones. Their mission will begin as scheduled, signaling the beginning of a new era for the world...the beginning of the end for Asao's family, friends, many of those living in and around Hiroshima... the beginning of a new direction and focus for his life.

Tomorrow, revenge will become unceremoniously plugged into the equation for his life's point of convergence. Once that is complete, it will induce the factor with which revenge and a final retribution can be the only answer.

CHAPTER 3

It is hot and muggy this early morning on Tinian Island. Months of fighting, thousands of lost lives, hours of briefings and debriefings have come down to this next mission. Everyone involved in the war believes they are fully prepared for what is about to take place.

Writing a letter, a man behind a small desk pauses to grab his face with both hands, indicating little sleep. The letter is one written to his wife and family in case the worst that could happen does. He signs, folds, and stuffs it in an envelope.

Outside, engines from three B-29s, firing up one by one, interrupt the silence of this particular morning. Mission Thirteen is about to begin. Three weather scouts make ready their departure, some seventy minutes ahead of the others. Their role, to radio up-to-the-second weather conditions surrounding the primary.

One at a time, each B-29 moves down the runway, engines roaring. The three advance planes lift into the air, systematically disappearing into darkness. Their early morning exodus signals the beginning of an event in time that will alter the course of world history, changing millions of lives for years to come. Innocent victims of a savage war, tens of thousands are about to lose their lives. Thousands more will suffer physically and emotionally...many of those wounds never healing.

As time passes and the first three planes are gone, silence reigns once again over the eastern shores of Tinian.

A few minutes later, at 2:00 a.m., floodlights persist; surrounding three additional B-29s as ground crews prepare each for its role in the continuing mission. One in particular receives additional attention over the others.

Popping camera bulbs resemble flashes of lightning from an electrical storm already on top of them. Trucks approaching from a distance, inject rumbling-like sounds of thunder into the early morning special effects, adding to the simulated appearance of the tempest. As the entourage and an expanding line of lights approaches, a press corps member yells out above all other clamor, "It's the crews!"

Headlights brighten the closer they come; vehicles slide to a complete stop on loose gravel just a few yards from idle planes. Men dressed in drab-gray flight suits step out of their "military" taxis, and walk toward a waiting press. Five hustle past a gathering crowd, moving instead in the direction of one plane receiving most of the attention so far this early morning. At that moment, it looks as though movie stars have stepped from the screen, out of the darkness, into the light. Flash bulbs pop once again with increasing rapidity, blazing a path to legendary status for those about to embark on this fateful journey.

Copilot Robert Lewis, weaponry assistant Norris Jepperson, and bombardier Tom Ferebee push their way through the darkness, the press singling each out for interviews and pictures.

Finally, two additional figures emerge from under and around their plane, completing preflight structural checks. One has silently walked the perimeter of his, stopping to pat the left side of the nose. As he removes his hand, a press member's camera focuses on two words recently painted on the side of that nose... Enola Gay. Facing the cameras once more, the squall intensifies. Reporters throw questions at the celebrities of the early morning, slinging one on top of another, barely giving time for even mere acknowledgment. Then again, there will be few answers from the crew this morning, the highly classified nature of this mission dictating their lack of response.

Suddenly, intense media interest escalates into a physical confrontation, momentarily separating the two from each other. Deke Parsons, mission weaponry assistant is literally slammed against the plane, fighting back by pushing through the now splintered media surge, ignoring their pleas for cooperation. One of the photographers tells him, "Smile! You're gonna be famous."

Colonel Paul Tibbets, mission commander and pilot of the *Enola Gay*, pushes his way through the crush and makes his way toward his plane named for his mother.

Twenty-two minutes gone since their arrival, it's time for crews to go to work. Parsons, realizing he has forgotten his pistol, required equipment for any mission, borrows one from a nearby

MP. Before climbing aboard the plane, he straps his just borrowed weapon around his waist. Tibbets, who is finally on board and sitting in the cockpit, leans out his window shouting, "OK, fellas, cut the lights! We gotta' be goin'!"

He begins phase two of the mission, ordering engines started, calling the tower.

"Dimples eight-two to North Tinian tower, taxi out and takeoff instructions."

A voice from the tower comes back.

"Dimples eight-two from North Tinian tower, takeoff to the east, runway A for able."

At 2:45 a.m., engines roaring times three, the *Enola Gay* and her two escort planes roll single file toward the main runway. One by one, each escort B-29 rumbles down the stretch of oiled-coral and takes off.

The *Enola* lumbers slowly onto the runway and settles into a holding position. The previous sound of three B-29s is now down to one. All remaining lights are off, with the exception of the tower, those lining the runway, and the lone plane sitting at one end.

Few on the ground or in the crew know much about this very important mission...contents of the cargo has been common knowledge for days; their primary target, by normal practice, has not.

In the history of the world, potential devastation of the payload they carry will be unlike any ever unleashed on a civilized people. Little Boy is projected to destroy almost everything in its path for nearly a three-mile radius. A briefing last night indicated that fact to be a somber reality. The briefing also unceremoniously declared the serious and profound effect their special cargo could have on the entire world in this war, their country, and its militaristic future in years to come.

Takeoff has been considered one of the most critical phases of this, or any other mission scheduled to depart Tinian this morning or in the past. In the back of everyone's mind rests previous incidents involving crashes of other B-29s during takeoff...reasons for concern generated by the fact all bombs are armed before each mission begins. The decision to arm on the ground before takeoff is as sound a decision as any other made in this war. However, should a crash occur this time, the payload carried by the *Enola* will certainly disintegrate everything surrounding them, including the entire air base...completely.

Tibbets turns to his copilot, Captain Robert Lewis, hesitating momentarily. A short pause, a sigh..."Let's go."

Slowly pushing her throttle forward, Tibbets holds a shaking plane back with both feet planted firmly on its brakes. As the engine's noise decibels increase with a deafening, thunderous crescendo, he awaits the moment only his judgment will determine to be the appropriate time for brake release. Reaching a vibration apogee that threatens to dismantle his warship from its frame, Tibbets lifts his feet suddenly and at once, allowing the plane to pull himself and his crew down the runway. Overweight at one hundred fifty tons, including five-ton Little Boy and seven thousand gallons of fuel needed to make the 2,800-mile journey, the *Enola Gay* begins its struggle to gain speed.

Only Tibbets knows of his decision to keep his plane on the ground until the precise, predetermined moment. By doing so, he will be able to build up to a speed necessary for the critically dangerous takeoff.

The *Enola* continues her journey down the lighted runway, coral dust flying from behind her tires. Using up nearly two-thirds of it, many of the crew believes they could be in trouble. Looking nervously out his cockpit window, Lewis loses it.

"She's too heavy, Colonel! Pull her off! Now!"

Tibbets says nothing, holding the B-29 steady on the runway. The *Enola's* speed, now exceeding one hundred and eighty miles per hour, has pushed every crew member deep into his seat. Every hole, every bump in the runway becomes more negligible as he pushes the plane's speed to its limits. The water's edge nearly at its nose, Tibbets pulls the wheel back into his groin, beginning the deliberate lifting of the large, grossly overweight ship into the air. The amount of strength required just to accomplish takeoff, to hold the wheel steady against his body, places a severe strain on his back and arms. Just inches off the ground, the runway beneath disappears, tires brushing across jagged rocks as they seem to reach for the plane in one last gasping effort to stop its momentum.

Standing on the observation deck of the control tower, General Farrell drops his binoculars, leaving them to hang about his neck. Heavy sweat rolls profusely down his forehead, as he finally releases air from his lungs held there during the *Enola's* almost entire takeoff. He stares into the early morning darkness, shaking his head in disbelief.

"Don't believe I've ever seen a plane use that much runway," he says to those around him.

And as all continue watching, the lights of the plane are simply engulfed by the surrounding darkness. The roar of her engines muffled by distance, all is quiet once again on the Pacific island's base.

Minutes into their mission, approximately ten minutes of three, Tibbets steers his plane in the direction of their proposed primary target. Now in the air, he can relax a little. His hand brushes across the pocket of his jacket, reminding him of a small black box he had placed there earlier, just prior to the flight. The twelve cyanide capsules contained in that box will be used should there be trouble of any kind for him and his crew. If captured by the enemy each will be expected to ingest one to avoid torture or even an outside chance anyone in the crew would be placed in a position to give up classified information.

At 2:52 a.m., Deke Parsons taps Tibbets on the shoulder. "We're starting."

Parsons moves toward the belly of the *Enola*, beginning an arming process of Little Boy. As he squats in the bomb bay, nestling himself into as comfortable a position as possible, he thinks back to the day before, and the time he spent, cramped in this same location. Time spent going through this process repeatedly in the sweltering heat would pay huge dividends for those left on Tinian had the worst occurred during takeoff. Only he, Farrell, and Tibbets knew of his plan to abandon normal procedure and arm in flight.

As he begins, the intricate process resembles that of a skilled surgeon in an operating room, albeit a very tight one. His assistant hands him the tools he needs, one by one. At 3:10 a.m., his work continues without a hitch. Gunpowder inserted, detonator connected; a critical electrical circuit is carefully left unattached.

4:55a.m.—Well into its mission, the *Enola Gay* continues in flight, on her journey through continuing early morning darkness. As dawn approaches this hemisphere, so does their primary. Lab and photo planes have joined them now, with Tibbets and his plane at the point position of the small V formation. Tibbets glances out both sides of the cockpit, acknowledging their presence with a salute. Mission Thirteen continues, on time and on course.

Just outside Hiroshima, Yuan Mei awakens to little Massey's request for water. She retrieves it, handing it to him. He places the cup to his lips, holding it with both hands, tips, then swallows. He hands the remaining liquid back to her. She gently strokes his head, calming an apparent uneasiness.

"I know; I miss brother too. He will be home soon. You must go back to sleep. It will soon be light, and we must be on our way to market. You will not be rested if you do not sleep."

Miki and her family, beginning their journey earlier, are currently several miles east of Okayama.

Not far away, Asao sleeps, though slightly restless.

AUGUST 6, 1945
THE ENOLA GAY, AT 26,000 FEET

Parsons returns to Little Boy for one last visit. He makes a final connection, this time fully arming the bomb. As he finishes, Tibbets' voice can be heard over the plane's intercom. The crew ceases all activities to listen to this important message.

"Gentlemen, as you know, we are carrying the world's first atomic bomb."

The roar of the engines, usual shaking, and rattling sounds continue, as if trying to drown out his message...a message given with a great degree of empathy, although somewhat matter-of-factly. After hearing Tibbets' statement, they will each sit in a personal silence, trying to determine the full ramification of this mission against Japan, not really knowing completely how this course of action will affect those in direct path of Little Boy's projected fury. Parsons sits without sound or movement, as do the others; hearing, digesting the remaining message with little show of emotion; emotions hidden within the cold, stark realities of a brutal war. He reflects back to the briefing that only Tibbets and he attended. He remembers a certain coldness with which the information was presented, hearing how this mission would be the first of many...one of nearly fifty planned in all. All would be missions scheduled to brusquely persuade Japan to halt their aggressions toward the United States. Making them pay for their surprise attack on Pearl Harbor where 2,403 of this crew's comrades were lost, is just the tip of the iceberg, as there have been many, many more since that fateful day. U.S. forces have had little trouble channeling all efforts into the all-out defeat of the powerful Japanese Empire since then. This would be no different.

Tibbets' statement has reminded them of the importance of what they are about to do, what they are about to be a part of; the importance of this particular mission now magnified tenfold, now projecting them all into a conditioned dark side of the war.

At this time of morning, the Ankawa's, minus Asao, are awake and on their way to Hiroshima's inner city. Always a happy occasion for the family, every member is no less excited about today's event than any past trip to market. There will be hundreds, maybe thousands, all there for the same general reasons. Many old friendships and acquaintances will be renewed today, as they are every month, with the prospect of new ones to be made. Many will arrive early to set up their temporary makeshift shops for a full day of selling and bartering. Although a world war rages within the hemisphere, life must still go on as it surely is in the States.

"Asao will surely be disappointed he missed this trip. He always has such a grand time," Grandmother tells her daughter.

A few miles outside Hiroshima, Miki and her family are closing in on their destination. Approaching the large city from the west, Miki's excitement continues to grow. The closer they are to Hiroshima, the closer she is to her Asao's home.

At 7:25 a.m., the *Enola Gay* leaves 26,000 feet, beginning its gradual climb to a final altitude dictated by pre-mission planning. Noise inside the plane is deafening as Tibbets nears completion of his last climb, passing through 31,000 feet. He looks out his cockpit window toward the completion of the oncoming sunrise to the east...deep in thought over all that is about to take place...convinced this must be the right thing to do. A thriving city is about to come to grips with a war of epic proportions. From *Straight Flush* comes an extremely important message. The weather plane's captain, Dutch Van Kirk, gives Tibbets one final piece of information, the final piece necessary in determining their primary's state.

"Cloud cover, less than three-tenths at all altitudes. Advise bombing primary."

Tibbets sends a final, chilling message to his crew. The intercom crackles with each word.

"Gentlemen, our primary is determined. It is Hiroshima."

Once again, a self-imposed silence immediately follows. Although they had been briefed on many different possibilities, his announcement has given their target a name, conferring a no uncertain finality to their mission. None knows much of the city or the people they will soon introduce to Little Boy. Knowing little helps keep emotions in check, extracting the human element as much as possible. This thriving city, virtually untouched by an all-out war, is about to see that change. With this one event unfolding, eighty thousand will die instantly...outright. Another sixty thousand will be dead in just a few months, by the end of the year, due to fallout sickness. In total, about two hundred thousand will die due to the massive explosion and subsequent inferno from the atomic bomb.

Tibbets levels the *Enola* back to 31,600 feet. He looks again out his window to the east as the morning sky takes on a new hue. The new day symbolizes many things. He cannot help thinking of the people 32,000 feet below. *What are they doing this morning? Where have their lives been taking them? What are their hopes, their dreams? Will death be instant? How many children will die? They are all about to pay for their country's militaristic aggressions toward my country,* he keeps telling himself; *it has to be. It will be their unfortunate sacrifice for a possible end to the war. It has to be, it is the right thing to do,* they have all tried to reason, he and his crew. If not the Japanese, then very likely their loved ones back home would eventually have to pay this extremely high price...justification enough for the entire crew it would seem.

At 8:05 a.m., Dutch Van Kirk radios to the *Enola* once again a reading that will take them to a point of no return, "Ten minutes to AP."

Tibbets' voice crackles over the intercom one last time. "We are about to begin our run! Goggles on, and do not...I repeat, do not remove them for any reason until further orders."

The crew's last check ritual continues methodically...unimpeded. The *Enola* approaches its rendezvous with destiny. Ferebee, the plane's bombardier, peers through his site. His target, the T-shaped Aioi Bridge at the city's center, has not yet moved into his view, not yet touched his site's cross hairs.

On the ground below, a large city is awakening from its summer night's sleep. In the center of town, very close to the bridge, those who have stirred early and are preparing for the day's crowds, work hard to finish those preparations. Yuan-Mei works diligently, arranging her display of the famous Ankawa berries. She steps back, proudly admiring her work. Asao would approve, she surmises. She watches as the rest of her family work in preparation for today's activities, finishing all tasks before them. Massey plays with other children his age, just a very few feet from his family's stand.

Yuan-Mei interrupts her thoughts momentarily, looking to the sky. She believes she can hear the sound of planes overhead. Using her hand to shade her eyes, she strains to pinpoint them, thinking...one must certainly be my intended returning home from battle, most likely some of Japan's finest. Almost everyone else around the market is too busy to notice.

At that moment, high above, Ferebee nervously shouts, "...Got it." The target he is searching for, the Aioi Bridge, slowly works its way toward the cross hair on his site...as it does, the precise moment for Little Boy's extrication is now upon him.

Swallowing hard, he presses the button, releasing the deadly weapon. The heavy payload drops from the plane, plummeting toward an unsuspecting city...its people below. The *Enola* shakes, lurching upward, as her heavy cargo is expelled from her body like the birthing of a newborn. Detonation will occur in a matter of seconds...forty-three to be exact, only a few feet above ground.

Tibbets immediately begins his predetermined, required maneuvers, steering the plane into a sixty-degree dive, at a one-hundred-and-fifty-eight-degree turn. The projected shock waves and flak soon to be ejected from the powerful explosion require these necessary and calculated flight adjustments to lessen their impact on the *Enola*, and ultimately her crew.

In the city and at the market's center, traffic has continued increasing with every passing second. Yuan-Mei, as do others, now hears a faint whistling, a sound growing louder, a sound many are not quite sure of. Increasingly, many more have stopped... stopped what they are doing to look to the heavens one last time.

"See anything yet?" Tibbets asks, turning in his seat to do so.

Jepperson had started his own countdown forty seconds ago. He stops at forty-five. *It's a dud*, he is thinking to himself.

Suddenly, the sky lights up as though the sun has exploded into a million pieces, throwing particles of light into every corner of the universe. If it weren't for what this truly represents, all on board would think this phenomenon to be one of the most beautiful sights they have ever seen. At ground level, early morning sunshine transforms into a fiery darkness, a contradiction of sorts. There is no warning. There is nothing anyone can do. The simple luxury of screaming out in pain is not an option for thousands. The onslaught on life at ground zero has begun.

Visible, initially blinding ultraviolet infrared rays blanket the city's center, a glowing fireball pouring down on its innocent people and members of Asao's family. The resulting raging firestorm incinerates life from inner Hiroshima, initiating an ultimate slaughter of thousands.

OKAYAMA, JAPAN

Awakened by what he thought was someone tapping him on the shoulder, Asao is finally able to revisit a less than deepening sleep. Soon his dream takes him back to a repeat of a battle he had just won.

Completing his mission, he stands before the emperor and a throng of well-wishing admirers. After receiving his medal of honor, he sees Yuan-Mei and Massey for the first time in any dream, stepping to the front of a very large crowd. They walk toward him, stopping just in front of where he stands. Looking past them, into the crowd, he can see his entire family, all apparently there to celebrate this great warrior, his tremendous accomplishments, their proud moment as well.

"Asao. We are all so proud of you," Yuan Mei tells him.

Asao watches as her smile transforms into a look of horror, one of severe anguish. Tears explode from her eyes.

"I will always love you, little brother." As Yuan Mei makes her final statement, Massey cries silently, tears streaming down his young face, changing to trails of blood oozing from his eyes, mouth, and nose.

"What's wrong?" he asks. "Yuan Mei! Massey! What is it? What's..."

Asao tries to walk toward them, attempting to get to them. But his legs will not move. Before him, Yuan Mei's skin literally burns, melts from her core skeleton, her skeleton disintegrating before his eyes as a massive barrier of immense fire explodes between them. He stares at Massey in horror, watching the same fate befall his little brother. Looking to the crowd, a crowd he later will trust represented the people of Hiroshima, he sees the same come to pass. The remaining members of his family disappear, screaming in extreme pain and agony; contributing to the nauseated feeling he will experience upon his awakening. None has been able to say anything more, as their mere existence is decidedly terminated.

"Mother! Father!" Asao cries out in such tremendous anguish and despair. He awakens, pulling the cover over his head, crying uncontrollably. Afraid to peer out for many moments, he finally gains the courage to do so, pulling the blanket from over his eyes, to just below his nose. His heart pounds harder than ever before, jumping erratically, almost through his throat and mouth as he sees what he believes to be his sister Yuan Mei, kneeling at the foot of his bed. He soon realizes it is his aunt, in his room to check on his condition, after hearing his screams. Extremely relieved it all must have been a dream, he uncontrollably vomits onto his bed and the floor, his sickness in actuality, brought about by many things.

As the *Enola* majestically completes her turn beginning an escape, light from the explosion fills her cockpit as crew members cannot look away from all that is about to consume them. Seconds later, the crew can see there is no cloud mass rising upward and outward at the top as expected. Instead, a stringer appears as those aboard the plane continue their witness to history.

"Hang on!" Tibbets shouts. The first shock wave overtakes the plane, catching her as she speeds away from the quickly approaching storm, jarring her and the crew aboard. It pushes the *Enola* upward, conversely slamming her downward. It's as though the floor of the plane drops from beneath as Tibbets struggles mightily to keep her steady. A few seconds pass before a second wave severely impacts the B-29, 2.5 g-forces sending them into a prolonged dive. With thousands of hours of flight time, Tibbets cannot remember ever encountering a set of conditions as severe as these. The plane and its crew continue to brace themselves, stopping everything they've been doing. Tibbets fights heroically to bring them out of the storm's determined push to their rendezvous with their death, a seismic alteration to their planned escape.

Yuan Mei has no time to reopen her eyes from a reactionary function as simple as a blink. Unable to complete even that, her eyelids are instantly sealed shut by intense heat, bringing a final darkness to her young life. Just a fraction of a second before dying, her senses trigger a scent of burning flesh and hair...her flesh...her hair. Rays from exploding fission slam into her fifteen-year-old body, penetrating her soft, youthful skin with ease, disintegrating her life into nothing more than millions of radiation-tainted particles. In her new life form, that will now be pulled farther upward into the air, farther upward into the rising cloud of dust and radiation, she will realize no change immediately. As she has tried to live life to the fullest during her fifteen years on earth, death becomes the catalyst for her next transition. Her soul, as do souls of all consumed this instant, rise into the air behind those particles; the angel of death at the controls of the carriage she, Massey, Asao's family, their fellow countrymen and women now ride in their final journey.

The traverse of time from life to death does not transpire in earthly seconds. Within this passage of time, severe pain and trauma escalate, but not likely in an instant. In that earthly splitting of one second, death becomes the mechanism slowing the normal process of life, casting these souls toward a most unfortunate lifetime of excruciating final physical moments on earth.

The penetrating prompt radiation emitted from the explosion travels across land, slamming through walls of buildings, pulverizing, disintegrating everything in its path. Asao's older sister, his six-year-old brother, his mother, his father, grandparents, friends...are all lost...forever!

Hiroshima is dying! Many within its boundaries are now waging a battle they cannot win. Heat from the radiation melts human flesh like butter. Shock waves from the massive explosion travel across land, pulverizing bodies, trees, buildings...anything in their path. In a matter of seconds, Hiroshima is transformed from a thriving city, full of life, into "Hell's Inferno"...death and destruction strewn about its streets everywhere. Trees, buildings, absolutely anything in the way explode inward then outward in a split second.

Little Boy carries out death sentences on the thousands who unwillingly, unknowingly stand in its path, further sentencing thousands more to a shortened miserable existence, followed by a painful early death. Those lucky enough to die instantly have been spared the pain and suffering, the emotional trauma, and the horrendous existence initial surviving friends and family must now endure.

Aboard the *Enola Gay*, everything is under control for the moment, all are silent. Mission accomplished; they are on their way back to Tinian, and what is sure to be a hero's welcome. Not everyone aboard will feel like a hero today. Sitting in the copilot's chair, Lewis works on his own private log of Mission 13. His next entry is amply profound, but triumphantly simple. "My God, what have we done?" Another shock wave suddenly engages the ship, driving its nose into a steep dive.

Mission 13 support planes systematically arrive back at Tinian. One by one, each will land to cheers and the expected welcome as news of the successful results of this mission has already begun reaching the base. Soon, all have arrived, with the exception of one.

Farrell, ground crews, crews from the support planes, members of the press, watch and wait. Few interviews are conducted and concluded...a more extensive debriefing awaits all participants in this monumentally historical event. Farrell anxiously looks *at* his watch. They all know it's highly unusual for the lead bomber to be so far behind its support group.

He turns to Dutch Van Kirk. "Did you see any sign of them after the explosion?"

"No, sir, we were already on our way and well ahead of their departure from the area."

Support crews make their way toward the base barracks, leaving their planes to be readied for their next mission. An aide to the general continues his watch through military-issued binoculars.

Minutes later, as most everyone else has given up, "General...I think I see them!"

Those left waiting look out over the water, eyes straining to see off into the distance. Seconds pass. Finally, landing lights come into view of the naked eye. The outline of one lone plane approaching the island emerges from the dark blue of the morning sky, gaining in size as its advancement continues completion of its mission nearly in sight.

August 6, 1945, just hours after Mission 13 began; momentum in the war has begun a massive, unalterable shift. The day is just beginning for many on Tinian, with little fanfare, with little change from the norm. For Hiroshima, this day is the beginning of the end for thousands. For thousands, their days, their lives, were over some time ago.

CHAPTER 4

L anding lights brighten in the distance as a large plane levels out following a left bank turn with adjustments, continuing its approach from the north. Southern Airlines' flight 1853 prepares to land on the east side of an ever-expansive Dallas-Ft. Worth International Airport. Captain Jack Yarbrough and his co-pilot work to keep their flight pattern steady and on course, adjusting flaps and airspeed in line with the controller's most recent instructions. One of hundreds in an ostensibly endless procession of planes through DFW daily, one of the world's busiest, 1853's landing seems insignificant at best. On the ground, it is business as usual, as ground crews hustle to complete their work at those gates occupied by other inbound and outbound flights. Thousands of travelers pass each other inside terminals on both sides of the airport, racing to catch connecting flights to destinations determined at the time of ticket purchase; moving from car to plane, plane to car. Others continue sitting on planes, awaiting their departure or arrival.

The controller assigned to 1853 from the time the plane entered DFW's airspace continues his job, guiding it through its approach to the airport. One hour and fifty-three minutes after leaving Chicago, this leg of this particular flight is almost over.

As the big plane approaches touchdown, Captain Yarbrough relays his final readings to the tower. One voice from that tower, a voice belonging to someone Yarbrough's never met—someone he places his complete trust in as he would a close member of his immediate family—continues guiding the person responsible for all passengers' lives on this flight.

On board, most of the one-hundred eighty-three passengers have raised their seat-backs to their upright positions, locking their trays into position into the back of the seats in front of them. Flight attendants complete their final passage through aisles, gathering cups and glasses in their final preparations for landing.

Sitting in seat 5B, courtesy of a frequent flier upgrade, Jason Cade lays his head back on his seat's headrest, closing his eyes momentarily. He's tired, apprehensive, but also very upbeat with this latest trip to Dallas. He will soon deplane, along with the other one hundred and eighty-two passengers and eight crew members. In and out of a dreamlike state throughout this flight, he again steals a sedentary glance at the person sitting next to him in 5A. Secretly stealing another quick look, he is not particularly eager to leave her side, not just yet anyway.

Rolling his head slowly into position to face the front of the plane, he closes his eyes again, revisiting the reason he's making this particular trip to begin with. This past Friday, his last day of work with the large conglomerate where he'd spent nineteen years, was the end of a tumultuous career, at least more so during the last couple of years. He realized when he finally mustered up the nerve to tell his boss, "Stick it up your ass!" he was making a statement...his statement, a fortuitous personal stamp on the end of a less than stellar career. Somehow, he had convinced himself he was making this drastic move on behalf of those he worked with. They had all had to put up with the boss from hell, the boss who didn't care about his people, was willing to sacrifice every one of them for his own personal gain. He had worked only there since getting his business degree, since marrying for the first and quite probably last time. At forty-two, divorced, a white male...he's in a world where being a white male may no longer be an advantage on the job-hunting front. The fact he didn't have anything lined up when he concluded his career with the now self-proclaimed infamous statement to his boss, is even more ludicrous; many would say idiotic. Calling his former boss a "dumb ass" to his face certainly wasn't a good move, never is, but it sure felt good at the time. He believes, fantasizes he walked out of the building a hero of sorts to his colleagues. Thing is, Cade knows he's probably the real "dumb ass" in this situation. Not for saying what many under his former boss's supervision had wanted to for so long, but for not having something lined up prior to that final blowup. Nonetheless, he's in search of a new career; no choice now. He's moving forward...has to.

Like smelling salts, her perfume rises, penetrating his nostrils each time she chooses to move in her seat, bringing him quickly back to the reality of the moment, a moment where he knows someone like her would most likely never be interested in a loser like him. Why would she be?

With the poor choices he's made in his life, walking out on a well-paying career, leaving his wife and two boys in Dallas almost seven years ago, and spending few physical moments with Jeff and Bobby since, just to name a few; no woman in her right mind would be interested. He can't help but wonder now if his trip to Dallas will be one more mistake, determination driving his character toward an increasing desire for some form of personal restitution.

He's on his way to Dallas, going to spend a couple days seeing his best friend, Mark Anderson, and his kids from his first marriage...his only marriage...and, oh yeah, there's the interview.

Thinking about his boys makes the decision to move back here the right one. A chance to spend more time with them, a chance to watch them continue through their teen years, grow into adulthood; something he thought he'd given up being able to do four years ago as a sacrifice for his career. *Shit, what career?* he thinks to himself. That's gone too. Now he has nothing, nothing whatsoever to show for those sacrifices. "I'm the so called dumb ass." Beating himself up for the umpteenth time, he figures he deserves it; little satisfaction available to his ego at the moment.

Maybe I'm being too hard on myself. I've got the job interview coming up; I've made the ultimate career sacrifice to be closer to Jeff and Bobby. I'm a good man...I've always provided for my family, financially anyway...when I could. I never ran around on my wife, well, maybe just once or twice. But, I really loved her despite all that. She just didn't understand how much I really loved her, sometimes believe I still do.

My third interview with the same company is coming up tomorrow. This opportunity could be a good one. The privately held corporation, a Dallas-based company, could be just what I need now. Working for a smaller company, settling down; no more moving, no more sacrificing to move up the ladder, all those things sound pretty good from here.

So it isn't just Chicago, the short hot summers, the seemingly endless frigid winter weather that's brought him to this point. The screw-ups in his life, the antics of "Corporate America" in general, his company specifically, all had something to do with the decision, that final confrontation with that "dickhead" of a boss. It really wasn't any one particular thing.

The numerous restructures during the last few years, one after another, were more than enough to chase him and many of his friends from the company. He reasons he's witnessed too many bungled attempts at upgrading internal systems, merging divisions, divestiture of businesses, work overload for those like himself left to do the job many getting laid off had done before. The degrading experience of being forced to re-interview for the job he'd worked so hard to get promoted to over the years. The fear of not being quite good enough to qualify for a job he knew he was good enough to do. Many did not get past that last hurdle.

I guess I was lucky though, or maybe I wasn't. Then, a few months later, there would be additional planned, cold, systematic elimination of jobs and people; the next phase devised to improve profitability...supposedly. *I'd seen HR's plans, by accident. Too many good people, many my closest friends, had lost their jobs, were going to lose their jobs. My job stability was becoming "iffy" at best.* Many were still unemployed due to the massive hordes suffering the same fate at the hands of "robotic," uncaring managers listening to the recommendations of hired guns...consultants; those who get paid big dollars to ruin people, careers, and families.

Tired of being forced to interview every time there was another downsizing, Cade was determined not to let it go on any longer. Somebody had to make a statement. He would stay in control of his own destiny...not leave the final decision for his life's direction to a bunch of arrogant, egotistical, highly overpaid assholes. That's the one thing he'd decided not to let happen; the one thing his father had taught him if nothing else. Stay in control of your own destiny.

I won't let 'em break my spirit. As hard as they tried to do just that, I still feel pretty good about myself. With a smaller company, I'll be able to settle in; work hard, maybe finally reap justified rewards for my efforts... further some personal goals and aspirations.

Yeah, the change I'm looking for is definitely in Dallas. I'm sure of that. I'm comfortable with my decision. I'm comfortable coming back here. I know my way around and I should be able to find someplace to live easily, although it probably won't be much for now. I loved it here before, when Janice and I still lived together, still had a semblance of marriage...or so I thought. I'm looking forward to taking the boys to see the major sport franchise games...all those things we used to do before...a few years back.

Again, like the effects of smelling salts, her perfume brings him back, forcing his eyes open. He turns his head slightly, trying to get another look at the attractive young woman sitting next to him in 5A. His unplanned glance...stolen, almost uncontrollable, reactionary, becomes one of longevity. He watches as she prepares herself for the landing. Laptop put away, she pulls a compact from her purse, readying to check her makeup, make sure she's presentable for the next planned event.

Cade doesn't see a thing she needs to improve on. His eyes focus on the small oval mirror within her compact. She's using the same mirror to catch another glimpse of him...checking out this slightly older man, slightly gray about the temples, appearing to be in fairly good shape for his age, no wedding band.

She allows their eyes to meet. She smiles...as he does in return. Oblivious to the remote possibility she could be interested or even remain interested over time, he turns away. He likes those little games that sort of come into play when it comes to the opposite sex. Occasionally slightly unsure of himself, still in need of a little confidence booster from time to time, a little self-appreciation, his recently developed shyness, a characterization not normally aligned with his persona may hinder him today. The young woman may read his reaction as a statement of non-interest.

Familiar landscape gradually moving closer to the plane underneath passes as they continue their descent toward the runway. Cade leans forward and to his left on the armrest; attempting to gain a little better advantage, a little better view out the window the two passengers share...trying to pick out landmarks he might recognize.

"Would you like to trade seats?"

"Ah...no. I'm fine." Jason rocks back into his seat, a little perplexed, thinking he's probably annoyed her and possibly just blown it. "Sorry. Didn't mean to crowd yuh."

Thinking now she's embarrassed him in one of these little games they seem to be playing with each other, she serves up the next volley.

"No, no. I didn't mean...I mean, just thought you might like to sit over here for a better view. Really, I don't mind at all."

She decides, almost too late, she'd probably be better off just not saying anything more. Based on experience in similar situations, nothing ever seems to come out right anyway. Besides, nothing can come of any new relationship now or ever anyway.

"I'm fine, thanks," Cade utters.

Man, I'm really blowin' it, he thinks to himself. He decides the best thing for him to do now is shut up. Settling back in his seat, he forces his eyes closed once again, throwing himself into a much safer environment. His thoughts review the past few hours, journeying back to the first time he saw her...O'Hare, just before the flight, energetic imagination combined with past realities not a problem here.

The first time he noticed her was when she walked up to the gate. She had on the typical "corporate" outfit worn by most women participating in the business community today...dark, two-piece suit. But, that's where typical ended. Her skirt was much shorter, and a little tighter than most he was used to seeing. Not really your everyday, axiomatic career woman's style. No, it was her style, her personal signature and stamp on business fashion for today. It was the way she chose to suit up, so to speak, the way she carried herself that set her apart from the others. He remembers thinking she was one of the few he'd seen who had taken your so-called fundamental "corporate" look, turned it into something attractive, something quite sexy.

She sat in a chair in the gate area, several rows away. He could tell she was quite confident in herself. He remembers wishing she was sitting next to him on the flight...hell, sitting next to him right now...never happen... seldom does. He usually ends up sitting next to another businessman, on the phone the entire flight, nose buried in his work. And too many times, when he can't get into first class, a young mother or father, traveling with a crying, squalling infant ruins the flight for everyone.

He can't help himself. He watches her every move, making his best attempt at being inconspicuous. She occasionally looks up from the book she's now pulled from her briefcase, pausing from her reading to look around. A couple of times, Cade thinks their eyes meet, is sure of it, fantasizing she's trying to watch him as well.

Sitting next to her now, her consistent fragrance, her mere closeness in proximity ignites another rush of adrenaline; pumping blood throughout his entire body's vein system, warming him above that which is normal. It reminds him of the way he felt at O'Hare each time their eyes met, at least each time he thought they had.

He remembers sitting there, imagining her standing, walking in his direction.

"This seat taken?" she would ask, stopping directly in front of him. He'd look up at her, to either side, unsure whether she was talking to him or someone next to him. Before he'd be able to answer, she'd sit beside him. Her smell would obviously be fresh...unforgettable.

Do I have a mint? Where are my mints? Digging in his pocket, he feels around, eventually finding the small foil wrapped remains of what was once a complete roll. Two left.

He'd had to do this before, matter of fact, he'd gotten pretty good at it; fake a cough to get the things to his mouth. He would turn away, covering his mouth with his hand obviously to prevent germ spreading, forcing the mints past his lips.

He turns back to face her. She looks him straight in the eye, smiling seductively, as he would expect in a dream-state like this where control was totally in his hands.

"You married?"

No. He isn't. Even if he were, he wouldn't be stupid enough to admit it now. But the truth made his answer an easy one.

"No. Matter of fact, I'm not."

She'd lean up to him, coming much closer, in a soft, sensuous voice "I've been watching you ever since I saw you. You're just what I've been looking for. I've decided you're the one. I want to have your baby."

He feels a warming sensation throughout his body. He leans toward her, within a fraction of an inch away from touching, mouth to mouth. He opens his mouth; she opens hers.

Danny, as she prefers to be called, looks at him sitting next to her. She is quite amused...his eyes closed, his mouth creeping open, he appears to pass into his subconscious.

Her breath is sweet...her taste like nothing he's ever consumed before. God what a woman! Then it happens!

The jolt from the landing brings him quickly back to reality, out of his dreamlike state, out of his incremental flirtation with fantasy. As he does, he glances over at her. She's grinning.

What's so funny, he wonders.

The captain engages reverse thrusters, slowing the large ship's initial landing speed to a crawl, then to a complete stop on a cross ramp between two active eastside runways. His first announcement follows the welcoming of the lead flight attendant. It will prove to be a very unpopular one for the majority of his passengers.

"This is your captain speaking. The good news is we've arrived a little ahead of schedule; unfortunately our gate is currently occupied. I've been told the plane is about to push back, but until it does, there's no place for us at the terminal. Looks like we're going to be stuck out here a few more minutes. I don't think anyone's in danger of missing connections at this point, so I ask your patience for just a few minutes more. I'll get us rolling as soon as I can."

Jason hadn't heard anything past the captain's initial announcement of delay, which he's personally quite happy about. Being able to spend a little more time with the woman sitting next to him was just fine with him, and a most fitting end to their flight.

She didn't seem very pleased with the prospects initially, glancing at her watch, swearing under her breath. Cade's about to say something, but she pulls a cell phone from her purse, hitting speed-dial, sending a call out to someone.

Cade closes his eyes again, relaxed, trying not to pay any attention at all to her phone conversation...no, really.

Back at O'Hare, the gate agent calls for pre-boarding, including those seated in first class. He notices the young woman stands, then makes her way toward the door. This could mean she's in first class...tremendously improving the odds of her sitting next to him. A fair level of excitement speeds up and down his body as he walks toward the door and the ticket agent's podium. But, instead of disappearing through that door as he had figured, she alters her course, making her way toward a bank of pay phones along the wall. Never looking at him, it's as though nothing had happened between them earlier...which of course, it hadn't.

Cade hands his ticket to the agent at the gate. With stub in hand, he moves into the walkway, onto the plane, closer to his seat. He imagines the young woman watching him closely, checking him out, as he walks past her.

One of the attendants approaches before he can slide into the seat he's assigned, asking him for his jacket, then if he'd like something to drink. He declines, telling her he'll wait till they are in flight, which is the way he usually does it. Pulling a USA Today *from his carry-on, he explores the cover page, searching for something interesting he hadn't already read twice.*

Passengers continue boarding at the front of the wide-body's forward cabin, many retracing his earlier steps, filing in one by one. He folds his paper, stuffing it in the pocket on the back of the seat in front of him. Nothing interesting enough to keep him from watching people coming on as they too begin their search for the correct seat.

People watching, something of a hobby for Cade, yet unrecognized and unofficial as such, something he thoroughly enjoys nonetheless. And this time there's additional excited incentive. Maybe he'll see her one more time. Surely, she's on this flight. She has to be on this flight. Additional time passes as she fails to enter the plane. Cade becomes more concerned, acting as though they are traveling companions in danger of not making their plane together, not make their lover's rendezvous.

He doesn't know it; but at this moment, she's making her way down the long walkway, from the terminal to the airplane, one of the last remaining passengers to board. The line onto the plane seems to be backed up a little, stopping her progress momentarily, giving her a little extra time to glance at her ticket; again reminding herself of her seating location.

Cade watches as she steps through the door and onto the plane; relieved...satisfied she has calmed his concerns. Bypassing the first aisle and what would have been her direct route to the row he was sitting in, she opts instead for the second on the right side of the cabin. He watches her every move, oblivious to all others on the plane at this moment. His eyes stalk her viciously as she slowly moves toward the back. At one point, she appears to glance at him as she makes her way down the aisle; smiling just before disappearing into coach. She too happens to be looking for him. Resigned to not seeing her again, he ceases the stalking and begins the usual "wait and see" game of "Who's Going To Take This Seat Next To Me"...one game he often loses.

An older gentleman, dressed in a well-tailored, dark-blue suit, makes his way toward row five, eyeing the seating numbers above each row, appearing to focus in on Cade's. He stops, looks at the number on his ticket, then the numbers above Cade, back to the number on his ticket again. Cade stands, smiling to be as pleasant as possible under the current circumstances, preparing to make room for the gentleman so he can slide into his seat...instead, the man throws his briefcase into the seat across the aisle; hands his coat to the attendant, then proceeds to settle into 5C. Relieved a little; thinking the next-best thing to having the attractive blonde next to him the whole flight would be to have the seat empty; he shrugs his shoulders, making his move to settle back in his seat. Before he can drop onto the seat cushion below, a soft voice, spiced with a slight southern drawl comes at him from behind.

"Excuse me. I believe that's my seat."

He turns to face the individual making the statement, to let the person in, and he can't believe his eyes. He finds himself face-to-face with her!

"Excuse me," she repeats.

He steps back to let her pass. She glides effortlessly into 5A, stuffing a computer bag under the seat in front of her, softly brushing against him. Still standing, Cade looks down the aisle toward the rear of the long plane. He feels the effects of her unexpected closeness. Like a kid, checking to see if everyone noticed who was indeed sitting with him on this flight. He just knows everyone, especially the men aboard, are watching him, envious of his great luck. He envisions every guy on the plane, up and down the aisles, giving him the thumbs-up, an "atta-boy Cade... way to go." "I'm never this lucky." An enormously stupid grin blankets his face.

Settled in her seat, she finishes stuffing her purse under the seat in front of her, next to her laptop then orders a glass of Chablis from the attendant, obviously not as happy about her seating arrangement as he is.

"Sir, you sure you wouldn't like something to drink before we depart?" the flight attendant persists.

"Sure. I'll have 'Jack n water'. Make it a double."

He decides he'll speak, say something really witty, but when his mouth opens, nothing remotely coherent comes out. His tongue has suddenly swollen to outrageous proportions.

"Excuse me," she says, obviously straining to understand what he has just said.

Before the plane begins backing away from the gate, he is able to manage a couple of coherent comments that she is finally able to comprehend. His nervousness subsiding, he finds her very easy to talk with. As the flight progresses, they are served a late lunch. During the dining, she continues sipping wine, accepting at least two refills, maybe three...his drink provides the needed calming effect, but as it does, the effects of a little too much alcohol hit him while he finishes his third as well.

The plane settles into a holding pattern, on a tarmac just to the south of the terminal. Cade's eyes closed, Danny checks her watch, concern about missing the meeting she was supposed to be back in time for subsiding with each passing minute.

She finds him attractive, almost cute, this man sitting next to her, this Jason Cade...especially the shyness. To her that characteristic is most refreshing. During the flight, she found him to be quite charming, unassuming; even unpretentious. His warm, quiet personality expounded few flaws, immediately attracting her to him; that is, if things were different. She'd noticed him in the gate area; one of several she'd noticed. But she wasn't really in the market right now, not with the problems she's facing here in Dallas. Besides, he reminded her a little too much of Robert.

An older man as well, at fifty-three, Robert works for the same company she does. In fact, he's her boss. Their mutual attraction began long before she began working directly as his assistant. His maturity, rugged good looks, and quite honestly, his status within the company, were all things she found attractive about him.

Considering herself no "gold digger," and certainly not a "feminist" as many of her colleagues always seemed to be labeled; thirty-one-year-old Danielle Wilson was determined to make it any way she could. She didn't get her promotion because of their relationship, she reasoned. She would've gotten it without the benefit of his help. She deserved the raises...she'd earned every one of them. This way, it just happened a little ahead of schedule. No, she liked to think of herself as a "realistic opportunist."

Their relationship had blossomed, maybe a little slower for her than him. She was a reluctant participant at first, feeling the way she did because of his marital status at the time. He convinced her, his marriage was crumbling...virtually on the brink of ending. He no longer loved his wife of seventeen years. And, finally succumbing to his personality and charm, she couldn't fight growing feelings for him any longer. It was a classic tale of modern romance...classic by today's standards, she reasoned. A romance spawned within the confines of "Corporate America," an aspiring young woman, all of thirty at the time, falling for her boss...an older, married man. A man who'd promoted her, bringing her into his department to keep her close...under his watchful eye. A man with slightly dishonorable intentions, a man who'd planned every event, every opportunity leading up to this point.

That was many months ago, a little over a year. Within the last few weeks, she'd finally come to her senses; realizing Robert would not give up his wife without conditions; conditions she wasn't willing to accept. She made the decision; took the action she should have weeks before.

Knowing Robert wouldn't handle rejection well, she planned to tell him just prior to her Chicago trip. Giving him a few days to calm down while she was gone...time to think about it; hopefully coming to his senses while she was away, agreeing she's right. She hoped she'd return to a reasonable, understanding man.

His initial reaction, although what she had expected generally, seemed much more abusive than she anticipated, considering the feelings and closeness they'd shared in their relationship all those months.

It didn't seem so much to be the breakup, the loss of someone he had shared a part of his life with, someone loving him unconditionally for over a year, someone he'd been untruthful to. Rather, it was the fact he'd lost control, had not been a part of the final decision. What she was doing to him hadn't been done before, or so he said. Robert was used to calling the shots in his relationships, in business; all of them.

He suddenly became belligerent, obnoxious, and extremely abusive. She hadn't seen this side of him; at least she didn't think she had. Maybe it had always been there. Maybe she was too blinded by what she thought was love to notice. She didn't want to accept it as real. She wasn't quite sure how to react.

"You can't do this! I won't let you!" she remembers him telling her tersely. "Just who the hell do you think you are?"

When she insisted it was over between them, he told her "You've just made the biggest mistake of your life. There'll be no breakup. It's over when I decide it's over! Not before...certainly not now. Do I make myself clear?"

He had. He had made himself quite clear...she understood all right. She understood she had made a big mistake all right, but the mistake had obviously been made early on in their relationship when she made the decision she couldn't live without the man. Obviously, her biggest mistake was agreeing to the relationship in the first place.

Admittedly, she still cares for him; her decision to take the steps to end their relationship seemed a tough one. But his violent outburst, his reaction, the threats...all finished off most feelings she'd once had. She'd look for her next relationship with someone a little closer to her age, not married, and the next time it would be just a flirtatious fling...nothing serious. But she'd also decided she wouldn't be looking for one anytime soon.

Now, she has to decide how she'll deal with a possibly bad situation awaiting her arrival. She'll need to assess Robert's state of being. More importantly, she'll need to assess the damage to her career. She'll ask for a transfer; that way, she'll be away from him...not see him almost every minute of the day. That has to be the first thing on her new agenda. Maybe he's calmed down since she last saw him. Maybe he's ready to accept what must be. No matter what awaits her, she'll have to face it...she'll need to be strong.

The plane begins to move; engines whining, quickly progressing to a higher-pitched sound, signaling to its passengers they are pushing ahead once again.

"Ladies and gentlemen, we are going to move out of the way. One of the planes behind us has a gate to go to. Unfortunately, the plane occupying ours seems to be having a mechanical problem, so we're going to try to find another open gate. In the meantime, we sit. I do apologize for any inconvenience. Our delay shouldn't last much longer."

Cade detects slight, but increasing frustration in the captain's voice. Most of the passengers aboard appear additionally irritated at the extended delay as well. He, for one, could not be happier. He has nowhere he needs to be today, at least not based on a predetermined time frame. He's sitting next to someone he'd like to continue getting to know, and now he has the opportunity to do just that. Danny doesn't seem angry at the prospects of an extended delay either.

This young woman, beautifully proportioned, everything in place...Her facial features, her hair, everything perfect...Well, with the exception of the small mole on her neck. He has decided he may like that the most about her. He thinks her hair is probably colored, couldn't be that perfect, he thinks. He is willing to accept any unexpected imperfections now hidden to the naked eye, no matter what they are. Articulate in speech, educated at UT, he imagines, slight southern drawl, with a sexy, slightly deeper voice than most women he was usually attracted to. He could go on and on in his mind. He needed nothing more to convince himself.

"Looks like I miss my meeting," she offers.

"...An important one?"

"Uh...not really. Gives me an excuse to go home early. Did you say earlier you were relocating to Dallas?"

"Yeah, regardless of how the interview goes tomorrow."

"You're moving here with nothing lined up...no job, no concrete offer."

"Yeah...'fraid so."

"Haven't you been reading the papers?"

"What d'yuh mean?"

"The job situation. You know Dallas hasn't been immune to all the downsizing. Aren't you a little concerned about finding work? I mean, a man your...your...uh."

"What...a man my age?"

"Oh no! I wasn't referring..."

"Yeah, I know. I don't look too intelligent right now for an old guy. Like I said, I've got kids here, from my marriage. I need to be close to them for a change. Don't guess it can get any worse."

She had just mentioned the one thing he knew would probably become the roadblock to any future relationship...their age difference. How could he have ever imagined she would even have the slightest interest in him anyway, regardless of his age?

"I didn't mean...I mean, obviously it's your decision. I just..."

"That's OK. Pretty dumb of me to think I have anything to offer over all the others out there looking for work, all those younger guys. I wanted to move back here...I've saved a little...I can hold out a few months. The interview doesn't work out, surely something'll come up. I'm not too concerned." Fact was, he was very concerned.

He's questioned this latest adjustment in his life many times. He doesn't need a stranger telling him what he's getting himself into. He looks at her, quickly refocusing out the window as the plane continues to hold, uncertainty, disappointment re-entering his thought processes.

"Actually, you sound a lot like my wife. She always had the common sense in our marriage." *And the way she continually presented her common sense was one of the reasons I left her,* he thought to himself.

"I didn't..."

"No, it's OK. This is just something I have to do. If for no one else, I have to do it for myself. I had to get out of Chicago."

"You didn't like Chicago?"

"Wasn't that...Living in Chicago was great. It's just that...that I was beginning to hate the company I was working for, the person I'd become. I guess I'm going through my change in life early." There, he went and did it again; inserting age into the equation. "I want more out of life...more excitement. I know there has to be something more out there...somewhere."

"You sound a lot like me."

"That so?" A little renewed excitement they might have something in common after all.

The captain interrupts their conversation with the announcement only one passenger is disappointed at hearing. He's found an open gate, and they're on their way. Cade prepares himself to say good-bye to the woman of his dreams.

"It's funny. I don't normally open up like this so early in a relationship."

Dead silence from both.

Shit! I can't believe I just said that.

What relationship, she thinks to herself. *I'm sitting here on a plane, talking to this stranger, a guy I just met a couple hours ago, and he's talking about a relationship. Here it comes; he's working up to say something witty...one of those patented "come-ons." Someone needs to teach these guys about the art of picking a woman up. I've heard it all. First he's going to tell me I'm easy to talk to, then he's going to tell me he's never met anyone quite like me...maybe.*

But he says nothing more.

The captain announces their arrival; walking through the subliminal sales pitch, filled with acknowledgments of how they can all fly with any airlines (and some probably will next time), and thanks them for choosing to fly Southern Airlines.

They're all the same, Cade thinks.

"Who's you're interview with?" she asks as the plane slows to a stop.

"I'm sure you've never heard of it. It's just a small, privately held company; not one of those larger-than-life, crappy Fortune 500 conglomerates."

"You're really down on Corporate America, huh."

"Don't get me started again," referring to some of their earlier conversation. "They could be the biggest problem facing this country today."

"Interesting you'd say that. How so...?"

"Big business doesn't care about people anymore. They've brainwashed management...their stockholders, the financial analysts...they're never happy. They'll all stop at nothing to get what they want. Improving profits at all costs...hurting millions of people, cornerstones of the very companies they've helped build; ruining their lives, handing them six-month severance packages if they're lucky...no thanks, no loyalty, no security."

"Sorry if I sound cold, but isn't that what being in business is all about? I mean, corporations have an obligation to their stockholders, an obligation to deliver those promised profits, improved stock values. Don't forget, a lot of those employees are stockholders, the very stockholders demanding more profits."

"You probably have a good point. But this corporate greed thing is out of control. On the one hand, you've got management, CEOs, boards, all afraid of their own shadows, even more so of Wall Street. On the other, the market analysts—they're the guys in control and they all know it. Someday though, the little guy's going to take it all back. The small companies will have their say. Our work force balance is shifting. Yeah, someday they'll all pay for what they're doing to people like us."

"Pretty idealistic attitude, don't you think?"

"So...? What's wrong with a little idealism?"

"If you think smaller companies, like the one I work for, Ankawa, for example...if you think for a minute they're not in business for profits, the almighty dollar—think again."

He hadn't heard anything after Ankawa.

"Did you say Ankawa?"

"Yeah...Why?"

What incredible luck, he thinks to himself.

"That's who I have an interview with tomorrow. I'm pretty excited about it. A little reluctant maybe, but excited." *Even more so now,* he thinks.

"Really...And why the reluctance?"

Not quite sure whether to answer, knowing he'll sound prejudicial, he decides to chance it, be honest anyway. She seems to be someone who appreciates honesty.

"It's Japanese owned, right?"

Danny's eyes reflect a much more serious posture with his last statement.

"What's wrong with that? If you feel that way, why work there? Why take a chance on getting a job there?"

"'Cause I guess I really don't consider myself prejudiced."

"Boy. You could've fooled me."

"No, you don't understand. I'm more than aware of the current attitudes toward the Japanese and other foreign investors in our economy. You know, the way they've come into America, buying up businesses, land, literally taking America from its people...using American money to do it...the Japanese attitude toward American products going into their country, or should I say, not going there."

He can see he could be ruining things between them, see Danny becoming more irritated with every word, so he attempts a comeback.

"Personally, I don't think the animosity is justified in any way. We've got to learn to take care of our own problems, take care of business in our own backyards...not blame the Japanese, or anyone else for our own problems. It's just that...right now, any association with one of these companies could be hazardous to one's health, considered unpatriotic by many standards."

"Bull! I can't believe you're saying that. That's typical American propaganda bullshit!"

He's beginning to forget all the other motivations, his initial reasons for generating this conversation to begin with. His beliefs spill out again.

"Why not? Americans feel threatened...are threatened. We're losing jobs by the thousands. The economy is in trouble, the Japanese are becoming more wealthy thanks to American dollars. Now they're moving in, buying large chunks of our country, taking over companies founded by American's...sucking us dry like 'economic vampires.' Yeah, excuse me. You're damned right I believe that! It's as though they're retaliating for what happened during World War II."

"Yeah, right." She laughs at the thought.

At this point, he believes it's probably over between them with little chance of taking this new friendship any further now. Over before it ever got started. But with this potentially new incentive, he still wants to do well on his interview tomorrow. He likes a woman who can think for herself; stay strong in her opinions... independent. That makes Danny even more attractive to him than ever before. He doesn't want to take any more chances on her walking out of his life now.

Man! What a piece of luck! This is incredible...my lucky day! he's thinking to himself once again.

She offers a smile, a sort of peace offering. She's enjoyed the conversation, the spirited discussion as it were. She really likes this guy, this Jason Cade. She doesn't want him walking out of her life just yet...until she can get to know him better. But that'll have to wait a bit...place this one on the back burner, so to speak. Give him just enough line; he'll hang around till she can unravel everything about to hit her on her return to Dallas. Once all that is behind, she'll be able to focus on this Mr. Cade, see what he's all about, see if there's something there worth going after. After all, she does like older men.

And Cade, he thinks he might still have a chance...although on life support, somehow he feels he's still got another "at bat" coming to him before the game's over. He doesn't see this potential relationship flat lining yet. Fully unaware of the events to follow, this chance meeting, this casual unexpected development in his social life, will bring excitement, danger, even intrigue to his relatively mundane existence. Just what he said he was looking for.

If he were to know of what awaits him, even minutes from now, he would probably end it right here, right now. But then again...maybe not.

CHAPTER 5

Despite Cade's hint of prejudice, Danny has to admit, the thought of this man working at the same company excites her. It seems she may have momentarily forgotten what may await her.

"What do you do there?" Jason asks, fulfilling his need to move on to a different subject.

"Systems technology...a senior tech analyst."

"That's great."

Of course everything is great at the moment. She could've told him the plane was on fire and he would've thought that was great. His excitement now is reminiscent of times when he was young, opening presents on Christmas morning at his grandparents'. His parents had little when he was a kid, couldn't afford much in the way of presents on Christmas, birthdays, etc. That never bothered him. He never knew any different. He'd decided long ago, what he didn't have or never had he could never miss. His grandparents always tried to provide what his parents couldn't, but he didn't know that back then. He does now, has for many years. Opening those presents Christmas morning at his grandparents' was a grand and happy time. Didn't matter what the gift; each one he opened was better than his last, not going to be quite as good as the next. His grandparents have been role models and inspirations in his life, his grandmother still living, his grandfather gone for three years now.

"Ugh, what's a senior tech analyst do at Ankawa?"

"Among other things, my primary responsibilities include visiting any company Ankawa takes over, reviewing their internal communication and technical support systems, retooling those to a level of compatibility with ours. I've been able to create several new programs, including software to make this task easier," boasting a little to impress. "The company's been using most of that new software to initiate the re-start of the new one. With my programs, any company's internal system is linked, then accessed and monitored from Ankawa's central system. What's exciting is we've found a way to get into a system without the use of a direct-line modem hookup. Beyond state-of-the-art; twenty-first century stuff...now."

She pauses only momentarily, apparently just to catch her breath as the excitement of telling someone about her work is obvious, telling someone who is interested in her and what she has accomplished.

"We can make sure the information flowing from top to bottom engages properly, and proceeds without any glitches. There are check-off programs I've built into the system that gives us the power to go in and pinpoint a glitch any time of the day or night almost before it happens. We can identify the problem, correct it, and be out before they know we're online dancing with their data terminal. With what I've been able to develop, we could probably tap into any company's internal system, monitor their day-to-day activities, and download a wealth of information from their data banks without bothering anyone, long before they know we're doing it, regardless whether it's an Ankawa subsidiary or not."

"Wow, sounds pretty incredible. Also sounds like your system could be dangerous in the wrong hands. If the government ever gets ahold of it, we're all in trouble."

"I think it's too late. Ankawa's negotiated some kind of trade-off for the government's use of that technology, as well as any other we develop in the future.

"Adding more power to Big Brother. Jesus, as if they needed anymore. You realize what you may be doing to us little guys, the common taxpayer, and God knows who else? Why in hell would you make a program like that available to the government?"

"Obviously, Ankawa can do what he wants with the programs. He owns them. Don't think for a moment the government doesn't already have the technology to do all you're accusing Ankawa of giving them the power to do. I don't know for sure where he's gone with the program, but I'm pretty sure he's shared them with Uncle Sam. Still a few bugs to work out though, before full-scale use can be attempted with confidence. Besides, I built and hid a self-destruct mechanism into the program should anyone get the wrong idea about what it should be used for. No one knows about that, not even Ankawa. With a simple push of a button, I could destroy it, and all the information data-banked. For anyone to stop that process once it's been set in motion is almost impossible. Anyone tries to defuse it, my program will unleash a virus so difficult to detect or stop, it'll have devastating effects on any system trying to control it."

"You're saying no one else can disarm it?"

"I can never say absolutely no one, but I can tell you it would be a most difficult and time-consuming process to figure it out—that is, after the time it'll take them to detect its presence in the program."

"From what it sounds like, you're telling me you might not even be able to disarm should that become necessary."

Danny decides she's told him enough...too much for that matter. All of what is out of her mouth now could be dangerous in the hands of the wrong person. An overwhelming feeling invades her senses, a comfort level with Cade, a feeling she can trust him with her life. Few men have ever had that effect on her...her father, when he was alive, most recently Robert. It's as though this new acquaintance has suddenly cast a spell on her; created an overwhelming desire on her part to share her excitement with him, her passion for the work she's doing; as though he's controlling her thought processes. Maybe she's just happy someone is interested in her work for a change, instead of the more common physical, sexual aspects of a prospective new relationship. But just to be sure, she'll say no more.

A passenger walks up to the two still sitting on the plane.

"Excuse me, but I think you're sitting in my seat." The man looks at his ticket, the number overhead. He shows Cade his ticket. Danny and Cade both already know they're in the wrong seats; they know they shouldn't still be on the plane. Other passengers are beginning to file on, as pre-boarding has begun for the continuation of flight 1853 to Miami.

Abandoning their seats after realizing what's happened, the two continue their friendly conversation, as they walk off the plane and up the ramp toward the terminal.

"What position you interviewing for?" she asks.

"Financial analyst."

"Oh, one of those."

"What do you mean?" he asks, not sure he likes the initial sound of her reaction. The two emerge from the boarding ramp into the terminal.

"You know. Accountant...Bean counter. Finance has kind of been my arch nemesis, especially throughout my program development. Never have much luck working with you guys. You always want everything laid out in black n' white, cost everything out to the nth degree. We can't justify every little expense, every little cent we need to spend; it gets axed with no consideration for the benefits to the company. You make everyone else's jobs so much more difficult, if not impossible."

"Oooo-kay."

Inside the terminal, they both look to the signs above, searching for the arrows and direction to baggage claim, continuing their journey side by side as though traveling companions and good friends.

Danny's just unloaded on him and his chosen profession, expressing a considerable amount of animosity and resentment. He could hear an umpire in the background bellow out, "Strike one!"

God, he hated being called a bean counter.

"Yeah...guess that's what some people prefer to call us." The disappointment in his voice detectable, yet unnoticed by her.

She looks at him, unsure of the meaning his comment represents, coming so long after her mini-attack on accountants. Instead, Danny's contemplating a move that could be totally out of character for her. She checks her watch. The meeting she was supposed to be attending should be over now...some thirty minutes ago. She's not usually in the habit of being so forward with a stranger, but the more time she spends with this guy, the more comfortable she feels, as though he's really no stranger at all. She thinks she'd really like to get to know him a little better.

"Can I give you a ride into Dallas?"

"Yeah, sure. I'd really appreciate that," he replies without hesitation. But Cade suddenly remembers Mark...Mark Anderson, his best friend since college at A & M. He should be here to pick him up. He glances around the terminal. Doesn't see him... quite frankly, doesn't want to. Maybe he was here and left. The delay reaching the gate took about forty-five minutes to an hour. Maybe he went home. Selfish thoughts run through his head as he and Danny Wilson continue their walk side by side toward baggage claim. The terminal remains very crowded, but it's slowly beginning to thin. He could still be here. Maybe Danny and I can sneak out without him seeing me. That'd be a dirty thing to do, but if he had the chance, Mark would do the same... in a second, he conveniently reasons. No doubt about it. Cade believes he may have finally broken through with this woman he finds so attractive.

Inside the walls of the tightly secured eighteenth floor of Ankawa Corporation, fifty-eight-year-old Asao Ankawa dozes during a midafternoon break. Racked with an obsession for revenge the past forty-some years, his hatred for the country unfaltering, its people provide his corporation and him the wealth to amass his silent, hidden efforts against her. He is in the midst of revisiting one of many dreams, or nightmares, this time remembering a happier time with his sister Yuan Mei. As he awakens in a profuse sweat, tears flowing from his aging eyes, he believes these dreams to be a just and most certain form of punishment. For the guilt he bears in soul, he cannot ever hope to eliminate it until his deed is accomplished.

"Southern Airlines paging Jason Cade...Please go to a red paging phone and pick up for an important message."

"Hear that?" Danny asks.

"What? Hear what?"

"I think someone's paging you."

"Southern Airlines paging Jason Cade...Please go to a red paging phone and pick up for an important message."

Entering baggage claim, he can readily see a bank of phones along the outer, partial glass wall. He also sees the red phone nestled among those pay phones. There's a bit of reluctance on his part to walk over and pick it up. It could be his buddy, probably is, somewhere here in the terminal trying to find him.

He forces his legs and feet to move in that direction. Luggage continues arriving from other flights sharing the same carousel as 1853. Danny watches for hers, in among the many pieces spewing forth from the depths of the loading area below. She finally sees hers break through the opening, as it rides the conveyer belt to the stainless steel carousel.

Cade rejoins her after retrieving the message from his friend. It was Mark.

"I really appreciate the offer of a ride. My friend's been detained at work. Hope it's not too out of the way for you."

"No. Have to go that way anyway," second thoughts now entering her mind. Maybe she shouldn't have offered him the ride; she could be making a big mistake.

"What's your friend do?"

"He's a photographer...owns a studio somewhere close to downtown Dallas. I think it's on Oak Lawn."

"That's perfect. Should be close to where I live."

Cade retrieves the two small bags he checked in Chicago, little clothing for what's in store. But he figures he'll be heading back there in a few days to pick up what's left, planning to be here for just a short visit initially.

"Ready?"

"Sure," she replies.

Walking out of the terminal, into the Texas-afternoon air, they can feel the August heat immediately.

"Man, is it hot or what?"

Not necessarily a brilliant deduction on his part, one she chooses to comment on.

"It's August, you are in Texas, or had you forgotten?" She smiles with her unsubtle reminder.

As the two quicken their pace slightly to escape the heat, entering the covered concrete garage directly adjacent to Terminal 3-E, Danny appears to have momentarily forgotten where she parked. Her growing uneasiness with what she is about to do with this man is totally screwing up her usual businesslike approach to everything. Pulling out her parking ticket, reading the number she'd written on it prior to abandoning her car a few days ago, she confidently moves in that direction. They soon find it...a white Volkswagen Beetle ragtop. A late sixties model, Cade only guessing, since that model of car has looked so much alike for so many years. It's a car she's very proud of; one she's spent considerable money restoring to near mint condition.

Unlocking the passenger's door, she tells her new friend to toss his bags in the backseat. She walks to the other side, doing the same, hers landing alongside his. She begins unsnapping the top of the VW; the initial process involved with taking it completely down. Jason follows her lead, doing the same from his side. He's thinking right now how well they work as a team. Insignificant conversation about the weather, etc., continues.

On the other side of the garage, a large man sits quietly and alone in a red Corvette. It took him awhile to find Danny's car, knowing the flight she departed on, the gate it left from, all those things helping considerably. He watches the two with interest as they work together, apparently enjoying each other's company. Completing their task, the top rests, folded neatly, and lying on the back of the car. The man conducting the stakeout continues to scribe mental notes of the two who appear to him to be more than just friendly acquaintances in his book.

She pulls out of the garage, pointing her car in the direction of the north tollgates. Small talk continues as they pass landmarks familiar to both, additional reinforcement for Cade's decision to come back to Dallas for good.

Driving through Las Colinas, past Cowboy Stadium, Cade relishes in just being here, being back. Several cars behind, mimicking the VW's lane changes to keep pace, the man in the Corvette keeps his distance, looking for the right opportunity.

CHAPTER 6

Cade lays his head back on the seat's headrest, soaking in the warmth of the late summer sun. Danny periodically glances over at him.

"What can you tell me about Ankawa? ...There anything that might help me with my interview tomorrow?"

She hesitates in her reply, a little unsure of her feelings about him working at Ankawa. "What do you mean? What do you want to know?"

"Anything...anything at all that'd help me. I really need this job. Can you tell me something about the company...the man behind it?"

"Why is working at Ankawa so important? I'm sure there are better opportunities out there."

Her comments disappoint him. Where's this all coming from? He's beginning to get the feeling she really doesn't want to see him working there. The exact feeling she's trying to influence him with.

"Why do you say that? Earlier, I got the impression you thought Ankawa was a great place to work...you're happy working there, right?"

Danny's mixed feelings are beginning to complicate the situation, confusing not only Cade, but herself as well.

"I know how important this job, any job must be to you, but I really don't think it's such a good idea, your working there and all." Her thoughts, her mind groping for the rationale he will surely demand.

"All I know is I've got a chance at a job, a good job. That's all I really want right now, a job, and a second chance...a second chance at a lot of things."

She doesn't want to admit it, but a part of her is glad he wants to go through with the interview...kind of. "OK. From your earlier comments, I wasn't sure you should be pursuing a job there, but if you do get the job, it might be good for you to see not all foreign immigrants are out to get us, so to speak."

Over the next few miles, she explains a little of Ankawa's history. How he came to America in the late sixties, about '67 she thought, from his homeland Japan. How his search for a dream landed him the opportunity to start a company, using money he'd saved since his childhood. She told Cade how Ankawa seemed driven by something in his past...driven toward success, toward a goal beyond that of any foreign immigrant preceding him. How he's been very successful building the company to where it is today, how it's all chronicled in an unauthorized biography written about his life.

She's about to give him additional information about the man, what she can remember anyway, when she notices something in her rearview mirror...something, or someone who shouldn't be there.

"What's wrong?" Cade asks after noticing her many glances, her sudden, piqued interest in what's behind them. He turns to look for himself.

She doesn't answer. She's too absorbed with the red Corvette, weaving in and out of traffic, gaining, closing the gap between them. The Vette seems to mimic every move of the little VW as Danny steers in and out of the eastbound traffic. She increases their speed ever so slightly, but just enough to send the message she wants, unfortunately not enough to keep the man in the Vette from gaining ground on them.

Almost past an exit ramp, she unexpectedly yanks the steering wheel to the right, catapulting Cade across the seat toward her.

"What the hell's going on?"

She refuses to answer, instead, continuing her vigil with the rearview mirror. Again, Cade turns to see what or who is drawing such a level of preoccupation, noticing the red Corvette quickly closing on them, performing menacing movement after movement.

Danny, her new friend, and the little convertible sputter down the pavement toward the oncoming intersection, as Cade turns back around just in time to see the light go from green to yellow. Danny's continuing moves push them toward an intersection about to fill with cars. He considers reaching over with his foot and stomping on the brake, but Danny slams her foot down hard, missing the brake altogether, practically forcing the accelerator through the floor. The little car responds once again as before. He was afraid of that.

The driver in the Vette tromps his accelerator in his attempt to try to catch them. Speeding down the exit ramp, cutting off several other cars to do so, he can see the light in the intersection ahead flashing to yellow as well, but more importantly, he also confirms he is closing on the VW.

Danny and Cade have quickly passed the point of no return. She swerves to the right of a stopping vehicle, taking to the shoulder to bypass the car with its brake lights flashing and turn signal on. That car hesitates momentarily, also moving to the right, unaware Cade and Wilson are flying by it in a very illegal move surely to bring the law down on them, as Cade imagines, hopes...silently prays for at this point. As she maneuvers around the turning car, missing it ever so slightly, Cade waves at the man behind the wheel, now honking loudly, figuring that to be the only appropriate gesture now. As they fly through the intersection, Cade digs his fingers into the new upholstery now covering the seat; figuring the handmade gash will be the last thing paramedics notice as they pick his and Danny's mangled bodies up off the hot pavement.

Behind them and gaining rapidly, the Vette's driver shifts gears, increasing his speed much more easily with the slightest touch of his foot.

To those waiting in their cars at the intersection, those about to accelerate north and south, it had to be quite a sight. A grown man screaming garbled obscenities from the passenger side of the topless VW as the car and its occupants navigate through the intersection untouched, onto the Highway 114 on-ramp. Within seconds, the light has changed and the intersection is filled with cars, blocking the Vette's path to Danny, Cade, and the VW carrying them potentially to safety in their getaway.

The intersection ahead immediately jammed with north- and southbound traffic, the Vette driver's reaction is just short of instantaneous. Slamming his brake pedal to the floor, he forces the Corvette into a three-sixty toward a certain collision. After a total spinout, the Vette finally comes to rest, facing the direction from which it had just come. The man behind its wheel looks over his shoulder, just in time to see the object of his chase disappear beyond the rise of the on-ramp, merging into continuing eastbound traffic. He pounds his steering wheel, totally disgusted with his inability to catch them. Other vehicles have already filled the once vacant lanes behind, and to either side, all very curious as to what has just happened. A small boy sitting in the backseat of one car beside him stares blankly at the angered driver. Several seconds pass to just before traffic begins moving again, with the man sticking his tongue out at the young boy in a childlike display of anger. The child's expression doesn't change as he raises his hand, flipping the Vette's driver off as he and his mother pull away with the changing of their light to green.

"Mind my asking what that was all about?" Cade asks.

"Wrong exit," she replies.

She continues driving, more determined than ever to reach their destination, more determined than ever not to see Kirk, the man she knew to be driving the Corvette, again today, more determined than ever now to unload what has suddenly become excess baggage sitting in the seat next to her. Turning south on I-35, she points her car in the direction of the Dallas skyline, keeping the little car at a top speed of seventy, seemingly pushing it to a point nearly beyond its limitation. As they drive, Cade notices a very large glass structure standing alone above all others surrounding it. Approaching it from the north, the building on the west side of the multilane expressway is impressive and complete with signage proclaiming it the Ankawa Corporation. Its design, although similar to others in many aspects, has an Asian flare, topped with what appears to be a very large Pagoda-like structure. Despite that difference, the building blends nicely with the numerous structures lined up and down either side of Interstate 35, or Stemmons Freeway, as it is known to the locals. He makes a mental note of its location.

"Nice building."

Danny's continued preoccupation with her concern over everything that's happened to this point, blocks out any and all comments from her traveling companion. They reach R.L. Thornton Expressway, running east to west, and to the north of downtown. She turns onto R.L., then onto Maple Avenue, taking a left turn back to the north. Cade's familiarity with Dallas tells him they're going in the right direction to reach his friend's studio. Cade continues to say nothing, watching the Dallas skyline slowly pass to his right before taking another exit ramp back to the north, toward a single high-rise in the middle of a group of much smaller buildings. He admires the Crescent Building as they approach it from the south.

Not sure if they will pass it, Danny surprises him when she slows to turn into the Crescent parking lot, driving through it, onto the ramp leading to an underground garage, burrowed below the building itself.

"Hope you don't mind calling your friend from here. We shouldn't be too far from his business. You can use my phone."

The prospect and unexpected bonus of being invited to her apartment excites and pleases him immensely.

Danny parks in a stall labeled appropriately, "Wilson," the numbers eight-fifteen printed underneath. Cade, apparently oblivious to their meaning, adjusts everything in his mind to prepare to launch himself from the car. The two climb out, Cade following her move to reach back inside the car to pull luggage from the backseat.

Arriving at the elevators of the combination apartment, office, and shopping complex, Danny depresses the only call button available, in seconds, opening the doors, exposing an empty car. Inside, she punches the number eight, and the doors slowly close. On the way up, the two engage in absent conversation, spending an entire elevator confinement trying to generate an appropriate conversation between two strangers. But neither is quite sure what should be said, much less why either is here. Almost there, Danny wonders privately what possessed her to ask a virtual stranger to her home. She remembers originally the thought had excited her just a little...must've been the wine.

Cade contemplates his next move, should there be opportunity for such. Is she really attracted to him, or does she just do this sort of thing with every guy she meets on a flight in?

The elevator finally arrives at the eighth with a couple who are physically on board, but somewhat lacking in emotional and mental presence. He follows her through the doors, down the hall; assuming their next stop to be her apartment. Soon, standing in front of a door, waiting for her to unlock it, he makes a mental note of the number..."Eight-fifteen." It's not too late yet. She may still ask him to wait downstairs.

She opens the door, walks in...He follows hesitantly, but with little reluctance. Cade realizes he's just entered a part of this beautiful woman's life he would never have dreamed possible today...you could say her "private world." He drops his bags off to the side, close to the door in case he needs to make a quick exit, quickly asking the one thing he knows he can't wait any longer to ask, something he feels he must know, has to know. There are a lot of things going on in his mind at the moment, but first things first.

"Where's the bathroom?"

"Through those doors, to your left..." she says pointing him in the direction of a double door. "Phone's over there," she adds, also pointing to a remote sitting in its stand and reminding him of the real reason he's here in the first place.

With priorities in order, he makes his way toward the bathroom...first things first. He disappears through the doors, following her strict orders, passing through her bedroom, introducing himself to an even more private side of her life.

Watching Cade disappear into her bedroom, Danny moves to open the drapes covering a large double-glass door, exposing a balcony, and an exquisite view of the Dallas skyline to the south... one of the big reasons she took this particular apartment. She forgets the man in her bathroom for a moment, thinking instead about Robert, the incident with Kirk during the drive in, finally back to the strange man she's invited into her home. He's now in an area only one other man has ever been. What if this man is a rapist...even worse, a serial killer? What if he's schizophrenic? Now that he's inside, he has her where he wants her, he'll walk through those doors, a totally different personality from before, brandishing a sinister, darker side.

Considering all the wild possibilities sends chills down her spine. She walks to the rolltop desk, a gift from Robert. She pulls a drawer open. The gun's still there...a Davis P-380...another gift from Robert, along with the lessons on how to use it. She feels a little better knowing it's there. She closes the drawer and walks into the kitchen, pulling a bottle of wine from the rack on the counter. She could definitely use a glass after the events of the last couple of hours.

Finishing what he'd come in here for, Cade zips his pants and looks into the mirror as he washes his hands. He too has second thoughts about the reasons she may have brought him here. She really doesn't know him. What if he were some lunatic thriving on unsuspecting young women like her? Is this the kind of thing she does all the time? He walks from the bathroom, into her bedroom, stopping momentarily to check it out. He sees an open door to her closet, glances toward the living room, and subsequently decides to take a quick look at its contents. Maybe this will tell him something about the woman he's become so infatuated with. Parting pieces of clothing with his hands, feeling, stroking many of the garments hanging there, he stops. This is sick! I shouldn't be doing this! It's perverted! ...must be the alcohol.

Taking a visual inventory, he determines there's the usual stuff you'd find in a woman's closet, he guesses, not necessarily sure what it is you're supposed to find in a woman's closet. Then...the not so usual...an expensive suit, a man's suit; a couple of silk ties, expensive silk ties...French cuffed dress shirts. And a shoe rack exposing several pairs of men's dress shoes resting comfortably between several pairs of women's. The disappointment he begins to feel is major...quickly overwhelming if not totally consuming.

He had hoped he and Danny would have a chance for something more. Obviously, she's doing more than just dating someone. He remembers the Corvette on the way home from the airport. Could that have been a jealous boyfriend, or worse... fiancé?

Before moving away from the closet, Cade notices initials embroidered on one of the shirt's cuffs. Upon closer examination, he can see the initials "R.C."..."R.C." Must be the Robert she mentioned?

As time continues passing on this day, Asao Ankawa is back to his work on the eighteenth floor of his building. Within his sprawling and complete total floor penthouse, designed and decorated with historical Japanese artifacts, Ankawa finds solitude and safety by seldom leaving what he believes to be his pre-World War II sanctuary. Yami, his friend from the old world and current right-hand man in this one, enters the area, showing Robert Carrigan in. Ankawa stands to address him formally, as he always does, though their personal relationship goes back years.

"Is the meeting set?" Ankawa asks.

"All set, sir," replies Carrigan.

"We cannot allow any form of interference at this point. I trust you have safeguarded the information regarding the presidency, his personal life, and the economy's wavering indicators."

"As designed, everything has been set in motion. Before our new president and the American citizenry have any notion as to what is about to happen, the infrastructure of the American economy will have sustained great and permanent internal damage. The new president's inexperience in handling these affairs will become this country's economic undoing. The world's confidence will once again find true reason for unrest with our domestic financial mentor."

"Are our people on the inside secure and ready to do what is necessary?"

"I believe our plan to be infallible, sir. As most will anticipate, interest rates will not be lowered to stop the trend as it gains momentum. It will be too late to forestall a recession. Your decision to bring Federal Reserve Chairman Landers on board was a crowning achievement. There is no other faction on that board with the power to control him. As we have previously discussed, the Reserve Board remains his puppet, as do the markets both domestic and abroad, and without his allegiance to you, we would have never been able to pull this off."

Ankawa's smile and body language indicate extremely calculated, though controlled pleasure with all he is hearing from his American front man.

"If anyone with an ounce of intelligence should believe the president is still the most powerful man in the world, Landers' actions and subsequent disclosure should quickly put any of that to rest. This country will soon see its economy and ultimate world standing in serious jeopardy," Carrigan concludes.

"It sounds as though you have performed your tasks perfectly and as intended. I will always be indebted to you and your son for your loyal support. As such, both of you will soon be rewarded beyond your wildest dreams. Your decision to eliminate Jensen as a warning to others was also a stroke of genius."

"Thank you. I must admit many of our tasks appear unpleasant, although completely warranted. But now, I have matters of the utmost urgency to attend," Carrigan states in matter-of-fact style.

"Is it something I can further help with?" Ankawa questions.

"No. This is a personal matter...a personal relationship issue."

Ankawa nods, smiles as though understanding."

As Carrigian is out the door, Yami re-enters the room where his boss and good friend sit.

"Do you believe he suspects anything?" Yami enquires.

"How could he? He is as greedy as the others. They are all blinded by the riches before them...too much so to see the lion in wait. For now, we remain in the background as planned, waiting for the right moment to step up during the president's great time of need. Because there will be no other choice, he will have to take everything offered him so he may survive in his politically ambitious state. Then all will be in place for the crushing blow no country in the world can withstand. Then and only then, may I begin to finally rest. The leaders of this country could never have anticipated retaliation this deep into their future, so far removed from the past."

Yami smiles in agreement, as he too has been driven by the same vengeance as his childhood adversary, friend, and now mentor.

"Their arrogance continues even today, long after taking my family from me. The one factor they never dreamed could ever have driven one man to the level of destruction I intend will soon be injected into their lives. As their weapon of mass destruction was used against my homeland, this country and its people soon must come to grips with the force driving me to theirs. Who could imagine I am the one person with the fortitude and ability to amass such an arsenal within their own boundaries, founded within America's greed and overt willingness to devour its own. Yes, as in any mathematical equation, my extreme need for revenge has remained the most important piece soon to be embedded, now hidden in the pages of their history books. Our answer for solving America's most important final problem will ultimately prove to be their complete and total economic annihilation."

"When will we return to our homeland Asao?"

"Only after I am quite sure my plan has been carried out fully... without any chance of reversing. I will stay here long enough to witness the financial collapse of America at the hands of its own leaders, from a great and most satisfying vantage point. This will be a collapse adequately and most imminently surpassing that of the Asian meltdown. The world's financial markets will begin their freeze out of this country soon after that. The crucial loss of credibility in the Fed's actions that will most certainly bring disaster to our new president's feet will render him completely inept in his attempt to regain control. The doom he or any other will not be able to curtail begins a new day for America. The leader of the Free World will have unquestionably signaled his death slide of epic proportions. As that collapse should trigger the unstoppable aggressions of America's true enemies, we will depart then and only then to watch the physical destruction of their democracy, the death of hundreds of thousands upon millions from a distance. As this country's people watched from a great distance when my people died helplessly that day in Hiroshima, we too will watch the same befall families of their own. When the time is upon us, our team will not step up to save this country with the riches it has bestowed upon us, as my current allies believe. What these men hope to gain in stature, wealth, and control will never materialize. They will be left behind, witnesses to their own nation falling to its knees, and branded as those most responsible in its death. Few in the world will shed tears for America. This country will finally reap an appropriate bounty from their seeds of death and destruction, the same it sows outside its borders daily."

Ankawa nods as he finishes his final sentence, quite happy with his oratory of what is to come as his plan moves America closer to its final day of reckoning.

Yami smiles as though understanding, then moves next to his friend as they now both gaze out over thc Dallas skyline.

At the same instance, Danny continues her contemplation at the same view, but from a different angle. She then calls out to her guest. "You OK?"

"I'm OK," Cade responds, entering the living room.

"Can I offer you a glass of wine?"

"Got a beer?" he asks as he walks into the living area of the apartment.

He can hear the refrigerator open and close...the sound of a cap popping off a bottle. He moves quickly toward the center, in search of some place to sit. She enters the room at nearly the same time, handing him his beer. She sits in an overstuffed chair, directly opposite to where he's chosen to land. He notices what looks like wine in her glass.

"Thanks." He takes a quick swig. "You have a nice place. I really like the skyline view."

"Call your friend?"

No beating around the bush. Man, she must really want me outta here.

"No, but I will."

"Phone's over there," she reiterates, pointing to the remote once again. "I'm gonna change into something else. It's been a long day." She stands and walks through the double doors, pulling them closed behind her. Cade thinks he hears her locking the doors. In a way, it relieves him to know she takes some precautions. But what if she didn't? What if he were to walk through those doors unannounced, just at the precise moment she's undressed, standing naked; they would run to each other's arms, embracing each other's mere existence. Man, gotta be the alcohol.

Cade reaches behind him, pulling his billfold from his back pocket, pulling out a piece of paper...on it, his friend's number. Picking up the phone, he punches the numbers, and waits for an answer. A few seconds..."Hi, how you doin', buddy?"...a short, but warm conversation between two old friends, followed by instructions about where he is.

As he hangs up, the double doors open and she walks out. If he had problems earlier, they are even more severe now. He can't take his eyes off her. She's wearing a pair of very short cut-offs, tanned legs exposed that seem to increase what he thought was her original height, with an amply skimpy, white laced top. She looks amazing! He decides immediately that he doesn't give a shit who the hell R.C. is. He's about to make his next move, exposing her to his surprising wit and charm, or something along those lines, when the phone rings. Danny hesitates before grabbing it, as though she knows who it is immediately, not sure if she should answer it.

"Hello...Hi! Just a second."

She leaves the room with the remote to her ear, her face appearing to Cade to be rushing to red very quickly. She disappears through the double doors into her bedroom, closing the doors behind her once again.

Cade can faintly make out her side of the conversation. What appears to begin as calm, rational conversation seems to quickly escalate to irrational. Within moments, her voice level grows many decibels above her initial tone. She sounds angry, apparently arguing with the person on the other end, but her words are still somewhat muffled by closed doors. Growing a bit restless, somewhat uncomfortable with the apparent changing environment, he stands, then walks to the balcony doors, fidgeting in the view of downtown.

Several seconds, maybe minutes pass, and the argument still rages over the phone. Danny startles her guest by wildly slinging the doors open, knocking over and shattering a porcelain figure sitting on a table close enough to feel the rush of air from the quickly moving doors. As she storms from her bedroom, the panic in her eyes is easily detectable.

"You gotta leave! Now!" The look on her face, the sudden inflection of her voice tells him she means business as in no other instance prior to this one.

"Hey. No problem...everything OK?"

"Yeah, I think so...I'm sorry...just need you to leave now! Please!"

The room suddenly very cold, quite frankly frigid, Cade sur-mises the air-conditioning must've just kicked in. Her sudden personality swing has totally caught him off guard, and he doesn't have to be hit over the head to know he is no longer welcome. Obviously, she's the schizo.

"My friend's on his way. I'll just wait downstairs. I can find my way out."

"Good."

Hurt by her sudden and most assured eagerness to get rid of him; he decides he'll return the coolness.

"Appreciate the ride...It's been good meeting you...I guess."

Later, she may feel bad about the way she treated him; but for now, she has to get him out of her apartment. She needs him out now! Caller ID told her the phone call came from his cell, and she has little idea how close Robert is at this moment. He could be riding the elevator to her floor as she and Cade speak.

Literally pushing him out the door, into the hallway, she slams the door to her apartment behind him. He makes his way back in the direction of the elevator, depressed and dejected, his visit to her apartment not turning out at all like he'd hoped, especially after what he thought was a pretty positive beginning. Punching the down button, he awaits the arrival of one of four working elevator cars. As he waits, one approaches the upper floors, carrying a potentially dangerous cargo—two men target-ing the eighth as their final destination. Slowing to a complete stop, Kirk and his father Robert, prepare themselves for their landing and very forceful departure.

The first of four available doors opens, the light above illuminating just prior to, yet almost in concert with the chime tone. A few seconds after the first, a second chime announces the arrival of another. Planted in the middle of the hall, strategically centered between the four doors, Cade turns to face the first to open, an opening exposing a lone passenger not yet ready to depart. As he steps on, doors of the second arriving car open across the hall.

Kirk and his father, Robert, step off, immediately turning in the direction of Danny's apartment. As the two pass the elevator Cade has boarded, Kirk glances inside, noticing who he believes to be the man he saw with Danny in the airport parking garage. Preoccupied with his own thoughts of what had just transpired and the cute woman standing across the elevator from him, Cade hasn't noticed Kirk.

The door closes.

"It's him!" Kirk tells his father excitedly.

"Stop him and bring his ass back to the apartment," his dad commands. "We need to find out what he and that bitch are up to! An unplanned reunion will be interesting." The door to Cade's elevator closes before his words are out.

The elevator stops at the seventh, picking up another rider... again at the fifth, the second, finally the ground floor. Kirk has long since given up on the elevators, and is now attacking the stairs, vaulting down two, three steps at a time.

Unaware he's being pursued, Cade takes his time walking through the lobby, stopping to pick up literature on the apartment complex, thinking he may look into the possibilities of moving here soon. Once outside the building, he looks down the street, resting his arms by placing his luggage at curbside. A car turns onto the street, passing in front of the building, pulling up, then stopping where he stands. He recognizes the driver through the windshield, and the two friends acknowledge the presence of each other with a wave and reciprocating grins. Stepping to grab the door handle, Cade accidentally drops one of his bags to the pavement again, delaying his departure momentarily, allowing his stalker a chance to gain precious ground.

Inside, Kirk has finally reached the ground floor, sweating profusely from his very physical descent from the eighth floor, breathing heavily due to his poor physical condition. Eyeing his quarry through glass doors at the front of the building, he quickly resumes his pursuit, breaking into a dead run, about to finish the stalking of his prey.

Cade tosses his bags in the backseat and crawls inside, grabbing Mark's hand in a firm grip, a manifestation of a renewing friendship, before sitting back to buckle his seatbelt.

Kirk slams through the doors of the building, practically tearing them from their hinges. His momentum throws him into the side of Mark's Volvo, rocking it from the force of his massive body. Cade jerks his head to the right, reacting to the blow from the body now pressed against his side window, to see what type of truck had just hit them broadside. Instead of a truck, he sees a slightly contorted face against the window, that face reminding Cade of a character from an old movie he watched late night, not long ago, *The Hunchback of Notre Dame.*

"Get the hell outta here! It's Quasimodo!"

The car still in gear, Anderson floors the accelerator, quickly pulling the Volvo away from the curb, and out of harm's way.

Not in control of his body, the man spins along the length of the car as it pulls away, falling to the street when there is nothing left to hold his torso upright.

"Who the hell was that?" Anderson asks his friend.

"I'm not real sure. Guess it could've been my welcoming committee."

"Shit. Looking at that face, he did look like a committee, but I didn't see anything welcoming," Mark responds, making light of the situation. Noticeable concern on his buddy's face, forces another comment.

"Do we need to go back?"

Cade glances back over his shoulder. The man on his knees, crawling to a standing position, looks to the Volvo with renewed interest for revenge. Cade turns back toward the front, concern for the woman he had just left. But, with the way she'd just treated him, plus a certain amount of understandable fear, his reaction will surprise even himself.

"Should we what? Go back? Naw, don't think so. Not now. Not this time. Nothing back there that would make me want to go back now."

As Mark steers his car around yet another corner, the Crescent, Kirk, and Ms. Wilson are soon out of sight and out of mind.

But, not really...

CHAPTER 7

Inside her apartment, Danny paces, awaiting Robert's arrival. Since initializing the breakup just before her departure to Chicago earlier this week, she's dreaded their first confrontation upon her return. Fear of what just might happen is one of the reasons she decided to bypass the office this afternoon. Now, the additional circumstances surrounding this next meeting will probably make it an extremely negative one.

She walks back to the desk; again pulling the drawer open as before, this time pulling the gun from its resting place. In her hand, its feel so cold, she drops it back to its home. She could never use it on anyone, especially Robert. No, a gun will certainly never be the answer, not in her hand anyway. She turns toward the door, toward the sound of a key as it is inserted into the lock. The key, she forgot the key...Robert still has his key. Before she can react, do anything, the door opens, exposing a man appearing surprisingly subdued. Maybe she overestimated his reactions. He steps inside...the confrontation she expected begins, only she begins directing this one.

"Robert, I want that key!"

Danny has initiated the aggressive posture of this meeting, not Robert as she originally anticipated. But he will not flinch and he will only allow her temporary control in this meeting, initially appearing very cool under fire. His coolness just a tactic, as he begins his somewhat restrained retaliation.

"Glad to see you too. What? No hello? No...sure good to see you, honey?"

"Robert, you have to know I wasn't looking forward to this...to seeing you again under the circumstances...after all that's happened."

"What's happened? You left town on a business trip a few days ago. That's nothing out of the ordinary. We had a minor 'lover's quarrel.' You're back...I forgive you...That's that. Case closed. No more needs to be said."

She can't believe what she's hearing. "Robert, it's over. I can't go on like this. I...I don't love you anymore."

Kirk unintentionally interrupts their conversation by stepping into the apartment.

"Fuckin' boyfriend got away...almost had the son of a bitch too!"

Kirk's appearance introduces a sickening feeling to her stomach. Now Danny knows Robert knows.

"Who is he, Danny? What's his name?" Robert asks, returning his focus to her. "I don't appreciate what he's trying to do to us."

"I don't have any new boyfriend. We met on the flight. He means nothing to me. I was just giving him a ride."

Robert turns to his son. "Meet me downstairs."

After Kirk disappears through the door, Robert closes it, then turns to face Danny. She quickly turns away, walking toward the glass doors to the balcony. Her view of the Dallas skyline isn't particularly breathtaking at the moment but presents her with an opportunity to look at something else, even if it is only for the moment. She turns to face her former lover.

"What d'you want from me?"

"My needs are quite simple. I want you...nothing less, nothing more. I want things back the way they were. That's all. It's very simple actually."

Danny turns away again, hiding the increasing frustration with the man standing in her apartment. Gaining some degree of composure, but still quite frustrated..."It just can't happen. I told you before I left for Chicago..." Her frustration level continuing to mount, she says, "...It's over between us. How do I make you understand that?"

Robert's anger surfaces with his reaction to her latest statements. "It's over when I say it's over! Understand?"

She understood all right. "Yeah, I understand. I understand you don't seem to be able to deal with someone pushing back...someone not needing you." Her emotions building, she says, "I loved you. I wanted it to work for us...I tried everything..."

Her sensitivity to the moment, embedded feelings, her eyes water as tears collect at the corners, everything threatening to explode. Robert's enjoying this confrontation, especially now that he believes he's broken through.

Still slightly in control of herself, she continues. "I didn't want to continue sharing you...you knew that. We've talked about it so many times. And all your promises...obviously, they've meant nothing. I had to learn that the hard way."

"Danny, I meant what I..."

"Don't even start. Your promises have just been words, words to help you get what you want. Not any longer! I'm through letting you manipulate my emotions with your lies."

"I know you still love me. You're letting this unwarranted mistrust take you where I don't think you want to go. This young man you've decided to take up with, whoever he is, is ruining everything we ever had. And I gotta tell yuh, he's not gettin' away with it. When I find out who he is, he will quickly see what a tremendous mistake he's making."

"Don't you dare! He hasn't done a thing. He means nothing to me. I know I'll never see him again. But it's over for us. You're just not the man I thought I knew. You can't control me like this. I don't care how we resolve this, but I can't go on. Transfer me to another department, whatever. That might make things easier for both of us."

"I'm not transferring you anywhere. As I see it, you have two choices: stay with me, or get out! Leave Ankawa! Besides, what makes you think any other department will take a chance on you now? You are considered substantially damaged goods. Nobody'll trust you."

"What do you mean? I'm good at what I do. Why wouldn't they trust me? Please, Robert, don't do this to me. Please don't take my career away from me. I've worked so hard to get where I am."

Robert laughs, providing a certain effect to successfully deliver his next message. "So that's what you think, huh. It does not surprise me in the least you think you're the one responsible for where you are today."

She looks at him trying to make sense of what he is telling her. "What are you saying?"

"Hate to burst your little bubble, but you wouldn't be where you are now without me."

"I know that. I'm well aware of what you've done for me and I know I owe you a lot, but I also know I've worked hard to get where I am. No one gave me anything. The long hours, the work I did developing my programs..."

"Your programs?" He smiles, forcing a chuckle as he turns away, then back to her. "Must I remind you, those are far from being your programs. Those all belong to Ankawa. And as far as your career goes, you wouldn't even have a career without me. You haven't been in control of that since I first saw you. Did it ever occur to you, you were moving up the ranks within the company's framework much faster than most. Hell, you passed people much more deserving, people who'd been here longer, deserved those promotions, the raises you got."

He pauses, knowing he's crushing her, his voice now softening. "But, none of them could ever do the things you could do for me."

Robert softly touches his hands to hers. Initially, she doesn't pull away. She's feeling anger, resentment, and tremendous disappointment at what she is hearing. His touch unfelt momentarily, it's as though her whole body has suddenly gone numb.

Robert knows exactly what he's doing as he continues the barrage of eye-opening attacks. "You could not possibly think you got all those plum projects because you were good at your job. Oh, you are quite capable. That made it much easier for me to justify the decisions regarding your career. But, lady, you knew I planned everything...including your seduction."

"You're lying. You're pissed at me and just trying to hurt me."

He was...he was trying to discredit her in her own mind, establish a new level of self-doubt, taking a calculated risk she wouldn't jump ship, not yet anyway at least until he's done using her.

"You need to see the truth before you go beyond the point of no return. You're bought and paid for, just like everyone else who's ever been involved with me. It's the way it is. No one's ever complained before. Difference is, I still love you, still want you. To prove it to you, I'm willing to do whatever it takes to make you happy. I'll give you anything, including a vice presidency heading up your own division. Walk out on me now—your career, any chance you ever had of having the kind of life you dreamed about, is gone...over for good. Understand?"

Not sure of anything right now, the revelations just heaped upon her crush the very essence of her existence. She shattered no "glass ceiling," as she once prided herself in doing. The independence, successes she thought she was experiencing, mean nothing, have little bearing on her life at this point. The swell of depression overtaking her at this moment pushes her into a depth of realism never before experienced. Like a bomb inside, exploding outwardly, destroying everything in its path she is beyond stunned, beyond feeling much of anything at this moment. She doesn't answer. Anesthetized by all that has happened since arriving back in Dallas just a couple hours ago, she can no longer make sense of anything. Could he be telling the truth? Is this just his way of getting back at her, hurt her at all costs? All this time, she'd made herself believe she was earning her way, earning the promotions, the raises, her accomplishments at work the reason for all her rewards. Instead, she'd earned everything she had...apparently in bed...Robert's bed. She was nothing more than a high-priced prostitute, a gold digger, a two-bit whore, all those things she'd vowed she'd never be, all those things she believed before, she really wasn't.

Sensing victory in this initial skirmish, Robert walks to her side. Feeling he'll soon be reaping the benefits of his triumph, he has calmed considerably. He places his hands on her shoulders, gently turning her to face him.

"Danny, I still care deeply for you, love you like I've never loved anyone. The first time I saw you, I knew we'd be together. Don't you understand, I had to do those things, everything, to make sure it all happened the way it was supposed to? Don't you understand? And don't forget, you never turned any of it down. You were always more than willing—eager, in fact, to take all that I offered. Not once did you complain. I have made sacrifices for you, as I know you have for me."

Danny momentarily regains her desire to fight; defend herself...albeit, against surmounting odds. She looks into his eyes, eyes once belonging to a man she was willing to give totally of herself; no questions asked, no looking back. At six foot three, he has a commanding presence when he walks into any room. She fell for his unmatched charm, his wit, his attractiveness. Despite the age difference, more than twenty years, she had no trouble channeling all her love and attention his way. She thought she knew him, thought she understood him. She heard all the negatives, had been warned many times, but she thought their relationship would be different.

"This whole thing...our relationship...my career, I finally realize it's all been a hoax, one big fantasy contrived to help you get what you wanted from me. From the very beginning, all you've ever had in mind was making me another of your many conquests...get me in bed. It's all been a game."

"Darling, that just isn't true...at least not entirely. Don't lose sight of the fact we both truly enjoy each other's company. Yeah the sex is great, but you mean much more to me than that. All that other stuff...just a means to an end. If I have to, to keep you, I'll end my marriage today."

"...And what about Barbara Dickson?"

Her question catches him completely off guard. She senses a direct hit. She can almost hear him asking himself...how'd she know? She continues sarcastically, knocking him further off balance, digging deeper into his emotions than she should.

"You know, the redhead on the fourth, in accounting. You help her get where she is? What the hell makes you think you could hide that from me forever? I know everything. I have a few friends in the company too. You want to tell me about that? Or you gonna continue your lies?"

He slaps her across the face, knocking her backward. Her line of questioning stirs deep anger and resentment that she would even question him about anything as personal.

"You do not ever question my personal life outside our relationship again! What I do is nobody's business, including you. I answer to no one, absolutely no one!"

His physical aggression catches her off guard...the sting of his attack very real...the pain prolonging her anger. He has never hit her before. She breaks from his grip, stomping into her bedroom, moments later re-emerging with an armload of clothes, his clothes. He watches her carry them to her front door and toss them into the hall. Expensive suits, shirts, ties, all of it landing in a crumpled heap. Turning to Robert, she knows she's made a decision, one he'd just made easier for her. She will end this conversation once and for all. A red welt works its way to the surface of her cheek.

"That's where I draw the line, Mr. Carrigan! No one...absolutely no one raises a hand against me like you just did! I had enough of that in my first relationship! Now, get out! Get out of my apartment!"

Quickly sensing he may have indeed gone too far, Robert attempts a momentary reconciliation. "I'm sorry...I have never...I mean, I didn't mean to let it go this far. It's just...it's just that you mean so much..."

"I said get out!"

She will tolerate no further discussion. She figures he's in her apartment, on her turf...she has rights she will now execute fully.

Robert walks to the door, hesitates, then turns back toward her. "You just do not get it! You are not grasping the gravity of what you are doing, the damage I can do to your career, your life, not to mention your new boyfriend. Because of that, I am giving you additional time. Remember, your decision not only affects you, it affects your friend as well. Believe me when I tell you this; I will most assuredly know who he is, and soon."

Danny's eyes water again, overflowing at the corners, pushing tears down her cheeks.

Robert walks back to her, coming closer than she'd like. She flinches slightly, still hurting from his last advance as he raises his hand to touch her, and leans forward to kiss her forehead.

Confused, bewildered, perplexed—all of those emotions keeping her from backing away, he misreads her reaction. He steps back and smiles.

"See there, I knew you'd make the right decision."

He turns, walking through the doorway, into the hall, over the pile of clothing. He stops, turns back..."Now you're gonna have to send these out to the cleaners...can't wear them with all those wrinkles. Don't forget, heavy on the starch..."

She doesn't wait for him to finish his sentence before slamming the door in his face, locking it. Then she remembers...he still has his key.

CHAPTER 8

The drive to Mark's should have been pleasurable enough for Jason, and would have, had it not been for what had just happened. He wanted to go back...help her, but some of her last words kept playing back in his mind, over and over, as though he were listening to a segment of a prerecorded tape; rewinding, replaying her final comments, over and over. "Stay out of this! It's none of your concern! You need to leave! Leave! Now!" ...maybe overdramatizing a little.

The "How've you been," "What've you been up to" questions have been asked and answered by both friends, while Mark continues driving toward their new destination, turning off Central Expressway onto Mockingbird Lane, heading east toward White Rock Lake, in the northeast quadrant of Dallas proper.

Mark, of Japanese descent, is a ruggedly handsome man in appearance. His good looks have been helpful over the years with members of the opposite sex. Despite the rash of Japan bashing in the States recently, he's been able to toil in anonymity for the most part, enjoying a certain amount of success on the Dallas scene...his success partially due to his looks and charm, primarily to his keen business prowess.

The two good friends met while attending college, A & M at College Station. Although it was quite difficult getting to know him in the beginning...once he did, Cade found him intelligent, likable, and very loyal to his friends. During their years of friendship, there has been little Cade could find out about Mark's family, or heritage for that matter, except for the obvious. Mark has always remained closed lipped where that was concerned, despite Cade's best efforts at unraveling the great mystery.

A bachelor all his life, Anderson had good reason.

"What brings you to Dallas this time? Thought you quit traveling here on business a little while back. What's the occasion, business or pleasure?"

Cade decides this is probably as good a time as any to let him in on his little secret...the one he's kept from everybody, everyone to this point with the exception of Danny Wilson... and Janice.

"...Got an interview tomorrow for a new job. If I get it, I'll finally be able to move back home."

Anderson turns his head quickly to get a good look at his friend's face, checking the status of expression, more to determine whether his latest comment was one of triviality or serious. As quickly as he checks that out, he must quickly refocus on the cars ahead. "You're not kidding this time, are you?"

"Not this time."

"Man, that's great news." Mark holds his right hand out. Cade lightly slaps it in the style they shared while at school together. "You're finally comin' to your senses and comin' back to big D."

"Yeah, finally. Took me long enough, huh."

"Too long. So what're you gonna do? Something I can help you with…transportation, character reference, phone calls? You know, I know some pretty influential people around here."

"Yeah, since you asked, I could use a ride to my interview tomorrow. I'll check into a rental after I'm through with that. I forgot to do that when I made reservations." He hadn't really; thought he'd try saving some cash for later. "I don't want to be a burden on you while I'm here. But I sure do appreciate the offer of a bed. Not having a job, I gotta watch my spending till something's a little more solid."

"No problem. You can drop me off at work in the morning, take my car, then pick me up after you're through doin' whatever it is you need to do. You don't need a rental this weekend. Once Sandy's home, we'll have both cars. You can drive one of 'em. I can drive the truck I've been working on. Fortunately, it still runs. You gonna see the boys while you're here?"

"Naw. Not this weekend. Janice and I talked. She thought it'd be best if they didn't know. Something about their schedules being awfully busy anyway; besides, she wanted me to wait and tell them what was going on after the interview and all. She doesn't want 'em being disappointed in case it doesn't work out."

"Still letting that woman dictate your life this long after divorce?"

"Fuck you!" Cade's follow-up comment, a delayed afterthought. "Sandy the one you were telling me about?"

"She's the one. You're not gonna believe this…I think I've found the one I could spend the rest of my life with."

"Bullshit! You're kidding, right? I mean, Mark Anderson, lady's man par excellence. God's answer to the lonely woman? Confirmed lifelong bachelor."

"That's all behind me now. Since I met this one, there's been no one else...can be no one else."

"Yeah? Is that right? How'd you meet?"

"She showed up at the studio one day, out of nowhere, looking for a good deal on a photo shoot. She was trying to get into the modeling business, didn't have a lot of money, needed a good deal on a portfolio. Once I saw her, I knew she'd come to the right place. I gave her a price she couldn't refuse. Told her I'd do it for nothin', on two conditions. First, she could reimburse me the cost of taking the pictures, after she'd made it big, and two, she'd go out to dinner with me."

"Know she couldn't refuse that."

"Not exactly...As hard as I know it is for you to believe, guess she decided the stakes were too high at first. She left. I didn't hear from her for a couple of weeks, thought I'd probably never hear from her again. One afternoon, I'm getting ready to call it quits for the day...she walks through the door. She tells me she wants to discuss the 'shoot' over dinner, her treat. Hell, she pays for dinner...seduces me that very night!" Mark's pride in that elicits another low five in front of the dash. "Can you believe it, she seduced me! The next thing I know, we're living together. It's been great ever since. End of story."

"Sounds like it's either too good to be true, or you just made it all up."

"To top that off, since doin' her shoot, a lot of her friends and peers use me exclusively. After meeting her, my business has sky-rocketed. I've got so many new clients; I'm considering bringing in another photographer. You know how to handle a camera?"

"Something doesn't pan out on the interview circuit; I may have to try it. Sounds great! Sounds like you got the world by the nuts right now. Don't let go, no matter what you do. I'm the one who's made all the mistakes in life. Learn from me."

"So, how 'bout you? What the hell you doin' at the Crescent? Looking for an apartment already?"

"No, but that's not a bad idea." His thoughts drift back to the young woman he befriended today, still wondering if everything is OK where she's concerned. The two buddies are now only a couple of blocks from Anderson's home.

"What's on your mind?" Anderson asks, after noticing his friend's thoughtful stare.

"Oh...I met someone today...on the plane coming in. One thing led to another..."

"Talk about me. It's just as I always remembered you. Never miss an opportunity with a woman. Still using the ol' shyness routine? Used to work for you in college."

"Actually it wasn't like that at all. We experienced a little situation together. Next thing, she's taking me to her apartment. That's why I was at the Crescent."

"Sounds interesting...A 'hot, aggressive' female..."

"That's what I thought at first, but don't think it's anything like that now. I thought she was being aggressive, really liked me. But as it turns out, she's already seeing someone else...matter of fact, they're living together."

"So—never known that to stop you."

"Normally, it wouldn't. But, I'm not sure now it'd be worth it."

Anderson turns, pointing the car south, driving along the west side of White Rock Lake.

"You finally get the home on the lake?" Cade asks him.

"Not quite on the lake, but close. Sandy and I can walk a block and be there in a couple of minutes though. We're really enjoying it."

Anderson makes what will be the final turn into a residential area, onto a street lined with older homes, most of them well kept after a certain amount of remodeling, a couple in a state of remodeling, most of them two-story, most of them thirty to forty years old, a few a little older. Guiding the Volvo down the street, Mark says little more, allowing his friend the opportunity to enjoy the beauty of their surroundings. As the car progresses along the brick-paved street, Cade can readily see it's a long cove, no way out except for the direction they've just come. It kind of reminds him of his home, where his folks live, back in southwest Tennessee. Before reaching the end, Anderson slows, pulling into a driveway.

"This is it," Anderson tells him. "Not much...yet. Still needs some work. But we're proud of where we are at this point."

"It's great! ...reminds me of home." He doesn't know why Mark thinks he has to apologize for it.

"Speaking of, how are your mom and dad?" Mark asks.

"Doing great...at least the last time I talked to them. Thanks for asking."

"What do they think about your move?" Mark asks as he opens his door to crawl out.

"Don't know...haven't told 'em. Wanna make sure I have the job first. You know my dad. He'd have a fit if he thought I'd quit my job before having another lined up. He wouldn't understand. They think I'm still in Chicago working."

"Yeah...the old people. Don't know what it's like to live on the edge." They both laugh at that one.

"The old security thing. They don't know anything else, had it most of their lives...can't imagine anything else. Don't know the kind of games big companies are playing with people's lives these days." Cade jumps on his soapbox again.

The two stop at the front door while Anderson fumbles for his keys. He unlocks the door, pushes it open, and leads the way inside.

"Toss your bags over there for now. I'll show you your room after we've had a beer and taken care of dinner. It'll probably have to be pizza."

"Not a problem here. You got a beer in the fridge, I'll be happy with anything else."

"You can count on that."

Cade finds a bathroom. At forty-two, one of the few things he thinks he can still do well. While standing over the toilet, he hears the phone ring. He finishes, and then walks into the kitchen where his buddy engages in conversation with someone on the phone.

"How's the shoot going? Great...When you comin' home? OK...Yeah, miss you too. Love you too." Although Japanese by birth, Mark's lived in America most of his forty-one years, picking up much of the jargon one can only call American, even southwestern American habits, good and bad, including some of the slang and drawl.

"Let me guess...your accountant, lawyer?"

Anderson hands him a beer. "Looks like pizza or burgers. Mind if we order in?"

Anderson picks the phone up once again, this time punching two numbers, speed-dialing a local pizza restaurant. While he's on the phone, Cade and his beer migrate out of the kitchen into the living room, conducting an unofficial self-guided tour.

Anderson completes his call, joining his friend. "Now that I've got dinner on, we can relax. And he does, falling into his favorite chair, slightly worn from overuse and age. Cade sits on the couch facing him.

"I was looking at some of the pictures on the wall…great-looking woman, man. That wouldn't be Sandy?"

"What do you think?"

"Nice looking. The biggest question in my mind is how in the hell did you get someone looking like that interested in you?"

"…Plain and simple. Talent. You know how we Japanese can perform. Whenever you hear about the samurai warrior's sword, they're not talking about a big knife. And I come from a long line of samurai."

"Yeah, right. If that's the case, there's nothing samurai about your ass."

"Oh, but that's where you are wrong, oh honorable one. My great-great-grandfather was a warrior for the Japanese emperor many years ago. My father's descendants come from a long line of warriors. We were major ass kickers back then. So don't fuck with me." Anderson smiles.

Cade laughs, pausing before speaking, "You know, that's about as much as I've ever heard you talk about your family. We've known each other for what, twenty years."

"Man, if I could've told you something before, I would've. I haven't known much myself. My father's always told me he was trying' to spare me the pain and hatred he's felt all these years. About what, I don't know."

"You've never really talked about your dad or your mother much."

"That's because my mother's dead…never really got to know her," Anderson answers, staring straight ahead.

"Hey. Sorry. I didn't know."

"I know you didn't. Anyway, she's been dead a long time. She died shortly after I was born. Like I said, I never really knew her… didn't really have anything…no pictures, no records of her existence, until recently."

"What do you mean?"

"Got a package in the mail several weeks ago…from my father. It was nothing more than a photograph album with a few old family pictures. But it was the first time I'd ever seen anything regarding my family, or its history."

Anderson stands and walks to the bookcase across the room, pulling the photo album from a shelf, handing it to Cade. "Here you go…this is all I know. Now you'll know as much."

Cade readily accepts the frail book, aged with its many years of existence. He takes it in his hands, carefully opening it as though it were made of the finest, most fragile crystal or material in existence. It kind of reminded him of some of his family's old black and white picture albums he used to look at.

"…Another beer?" Anderson asks.

Cade reaches for the one he's been nursing, shaking it. "Naw, still got some. Thanks." He gulps it down quickly. "Now I'm ready."

Upon his good friend's departure from the room, Cade turns the next page gingerly. The pictures, most discolored to a light brown, yellow, or gray, are primarily of people. Probably Mark's family, Cade assumes, from many years back. There are a few pictures of countryside somewhere, Japan, he assumes, but with the shape they're in and with the discoloration, you really can't make out much detail. He imagines with full color; the shots would've been very beautiful.

Continuing his browsing, he turns the pages, looking through twenty or so photographs, until he comes across a final photo. This particular one is of a woman holding a tiny baby. It doesn't appear to be quite as old as the others, the discoloration only beginning to take effect. Cade surmises it to be a picture of Mark, possibly his mother.

"Who's this?" he asks, pointing to the picture in question, as Mark re-enters the room.

"Can't you tell? That's me...me and my mother. It was taken just after I was born. Like I said, she died a few months later."

"What's it say here, under the picture?" Cade points to the words scribbled under the picture, written in Japanese.

"It's something my father says she wrote him before she died."

"Then it's private. I don't need to know."

"No, that's OK. You're my best friend...I can share it with you." And he begins reading: "You are my life. As Kami miraculously carried you to me, he will also soon separate us. Our son is my gift to you. Love him with all your heart. Care for him, as you have for me. He is the mixture of our blood, the symbol of our bonded lives. I will wait for you in the afterlife. Take care of little Massey. May Kami protect the two of you always. I love you. Miki."

As he finishes, the doorbell rings, announcing the arrival of their two-pizza—one pepperoni, one sausage—basic fare dinner.

While Anderson answers the door, pays for, and carries the food into the kitchen, Cade turns the page. There was nothing more in the book, with the exception of pages appearing to have had pictures there before, removed at some point in time. He wants to ask, but decides pizza and another beer are more important right now.

CHAPTER 9

Today, August 7, 1992, Jason Cade awakens early. It takes few seconds to remember what today is, and what today is all about. His initial moments of drowsiness are quickly replaced with excitement...and nervousness. The nervousness, somewhat uncontrollable...the excitement, although guarded, comes with the opportunity to start again in a new career, the outside chance he may get to see the young woman from yesterday. The job is important, but the opportunity to see her again, possibly work with her every day, intercepts any thoughts of improving his financial well-being. How easily a shot of testosterone helps him forget the events on the ride home from the airport, the Crescent, or what he saw in the closet.

Anderson makes good on his promise, lending him his car for the day. Cade drops him off at his studio as planned, noticing his friend is very quiet this morning, quite somber, in fact. Cade's not sure why, why the sudden change of attitude. He's feeling too good to let it ruin his day.

Minutes after dropping Mark off, Cade pulls the Volvo into the Ankawa garage next to the eighteen-story, glass-paneled building. The new day's sunrise reflects brightly off its eastside facing. Cade decides it's a good sign, an omen. Then again, he would probably interpret any sign as good this morning.

Checking his watch...now seven forty-seven, he realizes he's a bit early. His interview's not until eight-thirty, but he figures it won't hurt him to be early, show he's gung-ho, enthusiastic. Besides, maybe he'll catch a glimpse of Danny on her way to work. Being there a little early might help.

Inside the building, he stops at the security desk, telling them why he's there. One of the men on duty picks up a phone, announcing his arrival to someone on the other end, somewhere inside the building, Cade presumes personnel.

"You'll need to sign in." He offers Cade a pen, pointing to a registration book and the exact line where he is expected to sign. "There'll be someone here for you in a few minutes. You'll need to wear this badge at all times until you leave the building. If you'll have a seat over there, I'll call you when your escort arrives." Cade clips the visitor's badge to the lapel of his coat, finds what appears to be a comfortable chair, and begins his wait.

The couch and chairs in the waiting area are plush and comfortable. The large multi-story, open-air lobby reminds him of a large cathedral, a great deal more modernistic...striking, architectural artistry at its best...little indication this company is of Japanese influence. That's good, he thinks. The flow of people through the front door, arriving for work, increases as time approaches eight o'clock. Cade watches more intently with each passing minute, making sure he catches sight of every person, every entrance made through the many doors into the building, at one point trying to "will" Danny Wilson through one of them.

He hopes she'll be as glad to see him as he will her, not knowing she's already inside...been there since six this morning.

A few minutes after the human rush hour subsides, an older woman greets him; he guesses she is probably in her late fifties, early sixties. He notices the name on her badge almost as quickly as she speaks it in introduction. Greeting her pleasantly, he imagines she was once a very beautiful woman...still doing a good job of maintaining that beauty in her later years. Jackie takes him to yet a smaller, more intimate waiting area, through a door appropriately marked "Personnel." The receptionist here is a little on the heavy side, probably mid-fifties. She has the appearance of someone still trying to live out her life in the sixties; her clothing...her hair piled high on her head like a beehive. The color... blonde, definitely bleached, definitely not her normal shade... not even close. She is very pleasant, and seems genuinely interested in helping.

"And your name is, darlin'...?"

"Jason, ma'am. Jason Cade."

The woman doesn't look away once, having semi-memorized the morning's appointments. "Sweetie, you're here early. That's good. Very smart of you."

"Yes, ma'am. You know what they say about the early bird?"

"Sure do, but you're not the early one this morning. Another little birdie got here a whole lot earlier, and he's already caught that little worm, Richard."

Cade has no idea who Richard is; amused at the way the receptionist almost sings every word to him. She's undoubtedly one of the most cheerful and positive people he's ever met, especially this early in the morning. It's obvious to him that she really enjoys life, as well as her job.

"If you'll just pick you out a little seat over there I'm sure that grubby little worm'll be out to get you in good time. I'll let him know you're here."

Cade finds a chair, now a little concerned there could be another vying for the same job. Maybe not, he reasons. Whoever it is could be interviewing for another job in another department. Naw, with my luck, they'll have the job filled before I ever get inside. What a bummer. What am I gonna do if I can't work here? He quickly surmises it probably wouldn't be the end of the world. Just seem like it.

"Excuse me, honey. Excuse me. Helloooooooooooo," the receptionist tries enthusiastically to gain his attention, which eventually she does. "Honey, could I interest you in some coffee, juice, a donut?"

"Uh, no thanks, I'm fine." As soon as he says that, his stomach growls from hunger. He'd forgotten to eat breakfast, actually hadn't had time this morning. He looks up to see if she heard, as if it mattered. She smiles. She heard.

"There's a *Dallas Morning News*, *Wall Street*, or *USA Today* over there in the rack. Help yourself."

"Thanks." He stands, walks to the rack as suggested, although not interested in reading anything this morning. He's beginning to get a little irritated at her constant badgering. He drops into another chair, a little farther away from her, looking for some peace and quiet...just so he doesn't have to answer any more of her questions. "Please, God, no more questions," he whispers to himself.

He's accepted the fact he now has competition. Why should it have been any different? Why would I have thought any differently? It's normal to have several candidates for one job. He looks at his watch...around eight thirty-eight.

Since it's already late, and thinking he may have a few moments..."Is there a phone I can use to call someone I know in the building?"

"See the one on the table, in the corner over there? That's what it's there for, darlin'."

"Thanks." He stands again, walking to the phone, sitting next to it, picking it up, setting the receiver back on the phone. "How do I get out? Do I need to go through an operator?"

"Who do you need to call, sweetie?"

"Danny...uh, Danielle Wilson. I think she's in technology."

The receptionist, Lil', as she likes to be called, looks up. "Who'd you say?"

"Danny Wilson."

"You don't mind my asking, how do you know her?"

"Met her on my plane coming in for this interview. Why?"

"Just curious. I'll connect you to her office. When the phone rings, pick it up."

Which he does. As he listens, it rings her office, three, maybe four times. He hears the click; someone picking it up...he waits for an answer.

"Hello."

"Danny," Cade replies in normal voice though excited at the sound of her voice. "Jason Cade. You..."

The recording continues. "You've reached the office of Danny Wilson. I'm either on the phone, or away from my desk right now, so at the tone, please leave a number, a short message and I'll get back to you as soon as I return." After the short pause, a beep tells him to begin his message.

During the recorded message, Cade tries to figure out how to save face in front of Lil', attempting to hide the fact he's just been duped by a recording. He turns away, facing the wall, covering his mouth slightly. Lil' continues smiling.

"Danny," he says softly, almost in a whisper. "...Jason Cade; from yesterday. I'm in the building, waiting for my interview. Wondered if we might get together later for a cup of coffee, or lunch. I'll call back when I'm finished here." He hangs up, looks at the receptionist again. She looks up from what she's doing, smiling almost grinning, he thinks. God, how can one person be so damned happy?

"Everything OK? You able to get through?"

She knew. "Yes, ma'am. Got through. No problem."

"That surprises me. The girl's a very busy person, if you know what I mean."

"No, what do you mean? Obviously you know something about her. Care to share?" He's found renewed interest in Lil' Simpson. Maybe she can provide a little helpful information about the elusive Miss Wilson.

"Who, darlin'? Danny Wilson?"

"Yes, ma'am. I must confess, I don't really know her as well as I'd like to."

"You and all the other men in this building. Well, let's see. She's pretty. But, I guess you already noticed that quality about her. She's smart...real smart. She hasn't gotten where she is being a dumb blonde, brunette, whatever color her hair happens to be."

That coming from you, he thinks. "Where? Where's she gotten, I mean, what's she to this company?"

"Oh, honey, you don't know much about her, do you? She's one of the top women in this organization. Just more proof; it's not what you know, but who you know or who you're doing." That last part under her breath but heard. "She's Mr. Carrigan's "Girl Friday." She's probably good on the other days of the week too. I'm sorry, I shouldn't be..."

"Why do you say that? You seem to know more than you're telling. What's the deal with her?"

"She's trouble, big trouble. You gotta know she's seein' Mr. Carrigan. They're supposed to be a pretty hot item right now. Everybody here knows that."

"I didn't," playing dumb to get additional information. "Who'd you say she's seeing?"

"Robert Carrigan. He's a president, and her boss. He's supposed to be in line to head up the company. And soon, I understand."

Cade flashes back to the closet in her apartment. His mind restamps the image of the embroidered initials on the cuffs of the expensive shirts he saw hanging there. "R.C. Robert Carrigan. R.C."

"He's her boss, huh?"

"Yes, sir...and, baby, he's one powerful man! Not only in this company, but like Mr. Ankawa, around the entire U.S. of A. You really don't wanna get involved with this woman. You really don't wanna cross him. Tryin' to see her would be big trouble."

"I wasn't planning on doin' that at all. I just liked her... thought it'd be good to get to know her, strictly from a business perspective." He knew he wasn't convincing her. About to continue his questioning, a door opens into the waiting area. Richard sticks his head into the room calling Cade's name. This particular moment reminds him of the times he used to visit the doctor when he was a kid. Hearing his name like that always meant a rendezvous with some kind of shot, probing by a doctor, your standard unwanted childhood pain. He always dreaded the nurse opening that door, calling out his name as this "Richard" had just done. He never knew what awaited him behind that door. A piece of his childhood just revisited; he approaches the person awaiting his arrival.

Richard extends his hand, introducing himself...Cade reciprocates.

"You ready to go to work?"

Richard's first question catches him off guard. "Pardon me?"

"Work...you know, the reason you're here this morning. We've looked at your credentials, and we're prepared to make you an offer of employment."

Richard ushers a suddenly internally elated Cade to a small office, shows him a seat, and continues. Jason can barely contain his excitement.

"You'll start at $106,500, get an office and a secretary. You'll be working with Dickson, in accounting. I assume you'll be ready to start work on Monday."

"Hell...I mean, you bet! I can do that!"

"You seem a little surprised," Richard adds.

"I have to admit, I thought there'd be another interview, other candidates."

"You had two. How many you think it takes to determine someone's qualifications? We made our decision prior to asking you here. Your reputation precedes you. Why do you think we came to Chicago for the first two interviews? We wanted you. When it's someone we want, we go after 'em. You wouldn't have made it past the first interview unless you were good."

Cade's feeling pretty good about himself right now...no, damn good! He's about to step into a job making more than he made in Chicago and in the South where cost of living is cheaper. Get the opportunity to work alongside the woman of his dreams, well, in the same building anyway. He can't wait to get out of here; tell someone of his success. Danny. He'll try to call her again.

"Now, before you can start, we've got some paperwork to do. I need you to fill out a few forms...benefit selection, legal documentation, tax information. I've got a contract I'll need you to sign, standard operation for our higher salaried exempt employees. You'll also need to take a drug test. Won't be any problems there, I hope." Before Cade can answer in the negative, Richard continues.

"You'll have to gain final clearance with security, although most of that's done already. You're going to need a permanent employee badge. That part's easy and almost done and will be once final clearance is granted."

Cade's altered expression alerts Richard to the need for a little clarification of his most recent statements.

"Do I detect some confusion about something?"

"No, not really...well yeah, the security work you've already done."

"Again, standard procedure. There's some pretty high profile people working here, numerous confidential materials passing through here daily. In your new position, you'll be reviewing many of Ankawa's financial statements, not to mention those from company's we buy or are looking to buy, and there are many. We're the ones standing to lose should we not take the necessary precautions. I thought you probably knew all about that stuff with your experience. If it's a problem..."

The last thing Cade wanted to do now was appear stupid, out of touch, ignorant to the ways of big business. "No, no problem."

"I know you'll appreciate the need for confidentiality. Mr. Ankawa has much to protect in many areas of his operation. That's why we had to do a little background check and clearance before we got this far. Probably as no surprise to you, you came through with flying colors." Richard stands, telling Cade to follow, which he does...down a hallway, into a room containing three cubicles.

"We'll put you in this one. You do know how to operate one of these?" he asks, speaking of the IBM sitting on the desk. Richard assumes so and gives no time for an answer. "We fill out everything electronically from here on. Follow the instructions as they pop up on the screen, the information you enter will be channeled automatically to the proper department, where it'll be cataloged appropriately. If you have any problems, press this button here." He points to a small white button to the left side of the cubicle. "Now, I must check on my new security candidate."

Within seconds, he leaves Cade alone, staring at the screen before him. The first prompt tells him to enter his full and complete name, social security...on and on. He works diligently, completing each phase carefully and thoroughly. He checks his watch...ten forty-nine. Once he finishes the last piece, he depresses the "enter" key as prompted, sending all information entered along the Ankawa information link, traveling through the intricate internal system toward each respective department, so he presumes. *This may be one of the systems Danny designed,* he thinks to himself. Upon completion, he depresses the white button, but Richard is already on his way.

He arrives soon thereafter, handing Cade a folder with the proper papers for the next phase, the drug test. That, and the map of the building, will help him get to the company clinic located on the basement floor. Approximately thirty minutes later, his most recent test a successful one, he returns to the reception area, checking in with the new receptionist now stationed where Lil' once sat.

"Where's Lil'?" he asks the very attractive, much younger woman now seated at the desk.

"Lunch..."

"Lunch?" Cade glances at his watch for about the tenth time this morning, confirming to himself it is indeed approaching that time of day.

"By the way, don't believe we've met. I'm Jason Cade."

"Yes Mr. Cade, I'll let Mr. Saxon know you're here. If you'll take a seat, I'm sure he'll be right out."

Very attractive...very businesslike. He likes her name... Michelle. It seems to fit the way she looks. There's nothing wrong with trying to cultivate a backup, just in case. Amazing what a little success will do for your confidence. Before he can act on his decision, Richard Saxon appears, sticking his head through the door once again.

"Mr. Cade, come in. Let's see if we can get you finished before lunch. I'm sure you'd like to see your new office, meet your new secretary."

Among other things, he thinks to himself.

As the two walk the hallway, toward Richard's office, Cade comments on what he's seen so far. "I'm really impressed with the entire operation. Never expected it to be quite like this, the fact we have our own clinic."

"…One of the best medical facilities in the country, private or otherwise. One thing you'll find out after working here a short while, Ankawa spares no expense where his company and its employees are concerned. You should feel fortunate to be coming to work here. He's built a first-class operation from the ground up. Those doctors in the clinic, the best the country…quite probably the world has to offer. They're some of the top physicians, specialists anywhere. He considers everyone in this building family."

"How…why would a top physician work in a controlled environment like this, not go into the private sector where I'm sure the money would be much better, instead of…"

"Instead of what, fight the enormous competition for research dollars, fight the rules of some hospital being run by business-people, people who have no idea what's needed in a medical environment. These guys, and women, I might add, are paid extremely well to be a part of this staff. The hours are great compared to the near nonstop days they'd be fighting in the public arena, and the research dollars pour in, as promised from Ankawa's near endless funding."

Richard pulls out a diagram of the building, showing Cade where his new office will be, handing him keys, a semi-permanent badge, which Cade promptly clips to his lapel, replacing the temporary. He also hands him a brochure detailing the amenities available inside the building; restaurants, a health club, theater, a bowling alley...all those things added for the pleasure of Ankawa and his full-time servants, as well as his employees and their families. The final piece to the array of information is a six-digit code to use on the electronic entry system, and a magnetic stripped card, loaded with personal information, to guarantee access through the doors after hours. He leaves Richard's office more impressed than before, ecstatic that he's now a working employee for any company, re-entering the waiting area.

The young one's still behind the desk, eating her lunch from a brown bag, reading a book...a novel by some new author, a John Grisham. When he stops at her desk, she looks up.

"How'd it go?" she asks.

"Great! Absolutely great! Just need a few instructions." He really didn't; just using this as a means to converse with her, try to impress her a little.

"Congratulations, then. You got the job. I guess we'll be seeing a lot of you around here in the future."

This could be her attempt at a come-on. He thinks. Gotta handle this right.

"Probably will. Where do you normally work, I mean, this obviously isn't your normal work station."

"You're right. I'm an Ankawa temp. I float around the building, doing whatever needs to be done during the absence of regulars. I get to do this till something more permanent comes available. You're not gonna need an assistant anytime soon, are you?"

"Sorry, no." He wishes he were though. "Give me your name and I'll definitely keep you in mind should that change."

"You got a deal." Michelle Miller, she writes on a piece of paper along with a phone number. "This is my home phone. In case you need, you know, in case you ever have an emergency, if you know what I mean?"

He wasn't quite sure what she meant, but thought he'd act like he did. Cade extends his hand, as she does, meeting his halfway across the desk. Her hand soft and warm, he holds it a little longer than he should. She's fully aware of that, and doesn't seem to mind. He doesn't know how at this moment, but thoughts of Danny enter his mind.

"Listen. I need to try to reach someone in the building. I don't know her number, but if you could ring it for me, I'd really appreciate it. Her name's Danny Wilson. You know her?"

"Oh, I know her." Saying nothing more, she connects him, where the recording is still answering for her. Not fooled this time around, he declines leaving a message, not wanting to appear eager. He sets the receiver back on its stand and starts for the door that'll take him beyond personnel. Before he can exit, the receptionist stops him.

"Mind if I offer a little friendly advice?"

"Not at all."

"About Ms. Wilson," expounding her name a little sarcastically. "Be careful. There's more there than meets the eye."

"You're the second person to tell me that today. What's goin' on? Why do you say that?"

She appears hesitant to say anything further. "That's all I better say for now. Just be careful."

Fortunately for her, the phone on her desk rings, which she must pick up. Cade leaves the room, sauntering down the hall, leaving an area of the building he will never revisit.

Entering the elevator corridor, he stands before a row of ten doors, five on either side. He checks the call buttons, immediately recognizing the "up" arrow as already illuminated, probably due to one of two individuals already waiting on a car.

A chime sounds, announcing the arrival of the first. He boards, after politely waiting for all passengers to disembark, allowing the two waiting first passage. He immediately reaches for the panel, depressing the number "four," that process closing the doors. Three passengers, two obviously acquainted, ride the cavernous elevator to its next port of call. Cade looks around, thinking he's never seen one as large as this one, and he will soon understand why Ankawa installed such large cars.

Stopping at the second after a very short ride, doors open to a throng of people heading back to work after lunch in one of three restaurants inside the building. Before arriving at this floor, he knew he must have been close to food, the aroma permeating the walls and shaft of the elevator. He could smell it before the doors ever opened.

The crowd pushes its way onto the elevator, filling it as though it were the only one in service now. Cade finds himself pushed to the rear, a long way from the front and unbelievably, with little room to move. Pinned to the back, he begins planning a strategy for his escape as the fourth approaches. He knows it's not going to be easy. Looking to the front, attempting to gradually work his way from the back, he believes he sees someone; someone he knows; someone he's been looking for. He hadn't noticed her before now.

As quickly as he's seen her, she notices him. The elevator slows, stopping at the third. Several in the crowded elevator step off. Cade inches closer, his eyes on her, her eyes watching every move he makes. The color of her skin has paled at the sight of him working his way toward her. The man she had befriended the day before, the man she'd really hoped she wouldn't see again provides a slight tinge of excitement, though she is quite anxious over his presence at the moment.

Before he can gain additional ground in his battle to reach her, another crowd boards from the third, forcing him backward once again, allowing him little additional progress.

He strains to catch a second glimpse, trying to confirm his initial sighting. It was, in fact, Danny Wilson standing on the same elevator as he. She's smiling slightly, a forced smile. She carries on a conversation with someone standing next to her, that person blocked from view by a large man. She glances occasionally in Cade's direction. He hasn't figured it out yet, but she's trying to ignore his presence, virtually will him from the elevator and away from her.

He strains to see her, and the individual garnering most of her attention. While doing so, he leans into other passengers, accidentally stepping on someone's toes. The woman screams out in pain.

"I'm so sorry. I didn't mean..."

"Why don't you watch what you're doing?" the middle-aged, medium-built woman yells.

The moment has become quite embarrassing. Everyone on the elevator interrupts conversations to see what is causing all the commotion in the back. Cade tries being a gentleman, extending his hand to assist her, help her regain her balance as she hobbles in pain. Someone bumps him from behind, sending his hand into the woman's D-cup chest. Reacting by grabbing something, anything to stop himself from falling on top of her, he clinches the woman's left breast.

"How dare you...you...you pervert!"

Before he can do or say anything else, she slaps him across the face. The crowd immediately steps away, obviously distancing themselves from this poor excuse of a human being.

As easily embarrassed as he is, Cade's beside himself. No matter what he tries at this point, it's the wrong thing to do. He backs away from the woman, taking a long, hard look at her. He doesn't want to forget her face, so he can make sure he keeps his distance in the future. The woman may see his lingering stare as a stalking of sorts.

He glances at Danny. What must she think of him now? Their eyes meet. He smiles, halfheartedly this time, not sure of her reaction after what's just happened. She reacts by turning away; he presumes disgusted at the very sight of him.

Shit! I'll never be able to explain, he thinks, but he has to try.

Looking for a chance to say something to her, he decides he will, on his way out. Realizing he's missed his floor in all the commotion; he fights his way toward the front as the elevator approaches the fifth. He has little difficulty this time, most still aware of the incident before, now stepping aside willingly as he pushes his way through the crowd.

His approach signals trouble for Danny. In a near state of panic, she turns quickly, taking the only course of action available to her, nuzzling up to the man still standing next to her. The surprising show of affection is welcomed by Robert, especially after all that's previously happened with them. Cade reaches her side, stopping. Aching to say something, he cannot. An arm slides around her shoulder. With the same results as the recent slap in the face, Cade sees the initials embroidered on his cuff. "R.C."

"R.C.," the same initials on the shirts in her closet. He looks at the man attached to that arm. She quickly turns, Cade thinking she's about to acknowledge his presence. He can see it in her eyes, eyes saying it all. Their glance lasts mere seconds, long enough for Robert to catch them.

"You got a problem?"

Danny looks at Cade again, silently pleading with those eyes, knowing what lies ahead for the two of them should she acknowledge.

"No, no. Sorry. Thought I knew you. Guess not. My mistake."

The doors begin closing to the fifth. Cade slams his arm between them, forcing a second opening. Stepping off the elevator he hopes to hear her voice from behind, hearing only the "swoosh" of the closing doors.

Back on board the elevator. "What was that all about? Who was he?"

"No one. I didn't know him. I guess...I guess he thought he knew me."

Not ready to buy her story, he makes a mental note of the floor Cade got off on, figuring he'll make a trip to the fifth real soon...sometime very soon.

By the time Robert and Danny have reached the eighth, Cade walks off his second elevator at the fourth. Glancing at his directions, then at the floor directory on the wall, his keen sense of smell kicks in high gear, telling him he's not alone. The aroma of perfume filling the air around him is obviously that of a most expensive one.

"Can I help you?" The pleasant voice and southern drawl from the lips of a woman forces a quick turn to get a look at whom he will soon be talking with. Checking out its source, he comes face to face with a statuesque redhead. Her hair is actually closer to brunette, with a tinge of red deepening throughout. Her beauty is natural, her makeup barely noticeable. With her looks, she probably doesn't need any.

"Looking for my office, ma'am."

"Please don't call me ma'am. It makes me feel so old. Just call me Barbara. And you are...?"

"Jason Cade."

"Oh, you're our new analyst. I've heard a lot about you. If you'll follow me, I'll take you to your office."

Intrigued by her apparent knowledge of what he's there for, he asks, "How'd you know that?"

"Oh I make a point of knowing everything going on, on this floor. I'll bet you're looking for four fifty-five."

Sounds like a secretary, could be my secretary. They're usually in the know about everything that goes on in an office. They continue their stroll down the hall, Cade just a few steps behind. God, if this is my secretary Michelle can forget ever working for me.

He likes everything he sees, her curvaceous figure sensuously highlighted by the slick, dark green, one-piece outfit she's wearing. The way it clings to her body leaves nothing to the imagination, nothing at all. He decides once again and basically for the same reasoning, he's going to like working here.

She's been here before. Escorting a new male employee to his office, her trap awaiting his entanglement, her chance to devour yet another caught in her web. She can sense his eyes on her every move, then again, that's the reason she dresses the way she does, why she conducts herself as she does.

Cade steps up his pace, catching her, deciding he'll make some points with his new secretary.

"Great perfume."

"You're so sweet. Thank you, darlin'. I can tell you and I are gonna get along wonderfully. We should work very well as a team."

That's it. She's just confirmed my suspicion. She just told him what he wanted to know...in so many words, what he wanted to hear.

Like any other red-blooded male, his juices are flowing, aroused by the simple scent of perfume, the appearance of an attractive woman, the excitement of so many unknowns. At this moment, Danny Wilson is the furthest thing from his mind. His imagination generates endless possibilities, a mental visualization of him and this very attractive woman, now walking beside him.

She knows what effect she's having on this man. She knows, because she's done it so many times before. She stops in front of a door, and like a game show host, motions with a wave of her arm and hand, directing him through the opening.

"I believe this is what you're looking for."

"Thanks. I really appreciate you showing me around. If you have a few minutes why don't you grab us both a cup of coffee. We can sit; get to know each other a little better, talk about our new working relationship. I can fill you in on what I usually expect, and what you can expect from me." There, that sounded good. She should be impressed I'm so buttoned up, mature.

Her smile was very pleasant...at the moment, for whatever the reason, bordering on a grin. Obviously, she's excited about the prospect of working for him; as well what might be in store for their impending relationship.

"What? Is it something I said?"

"I guess you could say that. I love aggressive men. I'd love to sit and talk, as you suggested, get to know you better, all those things...but, I really don't have the time right now. I'm already late for a meeting." She glances at her watch. "In fact, it may be over by the time I get there." She turns to walk away, stops and looks back. "I'm looking forward to working with you too, Jason Cade."

Wow! No one had ever said his name like that before. They depart company for now. He walks into his new office; barren of the personal touch, those essentials he figures he'll add later. But he likes it. The huge corner window gives his office a spacious feel, a view with two distinct and differing perspectives. Beats the hell out of the cubicle he had in Chicago. He stands in one spot...turning a slow but complete three-sixty, making mental notes of how he will rearrange the furniture; add some of his own, when he can get around to it. He can see to the east, toward a huge white building. Admiring the architecture of the Info-Mart, he completes a half turn, checking out his other view to the southeast, a really decent view of a lone high-rise to the north of downtown Dallas, a building he believes to be the Crescent. Not quite the view Danny had from her apartment, nonetheless, a view he now cherishes immensely...Dallas, glorious Dallas. It's sure good to be home.

Reveling in his continued good fortune, his back to the door, he doesn't notice he's been joined by someone he already knows, has already met. She speaks first, catching him by surprise.

"You must be Mr. Cade."

The voice from behind startles him, forcing him from his near daydream.

Both are surprised as they face each other for the first time, but then, upon seeing each other, they realize it's not the first time. The woman standing inside his office is none other than the one from the elevator...the one he last heard proclaiming him to be a pervert, screaming the accusation from the top of her lungs; the very woman he'd vowed he'd stay clear of in the future.

Over the initial shock of their meeting and subsequent realization, she's able to regain a small amount of composure. "You aren't...you aren't Mr. Cade? Jason Cade...the new analyst?"

"As a matter of fact, I am. I don't believe we've met, formally anyway. What can I help you with? Back to file charges?"

"Oh no," she mumbles under her breath.

"Something wrong?"

"Sure hope not, sir. Mr. Cade, I'm Jenny...Jenny Compton... your secretary."

He tries to deal with the blow, deal with the thought of this woman as his secretary...the thought of working closely with her on a daily basis...the thought of ...After the elevator fiasco; she ought to be on her knees right now, begging his forgiveness. His thoughts quickly transfer to Michelle and the possibility of hiring her to replace this woman soon. But, he can be fair about this...give her another chance, show her he's not really the pervert she thinks he might be. And he's about to do just that, when another reality hits him. If she's his secretary, who the hell's Barbara?

"Let me ask you something. Did you see the woman I was just with, the one who just left my office?"

"Barbara Dickson?"

"That...was Dickson?"

"Yes, sir. She's the VP in charge of this department."

The ground begins to shake. Cade can't tell if it's an earthquake or his legs getting wobbly after finding out what an ass he's just made of himself in front of his new boss.

Jenny senses something's wrong.

"Somethin' I can get you?"

"Nothin'. Everything's OK...I hope." He sits back on his desk.

"Can I get you a cup of coffee, a Coke, something else?"

"What time you go home? I may need somethin' from you later."

God, she thinks. She imagines him coming to her later, wanting...no, demanding certain liberties. The way he touched her on the elevator, came at her so aggressively... *God, he must be an animal.* "I normally go home around four thirty...unless you need me to stay longer." *God, what'll I do?*

"I'll find you later. I know we'll get along just fine. We got off on the wrong foot. Our relationship will be a good one." He of all people can understand saying the wrong thing at the wrong time...to the wrong person.

Jenny leaves, going straight for the cubicle of her best friend Cassandra. She'll have quite a bit to tell her. In just a short time, it'll be all over the office.

Cade tinkers with his chair, trying to adjust it. He'll have time to figure it out later. He opens a couple of drawers, looking inside... to be doing something more than anything. He inventories the few supplies left from the office's previous tenant. He still can't get over it. Out of all the secretaries in the building...his luck, it seems, has finally run out. He stands, again turning to the window.

Another enters his office.

"Congratulations."

It's only one word, but he's heard that voice before. Turning, he sees Danny standing just inside the door. A little surprised at her appearance since he didn't figure he'd ever see her again. "Hi. How you doin'?"

"I'm OK, I guess. Doesn't look like you're doing too badly."

"I'm doin' good, real good." Seeing her brings back all the good feelings he had yesterday when he was with her. But he can tell something's wrong.

"I can see that. I've been with the company over three years, and still don't have my own office."

"Just dumb luck, I guess. I don't know." Cade can sense her resentment. "I didn't ask for it. Just came with the job."

A little ashamed of the way she's acting..."I know; I'm not blaming you."

"What I came by for...I got your message. I had a couple of meetings I couldn't get out of. I wanted to apologize for the snub on the elevator too." Now she's about to do the unpleasant. "We need to talk. The best way I know to say this, is just say it. I like you. I like you a lot. But, there's nothing here to work with, I mean, I'm seeing someone else. You know that."

"Yeah, I know. That was him today on the elevator, wasn't it?"

"That was him. You have to understand something about the man. He's very powerful. He's also very jealous."

"And possessive, I might add."

Her expression tells him he's right on target.

"That's OK. It's too bad though. I just thought we could be friends. It doesn't have to be anything else." His feeble attempt at presenting half-truths isn't convincing her at all.

"I can't afford a friendship with another man right now. It'll mess everything up too much, create severe complications for both of us. You have to stay away from me. It's important you do that."

He doesn't know her, particularly not enough to say what he's about to, but as usual he'll say what's on his mind. "Doesn't really sound like you have much of a relationship to me. How'd you get involved in something so screwed up? I've always thought a relationship had to be built on trust and understanding...sounds like you have neither."

"Look, I'm asking you...no, I'm telling you, don't push it! Another day, another time...if you'd come along earlier in my life...shit! Never mind."

Obviously telling him she's very unhappy, feeling trapped, she doesn't see any way out; her words appear wasted.

"Guess it'd be out of the question to think you'd be interested in going to dinner tonight."

She rolls her eyes to the top of her head, expelling a sigh of frustration. "What is it with you men? Damn it! Haven't you been listening? Leave me alone! We'll never be an item, never be a couple, and never have a relationship! Understand? Never!"

"All right, all right. You made your point. I was just having a little fun...trying to make you laugh a little. It was nice seeing you again, now if you don't mind, I have work to do."

She disappears abruptly, leaving Cade feeling shitty. He's suddenly lost interest in doing anything at the moment. Besides, his job doesn't start till Monday anyway.

Danny sticks her head back inside his office. "Look, I'm sorry. I couldn't go anywhere tonight even if I wanted. I'll be working. Thanks for the invitation anyway." She knows she's taking a big risk, giving him a little more line, a different signal than she had planned or wanted...but, what the hell.

Cade accepts that, considering it a good sign...hell, a great sign. His next step is to survey the relationship she and Robert really have over the next few weeks. He'll wait for the right opportunity...which he's convinced will come.

He walks out of his office, into the area housing administrative support. As he appears, a small gathering halts its chatter, reducing their conversation to a whisper. In the middle of it all, Jenny quickly emerges.

"Is there something I can do for you, Mr. Cade?"

"As a matter of fact, to start with, stop calling me mister. Also, see if you can get me a rental car delivered to this address by four this afternoon."

She looks at the slip of paper he's just handed her, "I'll need a credit card, at least a number. How long you gonna need it?"

"I'm not sure yet. Get me a weekly rate. I'll take it from there." He reaches for his back pocket, pulling his wallet out, trying to decide which card isn't close to its limit, handing her his American Express. "I'll be leaving in a few minutes."

"Yes, sir, I'll get on it right away."

Cade finishes straightening his new desk, leaving a list of things to do Monday, on top where he'll see it first thing. He takes a quick look outside his window, noticing Stemmons traffic beginning to build, beginning to slow considerably on the north-bound side. The sight of Friday's rush hour reaffirms his great fortune to be traveling in the opposite direction.

He moves toward the door, stopping momentarily...looks back one last time, and then walks to Jenny's cubicle to pick up his card and check on his reservations. She hands him the information he's seeking, forgetting to give him his card.

"I was able to get you a pretty good rate...corporate. I hope a full size car's OK."

It was.

Just before reaching the elevator, Cade runs into Barbara Dickson, on her way back from her meeting.

"Leaving so soon?"

"Yes, ma'am...I mean, yeah. I think I've done all the damage I can do today. I'll be in early Monday." His attempt to show her the courtesy and respect his comments were so lacking in earlier is apparent. "Listen, I'd like to apologize for earlier...opening my big mouth before knowing all the facts. I spoke before thinking. I hope you'll forgive me."

"I've already forgotten. Believe me, it's happened before. We'll do dinner one evening next week. You can make it up to me then. We can discuss...our future relationship," she suggests seductively.

Additional excitement invades his mind, making him a little uneasy as well. "Uh, yeah, sure...looking forward to that."

An elevator arrives. Cade steps on, turning around just in time to see her walking away. The doors closing...he watches until he can no longer see her. It will be the last time he'll see Barbara Dickson, the last time he sees the fourth floor. He'll not make it to work on Monday.

CHAPTER 10

ade leaves his office, driving to Anderson's Oak Lawn studio just north of downtown. During his drive, he reflects back to the second encounter with Danny, the one in his office. He's relieved she appeared to be unharmed in any way from everything that might have happened yesterday, at least physically anyway. Her stress level seemed elevated some, however, not much he can do about that he figures. Not much she'll allow him to. She'll need to deal with all of that herself, he reasons, though feeling a little guilty for thinking this way.

Enjoying a short drive, one taking him down the proverbial memory lane despite heavy traffic, he observes many familiar sites as he passes. All these reminding him once again where he is...feeling a continuing exuberance at being home...gaining the new job...meeting Danny...all the other possibilities still in his sight. Arriving at Mark's studio, he encounters slight difficulty finding a parking spot in the street, quickly taking the one empty space next to the building marked "Reserved," figuring it's probably Mark's. He pulls in, and upon entering the building, he can readily see his friend does indeed have what appears to be a busy, thriving business. People seem to be everywhere, mostly attractive women...some moving through the partially visible hallway, from room to room, apparently changing clothes, primping as they move about.

A young woman behind the counter looks up to acknowledge his arrival, smiling. "May I help you?"

"Uh, yeah. I'm here to see the samurai."

"S'cuse me?"

"The Samurai...the Jap."

His comments and attempt at a little best friend humor take her by surprise. "I beg your pardon, sir. There's no one here by either of those names. Sure you have the right place?"

"Yeah, sorry. Mark Anderson, I'm here to see Mark Anderson." He can see he's irritated the young woman a bit. What appears to her to be a racial/ethnic slur is, in fact, an affectionate tag he's used on Anderson since early in their friendship.

"How dare you..." the woman begins, about to rip him in defense of her boss.

"Redneck! How'd it go?" Anderson yells out as he steps into the showroom. "You get the job?"

Cade smiles, nodding in the affirmative; gives his friend a confident thumbs-up.

"Debby, would you get my best friend something to drink, and make sure he's comfortable."

The petite receptionist looks at Cade, who's smiling at the unpretentious, fairly attractive woman, who has already found a spot on Cade's personal attractiveness scale, now preparing to do a complete three-sixty on her previous attitude toward him. "You're Cade?"

"That's me."

"I'm so sorry. I owe you an apology..."

"Don't worry about it. You didn't know, besides, I admire the loyalty. I should've introduced myself in the beginning."

"Please, can I get you something?"

"No thanks. Can't stay...Got a car being delivered here any-time now. When it arrives, I will be leaving to go on to Mark's. He's busy, so would you mind telling him I'll see him later?"

Practically on cue, a young man steps into the studio asking if a Mr. Jason Cade is there. Soon after, paperwork completed, Cade's on his way. Despite making a couple of wrong turns, he eventually finds the house. The afternoon continues a streak of very warm and sultry ones for the Dallas area...approaching uncomfortable. Not sure where he should park, he parks the car in the street in front of the house. He enters his temporary home, using a key Anderson told him about, disclosing its loca-tion to him before leaving the house this morning. Inside, he spends the next few minutes collecting and organizing the few things he'd brought with him. Reflecting on all that's happened since his arrival yesterday, he makes several decisions: one involv-ing the use of the couch in his office until he's able to find an apartment, the other involving Danny Wilson.

After showering, he dresses partially, pulling on a semi-wrin-kled pair of pleated casuals, and one of his favorite pullovers, no shoes or socks. He lands in Mark's chair, that one looking the most comfortable, reopening the photo album left on the table last night. He'll spend a little additional time browsing through the history of Anderson's existence; maybe spend a little time getting to know his family.

Time passes quickly, and unnoticed as Cade's presence in a focused stage lapses intermittingly through the pages. A car pulls into the driveway...two climbing out and approaching the front door of the house quickly. Having now partially dozed into a daydream; the opening door startles Cade, making it too late for him to react in any way other than to open his eyes and sit up just before it hits him. The first to enter is a very attractive woman. Slightly groggy, Cade believes he could still be dreaming. He realizes she's no dream when she immediately walks over to him, happily acknowledging his presence.

"You must be Jason."

Continuing his emergence from a self-induced stupor, "And you gotta be Sandy. I recognize you from the pictures...but I was wrong."

"Oh...wrong about what?"

"I complimented Mark on his work last night. Told him it was high-quality stuff, but his work doesn't do you justice."

"You're sweet." She steps closer, wrapping her arms around him, as he willingly reciprocates.

"...Works every time," he tells her.

Anderson walks into the house, carrying her luggage.

"Hey! What the hell's going on here? Obviously, I'm not gonna be able to leave you two alone for a second." He walks past them, through the room, up the stairs, disappearing through one of the doors. Reappearing shortly after, he offers everyone a drink.

"Think I'll shower before we leave...been a long day. A hot one will do me good." She disappears upstairs, through the same door Anderson had just previously.

Cade follows his buddy into the kitchen, Mark reaching inside the fridge, grabbing a couple of beers. "What did I tell you?"

"Definitely choice...Still don't understand it."

"What?"

"…The attraction. I just don't understand what she sees in you."

"…Hidden talent." Anderson declares, grabbing a hand full of crotch. "The sword of the samurai."

"You're right about it being hidden." Sandy responds, making an unannounced appearance in the kitchen. "I've changed my mind. Make me one of those fuzzy navels…this time, with grape-fruit juice."

She walks up to Anderson, reaching down and grabbing his crotch, as he just had seconds ago. Leaning closely to him, "Why don't you bring that little pocket knife you keep calling a sword upstairs. I've really missed you." Her request and a wet, juicy kiss are all the enticements he'll need to follow her like a little puppy.

"Looks like dinner's gonna have to wait, old buddy," Anderson replies.

Trying to make the best of the situation as it continues to present itself, "Can't take too long. What's another thirty sec-onds?" Cade responds quickly.

"Kiss my ass, doughboy."

Cade laughs at Mark's latest jab and cut, a fun reminder of their time in school, when he was a little heavier than he should've been. Figuring he could be alone a few more minutes; he moves into the living room to finish his beer as Anderson prepares for his upcoming performance. He finishes making Sandy's drink, carrying it with him up the stairs, into the bedroom where she awaits his arrival. Soon after, some pretty strange noises filter through the closed door, down the stairs, and into Cade's ears.

Listening as long as he can stand it, he moves outside to the deck on the back of the house.

Heavy tree cover of the backyard, combined with that side of the house facing the east, cools the area slightly as this very warm summer day closes in on its final hours. Sitting there a few minutes, he decides he's bored, antsy; deciding to walk around, check out the surroundings. Obviously, Anderson has a lot more staying power than he gave him credit for.

A detached garage several feet from the house, out near the alley, indicates a little snooping might be in order. He wanders around, stopping at a window, looking through the tiny openings between the blinds. He thinks he can see some type of car, but it's too dark inside, plus whatever it is, appears to be covered by a tarp. He tries the door, attempting further investigation, finding it locked tight, forcing the discontinuation of any further meddling, unaware he came close to triggering an alarm. Concluding this short episode of super sleuthing, he walks back toward the house. Finding a chaise lounge to his liking; he slides to a semi-prone position, slowly sipping his beer; deciding, however, he better chug it after detecting a slight warming of its contents.

Sitting on the lounge, in the shade, on this early evening in early August, his thoughts finally find time to drift back to the young woman at the office. He glances at his watch, trying to imagine what she might be doing right now. His infatuation with her obviously isn't over.

"Cade...Cade! Where are you, man?"

Hearing his name brings him back to the time at hand.

"Yeah, man. Out here."

"Ready?"

He joins his friend and Sandy inside. Both are completely dressed and ready to go to dinner. Minutes later, the three are in front of the house, climbing into the Volvo. Top down, Cade prepares to enjoy the warm summer air from the backseat of the convertible.

"Remember the little gal manning my front desk? She's joining us for dinner," Anderson informs him as they slowly pull down the street, exiting the tree-covered cove, escaping the imitated early darkness, into the open reality of dusk. "I think she really liked you."

Anderson's grin forces a response from him. "Yeah, right. I could tell that right off."

The drive into downtown Dallas is enjoyable...Anderson and Sandy in the front; Cade and the little receptionist in the back after stopping to pick her up. Polite conversation seems to be the fare for the evening, including the two men continuing their reminiscing about college life and many days gone by. The girls say virtually nothing, enjoying the stories and anecdotes pouring from the guys' mouths, ad-libbing a little here and there to embellish toward more interesting lines.

Sandy feels a little uneasy around Debby. She's always felt she had an unhealthy interest in Mark. Since first meeting her, Debby decided Sandy's a fake. Not much of a basis with which to build a lasting friendship between the two.

Off toward the sunset, appearing as a backdrop to the skyline and slightly to the southwest, huge thunderheads build, the humid air around the evening travelers hinting at a possible late-night storm. Anderson steers the Volvo into the far right lane feeding onto R.L. Thornton. Aiming west, he accelerates slightly and quickly slows just before their exit onto Maple. Finally a quick left under the freeway, toward the so-called Gumby Tower, aptly named by Dallasites due to bright green argon lights trimming the skyscraper with a glowing perimeter visible for miles at night. Dusk fully blankets the beautiful downtown area now; lighting of the many buildings and the streetlights, all begin to take over from the end of a natural Texas daylight, illuminating the area adequately.

Prior to Anderson's turn off R.L., Cade glances to the north, catching a glimpse of the Crescent standing alone, no other building close to its size around it. He wonders if she could be in her apartment, there with her boss, her lover...Then he remembers; she had mentioned she would be working late tonight. He decides at that moment, he may go to the office after dinner, try out his new access number on the front door, check out his office further, maybe rearrange some furniture...whatever. Mentally looking for excuses, acceptable reasoning to do what he can't quite yet convince himself he should do.

Emerging from under the overpass, still on Maple heading south, downtown buildings and their lights are upon them, not nearly as beautiful as distance will generally dictate a view of much of anything ...although still sufficient enough to continue Cade's happy streak.

Weaving through the street system, Anderson seems to have a definite destination in mind. Approaching the West End, an aroma of Tex-Mex and BBQ fills the air, tantalizing their senses. The West End is a fitting location for Cade's first night out since returning to Dallas.

Soon parked, the foursome crawls from the car, waiting on Mark to put the top up and lock the doors. The walk down an alley toward the refurbished warehouse district is quick, pleasant, and tempting to their sense of smell. As Cade and Debby trail Mark and Sandy, Cade starts to notice the way his date for the evening looks at his buddy. He watches his friend, concluding he's probably considered attractive to the opposite sex; but in today's environment, most Japanese-American unions are still considered somewhat taboo, like so many other interracial relationships. He can understand many Americans feeling that way, but he's never really thought of his best friend as Japanese, not until recently. He knows Anderson's looks say Japanese, but his mind and heart are one hundred percent American. Cade has never had a problem with most issues of this nature. Not until reading the stories in the papers of Japanese businessmen buying American pro sports teams, huge chunks of American soil, American businesses, as their homeland turns its backs on American manufacturers wanting to export to Japan.

Out of the alley, into the well-lit West End, the smell of grilled fajitas has become quite more prevalent, and just what the doctor ordered. Seeing the restaurant, with its wooden-deck patio for outside dining, he knows immediately where he wants to eat. The usual Friday evening crowd is arriving, many already there... settled in for dinner, entertainment, or whatever the evening might bring. There will be a little wait for a table, this Tex-Mex establishment being one of the more popular restaurants in this area. A cold margarita on the rocks calls out Cade's name, and with that, the four head for the bar inside after leaving their name with the host. Twenty-five minutes and two margaritas apiece later, a table is available as their name resonates over the PA system. Seated, they continue enjoying the drinks, adding to that the flavor of salsa, chips, and nachos...all those things helping to make Cade's recent return to Dallas a successful one.

Back inside, a man sits with a few of his buddies, maintaining a low profile while closely watching the four out for a relaxing evening. Cade seems to be enjoying the evening too much to have noticed the man who plastered his contorted face on the passenger-side window of Anderson's Volvo yesterday, but then he probably wouldn't have recognized him at this point anyway...really hadn't seen that much of his normal face to begin with. Unfortunately, Kirk recognizes him and offers his barmaid a one hundred-dollar bill to get the host from the front door, offering her an equal amount to get him the table next to his dad's newest nemesis. Within minutes, his redneck buddies are being escorted outside, to the designated table right next to Cade, Anderson, and the girls. Kirk won't be joining them tonight; he'll let his friends do his dirty work.

As far as Cade's concerned, the evening to this point has been an unqualified success. He figures there's nothing that could possibly ruin it tonight. The first few minutes of their meal, they dine on enchiladas, fajitas, all the trimmings. The guys ushered to the table next to them, seem normal customers at first glance, barely drawing notice from Cade or Anderson. Before sitting, one stops, sniffing air as if smelling something foul. "This the only table you got?"

"But, sir, your friend..."

The man the others call J.D. interrupts. "Don't you worry yer purty little head, darlin', we'll just try to make the best of the stench and all. Unfortunately, these damn 'Chinks' are everwhare."

The conversation at Cade's table quickly ceases, Cade looks to Mark for a reaction. Anderson continues eating; acting as though nothing's been said. Good enough for him. If his friend chooses to ignore the comment, he can too.

A waiter arrives at the table of the "bubba brigade," taking their orders for drinks, J.D. ordering two buckets of longnecks.

"Shit, Chuck, you know, I could've gone all night without havin' to sit next to another damn Chink. You know how they smell n'all. Kinda ruins yer appetite, doesn't it?"

Anderson continues eating, although finding it more difficult with each insulting remark. Debby...tried and true and always ready for a fight stands eager to defend her boss' honor. Cade can't help admiring his friend's self-control.

"Debby," Anderson directly voices the girl's name, "let it go." His composure quite impressive, he won't be able to keep it in check much longer.

"Hey, gook...you. I'm talkin' to you. What the hell makes you think yer good enuf 'ta eat at a fine restaurant like this? You oughta be cookin' at a place like this, and eaten' in some shitty' Chinese hole, where you belong."

Cade can't believe what he's hearing. He knows he can't take much more, doesn't think they should have to. He continues looking to Anderson for some sign of reaction, a sign of anger. Everyone's meal is ruined, their evening not far behind. Others around the two tables have become annoyed with the developing situation. Sandy wants to leave...Cade decides he'll react whether Mark does or not, the best thing to do...summon the waiter to their table, ask for the check. He also decides he'll protest their treatment.

"Yes, sir?" the waiter responds.

"I'd like to see the manager. These guys are very offensive. They've ruined everyone's dinner," he tells him, referring to the table of rednecks sitting next to them. "We'd just like to be able to enjoy our meal in peace...without the swearing, the racial commentary."

"Yes, sir. I'll handle it, sir."

He steps to the table, asking the men seated there to please respect the rights and feelings of other patrons or he'll have his manager call the police.

"Sure, we can do that," J.D. tells him.

The waiter steps back to address Cade, apologizing. "Let me know if they cause you any more trouble, sir, and I'll have them removed from the premises."

"Thanks, man. Why don't cha go ahead and bring us the check."

Inside, Kirk's moved to a closer table where he will be able to see everything as it happens, scarfing down refried beans, rice, and tacos, and one beer after another, enjoying all he sees.

"Awe, c'mon, man. You and yer friends not take a little ribbin'—see someone havin' a little fun?" He looks directly at Cade. "You and yer gook don't like sittin' next to real Americans, you kin always leave!"

Sandy grabs Mark's hand as he rises from his seat. "Mark, don't. Let's just go."

"Shit. Will yuh look at that? The good-lookin' babe's with the Chink. You gonna let yer girl tell yuh what to do, Chink? By the way, girl, what's it like screwin' a gook?"

Anderson steps back from the table to face the redneck doing all the talking. The manager's already called the police, expecting a full-scale brawl to break out at any time. People in the restaurant, those who haven't already left because of J.D.'s offensive language, have begun distancing themselves from the impending confrontation. Anderson's physical stature has most believing he couldn't fight a fifth grader. But Cade knows differently, knows he's been boxing since college. He's used his boxing as a form of exercise, helping him stay in shape as he approaches his midlife. The sport has also been a good diversion from the rigors of work. As he puts it, "Americans have stereotyped all Asians, people with that ancestry, as skilled martial art experts. My skills in boxing give me an element of surprise, should I ever need it."

Actually, Cade's been the one trained in a form of the arts... Tae Kwon Do, specifically. Only problem, it's been several years since he's worked out, practiced, used it in any way. He's forgotten much of the technique, the moves necessary for the skill. On top of that, he's not in near the shape he used to be, back when he earned his black belt.

Cade quickly, though a little reluctantly, joins his friend at his side. Peering through the window at his table, Kirk enjoys all events taking place on the outside deck, grinning more with each additional movement toward an altercation.

The bubba brigade, all membership now standing for the inevitable, appears ready for battle. "Got a problem, Chink?"

Anderson looks at him, speaking calmly. "First of all, if any of you were of an intelligent species and knew anything at all—except how to order a beer, or use your four-letter words—you'd know I'm not Chinese or Vietnamese as you have so eloquently referred. I'm Japanese-American. I was born in America, just like you. It's just that my mother wasn't my father's sister or cousin. You wanna call me something; call me a Jap." He looks at Cade. "That would at least make me feel at home, and would indicate to everyone around, you were a creature with some form of advanced intelligence."

"What the hell yuh mean by all that?" He turns to his buddies, then looks at restaurant patrons still left, all now laughing... laughing at his expense. The level of his intelligence surfaces further with his next question. "What's so damned funny?"

"Let me put it to you in terms even you'll find easy to understand. Watch my lips and listen closely. I'm not Chinese. OK, you got that part, right? Now, listen closely to this one, I'm not Vietnamese either. OK, now what's that leave...Japanese? I'm also an American citizen, just like you. As hard as I know that must be for you to understand, or accept, we're kind of like brothers, so to speak. But that's OK. I wouldn't expect a dumb-shit redneck like yourself to be intelligent enough to figure this one out on your own. Hell, it's kinda been difficult for me."

Cade relaxes a little, temporarily letting his guard down, feeling Anderson's handling the situation pretty well.

"You fuckin' Chink, Jap, whatever the hell you are, nobody gives a shit! I didn't ask for no fuckin' lecture, and I don't appreciate a smart-ass foreigner calling me some name! There's nothing American about your ass, except fer that ugly-assed wart attached to yer side there next to yuh." Cade quickly realizes he's referring to him, ruffling his feathers greatly. "As far as I'm concerned, he's a fuckin' Jap lover. No red-blooded American would ever let himself love a Jap."

"I've told you once," Anderson's impatience growing, almost to the point of no return, "and I'm only gonna repeat myself once more. I'm American, and proud to be one, despite assholes like yourself. I'm also proud of my Japanese heritage. Guys like you also make that part easy. Now, if you don't mind, I'd appreciate your watching your mouth in the presence of the ladies and children. You don't, you're gonna force me to do something I don't want to do."

Cade still can't believe his friend's restraint with the very negative situation unfolding before them. Mentally, he's been prepared for the worst since the thing began a few minutes back. For most of the time, he's been searching his memory for the correct positioning of a side-kick; any Tae Kwon Do move he can still remember well enough to do.

Debby's already stepped up next to them, ready to join the fight, should there be one.

"Mark. They don't bother me," Sandy pleads.

"Well it's not about you this time. And they may not bother you, but they bother the hell outta me. No one should have to listen to this kind of garbage, or put up with this crap from anyone."

The cavalry arrives, minus trumpet fanfare. Two of Dallas' finest, assigned the West End beat, calm things considerably with nothing more than their presence, but then, things weren't planned to go any further at this time anyway. The brigade is just there to try to embarrass the group, to set Cade and Anderson up for a later showdown, something a little more private.

After discussions with all parties involved, the cops decide to excuse Anderson, Cade, and their dates, detaining Kirk's gang for further discussion. Their detention, gives Cade and his friends the opportunity to escape into the crowd. Kirk waits for the right moment, coming to the aid of his troops. "Jack, is there a problem?"

Jack Simon, one of the uniformed officers, looks up when he hears his name. "Hey buddy, how yuh doin'?"

"Doin' good…'bout yerself? Listen, these dimwits work fer me and my dad. Let me handle this. I promise you won't have any more problems with them tonight."

Officer Simon looks at his partner, shrugs, and then closes his book. "Sounds like a program to me. Didn't want to haf'ta fill out another report tonight anyway. Nothin' damaged. Whatta yuh think, Ross?" After his partner nods in agreement, the two leave.

Kirk watches them disappear into the evening crowd, turning to his gang. "You guys were great. Damn good work, men. Here's the reward I promised." Reaching deep into one of his pant pockets, he pulls out a wad of bills big enough to choke a bull. Peeling several hundreds from a roll the size of his huge fist, Kirk hands five large bills to each man standing there.

"There's more where that came from. Interested?"

"What do we need t'do, boss?" J.D. asks.

Kirk lays out the plan for the remainder of the evening, a plan designed to take Cade and Anderson out of commission for a long time. Kirk watches his men leave, walking in the same direction as their prey, disappearing into the crowd as they did, just minutes before. The night's certainly not over yet.

Inside a West End club Cade, Anderson, and the girls find a vacant table. Sandy's already found a few modeling friends, two guys and a couple of women, leaving her group to visit them for a few minutes, Debby, watching in disgust as Sandy dances with one of the guys. Thinking she'd like to dance, Cade asks her.

Initially balking at the overture, not wanting to leave Mark alone, she accepts at Mark's insistence. Approaching the floor, the fast music ends, and a slower one begins. During the dance, Cade notices her continuing stares back toward the table where Mark continues to sit alone.

"You're really fond of him, aren't you?"

She's a little embarrassed it must be so obvious.

"Look, I haven't known you long, but if you have feelings for him, why not tell him...tell him how you feel."

"No way! I couldn't do that. He has Sandy...he'd never...Don't you dare tell him."

"Hey, it's not my place to tell him something like that. I've always felt if you want something or someone bad enough, you have to go for it yourself, no matter what the obstacle. You can never rely on someone else to do it for you. You know, in life; there's no room for regrets...no regrets."

His words find their target, Debby listening intently to everything he says, because it's what she wants to hear...what she wants to believe...what she can't bring herself to do now, or any other time. His words are philosophically what he knows, what he believes; now, listening to his own advice, he decides what he now must do.

Music over, Cade and his partner return to their table and Anderson. Debby soon excuses herself, saying it must be because of something she ate...Cade knows better. Cade can tell something's really bothering his friend as well, maybe still feeling the sting of the redneck remarks earlier. He just doesn't quite know how to pull it out of him.

"You don't want Sandy partying with those people, why don't you tell her?"

Anderson smiles. "That's not it at all. That's not what's bothering me."

"What is it, then? Those assholes at the restaurant?"

"My father was right."

What do you mean?"

"He's always said there's much prejudice and hatred in the world. And there seems to be no shortage of that for my people here in America. My family's seen and felt the sting of hatred since coming here years ago."

"Come on, Mark. You know those rednecks aren't indicative in any way of how all of us feel. Those guys are illiterates from the backwoods, throwbacks from the dark ages, a race of people from another place in time."

"That may be true, but you don't live it every day, see it every day like I do...like my people have. I can truly relate to African-Americans, Hispanics, and their problems over the years."

Cade wants to change the subject now; wishes he hadn't gotten his buddy to open up. The topic's a little too heavy for him this evening, his next choice not much better.

"What about your family? I've never asked you much about them, never forced the issue. I know that's a private part of someone's life, and I guessed you would probably tell me what you wanted someday. How about now?"

"I've told you before...I've known little myself till recently. It's not that I didn't want to tell you; I just never knew enough to tell you. Despite what I know now, I don't think I'm ready just yet... don't think I want to share them with anybody. Hell, I just found out more than I've ever known. I need some private time with them...time to get to know my past. Make any sense?"

"Sure...kind of. I think I can understand that."

The two look toward the dance floor, Debby rejoining them.

"Great dancer isn't she?" Anderson inquires.

"Great dancer, great looking, successful business, very (emphasizing "very") loyal employees," Cade says, glancing at Debby as she stands to accept a dance from some guy she knows. "I'm proud for you, Mark. You've got a lot going for you right now."

"Things are not always as they seem, as they say," Anderson laments.

"What's going on? You and Sandy got some problems? Sure doesn't show. You both look happy."

"On the contrary, that's the best part of my life right now," he said, hesitating as though he won't say anything more.

"Then what? What is it? Talk to me, man...what's keeping you from being totally happy?"

Anderson sighs, not really wanting to answer the questions, about to do so anyway. "Incidents like tonight for one. I'm tired, sick 'n tired of seeing people like myself violated in public displays of racial hatred. It's enough just knowing how most people feel; without the taunting, the outward animosity displayed by people like those guys tonight."

"I'm telling you, Mark, those assholes don't speak for the rest of us."

"That...is where you are wrong, ol' buddy. They do represent the majority, at least the outspoken majority. And, sometimes I can understand their feelings of insecurity...really I can. But those who are willing to succumb to their inner feelings of hatred, don't really know us...don't really want to know us."

"Who's us?"

"The Japanese-American, African-American, Hispanic-American—we're all alike in one sense. What you fail to see when you can't look past our physical features is that we're American, just like you, inside and out. I'm an American. I want to be nothing more. I want to be left alone to enjoy all those things in life you all seem to take for granted. I'd do anything to defend those rights, anything."

Anderson takes a sip of his drink, saying nothing more, climbing off his soapbox.

Cade knows his friend is probably right, although he despises having just been labeled a bigot. Realizing his friend's comments followed an encounter with intolerance at its worst, Cade allows him his personal feelings, though dogmatic in many respects.

"You may be right. Guess I never thought about all that stuff. If I were in your shoes, I'd probably feel the same way, be just as bitter, probably more so." With that, Cade's decided he'll never call his friend a Jap again, ever.

"I'm not really bitter...yet. Just tired." Anderson contemplates dropping a bomb on his friend. Something he's been carrying around with him since finding out more about his family's past. Something he's wanted to share with someone, someone he knew cared about him, a friend.

"I've not told anyone what I'm about to tell you, not even Sandy. Can I expect you to keep this to yourself?"

"Sure," his reply quite easy. If his friend were to tell him anything about his past, Cade would welcome it with open arms.

"Just found out how my mother died...and now it seems it could have consequences for my life."

"You told me she'd died right after your birth, but how does her death affect your life now, other than from the obvious?"

"From what I know, she was a small girl, about ten or so. She was close to Hiroshima, Japan, when this country dropped the big bomb. She wasn't close enough to die then, but I guess she ingested particles of radiation impregnating the air around her and her family. Radiation invaded her body and I guess she carried it around for years, dying at a very young age...around nineteen, I think."

Cade couldn't think of anything to say to his friend, nothing to console him, but he had to try. "Man, I don't know what to say. That's terrible. So that picture you have, it has to be as your father and you need to remember her ...young and beautiful."

"Want to hear the real kicker? I've done a little additional reading on the subject. It seems I could be carrying the same shit around inside me. Someday, one of those little particles transferred from her to me while in her womb, could explode, like the bomb. When, and if it does, I'm a goner."

Anderson's revelation stuns Cade. "You sure about this?"

"Afraid so. I've talked to more than one specialist. It's kind of like this disease, AIDS. You don't have any idea when the shit's gonna kick in and take you down; you just know it's there and you know it will, someday."

"And Sandy knows nothing about this?"

"Nothing. I'm not ready to tell her yet either. She wants to start a family, something I can never let happen. I can't take a chance on one of my own kids having to deal with this shit inside them all their lives."

"But, don't you think you should tell her? I mean, you're sharing your lives now. Don't you think she deserves to know about this...at least have the opportunity to be in on your decision? Shit, what if she accidentally gets pregnant...then what?"

"Just after I confirmed everything, I took the necessary precautions. She could go off the pill now, and never get pregnant, not by me anyway."

Cade's expression probably says it all right now. He knows enough to know if Sandy finds out she's been lied to, Mark's perfect relationship could be doomed.

"I know what you're thinking...I'll tell her soon, I promise... just got to find the right moment."

Debby rejoins them again after the dance with her friend, and Sandy finally decides she'll leave her friends for the first time since coming here. "I've given you two enough time to catch up," she says upon her return. "Besides, from the looks on your faces, this conversation's getting far too serious. What're you guys' talkin' about anyway?"

Anderson smiles, standing to kiss her, holding her chair while she sits. Cade's smile is a phony. *If only you knew,* he thinks.

Cade looks at his watch, suddenly remembering Danny. It's eleven after nine...he's wondering if she could still be at the office. He'll soon find out, if he can figure out a way to hurry this little party along.

Anderson can't help noticing his friend's fidgeting. "We'd better go...I have some things I need to take care of early in the morning. Need my beauty sleep." Not really, but what he's actually doing is taking care of his buddy tonight.

After paying their tab, they wish Sandy's friends a good night then walk to the front of the club, near the front door. Sandy excuses herself, telling them she needs to pee before going any farther, deciding it's too long a drive home to wait. She tells them she'll join them all outside in a few seconds.

As the remaining three enter the humid night air, they hear voices from their not so distant past. "Well, look who we have here. The gook and his lover boy. You know, everyone ought to have his own personal gook."

Cade looks at Anderson. "What a bunch of assholes."

J.D. continues, "Where's your good-lookin' woman? She get smart and dump your gimpy Chink ass?"

Anderson quickly turns to Debby, who's standing behind him. "Find Sandy and get the car. Meet us back out here in the street, in front of the mall. Do it now!"

True to her spirit, and at no real surprise to either of the guys, she tells Mark she's staying put...to help them.

Anderson takes control immediately, "Do what I tell you! Now!" he says sternly. There's no questioning he means business. Apparently, he has a plan.

The brigade converges on the two friends, "When we get through with you two, there'll be one less fuckin' Jap, and one less fuckin' Jap lover in our city, takin' our jobs and our women!"

"Shit! Come on!" Anderson quickly tells Cade. "When we get inside the mall, you go down, find the elevator...take it to the top! I'll meet you there!"

Cade isn't quite sure where "there" is, but with the gang from the restaurant hot on their asses again, he didn't want to stand around arguing or asking any questions.

Looking at her watch, Danny's still dazed a little, realizing it's getting late. She leans back in her chair, still in total disbelief at what just happened. She knew she was taking a chance letting Robert think their affair wasn't over, trying to get his mind off going after this guy she'd just met yesterday. She must have been out of her mind, going through what she just had for someone she doesn't even know, a complete stranger. But, she was concerned about another human being's welfare, even more concerned about her own well-being, her career. She had to continue seeing Robert, she thought, convince him she's still interested in continuing their relationship. She doesn't; he and his asshole of a son can make her life miserable.

After the events of this evening, after what's just happened, she's more frightened than ever before. Appalled, angry, hurt... she still cannot help thinking about her career, her job. Anger pushes her to the brink of confrontation; maybe she'll threaten him with going to the police, maybe Ankawa himself. What if the power Robert yields is as strong as everyone says? He too is probably angrier now than ever before. He'll probably stop at nothing himself to ruin her life, Jason Cade's, and anyone else's around her before he's finished.

Valuing her job, her career more than anything...that being the most important thing she believes she has in her life, the only thing left of real value...she has to go to Robert. Maybe I am at fault for the whole thing...I did lead him on...a little. It was a long day for both of us. Maybe if I were to apologize...try to convince him this whole thing was a bad misunderstanding, maybe he'll forgive me, then we can go on as though all of this never happened. That'll buy me some time. No. Shit! That'll never happen. What the hell am I thinking? What's all this really make me? A prostitute, gold digger, everything I was ever concerned about becoming? I guess I really am all those things.

I've worked hard to get where I am, damn it! Why should I have to give up my career? I leave Ankawa now, where will I go? I'll have to start all over again...never again be able to achieve all I have. A transfer to another department! I've got to convince him that's the right step to take, the right thing to do for both of us. I love working at Ankawa.

Moving closer to the keyboard and unbelievably calm at this point, she prompts the print command, her decision to go to him and ask his forgiveness made. Command delivered; her LaserJet printer engages, beginning the print process on the final page of the project she and Robert have been working on all day...into this particular evening. As the printer continues its functional process, the pieces of paper quickly move through their printing process, discharging onto the holding tray one by one, the final page resting on top of the other completed pages. Not waiting for the finished product, she'd already begun organizing her desk so everything will be in its place on Monday, should there be a Monday...a continuing unusual amount of exhibited composure for what's just happened.

What a sobering thought, she thinks. *There might not even be any more Mondays for me here. A sincere apology, and after all we've been through, surely Robert will forgive me again; he has before.*

She pushes away from her desk, stands, quickly proofing her work. Once again...flawless work, gaining little solace at the moment.

Feeling a slight stiffness in her legs, partially from sitting all day, partially from the final move she'd made to free herself, she takes a couple of moments to stretch, using the same exercises she normally would just prior to beginning her usual early morning run.

She doesn't really know for sure if he's still in the building. Maybe I really hurt him. Hell, he deserved to get hurt for what he did, what he tried to do. She walks out of the large room, the one housing the cubicle she calls home thirteen, fourteen hours a day, almost seven days a week. Stopping in the hall, she looks toward his office at the end of the long corridor. The light's on...crap! He must still be here. She begins in that direction, stopping after just a couple of steps, the thought of having to apologize to him incensing her! But, that's the way their relationship has always gone. She's about to take that familiar walk, a walk she's taken time and time again during this relationship. She never really thought about it before, but she can't ever remember him apologizing once for anything since their relationship began.

"Damn it! He should be apologizing to me! But he won't! No, if I want to keep my job, I'll have to make the first overture. You son of a bitch! What did I ever see in you to begin with?" she admonishes slightly under her breath as though he were standing there next to her. "Why do you always have to make every-thing so damned difficult, you stupid jerk?"

Cold feet, or justifiable anger fueling her stubbornness, she decides she'll take a side trip to the restroom, not really sure if she'll be able to complete her walk into Robert's office. She steps into one of the stalls, relieving herself, then exits, standing in front of the row of mirrors lining the wall, leaning onto a marble counter as though losing her balance, still pushing back against her sense of reality. What she notices slams her back home.

"Crap, he ripped my dress," her visual assessment uncovers the tear in the side exposing her slip underneath.

She thinks back, her vision penetrating the barrier of time try-ing to remember the moment he ripped it...revisiting an episode in her life she will soon need to forget. She transgresses back to that moment, those surrounding it, as vivid as though it had just happened; which of course it had.

Robert enters her oversized cubicle...not a private office as she had once been promised, but one of the largest partitioned cubi-cles in the office. He claimed to be there checking her progress. Work on their project had gone well all day long. There would be no reason for her to anticipate what was about to happen; at least thinking about it now, she doesn't see any reason why she would have.

Danny knew he probably hadn't quite gotten over the events of the week, those surrounding the breakup, the confronta-tion at her apartment. Earlier today she convinced him she had changed her mind, at least what she thought she needed to do to buy time. At the very least she wanted him to think that, until she could come up with a better plan. She had to admit, she still had residual feelings for the man. Why wouldn't she? ...after all they'd been through. Problem is; she just doesn't feel the way she once did...in the beginning.

When he came to her cubicle that last time, he seemed very appreciative and quite complimentary of her work. He surprised her with an unanticipated reward, a neck massage. Innocent enough, she thought, the massage progressed quickly to her shoulders. He said it was a reward for a job well done, for her hard work today...a friend doing something for another. And she was naive enough to believe him.

His hands moved from her neck to her shoulders, back to her neck; manipulation disguised within a counterfeit innocence. Admittedly; it felt awfully good, especially after the long day. His soft touch, careful hand orchestration still had its intended effect on her, sending chills throughout her body, bringing back the memories of many moments of tenderness, moments they'd shared together...exactly what he was trying to accomplish. And frankly, maybe she really didn't want him to stop.

His hands moved slowly, more deliberately, from her neck to her shoulders. His moves converted more quickly with each passing second...He knew exactly what he was doing tonight...from her shoulders, to her back, to her neck again, moving back to her shoulders. She closed her eyes intermittently for moments of pleasure provided, falling into a false sense of trust. Instinctively, losing control, she emitted a soft sensuous moan. This was all the encouragement Robert needed, believing he was back. He leaned over, kissing her neck, ears, progressing further.

"Robert, please don't," she said in a soft, slightly pleading tone...her reaction not at all convincing.

He stopped momentarily, more to catch his breath than to positively respond to her request, continuing the massage.

Danny decided it had gone far enough, asking him once again to "Please stop!"

He quickly moved around to front her, sensing his short window of opportunity quickly closing. Facing her, placing himself between her body and the desk...he was ready. She was still seated in her chair when he grabbed her, yanking her up and out of it, pulling her to her feet, closer to him. She finally realized what was really happening, attempting to push away.

To gain additional leverage, he lifted her off the floor, spinning her around, slamming her down on top of the desk. She remembers landing painfully hard, very painfully. Standing in front of the mirror, she rubs her backside, a bruise already forming there, still hurting at the moment.

Robert quickly pried her legs apart, forcefully moving between them. By now, their breathing intensified, each for quite different reasons. He reached under her dress, grabbing her underwear, ripping her panties from her body, extreme sheerness making that task very easy.

A forced reality of where they were headed hitting her solidly, Danny fought emphatically for her freedom.

Still standing in the bathroom, she hyperventilates in the memories of the past few minutes, reliving the moment of helplessness she felt during the attack. Once again she finds a way to blame herself. Because of what she considers her feeble attempt at fighting off the unwanted, unsolicited advance, she can easily lay most of the blame at her own feet.

She can remember feeling his obvious excitement as he reached around her with both hands, grabbing her buttocks, pulling her against him firmly, his groin pressed to hers. She does the only thing she can...SCREAM! Unfortunately, there was no one there to hear her cries for help on this night, probably no one who would've helped anyway. Everyone home, with the exception of a building security skeleton crew, the cleaning service not coming in until Sunday, there was no one...no one to help her.

To muffle subsequent screams, Robert forced his mouth over hers, driving his tongue deep inside, raping her orally, his taste not the least bit foreign to her. He knew he would be in control soon, very soon...When he was, she would succumb; they all do.

Now in a state of shock, it took Danny longer to respond, but once she did, she was determined as never before! She remembered how she bit down hard, immediately recognizing the taste of blood, Robert's blood! Roles quickly reversing; he now became the victim, the person in retreat. He tried in vain to pull away, her teeth's grip not given up that easily. For the first time since this encounter began, she enjoyed a certain amount of control. When she finally released him, he fell backward.

His anger surged as he came at her again! His retaliation in the form of an open-handed left hook missed its target...barely. Seeing it coming, Danny quickly leaned out of the way...his punch close enough she could feel the trail of air as it passed her face.

Before he can come at her again, she jumped off the desk, quickly moving away. Robert reached out, grabbing at her... clutching a handful of clothing, tearing her dress. This act of retaliatory aggression knocked Danny sideways, forcing her onto her chair.

By now, her anger and desire to make him pay for his attack had turned to fear...and she was scared, very scared! Robert, furious she was putting up such a fight, reacted through hostile obscenities.

"You fucking bitch! What the hell's the matter with you?"

She had been seeing him this way more and more lately. Before she could reply, much less stand, he was straddling her and her chair, unzipping his pants, reaching inside, pulling out his next weapon of choice.

"What're you doing?" The obvious before her, horrified at how far this thing had gone. "Oh my God, Robert! No! Please don't do this!"

Her next reaction, spontaneous, immediate; she lifted her knee forcefully, driving home the only message she was sure he would understand, at this point, hope against hope he does. Connecting solidly, Robert reacted by straightening up, the pain rushing into his groin as he fell back on the desk. During his fall, he caught himself, throwing his hands behind him, grabbing the edge of the desktop.

Danny's final maneuver is a crushing blow to his manhood. She raised her legs, slamming her feet toward the desk to create the leverage she'd need to push away. As she did, her feet hit hard with the force of a runner's muscular legs behind them, catching a partially open drawer to the right, shutting it. Robert's left hand remained draped over the edge, fingers of that hand dangling in the path of the closing drawer. She remembers the sound and will as long as she lives.

It was like he was cracking his knuckles, only much worse. She wasn't sure whether his fingers were broken...probably were, but at the time she didn't really care. Robert yelled his loudest and most convincing obscenity of the evening, as he was the one to finally surrender to the attacks, doing anything he could to get away from his opponent. Despite his obvious pain, he would soon decide the war was just beginning.

Still standing in front of the mirror, most of the feelings she'd experienced just minutes earlier consume her once again. But she also knows she'll need to deal with it; she also knows she will have to deal with Robert, somewhere, sometime in the near future. One of those confrontations might as well be now. Her first concern, keeping her career in tact...damage control, at least until she's figured out where she goes from here, although she is closer to losing the desire to go on.

She finishes straightening herself, sighs reluctantly, and begins her walk through the bathroom doors, down the hall toward Robert's office. Determined this time to go through with it, her next confrontation will be her best attempt at a temporary artificial reconciliation, offering him an undeserved apology.

She stops just short of the open door, takes a deep breath, and knocks. "Robert? Excuse me. Robert? ...you in here? ...you OK?" Sticking her head inside, she sees no one.

Seeing the light in his private bathroom, she approaches with caution, once again forced to go through the same feelings, the anxiety she'd just endured in the hall. Her breathing quite labored, she digs deep inside for the courage to move forward.

Downstairs, inside the employee infirmary, Robert finishes applying ointment to his torn skin, bandaging his swollen fingers. He's been able to stop the bleeding, but he thinks his hand could be broken. The slight irregular angle his fingers' project would indicate that self-diagnosis to be a real possibility. He's decided he'll let his physician look at it in the morning. For now, the one-handed, unprofessional job of bandaging will have to suffice. A few aspirin should also help, he thought, grabbing a handful, popping four before leaving.

"The stupid bitch!" he mumbles, blaming her for the whole thing. *In the beginning, I thought she might be different from the others. She gets what she wants, uses me to get it, then when she doesn't need me anymore...*Thoughts of self-pity, coupled with extreme anger, although the anger is subsiding as nurtured deviation takes over, help him deal with everything for the moment.

She and her new boyfriend are going to pay. They'll both be sorry. His initial thoughts...to go back and fire her ass, directs his more devious side in its near complete takeover. *She'll soon regret she ever did this to me. There are better ways to handle a conniving bitch like her. She wants to break it off with me for some young "dick," I'll make sure she gets more than she ever bargained for.*

Still hurting and pissed at being defeated so easily, his decision to make sure the young man, whoever he is, doesn't work another day for Ankawa will be accomplished immediately. How he deals with him, will be quite unlike how he'll handle Danny. Knowing how important her career is to her, he decides he'll begin the gradual dismantling of her essence, her spirit. In time, he'll bust her all the way back to the secretarial temp pool. It'll be one rung at a time. At first, she'll think it a minor setback in her career...and she'll probably be quite happy with this; welcome it, in fact, thinking she will not have to deal with him any longer within the department. The transfer she mentioned will happen sooner than later. Then, the final move will kill her. But not before he makes her sweat a little. He'll enjoy watching every second of her painful fall. Maybe he'll also turn his son loose on the boyfriend, soon as he can find out who the hell he is. Hell, his son can have his way with Danny as well.

Danny walks into the private bathroom, knocking before she enters. She finds no one. Seeing the blood splattered on the floor and in the sink, she forgets her personal problems, concern for Robert's well-being surfacing immediately.

She quickly emerges from the bathroom, back into his office, over to his desk. Picking up his phone, she dials his car phone number, hoping she'll catch him there. No answer, except for the operator telling her it's not in service and the person cannot be reached at this time. She sits in his chair, contemplating her next move.

Sitting, thinking...her eyes quickly focus on a small leather binder to the right side of his desk. It looks like one someone might use to keep a log, a diary, and maybe important numbers. Laying there, its apparent easy access almost an open invitation, the book invites her curiosity to its pages. As though possessing little control over her arms or hands, she moves to pick it up, preparing a search through its as yet undisclosed contents. A quick inventory details the presence of four data disks, instead of initially suspected notes or words. Each labeled "Project Hiroshima I, II, III, or IV," she immediately sees one is missing from its pocket.

Considering his computer sitting on the desk, she can see a disk stuck in a drive slot. Glancing toward the door into the hall, seeing no one, hearing nothing...curiosity's gotten the best of her and she decides she'll investigate. Depressing the "enter" key, her simple action brings the computer out of "power save," the screen immediately coming on with information Robert must have accessed prior to their altercation, the information he must have been working with before deciding he'd come into her cubicle. What she sees initially intrigues her.

The particular format she is viewing is one she spent months designing. The closer she surveys the information displayed, the more she realizes she may have found something she will authenticate later as pretty incredible, something she has no clue as to its meaning now. She scrolls to the next page, to the next, and so on. Viewing the script and program displayed on the screen. With each new page she sees some pretty wild information.

The program she designed is being used partially for what it was intended, a tool for automatically downloading funds from a master bank account into individual accounts, an automatic direct deposit. She had programmed passwords and data into this particular program to make accessing of Ankawa's payroll account easier for executives like Ankawa and Robert, almost with a flip of a switch. However, this particular payroll resembles nothing like she's ever seen before.

Names listed are definitely not those of any Ankawa employees she knows. If this is truly what it represents, her employer could have much more power than anyone ever imagined. It had to be something Robert's involved in. Why would he have these disks if he wasn't? The list of "Who's Who in America" is staggering. Many monetary figures representing significant sums, she can only presume; actual amounts being paid out to each individual;

demonstrating some very large amounts of money. As she continues scrolling, the list is elite in nature, and assuming the numbers
are correct, the total dollar amount significant; larger than any one
individual or most corporations could afford. She recognizes a few
names, but not all. The list appears to be categorized by profession,
separated into government officials...federal and state; judges, lawyers, other corporate executives, from some of the largest corporations in the world, from the military...each list existing of only three
or four names per category. She recognizes the name of one of
the most prolific televangelists known in modern times—why him,
escapes her at the moment—the names of local law enforcement,
by rank, city office holders. Only Ankawa could afford such a staggering payroll.

Her first thought...write some of the names on a piece of
paper, deciding instead, to copy what she has onto another disk.
Not knowing where Robert keeps his blanks, she closes and pops
the disk out, grabbing the small folder with the others as she
runs to her cubicle, grabbing four new ones to begin the process. She accesses file manager, beginning the copying process.

While she waits for the extensive program to begin copying
itself, she wonders why such apparently important information
would be on a common, ordinary disk, and not on a more confidential hard drive, or stored in some data bank somewhere in
the building. Why no access codes or IDs, especially in light of
the current technological advancements of today? She can only
assume in Robert's case, a disk would be much easier for him to
handle, gain access to, and keep hidden until needed, considering his low level of technical skills. Or maybe, maybe he thought
no one would think to look on a plain data disk for such impor-

tant information. There was another possibility she had to consider, a possibility crossing her mind earlier...maybe he wasn't supposed to even possess this information.

Finished in the clinic; Robert begins his trek back to his office, his next move already being mapped out in his head. His tongue quite sore and swelling, a bandaged hand with the real possibility of broken bones, and walking with a slight limp, he makes it to the elevators, pushing the "up" button. His extremely angered temperament surveys the damage she has done to him, more importantly what he will now do to her. As the elevator approaches its destination, his anger is beginning to subside, however slightly, and he begins replacing that with a desire for a calculated revenge. His revenge, a required condition for his personal satisfaction, will come regardless of the cost to others.

The first disk finished, Danny ejects it and readies the next, popping "Hiroshima II" into the same drive slot. Unaware of Robert's location in the building; thinking he must have left in a hurry; she continues working toward her ultimate goal thinking she should go back to his office, clean up around his desk. There may not be time left for that, she reasons. She's taking too much for granted. She knows she's taking a big risk.

At one point, she thinks she hears something...a noise coming from the hall. Stopping what she's doing, she listens...nothing.

Robert arrives at the eighth. His plan, continuing its development with each step, includes a stop by her cubicle. His apology will surprise her, although meaningless to him. Just the first step...the first step of his deception designed to throw her off balance further until he can get control of the situation.

Danny continues her work. The second disk not yet completed, she decides she'll go back to his office, make sure she left nothing behind that would be suspicious, planning to drop his little book full of disks off as she is leaving the building.

About to arrive in the area of cubicles housing Danny's, he stops, thinking he hears something from down by his office. He turns to head in that direction.

Danny walks toward the entrance to her cubicle, about to enter the hall.

Robert continues on a path to his office, within seconds of entering. A bell sounds, announcing the arrival of one of the elevators. Thinking it could be her; he turns to address its passenger. As he does, Danny walks through the door into the hall, stopping in her tracks at the sight of him, fortunately his back to hers. The door to the elevator opens, exposing its lone passenger. Kirk steps off, seeing his dad, immediately looking beyond his father at an empty hallway. The two greet each other cordially.

"Take care of her boyfriend?" Robert asks.

"Not yet. My boys should be having a little fun with him and his buddies as we speak. I told them to do what they had to."

"Good, by that I am assuming we should not need to worry about his continued presence in her life."

"You can assume that."

"I need to take care of something before we leave. I will be just a couple of minutes. Wait for me in my office. I'll be right back."

Robert turns to head back to Danny's cubicle. She can see him as she peers around the corner, migrating instantly toward a state of panic. Rushing to her work station, she searches frantically for a place to hide, then remembers the disks. She grabs those, about to go into hiding, and then remembers the disk still inside her computer.

Figuring she's most likely gone home, he walks around the corner, entering her space just to make sure, and to see if there is anything he might be able to grab to use against her. Confirming his suspicion she is gone, he stands at her desk and surveys the surroundings. He notices something that arouses his curiosity.

"Stupid bitch left in such a hurry she forgot to turn her computer off," he mumbles as though speaking with someone. As he reaches to turn it off, he notices what looks to be shoes sticking out from under a partially covered table.

"Come on out, Danny. Did you really think you could hide from me under there?"

Knowing she's been caught, thoughts race through her mind on her next move as she is about to crawl from under her poor excuse for a hiding place to face her hunter.

Robert bends down to grab her, pull her out forcefully, but the shoes he sees are nothing more than an empty pair she has left behind.

"Well, young lady. It appears I am paying you so well you can just leave a pair of your expensive shoes anywhere." He finishes what he was about to do before distracted, turning off her computer. From her crouched position under the desk, Danny can see his feet and legs…sweat pouring off her, she has been thinking of an appropriate explanation for what she is doing.

Robert sniffs the air as Kirk walks into the cubicle. "God, I love that perfume. That stuff sure cost me a lot of money," Robert quips.

"Give it a rest," Kirk responds. "She's no longer interested. Look, you know you haven't been yerself since that bitch came to work here. You finally figured out what everyone here's known for some time. She's a two-timing whore, and she'll obviously screw anybody to get what she wants."

Disbelief at everything she is hearing, she struggles to maintain composure and to keep from crawling from under the desk.

Robert and his son depart, stepping beyond her sight as they disappear down the hall. Robert is glad she was not there. He was never any good at apologies anyway. The weekend will give him the additional time he needs to develop something sounding a bit more sincere. He walks into the hall, turning toward his office.

Danny stands, after pushing away from her desk, readying to walk toward the door.

She waits a few seconds to make sure she doesn't step into the open too quickly. Soon she is just as quickly down the hall and into an elevator, on her way to the ground floor. As she is about to stop at the appropriate garage floor, she's not really sure where either of them has gone. She must be careful entering the dimly lit garage and she must be quick getting to her car.

CHAPTER 11

Inside the aging, but renovated four-story brick building, Cade and his friend separate as planned, each minimally a few steps ahead of J.D. and his gang. At the base of the single flight of stairs leading to the basement of the multi-themed entertainment facility, Jason can hear the five-member group busting through the double-wide, solid wood doors at its entrance above all other clatter. The few patrons remaining in the arcade at this late hour continue dropping tokens into slots of their selected games as he quickly passes through looking for the elevator. Most patrons are unaware, oblivious to the incident beginning to unfold around them; enjoying their final minutes of play before the mall's closing pushes them out the doors.

The bubba brigade splits at the stairway; three continuing their pursuit of Cade, the key target in this revenge-inspired fracas. The remaining two after Anderson, retracing his steps of only seconds before. Cade finds his way through the maze of popular video and sports-themed games to where an elevator awaits. Arriving in front of the door, he depresses the only call button available, while those in pursuit reach the basement arcade, stopping momentarily to conduct a visual search. A decision to split up will probably be one of the more intelligent things they've done all night, all year, for that matter.

Cade will have a slight wait, as the elevator stops at the ground floor, and several teenagers unload there. Several seconds pass, the door finally closes, and the elevator continues its journey to the basement. Before it arrives, Cade's first confrontation is before him as one of those in pursuit challenges him.

"Thought you'd lose us, didn't yuh? I'm gonna kick yer fuckin' ass rat here...rat here and rat now."

Cade decides instantly he'll try one of the oldest tricks in the book. With this guy, anything's possible, he figures. "My friend behind you may have somethin' to say about that."

The moron turns, expecting to see Cade's imaginary friend; obviously he doesn't, and Cade's ready for him. As the big boy completes his three-sixty, Cade delivers a frontal jump-kick, or something closely resembling one. Instead of connecting in the facial area as is supposed to happen with this particular move, the years of no training, no practice, the years away from the sport, all produce less than expected results. This maneuver normally requires an extension of the leg above the opponent's waist. Instead, he can only raise his leg high enough to reach the groin. Cade's misdirected attack will fortunately be to his benefit, helping him land a most effective blow.

The guy says nothing, standing motionless. The sole indication of pain comes from his eyes...glassy, watering, his hands drop to a cupped position covering his groin. The door finally opens, and not a minute too soon, as the second of three initially venturing into the arcade rushes Cade. Leaving his feet, he flies through the air, through the opening. Standing at the back, Cade politely steps aside, letting him in, allowing immediate access to the back wall. After slamming full force into that, he falls backward to the floor, lying there with only slight movement. The doors try closing repeatedly, the man's body jamming them each time, stopping them from completing their designed function. While Cade attempts to remove their obstacle, a third redneck arrives like a thundering herd of armadillos. This next confrontation lasts just seconds; Cade grabs the closest weapon he can find, a two-foot-tall metal cigarette ash can, lying overturned just outside the elevator doors. Picking it up, he swings wildly, connecting on his first shot, the blow not taking the guy out completely after clipping him with the bottom edge of the can. Knocking him back into the elevator, the doors close, transporting two of the three to the floors above. Teenagers in the arcade, now called into the fray as spectators, cheer his accomplishments, elevating Cade to sudden rock star status.

His initial attacker appears to be making a comeback, pushing himself from his completely prone position, recalling his senses to regroup for a second assault. Cade decides he doesn't have the time or the inclination to deal with him again, bolting for the stairway leading back to the ground floor. Plans have changed... Anderson will just have to deal with that.

On his way up the stairs, Anderson has conducted a quick search for mall security at each level, with little time to do a complete job. The rent-a-cops are on duty, but inside one of the retail stores...a lingerie shop...interviewing, scoping out a new clerk, one that has renewed male interest in bras and panties. They won't see him rushing to the fourth, or the men close behind in hot pursuit.

Anderson arrives at his destination, the fourth...a food court with two additional venues of entertainment...one, a miniature golf course, the other, a laser-tag business gone belly-up. He's always enjoyed golf, taking up the game several years ago, not getting much time on the links since the successful growth of his business. He grabs a putter without paying the customary fee, deciding he'll take a couple extra, just in case he busts one in a fit of anger. The kid at the counter asks what the hell he's doing, something about closing in ten minutes, there not being enough time to finish a round. Anderson informs him he's the fastest golfer in the world; reassuring him he'll be off work in time, slapping a twenty on the counter, telling him to keep the change.

Two in pursuit of Anderson arrive at the top, carefully canvassing the floor when they don't immediately see him. J.D. and one of his gang members split up, each taking opposite sides around the railing of the stairwell in the middle of the floor. The one farthest away from the miniature golf course will be the luckiest for the moment. As Anderson awaits his first encounter, he lurks behind a partition, in place because of the original builder's need to brace the roofing structure. Anderson will use that to aid his ambush. It will become a hazard, so to speak, for the man about to play through. He strolls around the course, careful not to trip over the miniature man-made fairways and greens boxed in by two-by-fours protruding from the floor; Anderson's stalker finds his prey's golf swing to be a thing of beauty. No hook, no slice...straight down the middle, the middle of the man's head. "Four!"...One down, one to go.

J.D. hears his sidekick crash to the floor, falling on top of hole number eleven, splintering the wooden frame around it.

The kid working the game, left moments before to go to the bathroom and is parked in a stall, his money box sitting on the floor under his feet. When he hears the clamorous sound of Doug falling, he quickly finishes his "paperwork," leaving the bathroom.

J.D.'s arrival is not unexpected and Anderson confronts him, dropping his remaining metal putters. Anderson's already decided he'd enjoy getting a piece of this dumb-ass, flesh on flesh, a more intimate encounter, especially after what was said in the restaurant. This time he allows his personal vendetta to get in the way of more practical, sensible tactics.

"You should' a kept those things, 'cause yer gonna need 'em to keep me from wearin' yer ass out. And don't think I don't know about that shit you Chinks use...that Kung foo crap, or whatever the hell it is. Come on; give it yer best shot, China boy."

Anderson obliges his opponent's latest fantasy, going through several wild, exaggerated, near-comedic gyrations with his hands and feet, accompanied by a high-pitched chant like you might see in an old Japanese martial arts movie. J.D. watches him closely, waiting for the right opportunity, about to step up and coldcock his ass.

Cade finally arrives at the third, one of three trailing him two floors below, the other two slowly making their climb to the fourth via the elevator.

Anderson surprises J.D. as the redneck comes at him. No martial arts as J.D. fully expected, instead, Anderson pelts the big man about the face and body with shot after shot from his doubled fists. Boxing's his game, and J.D. will manage to recover only once, delivering a shot to Anderson's midsection, knocking him back against the partition.

Mark's resiliency comes through as needed, coming out of that blow, delivering shots with the rapidity of a thousand bees stinging their target repeatedly. The shots arrive so rapidly, J.D. no more than receives one to the face or body, before another is already on its way.

Cade reaches the fourth, picking up a chair at a table in the food court, slamming it down hard on the back of the head of Anderson's punching bag. That surprise shot finishes the big man, sending him to the canvas for the final ten-count, one he'll not be able to respond to anytime soon.

Apparently defeating the brigade with surprising ease, they're not completely out of the woods yet. Hearing footsteps accompanied by heavy breathing of the man following Cade from the depths below, the two friends decide their luck may be running out, hiding behind a counter in close proximity to the open central stairwell. The elevator arrives, both passengers on their feet, exiting the fourth. Once the three have cleared their access to the stairs, Anderson and Cade make their escape, striding two, three steps at a time, down the first flight, readily attacking the next.

The cavalry's been called; the kid working miniature golf hanging up after alerting security to a situation on the fourth. Reluctantly, the guards leave the lingerie shop, headed for the stairs at the center of the building. Before they can reach those, Anderson and Cade fly down the steps, past them, circling around to the next flight, attacking those with little hesitation.

"Stop! Hold it!" one of the guards yells.

Right behind them, J.D.'s compadres...separated from their prey by only seconds and just a few steps; continue their pursuit, minus J.D. who remains on the fourth...still down for the count.

"What the hell? Hey, stop, Goddamn it, somebody stop!" the other guard yells to no avail, both now joining in on the chase.

With their following back up to five, Anderson and Cade enlarge their steps, increasing the rapidity with which they take them. Grabbing the railing on the final flight of stairs, they pull themselves up and over, catapulting their bodies onto the ground floor below, the full force of their weight slamming them hard to the wooden surface. As Anderson hits wood flooring, he falls to his knees, coming up with a slight limp, struggling slightly just to make it to the outside. The girls sit in the street, in the Volvo, waiting patiently. Descending the cement steps outside the mall, Anderson yells, "Top down! Put the top down!"

"What'd he say?" Sandy asks.

"He said put the top down!" Debby yells.

Sandy quickly unlocks a latch above the windshield, flips the switch, and the top begins lifting up and back, folding itself toward the back of the car. As their guys fly across the green belt in front of the building, the sound of human bodies slamming the double doors open can be heard to their rear.

"Take off! Take off! " Anderson yells, neither he nor Cade slowing as they approach the car. "Now!" Sandy follows her orders, shifting into "drive," pushing the accelerator to the floor. As the car begins moving, screeching tires announce its intentions. Side by side, stride for stride, the two buddies leave the ground simultaneously, slinging their bodies through the air, toward the backseat.

Landing with a thud, Cade makes it completely inside the car, his body rolling across the seat, slamming against the inside wall on the driver's side. Anderson hits the intended target, partially...partially in, partially out, but he does manage to pull himself inside completely by the time they've reached the end of the street.

With distance growing between them, the gang, and security, everyone inside the car relaxes a little, negotiating the next street corner, leaving their trackers out of sight if not completely out of mind. Sandy drives to the end of the block, turning left, heading back in the direction from which they'd come earlier that evening. Pointed in the right direction, the car passes a dark alley between soon-to-be renovated buildings, an alley connecting directly to the front of the mall. The Volvo is suddenly rocked by a large body emerging from that darkness into the light. Another follows, slightly missing the car, turning to chase on foot.

Before Sandy can react by accelerating once again, the man still on foot catches them, lunging for the back, the weight of his body pushing the car's rear end downward, causing it to rise in the front. The first to hit the car is inside, crawling into the backseat in a matter of seconds. His first effort places him over Sandy, grabbing the steering wheel, while Debby slaps him continuously across the face, head...pounding his shoulder, back, whatever she can reach at the moment.

Anderson wraps his arms around the guy's waist, able to loosen his grip on the wheel by pulling him back into an upright position. Cade...already standing; delivers his best two-handed backhand to the face, knocking him onto the back of the car.

As his body hits his partner, still trying to crawl inside, the intensity of the blow loosens his grip, forcing his fall from the car to the pavement. The lone attacker remains, his feet draped over the backseat's backrest. Anderson grabs those, throwing them up over his head, flipping him off the car onto the pavement behind.

Anderson and Cade turn to make sure there's no one else. The guy in the street rises to his knees, appearing a little wobbly from his fall, but not so wobbly he can't flip them off before they can manipulate the last corner, finally taking them out of sight and harm's way. Taking the street that'll carry them out of the downtown area and away from any further potential danger, the foursome leaves a very interesting evening in their rearview mirror.

The two in the backseat are out of breath, sweating profusely. Cade turns to his buddy. Anderson smiles..."Man, that was fun." His shit-eating grin tells it all...

"You're outta your mind," Cade tells him, breaking into a smile of his own, before the two high-five each other.

"You're both crazy," Sandy tells them from the front seat.

Sporadic lighting casts an unusual darkness on the area. She can't remember if they were out when she came in this morning or not. She hesitates, visually scanning the immediate area between her and where she remembers parking her car, although it's been some time since she arrived this morning, and her acute mental faculties not operating so well at the moment. Catching a glimpse of her car about halfway toward the end, she pulls keys from her pocket and approaches the VW, inserting them into the keyhole, unaware a lone figure quickly approaches from behind. She hadn't seen him coming, didn't sense his approach, although she felt something was just not right at the moment. He reaches out, grabbing her shoulder. She screams, whirling around to face yet another attack, going face-to-face with Cade. He's managed to get through the recent mess at West End and, despite all that has happened up to this point; chose to return to Ankawa's to check out a few things.

"What the hell are you thinking sneaking up on someone like that?"

A little startled by her reaction, expecting to gain a little element of surprise playfully, he instantly recognizes the level of unadulterated fear projected through her expression. And unaware what had happened earlier, he responds… "God, I'm sorry. I wasn't thinking."

"Yeah well, I haven't done a whole lot of that of late either so I can't penalize you much for doing the same, I guess. What are you doing here now…so late?"

"I just decided to come in and see if I could get a few things done before coming in on Monday," Cade responds with a lie.

"Listen, you can't…you got to resign. Please don't come in Monday," she pleads.

"What? Resign? Hell, I haven't started yet. What the hell is the matter with you? I need this job. And honestly, I really need the money. We've already been through this. I'm working here so get that out of your head."

"Jason, I'm telling you…you're committing suicide if you show up Monday. Listen, we can't talk here. We need to get away from here as quick as possible. Do you know where the Anatole is?"

"Yeah, sure. I mean, I think so. It's been awhile."

"Follow me and we'll go to the club there. We need to talk in private. It'll take us about five minutes to get there."

"You got it!" Cade responds to the best offer he thinks he's had yet. Cade is sensing a very good end to what he thought would be a very bad night. No one ever said he could think rationally when there was an attractive woman involved.

As they pull out of the garage, Cade following her, a third car follows at a safe distance, lights out for now until the Corvette rolls out of the garage, onto the street.

On the short drive, both run through things in their minds, both thinking about the events of the night for each personally, neither aware of the other's situation, both intertwined and about to bring the two of them together in a way neither may be able to handle.

Parked, stepping from her car, Danny checks her watch... around ten-fifty. The club should be busy. Good cover for two who need not bring any undue attention their way anymore tonight. She waits on Cade to park and join her, which he soon does under the canopied walkway into the hotel. Once again made aware of her natural beauty even on the dimly lit path to the front door, he again reinforces his decision to continue his pursuit. He can see the valets looking her over as well, generating great pride in just being seen with someone as amazing as she is.

As they walk through the lobby, both view activity as brisk; late-night check-ins at the counter, a young couple, make Cade wish they were about to do the same. She looks at him, him at her, both oblivious to the other's thoughts this moment. Inside the club, he remembers it a little from some of his earlier visits as a patron on business while staying here, using the venue as a means to meet new friends, female and otherwise.

The place has always reminded him of a plush lawyer's office. Bookcases lining the walls, expensive accents giving the place its stamp on its name...The Office. Large leather couches, oversized chairs, call to his sense of the importance of finding one they both would be able to get comfortable in, maybe snuggle up close to one another and see what happens. But that is not apparently on her agenda this time as she leads him through that room, past those, and into the bar area. Before moving on, she waves at the bartender, walking up to him to give him a hug and peck on his cheek. Done with that and speaking to a few others, she continues taking him through a very busy, jammed dance floor, where lucky couples closely hold each other as the DJ plays a soft song he's heard before, just can't remember what it is.

As they continue, Cade's impressed, though a little jealous. Knowing he has no right to those feelings with her, he can't help wishing he were on the receiving end of her casual affections. As it seems, many in the club know Danny, one reason she selected this place, feeling comfortable and safe among friends. Figuring she is not interested in dancing, or anything but being the official club greeter, he embarks on a search for a table. Unfortunately, there are few available, but he soon finds one.

Danny finally rejoins him after making her rounds. Hell, it seems she knows just about everyone in here tonight. Drinks ordered, a couple of pleasantries exchanged, they sit a few seconds in silence, at an apparent loss for words, much less anything meaningful.

"...Thought you had something important to tell me," Cade finally begins.

"I do," she responds, saying nothing more.

"...Could've fooled me. You appeared to be more interested in making your rounds. Maybe the two receptionists were right about you."

She stares at him and if looks could indeed kill, he would be one dead SOB.

"Just what the hell are you talking about?" she asks.

"Never mind. I shouldn't have said that."

"No, you started it this time. I want to know what they are saying about me."

"Let's just forget I said anything. I should never have made the comment. Nobody's saying anything about you. I was just being childish about your lack of attention to me since getting here. I have no right..."

"You're right! You have no right to control me! No one does! I am sick to death of men who think they can control me at every turn! That shit is over for you, Robert, Kirk, Ankawa, you name it!"

As they sit in silence, Cade has figured out he has blown any chance he might have ever had. Thinking with something beside his brain, he decides to try to change the subject.

"How's the work on the project going?" he asks.

"What project?"

"Uh, the one I thought you were working on late at your office tonight. You know, the one you mentioned this afternoon.

Danny is trying to be pleasant; although she is not now sure inviting him here for whatever reason was the right thing to do.

"OK, I guess." Second-guessing herself continuously it seems; she tries to make sense of what she has done tonight.

Cade continues a gallant effort to keep options available and this night positive. "You still have a lot to do on it, or did you finish?"

In and out of her trancelike state, she continues, preoccupied, looking toward the entrance as though she were expecting someone. "It's uh, it's done."

"OK...we seem to really be rollin' here now. Is there something else you'd rather talk about?" Almost ready to give up and now believing as well this was a mistake. Danny's thoughts obviously elsewhere, he wants to do more prying into the depths of wherever it is she has fled mentally.

"You OK?"

She shows signs of coming back. "I'm sorry. What did you say?"

"I asked if you were OK. I'm trying real hard to carry on a two-way conversation here; obviously, I'm not doing too well."

"I really need to tell you something." She pauses a few seconds. "I need to tell someone." Deciding instantly he's not the one she'll tell, she immediately crawls back into the hole she had just exited.

Feeling a little excitement, he'll take anything he can get at this point. "OK, tell me....Jesus Christ! What's going on?"

"You absolutely cannot work at Ankawa's!" There, she said it, although, in fact, nothing close to what she was going to say originally.

Shit! That's not what I wanted to hear, Cade tells himself. "That's what you wanted to tell me? That's what you asked me to come here to tell me?" His disappointment more than obvious to her, there's a decisive pause in their conversation. Something they're both beginning to get used to.

"OK. That makes about as much sense as when you told me this before," he says sarcastically. "You mind telling me why, all of a sudden, you feel compelled to push the issue again?"

"My boss, his son...the guy following us from the airport... they're planning to come after you. They know you're working there now."

Cade sits quietly, no reply, no sarcasm coming from him at this moment, considering what she's just told him.

"They're convinced you're the reason behind Robert and my troubles, the reason I broke up with him. Plus, Robert's pissed at me now more than ever, and he's going to try to hurt me any way he can, even if he thinks that means hurting you. Robert told Kirk tonight to go after you, do whatever it takes to get you out of the picture."

Cade knows he has to say something, but all of a sudden, he's feeling anxious, fearful. His ego won't let him show fear in front of the person sitting across from him. "I can take care of myself." A sudden chill overcomes him as he says it. He knows nothing could probably be further from the truth. And he knows, more than likely, she knows the same. He comes to his senses momentarily, "Did you try to explain to them that's not what this thing's all about?"

"I told them, told them both. Robert thinks I'm lying to protect you. That's why I've reacted so badly toward you. I was trying to discourage you, run you off. Something I'm obviously not very good at, but it's not fair to involve you in all my personal problems right now."

Again losing all sense of practicality, trying to appear noble, Cade responds, "Don't worry about me. I told you, I can take care of myself...now, I guess I'll have to. What about you? Why don't you just quit, get away from those two?"

"I can't. I can't give up everything I've worked so hard to achieve. I'm not letting Robert, or the likes of Kirk Carrigan run me off. It's a matter of principle. Besides, I don't think Robert'll really hurt me, or let Kirk either." She feels lousy...lousy about everything going on in her life personally, lousy about what she's having to do tonight where Cade's concerned. She's glad of one thing though, she's glad she didn't tell him everything she knows...about what she'd found tonight. He didn't need to be involved in this thing any deeper...besides, it's not something she can just go out and share with the first guy that comes along.

Kirk's entrance to the club goes unnoticed for the moment. He followed them from Ankawa's, got ahold of a couple of his buddies by car phone, waiting outside till they finally showed. The three enter together, not looking for a good time, in the sense that most would be in a club like this one. Tonight, a good time will be had at the dire expense of another.

Kirk sees Danny and Cade through the crowd, beginning his walk toward their table.

Danny notices them first. "Oh my God!" she gasps, looking as though she's just seen someone rise from the dead.

Hearing her words, seeing her face, Cade traces her stare into the crowded dance floor, picking up her target as they emerge through the mass of people. If he could've done anything different tonight, it would've been to wear a pair of Depends, which he drastically needed right now, 'cause he was about to shit in his pants! He quickly recognizes JD from the situation at West End earlier this evening.

"Jason, let's go!" she says standing immediately.

"Where y'all goin'? We just got here," Kirk tells them, ambling up to the table, addressing them as though nothing had happened before tonight. "Sit down!" he commands. "The fun's just beginnin'."

"Kirk, don't you dare start anything."

"What d'yuh think I am...would like to ask you a question tho'. Why you dumpin' my dad for this piece o' shit, low-life asshole here?" Carrigan turns to Cade, words just not there at this moment. "Understand yer from Chicargo. What'd they do, shut down all the gay bars on Rush Street? So now you faggots think you can come to Dallas, mix in with the girls..." Kirk's message comes out loudly enough so everyone in the club, at least in close proximity to their table, can hear.

"Kirk, please, I'm begging you, please don't do this. Just leave us alone, please."

"I tell you what, darlin'. You dance with me right now; we might just be able to let this thing slide tonight. Yeah, one dance, then I'll think about lettin' you and pretty boy outta here."

"Danny, you don't have to..."

Before Cade can get a whole sentence out of his mouth, Danny's already up and on her way to the dance floor, hope against hope that Carrigan really means what he just said. Kirk follows, on his way stopping to tell his friends to join Cade at the table, keep him company.

"Uh, hey, guys. Sit down, be my guest," Cade tells them.

Neither smiles nor says anything, sitting, staring at their new friend.

Cade notices the doors to the restrooms opening, closing, as patrons file in and out to use them. He also notices a couple of pay phones just inside, in the hallway.

"You guys don't mind, I need to relieve myself."

"No problem, we'll just go with yuh," J.D. tells him.

Cade's quick mind stops them dead. "Great. We can take turns holdin' each other's. It'll be fun," he says, adding the necessary slight feminine touch to his voice, getting his message across.

"Uh, OK, but don't be long, we'll be watching the door. I know for a fact there's no other way out so you can't run and hide like the little pissant you are."

"What? ...you naughty thing? Trying to sneak a peek?"

Danny's dance with Kirk is obviously traumatic, Kirk forcing her to dance closer than she wants, wrapping both arms around her. He kisses her neck, and when he does, she squirms to free herself. Kirk warns her not to put up a fight, telling her it could be detrimental to her and her friend's health right now.

By now, Cade's dialed the number written on the slip of paper he's pulled from his wallet for the second time since arriving in Dallas. The phone on the end rings...once...twice...a third...a fourth time. "Come on, Mark, pick up the damn phone!"

"Hello."

"Sandy! Jason! Let me speak to Mark, please...hurry!"

"Jason, what's wrong?"

"Just let me speak to Mark, now!"

A few seconds pass, Kirk noticing Cade's absence from the table, breaking his hold on Danny, grabbing her hand, pulling her from the dance floor to their table.

"Hey, buddy. What's up?"

Anderson's voice on the other end creates a slight, but quickly passing sense of relief. "Man, I'm in big trouble!"

"What's the problem? Where are you?"

"The club in the Anatole...The Office. The guys from the West End earlier tonight...I've just run in to 'em again. The guy at the Crescent yesterday, the big guy, the one who slammed into your car, he's with them. I don't think they're planning to let the night pass without kicking somebody's ass. Looks like I may be their man."

During the seconds passed, Kirk and his boys are on their way to the bathroom. Danny's bolted for the bar and her friend behind it.

Cade peers through the door as a woman exits the hallway. He sees his three friends on their way, and almost there. Kirk pushes the door open, stepping into the short hallway leading to the restrooms. A man walks past him, out of the men's room, back into the club.

Carrigan stops him. "...there anyone else in there?"

"Yeah, some other guy, I think."

Carrigan turns to his buddies, "You stay here...don't let anyone past you. I'm gonna enjoy this one myself."

Danny's recruited help...her friend the bartender, and the club bouncer. They decline her suggestion to call the police, telling her they handle this kind of thing all the time. In seconds, they are both dumped in a heap, piled on the floor in front of the two hulking figures standing guard at the door.

Inside the men's room, Kirk slows his stalking, cautious when he is unable to immediately flush out his prey. As he arrives at each stall door, he pushes it open, expecting one to produce what he's looking for, finding nothing, until he comes to one that's locked.

Stepping back, he slams the bottom of his foot into the metal door, bending the lock, forcing the door open. A man sitting on the commode, taking care of business is shocked and surprised.

"Hey! What the hell you think you're doin'?" the man yells.

"Shut the fuck up!" Kirk yells back.

"Hey, no problem," the man answers willingly.

Continuing his campaign toward the final stall, Carrigan reaches for the door, thinking he's got to be here, lunging inside.

After the negative results from the bartender's attempt to help, Danny's on the phone dialing 911. Many in the club quickly file out, trying to escape before all hell breaks out.

Going through the door, Kirk hasn't planned for what awaits him in the final stall. Cade swings the fire extinguisher, taken from the wall moments earlier, in Kirk's direction, unleashing an uppercut Holyfield would have been proud of. As the big man straightens, Cade turns the chemical spray on him, hitting his face, open eyes and mouth. Kirk yells in pain, experiencing great discomfort from the chemical. Cade slams the extinguisher into his stomach, up through his jaw again, the combination taking him down, pushing him back into the urinals behind him. The finished product lies on the floor, covered in CO_2, mixed in with his own blood.

Cade appears to have won this battle, but he's severely rattled just the same, though quite proud of his work. Not used to spending his Friday nights in such a violent manner, he's thinking now maybe he'd be a lot safer back in Chicago going up against his old boss. He steps over the defeated enemy, only to immediately face the other two from outside. Neither can believe their leader's quick and decisive demise at the hands of this guy. Reacting to Cade with caution, unsure how he might have pulled it off, they figure he must be dangerous.

"Come on, guys, I don't want any more trouble. Let's call it even."

Cade takes a blow to the stomach. Pain surges throughout his body; air forced from his lungs making him feel as though they're about to collapse, as he gasps for oxygen. The next blow comes too quickly for any reaction, catching him in the face, rocking him backward. He knows he's falling, but he's lost all muscle control in the process, unable to break or cushion the fall. Lying on the floor, barely able to move and barely conscious, he can feel the body next to him moving.

Picking Cade off the floor, the two continue administering the beating. He's now totally at their mercy, soon surrendering to his subconscious. His only achievable reward will soon be within his grasp...as his pain will soon subside.

Knowing he's about gone, doesn't seem to stop the three on top of him, Kirk now conscious and standing, joining in on the fun. As his two sidekicks hold Cade upright, Kirk pummels his lifeless body into a horrifying state. Cade can no longer feel anything...reaching well beyond his limited threshold of pain.

The four are joined in the men's room by others now entering behind them. Anderson and some of his friends from the "Boxing Club" have arrived. The ensuing battle is a bloody one. Although Anderson and his friends are skilled with their fists, no one appears able to gain the upper hand immediately. The fight is soon shortened by the arrival of some of Dallas' finest. All involved are shoved against the wall, frisked, and cuffed for transportation to jail. All accept one.

Paramedics enter with Danny close behind. The officer bent over Cade's badly beaten body, looks up as they enter. "Check him out, but I think he's almost gone."

Paramedics drop to their knees, immediately checking for a pulse, verifying the officer's diagnosis, springing into immediate action, initiating CPR. Danny reacts, as does Mark, who's been released from his handcuffs after several say he came to Cade's defense.

"There's a pulse, but we're losing him fast." Their work continues feverishly, placing an oxygen mask over Cade's face, preparing him for transport. On the gurney, they push Cade's near-lifeless body through the door, monitoring his heart rate continuously. Outside the club, in the courtyard of the Anatole, one of them stops their progress. "I've lost him. We gotta hit him." Pulling the paddles from his box, the other cuts through his pullover, preparing for a defib. Ready to slam the paddles onto Cade's chest, the paramedic in charge begins his countdown..."Three...two...clear!" The electrical shock feeds through Cade's body, forcing a convulsive surge.

"Nothing!" the attending paramedic hollers.

"Again...three...two...clear!"...Similar results. Moments pass. "He's back! Let's get him to Methodist before we lose him again."

Toward the hotel's exit, through the sliding glass doors, Cade's body is wheeled to what a few of those following hope will be life-sustaining help.

Kirk and his friends follow, handcuffed, being led away by police. His smile sickens Danny. He knows the guy may no longer be a threat to his father's activities. His dad will be proud.

"You sick son of a bitch!" Danny yells in his face. "He never did anything to you! Why'd you have to take it this far? Why?"

Police pull Kirk and his gang to the outside. The detective in charge, Jake Schuler, pulls Kirk away from the others, pushing him against a squad car. He steps closely enough to get in his face. "What the hell were you thinking? He dies, no one can help you."

"Don't be too sure about that, Jake," Carrigan answers.

Preparations for transport complete inside the ambulance, the doors close. Mark and his buddy leave the Anatole, Danny, and Carrigan behind as the ambulance pulls away, sirens wailing, rushing into the night on a mission to save one life. This will be only one of many converging on the many hospitals in this sleepless metropolis tonight.

Standing under the canopy where she and Jason met tonight just before going in, she remembers her second-guessing. Why didn't I do what I thought was right? Why didn't I leave him out of this? This is all my fault. God, if he dies...Once again, accepting the blame for all that's happened.

Schuler walks over to her. "You feel like talking?"

"Detective..."

"Schuler, ma'am, Jake Schuler," he says, lighting a cigarette.

Schuler...Where has she seen that name before? She won't meet with him tonight. "No, I really don't feel up to answering any questions tonight," she says, hoping she can avoid the immediate confrontation, needing time to sort everything out.

"I will need to talk to you soon...we may have a homicide on our hands before the night's over. Here's my card. Call my office in the morning to set up an appointment," he says, letting her go, thinking he'll be able to get enough information from everyone else involved.

His remark about a homicide represents stark reality, upsetting her intensely. She hadn't had time to think about her friend of only two days not making it through the night until now. Hadn't been forced to...until now.

"I'm sorry, I didn't mean to upset you, but we gotta face the real possibilities here. Your boyfriend suffered a severe beating tonight. You and his friend may have to face that fact."

Danny asks which hospital Cade was being taken to, but instead of going there, she drives straight to her apartment. She has much to think about. She'll call the hospital later, to check on him. Today's been one of the toughest of her life...before it's over she'll make the only decision she can. That decision will change many lives.

CHAPTER 12

A short drive from the Anatole to the Crescent, Wilson arrives in less than ten minutes. She stops in front of the door to her apartment, unlocking it, entering cautiously. He could be here, right now, anywhere. I have to get the locks changed soon, she tells herself once again. Inside, satisfied she's alone, she fastens the dead bolt and settles down, deciding a glass of wine will help take the edge off a horrific day. Opening the drapes, she chooses to sit in the dark, staring out the window. A glance at the digital LCD displayed on her stereo tells her it's already Saturday, placing a very long Friday in her past. The last time she just sat like this, had to have been months ago.

The disks! She quickly grabs at her pockets...still there. With all that had happened tonight, she'd almost forgotten them. She continues, embedded in her solitude, disks in hand, staring into the early morning darkness. Traffic on R.L. Thornton, Stemmons, and Central feeding into and out of downtown appears brisk. She's never noticed before, not at this time of night, but doesn't anyone ever sleep in this town?

At Methodist, ironically only a few blocks from the Crescent, Jason Cade lies in "intensive care." The only one there in support, his best friend Mark, sits in the waiting room, on the phone.

"I just talked with the doctors. He makes it through the night, his prognosis looks encouraging, but they won't know for a couple of days on the amount of damage to his ability to think, walk, and do the normal things he did before...Yeah, I think I'll stay here awhile, make sure he's OK before comin' home. No, haven't yet. Don't think I will till I know something for sure. I'd like to be able to tell them he's gonna be OK. Yeah, somewhere in Tennessee, I think. His dad doesn't even know he's left his job in Chicago yet. OK. Love you too."

Mark sets the receiver down, and walks up to the nurse's station again.

"Can I see my friend now?" he asks Kathy, so her name badge says, one of the attending RNs on duty tonight.

"...you family?"

"Only family he has here."

She glances at a chart; Anderson assumes Cade's. "I guess it'd be OK, but only for a very few minutes. He's under heavy sedation and really needs to rest. He won't know you're there anyway."

Anderson walks toward the room, stopping in the doorway, stunned at what he sees. Tubes, life support, sounds of a machine pumping air into his friend's lungs overtake and consume him. He moves closer, standing at his bedside.

"What the hell happened tonight, man?" he asks, expecting no reply; getting none. "God, so much for a welcome home, huh?"

Cade is out cold, in a coma, and Mark can only assume the drugs are doing what they're supposed to. Anderson leaves. Back in the waiting room, he thought he'd eventually see the young woman he blames for getting his friend into all this, but she's not there. Never comes. Doesn't matter, he figures, Cade's better off without her hanging around. God, he hates this place. Never has liked hospitals. With little he can do at this point, he decides to put this place in his rearview mirror for now.

Danny remains awake. She's moved from the window to her computer. She's accessed much of the information from the disks, printing it off, now studying what she has. There it is. She thought she'd seen the name. Jake Schuler...bought and paid for. Like so many others in this city.

Anderson leaves the hospital, instead of going home; he plans another stop. This one's a little out of the way, but one he's determined to make, regardless of the hour. Pulling onto Interstate 35, he heads north, in a few minutes taking a specific exit. He knows what he's doing, and he knows where he's going.

Bringing his car to a complete stop, he steps out, taking a moment to look toward the top of the building. After regular hours, access can be gained only by swiping a magnetic card and entering a six-digit access number given only to members of the organization, or immediate family. He looks at the small electronic box attached to the right of the door, swipes his card and punches his code. The lock disengages with a clicking sound; Anderson pushes through the door to the inside.

Danny continues her vigil, working at her computer, weary from being awake nearly twenty-four hours straight. She tells herself she must quit soon. She knows there's something wrong with all this...Ankawa's paying a lot of people a lot of money. To do what, she hasn't a clue yet. They all seem to be outside his company, so she thinks...Why? What for? What kinds of services could all these people be providing? Numerous questions...few answers. She revisits the time before the incident in the club...in Robert's office. She recalls the leather binder, the four disks, two of which she now has copies. What's on the others? What are Ankawa and Robert up to? What are they involved in?

Worn out, too tired to sleep, she closes the function and pops the disk out. She quickly moves toward the door after she believes she's hearing something just outside. She checks the deadbolt making sure she secured it. Her memory doesn't seem to be working properly right now...hell, not much of anything is. Peering through the peep hole, she sees nothing, hears nothing more. Settling back into her chair, she faces the window again, deciding another glass of wine might help start the new day off right.

Anderson walks by security. No badge needed. As he does, security at the desk picks up a phone, making a call to some point inside the building. He steps on an elevator, inserts a key on his key chain, turning it clockwise. The panel lights up, flashing "RESTRICTED ACCESS APPROVED" across the miniature LCD screen; doors close. The elevator carrying its lone passenger ascends the shaft toward the top, passing all floors. At the eighteenth, the doors open, exposing a beautifully decorated reception area. The man at the desk greets him cordially. "Go on in, Mr. Ankawa, your father awaits your arrival."

Anderson enters through double doors, ornate in design with ancient Japanese architectural influences, into a very dominant realm of Pre-World War II Japan. It's like entering a museum of Japanese historical culture. Wall art and artifacts displayed throughout this two-story penthouse depict the way of life as it existed, during and before his father's childhood.

Anderson continues waiting, taking the time to view the pieces his father has managed to collect over the years as he usually does under similar, past circumstances. Beautiful pictures of people of that time and era, people he has just recently come to know. His mother, when she was young...his father, many years before now...his great-uncle Tomoko and wife, his Aunt Yuan Mei, Uncle Massey, his grandparents, great-grandparents. As he has tried to maintain a certain distance from what his father now represents, he is just beginning to feel a definite closeness to his extended family and now, it's past.

"You are awake at a very early hour, my son," his father says immediately upon entering the room. "What brings your visit at this time of morning? It must be quite important for you to step into my home at any time. As ashamed as you seem to be called my son, I am grateful you have decided to visit, regardless of the reason."

Anderson remains cordial, respectful, despite the critique and commentary from his father. Mark knows the timing of this visit is indeed quite unusual, but there is quite a definite reason for being here. Yami enters the room, interrupting them with delivery of a pot of tea and two cups. Mark stands to greet his old and dear friend from his childhood days.

"It's good to see you, Yami. It has been too long," Mark tells him.

"As always, I am glad and honored to see you as well. You must visit us more often."

Mark declines Ankawa's offer of tea, as the visit will last just a few minutes.

"This personal favor you have in mind...please...ask it. I am intrigued to know what is so important to you, that you would humble yourself by coming to me seeking favor."

"My best friend, Jason Cade..."

"Yes. The one you spent your college days with."

"The same...He is in a hospital tonight, fighting for his life. He may not live to see daylight."

"I am saddened to hear that. He seems such an honorable young man. How may I help in his great time of need?"

"The man responsible for his problems I believe is an employee of yours. I recognized him from other associations with your company."

"I cannot be certain. What is his name? If I find that he is indeed, I assure you, he will be dealt with in a proper manner."

"Kirk Carrigan...Do you know him?"

"His father is a valued and trusted employee. Are you sure it was Carrigan?"

"Quite positive...You know, my friend is also an employee of yours...as of today...I guess maybe it was yesterday."

"I will see that he is taken care of. Your Mr. Cade will not need to worry about or want for a thing...neither will you. My personal physicians will be dispatched to his care as quickly as you step onto the elevator taking you back to your car. I will also look into this matter you speak of, the one with Carrigan."

"That's all I'm asking." Mark stands, turning to walk from the room. His father follows.

"I would ask from you just one thing in return...a favor of my own."

Mark stops before entering the outer reception area. "And what would that be?"

"I would like as well as ask that you visit more often, not wait until a favor needs to be asked."

"Actually, that's two things, but I'll think about it." He already knows the answer to his father's request, an answer he will not share at this moment. He believes that will be all he will be able to give in return for his father's help. He disappears through the doors, stepping onto an awaiting elevator.

Ankawa immediately picks up a phone, dialing a number he knows, one he has memorized and used often. He waits patiently for the one he seeks to answer...and finally, she does.

"This is Ankawa. (pause) Yes, I am fully aware of the hour. (pause) That's not why I called. My patience is growing thin and your time is quickly running out! I am paying you well enough to expect delivery of what I have asked, soon. (pause) Yes, I am aware he can indeed be quite difficult. However, you have gained his confidence as you said you would. That is where everyone else has failed. I will continue to monitor your progress, but I must see substantial advancement toward our mutual goal soon...very soon. Good-bye." Ankawa sets the phone down, returning to bed. It is much too early to begin a new day of work without sleep.

The young woman on the other end sets her receiver down as well. She decides she must step up her efforts, not only for her sake, but for Mark's as well. She has one secret she cannot carry alone much longer.

LATER THE SAME SATURDAY MORNING...

Danny's awakened from a very short sleep by her phone ringing. Curled on the bed, she slides off to reach it. Before she can, the answering machine kicks in; the voice on the other end; not one she really wanted to hear this early. After hearing the man's voice, she thinks about the horrible nightmare she'd experienced in her sleep. Jake Schuler's voice, stating his name and why he's calling, triggers a bad feeling, producing slight nausea, telling her it was no dream, but a real nightmare that will continue into today and beyond.

She picks up. "Hello," she answers; a little raspy voiced.

He can easily tell he's most likely awakened her. "Ms. Wilson?"

"Yes."

"Detective Schuler..."

Danny's memory is beginning to engage, unfortunately bringing her mind's data banks to their full operational capacity too quickly for her. "Yes, what can I do for you, Detective?"

"I decided not to wait. There's been a change in the situation. I need to speak with you right away."

"Why? What's happened? Is Cade..."

"No. He's not dead, if that's what you are asking."

She is, and his reassurance relieves her. She looks at her clock, anticipating his need to set a specific time.

Schuler fails to disappoint her. "Let's say...later this morning, around eleven. Can you make that?"

"I'll make it," her answer showing little enthusiasm, but then, none was expected by her caller. Hanging up, crawling from her perch on the bed near the phone, she realizes she's still fully clothed, including shoes.

Anderson gets a similar call seconds later. He's awake, with little sleep behind him as well, making plans to go by the hospital after a shot of caffeine via a strong cup of coffee. He agrees to the meeting instead, unaware Wilson will be there as well. He showers, dresses, and grabs another coffee in the kitchen, sitting at the table for a couple of minutes. Sandy joins him.

She bends to kiss him on the forehead, telling him "good morning. What time did you finally get in?"

"About three, three-thirty I guess. Somewhere around there... Haven't paid much attention to time since last night."

"I tried my best to stay awake but just couldn't. I'm sorry. You call the hospital yet? Thought I'd go with you today."

"Haven't had time, besides, I left my number with strict instructions to call me should anything change. I'm going by to check on him, but before that I got to stop by the police station. You're welcome to come if you want."

"What're you going there for?"

"The detective in charge of the investigation called. He wants to get a statement from me about last night."

"What can you offer they don't already know?"

"Don't know. Don't know what he's looking for, but if I can help nail the assholes responsible for Jason's problems, I'll talk with him all day."

Sandy sits silently just a few seconds before speaking again. "When Jason gets out of the hospital, and when he's feeling up to it, let's throw him a party."

Mark doesn't answer.

"You hear what I just said?"

"Yeah, something about throwing a party in Jason's honor. Sorry, my mind's somewhere else today."

"Don't you think it'd be a good way to get him back in the swing of things, help him get all this behind him?"

"Yeah...Guess so. I'm sorry, honey. I think it would be a great idea."

"And, this might be a great time to invite your father," cringing with anticipation of total rejection about to hit her, something she was quite used to when it came to even mentioning his father around him.

"Yeah, that might be a good idea. Neither you nor Cade have ever met the man. It's time for that to happen." *Then maybe you two will finally understand my feelings,* he thinks to himself.

Danny walks to her desk where her personal computer sits idle, on power-save since early this morning. She reaches for six envelopes. She will finish addressing them, all to the *Dallas Morning News* in care of Allison Mickelson. *If I can get just one of these to Allison, she'll know what to do with it,* she thinks, sliding copies of the two disks into each one. A close and longtime friend of hers, Allison's a reporter for the paper, winning numerous awards for her in-depth investigative reporting. She's relentless in her work, more so on assignment. She's one person Danny feels she can trust, and she needs these disks in Allison's hands should anything go wrong or happen to her.

She carefully types a short note, copying it six times, placing one in each of the envelopes, sealing them, packing them in a bag. The bag hidden away, she leaves for police headquarters, about a mile and a half by direct path, a little longer via the street system.   Arriving minutes later, there's little parking available near the station, so she'll have to park in a lot just down the street, a ways east of the building. Anderson's already arrived, and is inside waiting for Schuler. When Danny finally steps into the room, she thinks she recognizes him from last night. She extends her hand, Mark politely standing, offering his.

The two quickly detach, sitting in chairs along the wall, leaving one separating them.

"You got a call too, I guess."

"Yeah," Mark answers.

"You sure came to Jason's rescue at the right time last night. Without you and your friends, he might be dead."

"I guess. I was almost too late." He doesn't elaborate with further comment. He sits wondering what her angle could be...what interest she has in his friend.

"Your name wouldn't be Danny by any chance?"

"Yes it is. Danny Wilson."

"Jason's mentioned you. What interest if any, do you have in him, you don't mind my asking?"

"Just an acquaintance, that's all."

"Guess someone should've told him that's all it is. Looks like he just took a hell of a beating for nothing."

"Look..." She could say no more, before being interrupted by the appearance of Steve Jamison, an Ankawa attorney.

Jamison, very well dressed; has a reputation as one of the best in the business, bar none. His smile, his greeting directed at Danny, seems innocent to Mark and means little more than a guy flirting with a good-looking woman, until Kirk and his friends from the club walk out together. Carrigan doesn't look too good this morning, bruises, cuts, swollen areas about his face indicating the extent of damage he and Cade were able to inflict on the big man last night. Having spent the night in jail, their clothing's severely wrinkled. Anderson stands to face Carrigan, although he'll have to look up to do so.

Schuler's the last to walk from the office, extending his hand to Anderson.

"What the hell's going on?" Mark asks. "Why aren't these dick-heads still in jail?"

"Their attorney posted bail...can't keep 'em," Schuler answers.

"And let me guess," Mark continues. "You're their lawyer." Turning to Danny, "And you all work for Ankawa...how nice and convenient for all of you," his sarcasm just the beginning of his protest.

Danny looks at Mark, wanting badly to immediately and vehemently deny any involvement with any of these shitheads, deciding she better not at this point, hanging her head, a little ashamed.

"This the one doing all the damage to you last night?" Jamison asks Kirk and his sidekicks, referring to their obvious injuries.

"He got lucky," is all Kirk would say.

"You're lucky I don't file charges against you and your friends for assault and battery," Jamison tells Anderson.

Danny can't believe what she's hearing. She wants to tell Jamison, Carrigan, all of them, exactly what she thinks of them, but she doesn't. Mark assumes her silence means collaboration.

"You got to be kidding me? Is he for real?" Anderson asks, turning to Schuler.

Schuler shrugs.

"By the time the courts get through with you guys, you won't see the light of day for some time," Anderson says, fully aware he probably just misstated the obvious.

Carrigan and his buddies laugh at his suggestion they'll be punished for anything.

"I'm afraid that's where you're wrong Mr...Mr...I don't believe we've been properly introduced," Jamison responds on his client's behalf.

"No, and don't believe we ever will either." Anderson turns to Schuler again. "What the hell's going on here? What's he talking about?"

"Not here. I think we better talk about this inside," Schuler tells him, showing him the way into the next room.

"Yeah, let's do that. Let's go inside. I want to hear this."

The two disappear through the door, Schuler closing it behind them, leaving all others in the waiting area.

Jamison speaks next. "What're you doing here?" directing his question at Danny.

"I was there last night, at the club, with the guy these goons beat up. I had to come in this morning to make a statement."

"Then you'll need my services."

"No, I won't. I'll be just fine. I can handle this myself."

"You can't trust her." Carrigan offers.

"I think we can trust her to do the right thing, keep the best interests of the company in mind. Am I wrong, Ms. Wilson?"

Danny starts to tell them all to go to hell, but doesn't feel she has that luxury today. "Yeah, you're right, as usual. I'll handle things appropriately."

"See that you do. We don't want your career jeopardized for any miscalculations on your part, now do we?"

Danny's reaction is one of contempt at what's just been said. The four walk out of the room, leaving Danny to wonder what implications her telling the truth would have on her, versus Jason. Who would be most likely to get hurt now?

Inside, "Mr. Anderson, I don't think you or your friend's best interests are being served with reactions like the one you just displayed with those guys. Every one of the men you're involved with work for Ankawa. And as such, that company's only providing legal counsel and arbitration for its employees. There's nothing irregular about a company doing that. If you and your friend can resolve this thing without going to court, I'd recommend it."

"Bullshit! You're telling me you're not going to press charges against those guys for putting my friend in the hospital and near death?"

"No one has admitted to seeing anything. At least to this point, no one has stepped up to offer any information. We can't press charges when we know little about the altercation."

"How long you lived here?"

"Most of my life. My father was on the force. Why? What's that have to do with anything?"

"You're telling me, you don't think there's something irregular about this whole thing? Hell, the fact Ankawa's involved says that. When Ankawa's involved, everything's irregular, and you know it!"

"I'm just trying to help. I'm trying to tell you what'd be best for you and your friend. And I think it would be best for you to drop it."

"I could care less about what's good for me. My best friend was almost killed last night, or have you forgotten. And we're sitting here about to brush this whole incident off like it was just some little tiff among friends. No way! No fucking way! What are you—on Ankawa's payroll like everyone else around this fucking town?"

Continuing her wait, Danny can hear the yelling coming from inside, but not clearly enough to hear what's being said. She goes over and over in her mind what she plans to say to Schuler. She's come to the conclusion she's going to lose no matter what she says. The pressure from her anticipation of going into that room with Schuler, knowing what she knows about him, knowing he's an employee of Ankawa, is great. Then she thinks about Cade, lying in a hospital, possibly near death.

His feathers severely ruffled after the accusation, Schuler is sick and tired of putting up with all the crap today. "Another comment like that, I'm gonna throw your ass in jail! I'll let you sit your butt there a few days to help you think things through a little more." Schuler stands, beginning to pace; obviously irritated at Anderson's comments on top of all else happening behind the scenes. "Now, you can either accept what's going on, or sit behind bars. The choice is yours."

Anderson slams his fist down hard on the desk...he stands, throwing his chair back into the wall. Schuler reacts by grabbing his gun, ready to snatch it from its holster if Anderson takes his aggressions any further.

"There's no fucking way you people are going to pull this off! I'll go wherever I have to, do whatever I have to, to get satisfaction! You don't help us; I'll take it over your fucking head!"

Schuler has finally had enough and pulls his gun from its holster, to scare him a little, and to make his point. "Sit your Goddamn ass down! Now!"

"What're you gonna do, shoot me?"

"If I have to." Schuler further responds by cocking his gun, finally getting Anderson's attention. "I'll help your friend. Matter of fact, I want to help your friend, if you can find me a witness who'll talk. These assholes have had their way around this town too long. But I gotta have a witness willing to step up, and take your friend's side. So far, I have nothing. What about you, you see anything? You got anything at all that'd help me in my investigation?"

Anderson doesn't answer immediately. He knows Schuler knows he didn't see anything. "What about the girl? The one in the waiting room...What's her name? Wilson, I think."

"Ms. Wilson? Give me a break. She works for Ankawa. You think she's gonna help your friend against her own company and boss?"

"She might...she's here, isn't she? Maybe she and my friend have something going...something that'll cut through all the corporate loyalty bullshit."

"Don't count on it. I can't make her. It's gotta be her decision, beside, it's not like she's here of her own volition. I made her come down this morning to give me a statement, just like you, which, by the way, we need to get started on." Schuler's already holstered his weapon, satisfied there'll be no further outbursts.

Anderson gives his statement about the phone call he'd received from Cade...he and his friend's late arrival after most of the damage had already been done to his friend. Finished, Schuler escorts Anderson through the door into the waiting room, seeing no one.

"Guess our Ms. Wilson got cold feet," Schuler's observation qualifying the obvious.

Anderson leaves the building, headed in the direction of the parking lot where he too had to leave his car this morning. He can see Wilson and the shyster lawyer talking just a short distance down the street. Involved in their conversation, neither notices his approach, as he catches the tail end of their little talk.

"You made a wise decision, Danny. Robert will be very pleased you won't be implicating his son in any of this." Seeing Anderson stepping up behind her, he adds a little comment to finish it off. "I'm sure there will be a great deal of gratitude expressed for your help once again."

"Yeah, Ms. Wilson," Mark interrupts, "You've really done yourself proud on this one."

"Mr. Anderson, is it? You must learn to control your emotions."

At this point, Mark is ready to deck the guy, take out his frustrations on somebody, and Danny can sense he's about to do something.

Jamison continues, "Look, my friend..."

"Let's get one thing straight, asshole," Mark responds, "neither you," he looks at Danny, "nor anyone else at Ankawa is any friend of mine!"

"I have no time for this frivolous chit chat," Jamison offers. "I have many more pressing engagements to attend to. May I give you a lift, Ms. Wilson?"

"No thanks, I have a car."

The lawyer departs, leaving the two standing on the sidewalk, Danny wanting to explain what's happening, how she really feels. "Let me explain something to you."

"Go to hell, and stay away from my friend. He can't survive friendships like the one you're offering."

She walks away without any further attempts at reconciliation. *I hope you know what you're doing, Wilson,* she thinks to herself.

Mark sees she's doing exactly what he thought she'd do, save her own ass. Almost to his car, a red Vette glides into the lot, stopping right next to him, almost bumping him. The driver's side window lowers to the open position.

"Your fuckin' wart dead yet?"

Anderson can't ignore the question, or the shit-eating grin on the man's face. Like a cat, he strikes out quickly. Kirk's smile evaporates as he opens the door to oblige, engaging Anderson; initially sucking the reaction from him he wanted...was counting on. On his way to lunch, Schuler and another detective quickly converge on the two, their battle now drawing a small crowd of fight enthusiasts.

Surprisingly, Anderson's able to land the first blow, the second, a third, all uncontested. Kirk drops to his knees. His plan to offer little resistance moves forward, since noticing Schuler just before carrying out his hastily intended entrapment. The shot's he's received to this point come harder than he thought they would, air exploding from his lungs, forcing sounds of pain he is not faking. Anderson's frustrations at its peak and antagonized by the culmination of all events, continues delivering his attack.

Schuler steps in, grabbing Anderson, pushing him into the side of the car, bending his arms behind him, and placing the cuffs around his wrists. "You just wouldn't listen. Now you're gonna spend some time with us."

Handcuffs on, hearing his Miranda rights as quoted by Schuler, he realizes too late he may have been set up.

Carrigan watches as he's led away, still restrained. He has great feelings of satisfaction with his recent accomplishment.

Schuler stops and turns to address the big man standing next to his Vette. "I see you around here anytime soon; I'll throw your ass in jail for a long time. Now, get outta my sight!"

Anderson's allowed one phone call, calling Sandy. Explaining what's transpired, he asks her to make several calls, including one to his lawyer. After hanging up, her first call is to none of those people requested by Mark.

She and his father's conversation almost concluded "It will not hurt my son to spend one night in confinement. He must learn to settle his differences in other ways. I will make the necessary arrangements to see that he is freed first thing tomorrow morning."

Danny pulls into the lot next to Methodist. She enters through the doors, into the huge lobby and waiting area. Inquiring about Cade's location, she is told he is in the Critical Care Unit.

On the third, she leaves the elevator, after looking both ways as though she's about to cross a busy street. A double door stands before her, the last obstacle before entering CCU. She stares; holding back any further progress as though the door will not open.

Realistic thoughts and memories of the last time she came to an ICU or CCU of a hospital. It happened months ago, as her mother lay in a unit much like the one she's having trouble entering now. She remembers walking through similar doors, seeing her mother take her last breath. She has not been able to forget the feelings now resurrected by her presence on this floor, in this hospital, in front of these doors. She can't forget the night she and her father decided to take her mother off machines sustaining her life, pumping air into her lifeless body. Her entrance, should she make it, will be a personal triumph of epic proportions. That is, if she is able to overcome her emotions. From behind, the voice of a doctor about to walk through those doors interrupts her inner struggle.

"Can I help you find something?"

"I'm looking for a friend. I think he's in CCU."

"Let's see if we can find someone to help you." He hits the large round disk protruding from the wall to the right side, opening the double doors simultaneously. She cautiously enters the large room, surrounded by private rooms with large glass windows, a nurse's station in the center.

"I think someone here will be able to help you," the doctor offers.

"May I help you?" A nurse's friendly smile helps a little.

"Yes. I'm looking for Jason Cade. He was brought in here last night."

The nurse looks at a chart, and then glances toward a darkened room to her left. "I'm sorry, but he's no longer with us."

She hears the words, but what she'd just been told didn't register immediately. As it did, it brings back some of the same feelings she experienced the night her mother died.

"What? What'd you just say? What do you mean he's no longer with us? I thought...Are you telling me he's dead?"

"Oh no, I'm sorry. I didn't mean...he's just been moved. That's all."

"Moved? Where?" Danny's hands continue to tremble slightly, as she is not yet calmed down after the initial shock of the nurse's previous misguided miscommunication.

"Your friend must be someone very important. He's been moved to a private suite on the seventh floor. He has personal physicians looking after him."

"You're kidding."

"No ma'am. The transfer came in before I started my shift. Someone's taking very good care of him. With the personnel assigned his room, he'll get around-the-clock care, as good as, if not better than what he could've gotten here."

"Can I see him?"

"I'm not sure. Are you a member of the family?"

"No, just a friend." She says it, but knows she has just lied once again.

"You can try. You'll have to check in at the desk when you get to the seventh."

Boarding the elevator, Danny descends to the ground floor. She's decided not to take her attempt to try to see him any further; soon in her car, she is on her way home.

On the seventh, Cade continues his grand battle for life. Doctors spent nearly seven hours last night stopping all of his internal bleeding. He continues on life support, with close monitoring by the special staff placed at his side courtesy of Ankawa.

Anderson sits confined in the Dallas City jail. He anticipates his release sometime soon, awaiting the arrival of Alex, his lawyer and good friend.

Robert Carrigan meets with his son over a late lunch, discussing the events to this point, the plans they will continue to initiate. The meeting takes place in the Carrigan home, in the posh Dallas suburb of Highland Park.

"Almost made a mess of things, huh? What were you thinking? You could've ruined everything. I want some reassurance you'll not make any more dumb-ass moves like that without clearing them through me first, specifically against Cade. Understand?"

"I thought you'd be pleased. You forget...Cade's the one responsible for breaking you two up in the first place."

"The old man is involved now," Robert says, referring to Ankawa. "I have to be careful...as do you. Danny and I should be getting back together soon, and our Mr. Cade will be the pawn I use to arrive at checkmate. I need him alive and healthy, if I'm to make this whole thing work. Now you've forced me to have to make a few adjustments in my plan. She'll come to me, begging forgiveness before I'm through with her. I'll have her believing I'm the martyr, but because of my sense of fairness, I'll relent and give her another chance. That's when I take her two-timing ass down. When she least expects it."

Outside the study, where Kirk and his father continue their meeting, Mrs. Carrigan listens intently. She will not leave her post before learning as much as she can about her husband's planned activities—a plan to use Wilson and Cade, as he has used his wife all these years.

"I'm firing you from your job at Ankawa. I don't have any choice."

"What? You can't! What the hell's goin' on? I thought you'd..."

"Your job for the next few weeks will be to monitor the activities of our two young friends very closely. I want you to begin around-the-clock surveillance of both, starting tonight. The boyfriend will be pretty easy. He's going to be in that hospital a long time. Nonetheless, put somebody on him, watch who visits. Spend whatever you need to do the job, use whatever equipment it'll take. When we're through with this little operation, you'll get a new job back at Ankawa at a much higher salary. Right now, this is the best thing. I gotta' look good if this things gonna work."

"Yeah, I see what'cher doin'. This is good, Dad, real good. It'll take a little time to get things set up properly."

"I don't care, just do it! But we don't have a lot of time. Do whatever it takes. Watch the hospital, her apartment, wherever those two go."

"Just so I'm sure. You want her place bugged?"

"Already done. Did that when I brought her into my department."

Kirk can't believe his father's infatuation with the woman. She must be one fantastic lay, he assumes. His mind can't imagine the attraction being anything else. He will soon devise his own plan to find out for himself, then he'll know what it is his father finds so special about the woman.

CHAPTER 13

TWO WEEKS LATER...

Around eight o'clock, there's a knock at the door. Wilson peers through the peep-hole, discovering someone she never thought she would see again, much less standing at her front door. Greeting him cordially, considering their short, somewhat unfriendly past, she invites Mark Anderson into her apartment.

"It's Jason, isn't it? He's not doing well, is he?"

"You're partially right. Physically...he's mending about as well as can be expected. Mentally, he's not doing so hot. He needs to see you. And as much as I am against it, whatever you two have between you..."

"That's just it...there's nothing between us! Never was. I tried to explain that to him the night he was beaten. We never really had a chance to develop a relationship, even if I had wanted to. I like him. I like him a lot. But it just can't be anything more than a casual acquaintance."

"I guess I don't understand. Your conduct at the police station...What was that about?"

"Look, I had my reasons for leaving, none of which you or Jason would probably understand. As much as I want to help put those assholes away, I can't. I just can't."

"That's kind of what I figured you'd say. I mean, two weeks and you haven't gone to see how he's doing, or at the very least checked on his condition? Lady, unless I am wrong here, he almost lost his life trying to help you."

"Look, you have absolutely no idea what is going on here. If I show up at the hospital, the people responsible...no, I just can't. The man I work for, he's responsible for all this. You have no idea what he's capable of doing, how powerful..."

"Carrigan?"

"How'd you know?" Wilson asks.

"Never mind...So that's your answer..." Anderson vacates her apartment, dissatisfied with her answers, her comments, the total package, as it were. Descending in his elevator, another approaches, the two passing each other within the adjoining shaft.

Wilson is left to stew over her recent visitor, one more seemingly in an increasing line of those unhappy with her for multiple reasons. Once again, she stares blankly into space, through the glass door to her apartment's balcony. She's really getting tired of hearing what everyone else thinks of her or her actions. She doesn't feel she owes Cade, his friend, Robert, or anyone else, for that matter, a thing. What she does next, she figures, will surprise them all.

A man walks from the elevator, approaching her door.

Wilson sits on her bed now, another drink by her side, this time hard liquor and something she seems to be doing more of lately. She falls back staring at the ceiling. She believes she hears something, holding her breath, concentrating on the sound of metal against metal...a key inserted into the lock. She sits up quickly! Her pulse races! Her breathing quickening, suddenly heavy, shoots her internal system to the point of hyperventilating.

"Damn it!" is all she can spit out at the moment.

The door to her apartment opens, her reflex reaction guiding her vision into the next room, slicing through the darkness of her apartment...toward the desk holding her gun. Robert has entered quickly and moves directly into her view. There is apparently something very wrong, but she has not yet detected that... can't see well enough in the dark to know anything more than who it is.

"What are you doing here?" she blurts out.

Robert hears her voice, moving toward the sound. "Anna's dead!" he almost hysterically states.

"What? Robert...are you kidding?"

"Wouldn't joke about something like that."

She goes for the door, flipping the ceiling light on, seeing immediately how shaken he appears.

"I found her body when I came home tonight. She was already dead. Police believe she surprised a burglar."

Danny lets her guard down, quickly immersed in sympathy for her former lover and more importantly, a woman she never really knew, other than stories she'd heard from Robert. Recognizing he is now experiencing at first what looks like genuine grief, she goes to him, wrapping her arms around him, embracing him in his time of dire need. As he would, he reads her gesture as more than that, kissing her, his mouth engulfing hers. Sickly enough, she responds in kind before catching herself.

"What's wrong?" he asks.

"Everything! This is so wrong of us. Your wife's just been killed, for God's sake!"

Disgusted with herself more than anything, she walks away from him back to her bedroom. Left standing alone in her living room, he sits on the couch; hearing the bedroom door close, then reopen. Waiting for an apology, her remorseful return to him, hope fades as a pillow and blanket fall in his lap. Sitting alone in the apartment, he reaches for and turns the lamp off. With that illumination gone, darkness lasts few seconds before the glow of city lights invade the area. His mind reviews the last couple of hours, unable to flush them from his mind.

His flashback carries him to the moment he pulled in front of his home in his black Mercedes. As he stepped from the car, he could never have imagined what he was about to stumble upon. Walking through the front doors as he had so many times, he could sense almost immediately that something was not right. The door to his study unlocked as it should not have been, he pushes through the partially opened door, anger surging, seeing her rifling through papers on his desk.

"What the hell do you think you're doing?" he startles her.

She's caught, but the alcohol supplies a necessary additional level of courage. Fed up with the endless encounters with other women, fed up with the lies, deceit...she will stand up to him tonight at all costs. Slurred speech compliments of the alcohol she now consumes daily, "Well, well...none of your whores able to satisfy your needs tonight?"

"Get out of my office!" his only response at the moment.

"No. Not this time you son of a bitch. I've found me some real interesting information."

His wife picked up a handful of papers, grabbing the first thing she can get her hands on, a leather binder containing disks.

"You're drunk. Put that down and get out of my office. You have no idea what you're talking about," Robert continues.

"I'm not so drunk I don't know what's goin' on with our marriage. And I'm sick of it! This time, I'm taking your two-timing ass down. Everything will come out now. The *News* is going to love this! You'll be a huge liability to everyone in this town, including Ankawa once I'm through with you." As she finishes the sentence, she takes a quick sip from a half-empty glass of scotch. "Or should I say you've just screwed yourself out of everything, including those plans you and Kirk have for that home-wrecking slut."

"What the hell are you talking about?"

"Your plans for Ankawa...the takeover; I know everything."

Carrigan begins an advancement she's too drunk to realize he is now making. "What plans?"

'Don't you play innocent with me! You know exactly what the hell I'm talking about. The plans for Wilson, Ankawa, this country...I know everything. This time, I have proof!"

"No one will believe you. You don't have proof of anything. Besides, what if you did? You are not as smart as you seem to think you are. You think I don't have friends in places to control anything you throw at me?"

He has moved closer to her and she is now a little uncomfortable in that she may have pushed this little scheme of hers too far. "Don't...don't you come any closer!" She reaches inside her pocket, producing a small, shiny object, pointing a handgun at her husband. "I wouldn't have any trouble convincing the police you attacked me. I could tell them I confronted you with what I know." Her eyes on fire with a renewed confidence that she is now back in control of this situation. "You suddenly become irate. Yeah, you come at me. You know...all the stress you've been under lately. I feared for my life and I had no choice. I had to shoot you. That's perfect!"

Robert applauds his wife's creativity. "...Got to hand it to you. That's pretty good. I'm proud of you. Didn't know you had it in you. But you didn't count on one thing. You didn't count on me owning the police like I do. Ankawa? He trusts me explicitly. None of them would ever buy your story; as good as you think it is. You could shoot me...you could. But no one in this town is going to lift a finger to defend you. There is enough in that information to ruin Ankawa. You think once he knows what you have; he's going to let you do anything to stop him? The contract on your life would be signed as quickly as my body hit the floor."

Sensing her renewed weakening status, he moved around his desk.

"On the other hand, I could take care of you, do anything I deem necessary to stop you right here right now and no one would touch me. So, go ahead...pull the fucking trigger."

Anna, now in the sobering process, was entering a dominion of reality that had begun some time ago. At that moment she began fearing for her own well-being, sorry she'd come this far. Tears flowed from her reddened eyes.

"Robert, I love you. God help me, I do. All I ever wanted was to make you happy."

"You stupid...you've entered an extremely dangerous region of vulnerability where there's no room for error. Unfortunately, for you, you've just made the biggest mistake of your life. This is serious business woman, with global implications for a lot of people, including me."

Within inches, he grabbed her and the gun she was holding. Moving it to his right hand, he turned it toward her.

"You are one stupid...." he stopped to release the safety. "You never try to play in a game unless you know the rules, or at the very least, how to play. With you gone, Danny will marry me. For that reason alone, I should have done this long before now."

"Robert! Please don't! I'm begging you!" Sobbing uncontrollably, she placed her arms around his neck, trying to kiss him. "I'm your wife. I love you. I would never do anything to hurt you."

He placed his mouth gently on hers, pulling her closer. She relaxed, realizing he would not be doing what his actions had just suggested. Wrapping her arms around him, she now felt safe from harm. He pulled the trigger three times, no emotion displayed, hearing no sound. His eyes locked open; he could see an explosion of pain...his mouth still on hers, muffling screams all the way down to light grunts. Her body jerked from the entry and subsequent trauma of each bullet entering flesh. Within seconds of the first shot, her life had ended. With that realization and subsequent confirmation of her successful execution, he dropped her body to the floor, calling the police. He made no attempt to clean prints, or eliminate numerous tracks that might implicate him in his most recent of all heinous acts.

Robert stands to leave, migrating toward the balcony doors. He walks toward her bedroom door, reaching for the handle to open, but it's locked. Danny is almost asleep, her Davis P-380 close by her side. Jiggling the door handle awakens her fully. She then hears what sounds like the door to her apartment slam closed. She waits for any indication Robert could still be in her apartment.

"Robert?" She waits for an answer that never comes. "Robert? You still here?"

Ample time elapsing, she enters the darkened room, deciding she needs a cup of tea, maybe a glass of wine instead. She pauses at her balcony doors, peering into the night. Refocusing momentarily on its glass surface, a reflection of a man standing behind her startles, shocks her into action, recoiling her fingers like a cat readying to defend itself in battle. A physical encounter imminent, there is none. Robert is not there, his reflection, a product of her imagination.

Cade sits up in bed, finishing breakfast an orderly had left minutes before. He has had several visitors today, including Angela, a very attractive nurse, therapy enough for anyone. She leaves the morning paper, the usual front page stories of murder and mayhem in the Dallas area.

The next to visit...his therapist James. As they go at each other in their persistent daily routine, Cade suffers through continuing pain, as he has each day since therapy began. Their daily "courtship," as it seems, has given the two great incentive for developing a relationship of sorts.

"Why don't we just forget about this today," Cade begins, as he has each day of therapy since it began.

"Man, you still feelin' sorry for your ass today?" James responds.

"Why did I have to get the one black man in your profession, hell-bent on making every white man who can't fight back miserable?"

Let me tell you something..." as James begins his daily chiding. "When you decide to quit feelin' sorry for yourself, we might begin to make a little progress here. We're gonna get you well despite the endless self-pity you continue to heap upon yourself."

"Kiss my everlovin'..."

"Uh, uh, uhhhh. You gonna make me have'ta get physical with your ass again today. I guess I'll have'ta whip your butt in front of all these beautiful ladies."

James has just wheeled Cade to the elevator across from the nurse's station, all on duty stopping momentarily to listen to the usual conversation they get to hear every morning between these two who are becoming fast friends. Later, therapy for the day concluded, James wheels Cade back to his room, returning to a visitor, someone he's wanted to see for some time. Her reason for being here today...see how he's doing...guilt still hitting her harder than she imagined it would after what happened and especially since Anderson's visit late last night. She's wanted, needed to share what she found with someone, anyone, and since he's been through all he has, she decides strangely enough he deserves at least to know what put him here. Knowing he's an accountant, he may understand it...offer some insight she might not have yet considered. She pulls it from her bag, giving him several minutes to look it over.

"Well?" she asks.

Silence in the moment of initial perusal, "Well what?" he responds.

"What do you think?"

"I guess its innocent enough. Looks like some sort of payroll, I guess."

"You think it's innocent? Look at the names." a sense of slight frustration surfacing on her part.

His hesitation to answer, a frown forming over his face, tells her he sees something more now.

"What?" she responds to his expression.

"Looks like Schuler is making more than any detective should ever make in law enforcement." Cade responds.

"See anything else?"

"Uh...not really," Cade finishes as he hands it back to her. "Guess I'm not seeing what you want me to."

Resignation growing with his unenthusiastic analysis of her treasure, she begins a disqualification. "Look, your friend came by last night. Seems you...he thinks there's something between us."

"Yeah, well, I sure hope you set him straight. No one asked him to speak for me. He had no business..."

"I told him there was nothing between us...I mean, you know there's nothing...right? You know there can't be? Robert and I are back together now."

His silence is hard for her to read. She wants to believe she's hit the right spot.

"I better go," Danny tells him.

She turns to leave him, pass through the door that will take her away from him and out of his life, finally.

"You know some people are never as they seem," Cade proclaims after her.

She turns to address his commentary, fully believing she knows what he refers to, but playing coy to test the air.

"What're you talking about?"

"Carrigan...I just don't believe you should trust him."

"What are you talking about? You don't know him. How do you sit in judgment of someone you know little about?

He wants to discuss it further but decides to keep his thoughts to himself. Her continued arrogance and stupidity, as well as a direct unwillingness to accept even the possibilities are suddenly turning him off towards any eagerness to engage her further.

"Just be careful." And with that, he turns his back on her as she does him.

TWO WEEKS LATER...

Cade's stay at the hospital is now at four weeks and counting.

Robert has announced he is leaving town on a business trip, inviting Danny to accompany him. She declines, looking at this as the opportunity she's been waiting for. Today is the day he leaves.

Shortly after his scheduled departure, Danny works on a letter of resignation. It is a decision she has struggled with, but considers the only option left. It'll be on his desk when he returns. She'll be long gone by then. Her scheduled dinner meeting with her friend Allison Mickelson is tonight. She plans to tell her she can expect enough information to keep her writing stinging news articles for years to come if anything should happen to her.

Entering the restaurant in a suburb north of Dallas, she finds Allison quietly sipping a glass of wine. Their waiter strolls up behind her as she settles into her seat.

"Can I get you a drink, Ms. Wilson?" obviously recognizing her as a frequent patron.

"I'll have a glass of Merlot," she responds in kind. Looking at Allison, she forces a smile, and then emits a near uncontrollable sigh.

"What's going on?" Allison asks.

"Nothing. Let's enjoy dinner," Danny responds.

And they do, ordering, laughing, and catching up, as it has been some time since they were last together. Finishing their meal, Danny takes a long, hard look toward the middle of the restaurant, suddenly in another world altogether.

Allison has known her long enough to know something just isn't right, hasn't been all evening. "OK...There's something bothering you. I haven't known you all these years to not be able to figure that much out."

"I can't tell you much now, except to tell you I think I've stumbled onto something big, something really big."

"What? It's Ankawa, isn't it?"

"There's something going on there I can't quite put my finger on just yet. I'm close, just not close enough."

"You have to fill me in with at least what you've found at this point. You can't ask me to meet you for dinner then bring something like this up in the conversation. Tell me what's going on."

"I can't just yet. You're gonna have to wait. If I figure it out, I should be able to get you something in a few more days. I just needed to have dinner with you tonight..." she takes a sip of wine, "to tell you if anything happens to me..." another sip and a pause as if struggling for the right words.

"What? What's gonna happen?" Allison is now leaning into her friend from the other side of the table between them.

"If anything happens to me, you'll receive enough information to blow the lid off whatever it is Ankawa, Robert, his son, and God knows who else is planning."

"Danny...if it's as big as you say, shouldn't you get help? I mean, wouldn't it be better to get the police involved now, before it is out of control? I have a friend..."

"No! You have to promise me! You can't mention anything I've said tonight to anyone, especially the police! Promise me! If you do, I'll deny everything."

"That should be easy enough, since you really haven't told me a whole lot. But, yeah, against my better judgment, I promise nothing will be said to anyone," Mickelson responds.

Leaving the restaurant shortly after, Danny drives Interstate 35, glancing at her digital clock display on the dash. Eight forty-seven...no eight forty-eight as the numbers change before her.

Not far from the hospital, she decides she will make one last stop before going by the office. She has decided she will bid one last good-bye to Cade. She doesn't know why she feels she needs to do this, but maybe it's because she can't flush the feeling of responsibility she has for him being there. Although unable to fully admit it, she also can no longer deny she has inexplicably developed feelings for him, needing to see him one more time for some strange reason. Pulling into the parking lot, she parks her VW and walks inside. On heightened alert by his father, Kirk Carrigan has stationed himself on surveillance inside an SUV in the parking lot near where she left her car parked.

Her visit a short one, he reacts very coldly toward her. A much-deserved display of attitude she will feel as she walks into his room unannounced.

"What are you doing here? Forget to tell me to go to hell or stay out of your life?"

"I knew it was impossible for you to understand…"

As she retreats to the hall outside his room, he realizes he's been the ass he didn't really want to be, especially with her. Still in much pain, stiff and sore, Cade wobbles toward the door to catch her and reaches a turn in the hall just as she walks onto an elevator. Seconds after disappearing, she reappears, this time in the clutches of Kirk and one of his goons.

"What the hell are you doing, Kirk?" Danny asks.

"I feel a great need to pay yer friend a little visit tonight, dar-lin', if that's all right with you?"

"Kirk, what are you planning?" she speaks in winded fashion, about to scream.

Placing his mouth close to her ear, "You do; you and several others on this floor are dead. Right now, I got nothing to lose. Don't believe me—do it!"

The threesome stops just outside Cade's suite; the guy with Kirk pulls a gun, screwing a silencer onto its barrel as he pushes through the door, disappearing. The sight of the gun stirs an emotional panic to a level she's never experienced before.

"You said no one would get hurt if I kept my mouth shut!" Danny says in a continuing panic.

Carrigan chuckles in sinister fashion.

"So I lied. Shoot me...but then, I guess you'd have to have a gun to do that, now wouldn't ya?"

Inside, the hit man moves quickly through the front room, into the bedroom. Lights are out, with the exception of a small lamp in the corner, casting a low contrast over the room. He sees his target lying in bed, covered in blankets, obviously asleep.

CHAPTER 14

He moves without hesitation to the side of the bed; aims his gun pulling its trigger repeatedly, emptying four or five into the dormant torso, losing count after two. He stands quietly next to the bed a few seconds, seeing no blood as it should be oozing through the sheets. He then quickly pulls the covers from the body, seeing only blankets and pillows waded up on the bed. He straightens back up, pissed he's just fallen for one of the oldest tricks in the book, more importantly sensing he may be in trouble.

As he turns, an autographed wooden baseball bat, the one Anderson had delivered to Cade earlier, flies through the air from the shadows, connecting solidly with the man's forehead. The blow to the head, substantial, though the big man remains standing as though weathering Cade's best shot. Cade recoils, taking another cut, swinging for a homerun and connecting at the sweet spot.

Carrigan and Wilson enter the room a couple of minutes later. Danny continues her weak struggle for freedom as she is pulled into the room.

"Let's check out my friend's handiworks," Carrigan suggests.

The flush of the toilet coming from the bathroom tells Carrigan his friend must be in there relieving himself. Two differing reactions greet blood-stained sheets covering a body lying on the bed. Danny can only close her eyes as Kirk is about to pull those sheets away, relish in his dad's enemy's demise.

He quickly realizes what has happened, but it's too late. Released from his grip, Danny's eyes open. Cade's trusty bat slams Carrigan across the back of his upper torso, connecting partially across his neck, knocking him onto the bed, on top of his other would be accomplice. The current job incomplete, Carrigan tries to push himself off the body underneath. Before he can, Cade delivers another blow to the side of his head, finishing the job for the moment at least, a final upper cut knocking him completely unconscious.

Her rush of adrenaline, excitement, and sudden relief to see Cade alive and well overcomes her. Her initial reaction is to hug the man, kiss his neck and face. As suddenly as she began this welcomed show of affection, her aggressive approach is ended. She backs away, but Cade reaches out to pull her back against him, landing his mouth on hers. In the moment, she responds willingly.

"Oh my God, we have to leave!" Danny tells Cade, strongly pushing away from him.

"It's OK, the police should be here any second," Cade responds.

Still in his arms, her eyes explode open further. "Oh Jason, you didn't?"

"I called them when I realized Carrigan was here. I knew he had nothing great planned for me. Why? What's wrong?"

"You might as well have called Ankawa or Robert. Half the force is on the take. You forget Schuler?"

"We got to get out of here!" Cade agrees.

Quickly dressed, though in pain during the process; Cade moves through the suite toward the door to join Wilson, who is looking down the hall to make sure it's clear. In the hall, they turn in the direction of the elevators. Rounding the corner and in full view of its doors, Danny abruptly stops in her tracks. Armed with backup, Schuler walks off one of them onto the floor.

Moments later, at the door of Cade's suite, Schuler glances down the hall toward its stairway exit door and illuminated light above. He notices the door appears to be just closing, thinking nothing of it at that split second. He and his men cautiously enter, finding Cade's handiwork. Suddenly, a light comes on in his head, as he remembers the stairway door. Barking out orders to his second in command..."Call Jake and tell 'em to cover every exit out of this place, now! Steve, take the elevator to the ground floor. I'm taking the stairs. Let everyone know this guy's dangerous. Shoot first, ask questions later."

Schuler's orders, contradictory to department policy, won't be the first time he's strayed from policy or his sworn duty. Busting through the door into the stairwell, Schuler looks over the railing to the floors below. He can make out an arm and hand sliding along the railing several floors below, hear the echoing voices of two who sound a bit out of breath, one who sounds in pain at each turn.

"Cade! Hold up before this thing gets any worse!" Schuler yells, pulling his gun, aiming at the visible arm, pulling back on the trigger, just as quickly releasing it.

As he continues his descent, backup hits the front of the building. Reaching ground floor, he bursts through a door into a busy waiting room, drawing his gun down on other officers now entering the building, as well as several surprised and unsuspecting visitors and employees.

Outside, the VW pulls out to the street, lights off, moving quickly and deliberately away from all the commotion before disappearing around a corner as squad cars pass, emergency lights on, heading in the direction of the hospital..

Back in the hospital suite once occupied by Jason Cade, one man is awake and hurting greatly with a king-sized headache. He seizes the moment to swear revenge, his ultimate driving force one factor he will not be able to dismantle in his effort to gain satisfactory retaliation for what has just been done to him tonight. He pulls the cell phone from his pocket, dialing a local number. It rings several times before anyone answers.

"Yeah?" a voice answers on the other end.

"It's Kirk."

"What is it? I'm busy."

"Things...got pretty screwed up...tonight." Kirk's halting speech indicates the pain he is still in.

"What do you mean?"

"Just...just what I said. They...they got away."

"Who got away?"

"Wilson...her boyfriend...Cade. He's...he's out of the hospital and...she's with him," Kirk states matter-of-factly.

"What the hell is this all about? You were just supposed to watch them."

"I was. I mean...she came to the hospital tonight."

Just as I suspected. Where is she now?"

"That's what I've been...trying to tell you. They're gone...both of 'em." Kirk continues.

"Then you get your ass out there and find them."

"But Schuler..."

"Hell, I own Schuler! You don't worry about him. Put some men on the street now! Find them. I don't care how. Don't care what it takes, get it handled!

Robert slams the receiver back on its stand, rolling over to face the back of the woman sharing his bed tonight, the back of Barbara Dickson.

Danny pulls her car into the parking garage adjacent to the central building in this complex. Cade's not real sure why they're here, since she's not confiding any of her plans. If she is able to pull off what she does plan tonight, there'll be no turning back. The woman sitting next to him at this moment is about to make the ultimate commitment for both.

She tosses Cade her keys and a piece of paper. On it is written the floor number of Robert's office.

"I'll be here for the next fifteen minutes or so. What I have to get my hands on is there."

"What do you want me to do with these?" he asks her holding up the keys.

"If Carrigan, Schuler, any of them show up, get the hell out of here," as she throws him what could be one last look between the two. "I've got to get something from Robert's office.

"What if one of them shows up? What if Robert shows up?"

"Robert's the least of our worries. He's out of town on a trip," she confidently responds as she walks away.

Danny reaches the floor housing Robert's office, elevator doors opening, exposing a quiet, eerie serenity of an empty floor. During her march to his office, she's not certain why, but as she treks down the hall, her short journey makes her think about how those on death row must feel as they make their way toward the execution chambers. She stops at the door, as nervous and as sick to her stomach as she has been all day, anger pulling her headlong into something she has no idea how the final outcome will play out. Her breathing quickens as she reaches to insert the spare key she'd stolen from his desk over a week ago. She falters a little, slightly off balance, into the door's frame; moving through it after turning the key and pulling the door tight. The click of the key engaging its lock mechanism seems extremely loud. Thank God she found out Robert had had his lock changed, otherwise the continuation of this task would be rendered a quick and complete failure. After being in his office so many times in the past, any normalcy of those moments is now completely gone. A chilled feeling reminds her how serious everything she is attempting has become. The finality of this moment, she can share with no one. At his desk, the drawer where she knows other disks must lie is unlocked.

Minutes later, Robert shows up in the parking garage, Dickson in tow, on the same floor where Danny's car sits with Cade sitting uncomfortably inside. Parked in a dark corner but in sight of Robert's reserved parking spot, Cade is in the beginning stages of hyperventilation. A sudden injection of urgency dictates Cade's next move, as he makes the effort to crawl from the VW to venture into the building he still knows so little about, find Danny, and warn her. Not doing as she had instructed, and in his condition, he is just about to jeopardize the safety of both.

Finding what she believes is additional information, ammunition, whatever it will eventually end up being; she decides copying and loading to other disks will once again be too time consuming. As she quickly inserts one after another to peruse what it is she has found, she must admit it is all most astounding, unbelievable, implausible; as it all pulls her full attention completely into the material. Government codes, access formulas and passwords to files contained within Ankawa's mainframe she never knew existed, despite the fact she designed the program, leave her dumbfounded. Incredulous feelings of excitement, then fear of all she is seeing before her, especially the information regarding the United States Treasury have quickly engulfed, depressed, as well as confused her.

"What in the world could Robert be planning to do with all this?"

She continues looking over all materials. She sits at Robert's computer, so engrossed in everything before her; she is oblivious to anything going on close by.

Robert and Dickson enter the building at the fourth, access gained through executive privilege and the entrance to the walkway connecting the parking garage with the central building. Inside the elevator, he depresses his floor number, as she does hers. Doors close.

Danny's curiosity has the best of her. Going back to codes listed, she jots a couple on a piece of paper that may help her access the Ankawa mainframe containing this data. As she easily gains access there, Ankawa's internal security is alerted to an unscheduled breach, pinpointing that breach to the exact computer location in the building.

Elevator doors open at the eighth. Danny continues, unaware someone else has just landed at the floor. Internal security has dispatched two men to check on the alert and to make sure whoever is accessing the mainframe is an approved user.

He wastes little time moving down the hall toward the open door where an inside light casts a faint glow into the semi-darkened hallway.

Danny continues, stopping to look at the door momentarily. She turns back toward her screen as a man enters the room.

"You always this dedicated to your work?" a young security guard asks.

Danny jumps, initially startled, but relieved it's him. He's shown considerable interest in her since their meeting a few weeks back.

"Don't sneak up on people like that!" her heart racing in the moment, elevated breathing hidden from Tommy's scrutiny.

"Sorry, Ms. Wilson."

"I told you to call me Danny."

He smiles at that.

"Making your rounds?" she asks him.

"That's my job. You gonna work all night?" the young guard asks.

"No. I was just finishing up, as a matter of fact." With that, she starts to pack up. As she does, the security guard departs, Cade arriving via the stairs. Danny is startled once again at this unannounced arrival.

"God! What is with everyone tonight?"

"I thought you said Carrigan was out of town."

"He is...or at least he is supposed to be. Why?"

"He's here...in the building."

The very strange face she exhibits initially, quickly takes on new status of panic.

"Then he lied to me. Why? What's going on?" As quickly as she comments, the proverbial light goes on in her head.

"What have you pulled me into, Danny? What are you doing here tonight?"

"No time for that right now! We have to get outta here!" she tells him sensing their window of opportunity quickly closing.

Their escape will be, once again, down several flights of stairs. This time, she is not concerned about leaving a mess. Just moments later, Carrigan enters his office at about the same time as Ankawa's security team. Shortly following that rendezvous, a pursuit begins.

"Don't let them out of the building! Do whatever you have to, to stop them. They have stolen very important, classified documents!" Robert declares.

Soon inside the VW, Wilson and Cade travel to the fifth level of the parking garage, momentarily detoured, but heading for the exit available on the ground floor. Carrigan is on the phone to Ankawa's security.

"Get your men to the garage! They have information vital to the survival of this company and consequently, your jobs. Use whatever force is necessary to stop them." Carrigan once again orders them to escalate this situation to a worst-case scenario.

Dickson has entered his office to join him. "Sure hope I never piss you off."

"You can't afford to."

Cade rides along with Wilson, speechless since crawling inside the car. He's not sure what he's involved in, as he glances at his attractive accomplice.

"I'm so sorry I ever pulled you into all this," Danny laments, her eyes focusing on all that may be ahead of them.

Cade continues starring at his driver, this time for the first time, seeing what looks like tears streaming down her face. Scared shitless as well, the feeling in his stomach is unlike anything he's ever felt before.

"My God what have we done?" Cade asks not only her, but himself.

Beginning to wish he'd never met the woman, he knows it's too late now, besides; any common sense once in his possession had left him completely at this point, or he wouldn't be here to begin with.

At ground floor level of the garage exit, security awaits...each member of the welcome committee preparing for an eminent arrival. Within seconds, the unmistakable sound of a VW's engine grows louder on its approach. Heard above the final commands from the man in charge, tires screech loudly, signaling a final turn before its maneuver into a straightaway run at the blockade. Men raise their guns standing ready. Robert now behind them, his next order is about to be given. As the little car completes its turn, headlights momentarily blind those lined across the path to their exit.

"Take 'em out!"

Gunfire shatters the windshield; bullets riddling the car's thin metal body covering. The VW careens out of control, into parked cars, bouncing back into several of the fleeing army, as they run from a certain death. A crash, an explosion, the smell of burning rubber and flesh is overwhelming to those left standing, and those lying on the cold, hard concrete still conscious, nonetheless, fighting for their lives as well.

Anderson listens to his stereo, pacing back and forth, while Sandy prepares for a modeling assignment at a local shoot tomorrow, albeit a degree of mounting anxiety controlling her inner thoughts at the moment, constantly. Anderson was about to retire for the evening when Schuler called, asking of Cade's whereabouts, telling him his friend could be in serious trouble. Since then, he's not been able to relax; neither has Sandy. A knock at the door signaling a late-night visitor pulls Sandy to the door. Opening it, she's greeted by an extremely shaken, significantly upset recent acquaintance. Wilson steps inside ahead of Cade. Mark turns the stereo off with a remote after seeing his friend.

"What the hell's going on? Schuler's looking all over for you."

"Schuler called you? Shit!"

"Yeah...something about some mess you left at the hospital. What the hell'd you two do?"

The two fugitives sit; weary from a very busy, frightening first date. Mark remains standing, Sandy joining him by his side, her interest in this evening's events peaking since the call from Schuler about an hour and a half ago.

"Thanks for the weapon. It just may have saved my life tonight."

"What do you mean? What weapon?"

"The bat...unfortunately I busted it. Don't suppose I could get a replacement?"

"Mark," Danny jumps in uninvited, "I know we haven't hit it off from the beginning, and I know you don't agree with everything I've done, but after tonight I think you'll understand."

"OK. I've got nothing but time. What's going on? Hold it... before that, first things first. What happened at the hospital?" Both Sandy and Anderson sit to hear their story.

"A couple of men paid me a visit. Remember the gang at dinner the night I was sent to the hospital? The big guy at the Crescent the day you picked me up? He and a buddy came to finish the job tonight. As a matter of fact, a few more of their friends just tried to eliminate both of us over at Ankawa. I guess you could say, we're in deep shit."

"The big guy...Kirk, is it? What did you do to him?" Anderson queries.

"Like I said, I broke my bat...took him out with it...left him lying in my room. Hell, I may have killed him. I don't know. Schuler didn't give us any time to check to make sure."

"Far as I'm concerned, couldn't happen to a nicer guy. What do you think's going on? Why's this bunch so preoccupied with you two?"

"Danny's found something...something big...something Ankawa can't afford to let get out of her hands and into someone else's beyond his controlled environment."

Sandy appears extremely uneasy. She gets up to move to the kitchen, coming back a few seconds later with four beers.

"What're you talking about? What could be going on at Ankawa that's big enough for someone to die for?"

Cade glances at Danny..."We're still not sure what all the shit is about, but she may have found some answers tonight. We need to use your computer. I think you need to see this for yourself... help confirm our suspicions."

"And why me, if you don't mind my asking?" Anderson asks.

"We just need someone else's opinion. We may be looking at some of this all wrong," Cade tells them.

"You believe that after tonight?" Danny asks, a little pissed at his comment. "Listen, we...you and I crossed over tonight, to a dangerous point of no return. At this point, I'm not sure what they'll do now, but I know one thing's for sure, we both have targets all over our bodies after tonight."

Cade glances her way, saying nothing more, but then cannot help himself. "Wished I'd known all of this before you pulled me deeper into it."

"What are you talking about? I showed it to you at the hospital. You knew what I had before tonight," Danny reminds him. "You kept showing interest, kept acting like you wanted to venture further with this thing, with me."

Looking at his friend, Anderson can't believe what he is hearing. "You mean you knew all about this but you still chose to get involved? I have to say, sounds like the Cade I've always known."

"Mark, I had no idea it was going to get this bad. You think I'm looking for this kind of trouble, you're out of your mind," Cade responds without much additional thought, now wishing he hadn't gone there either.

Anderson looks at Danny, then his friend, fully understanding what Cade used to be all about, the fact he has not changed one bit, even though he should now be much more mature than those crazy days back in college. "You're both out of your minds."

It's like someone losing her best friend, realizing with Cade's comments, she may still be on her own.

"OK," Mark answers. "I'll bite this once."

Sandy's heard enough, butting into the conversation. "No Mark! You don't have to do this! You really don't need to be a part of this! You have no idea what they're pulling you into!"

"...And you do? A part of what? So far, there's nothing here to be a part of. What're you talking about? What the hell's anybody talking about tonight?" Mark's confusion mounts with each passing comment.

"Nothing, nothing...never mind." Sandy's overzealousness nearly draws unwanted suspicion.

"I want to see what she's got. OK with you?" Mark responds, slight sarcasm putting a quick end to Sandy's current objections.

"I wasn't sure it was anything at first. Still don't know if I totally understand exactly what it is," Danny responds.

"Then what good is it gonna do to expose all of, whatever it is? You don't know what you got, how do you know it's something Mark needs to see?" Sandy jumps back in again.

"Well, the more I study it, the more I'm beginning to believe this is something really big. Then tonight, I may have gotten the rest of the story."

"Yeah, no shit. Almost cost us our lives in the process," Cade adds.

"Hold it, hold it, hold it...Let's back up a little. What happened tonight? What the hell are you two talking about...almost cost you your lives?" Anderson asks.

"Danny and I paid Ankawa a visit."

Anderson snaps to attention, as does Sandy. "...And..." Anderson prompts continuance.

"She was able to access additional information we think can shed some light on this whole thing."

Danny jumps in, "If you'll allow me to use your computer." She pulls the disks from her pocket, finally exposing her treasure to someone else excluding her new comrade-in-arms sitting beside her.

"Be my guest."

She stands, walks to the corner of the room and sits in the chair facing the PC, but before flipping the power on, she makes a comment. "...this thing ever get used? There must be an inch of dust."

"Yeah, well, guess I haven't used it much lately. Never been much of a computer geek. Never really been any good with one."

"...Japanese and not proficient with a computer? That's almost..." Cade stops himself before saying anything more, remembering their earlier encounter with prejudice.

"I know, I know," Anderson interrupts his best friend. "Kind of like the karate crap...get off my ass, redneck!"

Danny bends over slightly, blowing dust from its top, flipping the switch on, then waits for the thing to run through its program check. She discovers few modern configurations or programs of any kind installed, forced to use the basic, almost primitive methods to access the disk's contents.

"This is gonna take a few minutes."

"...You two hungry?" Sandy asks to try to give her an excuse to escape all of this madness for a few seconds.

"Yeah, man, I'm starving," Cade answers, then disappears into the kitchen where Sandy's already retreated to pull cold cuts, cheese, and other stuff from the fridge. She says nothing the entire time she and Cade work side by side. Cade easily notices the frigid weather in the room, getting used to that style of treatment lately. After getting everything out, she abruptly leaves him to fend for himself, moving back into the room where she can monitor the late-night activities.

"Anything else you'd like the maid to get your friends?"

"Hey...what's going on? I didn't ask you to get the stuff out... you did that on your own. Don't go getting weird on me now."

She stands, walking toward the stairs, then stops to turn around. She has second thoughts about walking away from all that is about to unfold before her. She cannot afford to miss any of it. "Sorry, honey. I'm just nervous about tomorrow's shoot, I guess. It's pretty important. Now all this cloak 'n dagger crap dumped in our laps tonight..."

"Damn! No wonder they came at us tonight! Look at this!" Wilson yells out.

All converge on the computer from each corner of the house they've been occupying, to where Danny has just exclaimed surprised confirmation at what she's seeing. She offers Anderson her place in front of the computer, which he takes without hesitation. As Danny, Sandy, and Cade all stand around, he scrolls through page after page of some very intriguing information. Anderson's fortitude continues as he works through the information, reading everything before him very carefully for at least an hour after the original declaration from Danny; extraordinary interest driving his desire to find out all he can. Cade has dropped to a chair, succumbing to his fatigue and Danny finally falters, collapsing next to him.

They look at each other, Danny offering a sweet, silent smile at her new comrade. Cade reciprocates. They will both discover tomorrow why no one has pursued them further. By 2:00 a.m., Danny's asleep, her head on Cade's shoulder. Mark finally pushes away from his work, breaking his long silence.

"You've got some bad shit here. Did you see the names, our man Detective Schuler, looks like half the city's police force...a bunch of important people from around the country, hell, the world. I should've known my fa...anyway, this explains everything."

Still half asleep, Cade nods in the affirmative, missing completely his friend's near snafu.

"Sure would like to know what this board is that the documents refer to. I mean, I wonder who the members are, what they are set up to do, where they meet. Some of this looks like abbreviated meeting minutes...not enough detail. And what's all this about 'Project Hiroshima'?" Anderson continues to question his near-snoozing guests.

Cade and Sandy both stand, move closer to the desk to position themselves behind Anderson for a better view; Cade, yawning and stretching his arms into the air. The three continue their search for information, reading through each page at a slower pace, Anderson scrolling through the material after asking each of his partners if they are ready to move on. After several additional minutes of research, Sandy's evidently seen enough, and lands on the other unoccupied couch, stretching out in search of immediate comfort. After a few more pages into the next disk, Anderson pushes away again, flipping the switch off.

"Hey! What the hell..." Cade questions his sudden move without approval.

"You need to see more? Hell, be my guest. I'm tired." Anderson stands, walking toward the stairs, but not before gathering up a very sleepy bed partner. Cade's friend is deeply disturbed by what he's seen, but decides it can all wait until tomorrow, especially after glancing at his watch. Halfway up the flight of stairs, he stops, turning toward Cade. "You realize what you've just done?"

"What're you talking about?" Cade asks.

"I'm talking to your friend. Do you?"

"Yeah," she responds tautly. "I've uncovered a plan to control our government's finances, create an economic holocaust, for lack of a better term. If these people are allowed to carry out these plans...if Ankawa is allowed to accomplish everything on those disks, we're all in trouble. If he can pull it off, sometime between now and the end of President Stephenson's second term, should he win another term, this country could be facing its most devastating social and economic crisis since the Depression and the last world war. Yeah, I know what I've done."

Anderson chuckles lightly. "No, I don't think you do, don't think either of you do. Let me enlighten you. You have just single-handedly signed all our death warrants! Cade, she just placed a very high price on your head, one many a hit man would love to collect on. Once Ankawa and his group know who has this information, they'll stop at nothing to make sure none of us are left to talk about it. That's what you've done."

The room suddenly grows dark with a deathly silence, differing thoughts on the matter pervading each one's mind.

"Aren't you being a little melodramatic?"Cade offers.

"I know what this man is capable of. I know how ruthless he can be. I…"

"How…how do you know all that? What makes you the expert all of a sudden? Just because you're both Japanese you think…"

Anderson doesn't want to answer, so he doesn't. Sandy, recognizing his inner struggle, comes to his rescue. "Living here in Dallas as long as we have, if you read at all, you can't help but feel like you know some of these high-profile people almost on a personal level. Ankawa's as newsworthy as it gets. His coverage here at times can exceed that of the president's, the sports teams, you name it."

"She's right," Danny adds. "I'm sorry. You're right, Mark. Guess coming here was a big mistake. I should never have involved any of you. This is obviously a battle I'm gonna have to continue fighting alone."

"Hold it," Cade responds to all of the flying comments. "Come on, Mark, cut her some slack. Finding this stuff was an accident. Now we have it, we can't just turn our back on it."

"Where's that shit coming from? Fuck! What's made you want to be a big hero all of a sudden? You think you're some kind of cat with nine lives or something? You almost got killed once already. Or have you forgotten that in your quest to bed her down?"

Danny's incredulous look could kill anything in her path as she storms toward the computer to retrieve her things. "Just what the hell are you talking about? No one is bedding anyone down over this. I couldn't be more done over this than I am right now!"

"Come on, Mark. I never said anything of the kind. I, I..." Cade's slight stutter speaks the truth.

"You think you can survive another attack? I'm not talking just to her; I'm talking to you too. Hell, I wish you'd never come back to Dallas! Wish you'd stayed in Chicago." As Mark finishes, Sandy emits a silent sigh of relief he might finally be coming to his senses. "All you are interested in is getting in her pants, fulfilling your animal instinct and urge to conquer one more good-looking bitch!"

His best friend's latest statements further stun Cade, standing now as if preparing to leave. "I can tell you one thing for sure; you don't have to worry about it anymore. You're right, Danny... we should never have come here. Forget you saw any of this...forget we ever showed up at all tonight." He hesitates momentarily before making his next statement, "This shit's fine with me. Let's end it now. Let's just forget we were ever friends."

Danny grabs her disks, meeting Cade at the front door of the house, walking through to the outside. Anderson has since descended the stairway and now stands in the middle of the room, beside himself that he may have just lost his best friend. A part of him wants to go after them; another says let 'em go. He starts for the door.

"Mark! Where're you going?" Sandy yells after him.

"I can't let them do this on their own. I've gotta help 'em. I don't...they'll never make it."

"Think about what you're doing. You help them, you not only endanger yourself, but me as well, and..."

"...And what? Sandy, I don't have any choice. My friend needs my help. I can't turn my back on him. I can no longer look away from what my father is planning. Frankly, I'm in the best position of anyone to help him."

"I thought I was your best friend. Please don't do this," she pleads.

Without saying another word, he also disappears through the front door. What appeared to be her initial victory, has quickly turned into a major loss for Sandy. Outside, Anderson looks toward the cove, then down the street as he walks off the porch.

"I knew you wouldn't abandon us, but you had me a little worried," Cade's words coming from the side of the house and startling Anderson who expected they had departed the premises.

"...Thought you'd left."

"Another couple of hours, we probably would've. I told Danny you wouldn't let us down."

"This is probably one time I should. This one's gonna be tough. You gotta know none of us may come outta of this."

A thoughtful silence once again permeates the moment.

"First thing we gotta do is find out who all knows you have this stuff."

"After tonight, I'm sure Ankawa does," Danny answers.

"We all need some sleep. Let's take care of that first. Besides, I don't think anybody will bother you here. There's no way they could think you would come here." Anderson's statement exudes an extreme amount of confidence; the other two buy in totally, driven by the fatigue both are now succumbing to. "Looks like we're going to be very busy over the next few days."

Back inside, Sandy's taken this opportunity to make an early morning call to a local number. "I'm so sorry to call you so early, but he left me no choice. No, sir, they're here...alive. He's agreed to help. I gotta hurry. I think they're coming back in. I don't think I can stop him. You know how stubborn he can be. I'll do what I can. Yes, sir, I understand completely." She sets the phone down, looking up to see Mark standing in the doorway.

"Who you talking to this time of the morning?"

"I called to try to get out of my shoot. I wanna be here with you."

"No, don't do that, we're probably gonna spend most of the day in bed around here anyway. They need some rest. Quite frankly, so do I."

"You sure?"

"Naw, seriously, go ahead. We'll be here when you get back." Anderson drops to his bed, wondering who she was really talking to, what she could've meant by "You know how stubborn he can be."

It's almost five thirty by the time Anderson's able to fall asleep. Outside, a car approaches the cove, slowing as it pulls up in front of the house. A lone arm extends through the open window, a newspaper flying from someone's hand onto the driveway. All the way back down the cove, the process continues as the *Morning News* is delivered to each house one by one. Its front page may soon reveal what happened at Ankawa last night.

CHAPTER 15

Sleep for all is sound, even considering the harrowing night two had the misfortune of going through, with the exception of Sandy. She never really had much of an opportunity, needing to leave for her shoot at seven, although she'll be able to catch a little nap on the forty- to forty-five minute ride in the limo. She will not have to worry about makeup; that is usually applied at the shoot location. Her work today takes her to the Las Colinas area, photographers waiting there to shoot her and three other models in and around the locally famous fountains and longhorn sculptures. Today, she and the others are schedule to model bathing suits, next summer's styles, for fashion magazines and stores this late winter and early next spring.

She is out the door and gone by the time the first of those she leaves behind begin to stir. The usual early morning departures for most local shoots...a product of the tremendous rush hour crunch beginning to build as the car leaves the cove. Anderson, reminded of her early departure after a quick peck on the cheek, falls back asleep easily. By eleven, all are awake, one working on a couple of two-day old donuts, Danny searching the freezer and finding a frozen cinnamon bagel to toast. Coffee appears to be the predominant beverage of choice for the guys this morning, Danny opting for a glass of OJ. Outside, the late September weather is perfect for just about anything. Cade joins his buddy on the back deck.

"Sleep well?" Anderson asks.

"Matter of fact, I did. Just feel like I was out on an all-night drunk." Cade continues, "Tell me last night was a nightmare. Tell me it never happened."

"OK...last night was a nightmare. I think I'd call it more like the beginning of a nightmare."

Danny joins them, saying little more than "morning."

"Morning," Cade replies, Anderson offering no response. He picks the paper off his lap, tossing it into the middle of the table. "Take a look at that, then tell me what kind of morning you two really think it is."

Cade picks it up. Danny stands behind him, bending over slightly to view the headlines of which Anderson has spoken.

TWO KILLED DURING THEFT AT ANKAWA CORPORATION

As the article reads: *Late last night, two former employees of the Ankawa Corporation were killed in a failed attempt at high-tech thievery. Danielle Wilson and Jason Cade were burned to death in a fiery crash inside the parking garage of the Ankawa Corporation. Details are sketchy at this time, but it appears the two were disgruntled employees, who had obviously been planning the heist of valuable proprietary information for some time, according to Dallas Detective Jake Schuler.*

Schuler credits Ankawa's internal security of the multibillion-dollar corporation with uncovering and thwarting the efforts of the two.

Unfortunately in the melee surrounding their escape, two of the company's valued employees, security guards Sam Spencer and Tommy Phelps were killed as they tried to stop Cade and Wilson's speeding car.

The apparent perpetrators' demise came as a result of their reckless attempt to escape authorities around 11:30 p.m. Although there was little detail available at press time, it is known both had recently lost their jobs with the nationally known company. Ankawa spokesperson Robert Carrigan cited "obvious revenge as the motivating factor leading up to this unfortunate series of devastating events for our company and its corporate family."

Corporation CEO and primary stockholder Asao Ankawa was not immediately available for comment. Carrigan termed the incident "most tragic and unfortunate that two young lives had been wasted" for what he termed proprietary, yet frivolous information. He also said, "The loss of two highly regarded employees, (Spencer and Phelps), who had the misfortune of being on duty last night, was most devastating to everyone who knew and worked with them."

"Shit! Can you believe this? We're dead." Cade looks at Danny with a wry smile.

Danny's immediate concerns are not associated with his at the moment, especially after seeing Sam's name. "Oh my God!" she begins to cry softly. "What have we done?"

Reading through the article, she reaches the paragraph about the security guards being killed in the melee surrounding their escape last night, a close and dear friend of her father's, a man she'd helped get the job only months ago, the other, the young man who had confronted her in Robert's office last night. Their deaths were their obvious punishment for allowing their escape unharmed.

"Both of you need to look on the bright side. This is good. It could really work to your benefit, to our benefit," Anderson comments.

"What're you talking about? Two innocent people lost their lives last night! How can you be so nonchalant?" Danny jumps in. "Jason, Sam and the other guy were both alive when we left last night. How could they have been killed? If I had anything to do with their deaths, I don't know what I'll do."

"What about us? If we hadn't done that little trick with the bat pinned against the accelerator, we'd be the one's everyone would be reading about this morning...well, in reality anyway. I'm sorry about your friends, but you gotta keep this in proper perspective. Let 'em think they got us. I'm with Mark. This gives us some badly needed breathing room and time to deal with this whole thing, without worrying about Ankawa or the Carrigans breathing down our necks," Cade adds.

"This is good," Anderson adds. "I mean, not that someone had to die, but face it, better someone else than you. And what if they were both on the corrupt side? What if they were nothing more than a couple of Ankawa's goons?"

"As hard as it may be for you to understand, I just don't share your feelings," Danny interjects.

"I don't mean any disrespect or anything, but if what you two have is that important, this buys you time before they realize it wasn't you they got."

"You really believe they don't know? They have to know we're still alive and in control of the disks. Don't you guys get it? We're not dealing with a bunch of Texas hicks. They want the authorities to believe we're dead. How easy does that condition make it for them to kill us now, come after us with all they got? If we're already dead and we died trying to steal from Ankawa, it becomes all too easy for them to actually eliminate us now, with no fear of prosecution."

Neither of the guys had thought about it from that angle. "I see where you heading. OK, then, maybe we do have more of a problem, possibly a more immediate problem than we thought. Just in case, we better get moving. The best thing to do at the moment is find someplace where you two can hide, a place they'll never think to look...another city, maybe even another state." Anderson offers his opinion.

"Before that, I've got to get back to my apartment. There are still a couple of disks there and a few other things I need," Danny tells them.

"I don't think it'd be smart for you to go back there now," Cade tells her.

"I'll be OK."

"Yeah but, you said yourself you didn't trust them. If they know we're still alive..."

"Cade's right; it's too dangerous. They'll probably have someone watching your apartment."

"I don't have a choice. This is my problem, my decision. You guys don't have a say here."

"OK, fine, let her go! You feel that way, go!" Cade shows signs of anger with his new partner.

Danny leaves shortly after, the guys sitting down to discuss their plans; Cade's fidgeting a clear sign of his concern for Danny, now she's departed their company. "Look, I know you hadn't planned on getting involved in this shit," he begins.

Anderson sits quietly saying little, allowing him to open up.

"I was ready to write her ass off, I mean, she's done nothing but cause me grief since I met her." He looks at his friend, hoping for some kind of support. "You not gonna say anything?"

"What do you want me to say? Everything's OK, it's all just a bad dream, we're gonna wake up and everything will be OK?"

Cade's hesitation indicates a continued tenseness, a little annoyance with Anderson at the moment.

"Look, it's not the first time a guy's fallen for some woman he shouldn't have and it won't be the last. But damn, you sure can pick 'em."

"Listen," Mark continues, "About last night; I lost it in the moment, but there's something I need to discuss with you... before we take this thing any further. I'm not sure where to begin. You may not want me involved after I tell you what I'm about to. Hell, you may never want anything more to do with me."

Cade senses immediately his friend is greatly bothered by something he's obviously been holding back from their renewed friendship. "Just tell me. We've been friends a long time. You can tell me anything."

"You may have a little trouble with this," Anderson begins, his explanation coming slowly, dreading this moment since he'd seen what he saw last night on his computer. "All these years, I've had to keep my family, my past, pretty much to myself."

"I know. I understand how you didn't know anything about your family and all."

"That's not been the entire truth. I...I haven't been totally honest with you."

"What do you mean? What's going on?"

"All those years, I've kept a lot of things from you, things I didn't want anybody to know. The years we roomed together in school, the times I met with the man I told you was my father..."

"Yeah, I remember."

"That man wasn't my father. He's my father's best friend, his closest confidant from the old world. It's true, he's probably been more of a father to me than my real one, nonetheless, he is not my father."

"OK. So you lied to me. What's the big deal? Friends lie to each other all the time. I promise you, it's no big deal. Forget it."

"I need to tell you about my dad," Mark begins, fidgeting nervously momentarily.

"OK. I'm listening. Your father...he still alive...dead...what?"

"Ankawa."

It takes a few seconds to sink in, then Cade laughs. "That's a good one...really, who is it?"

Nothing more needed to be said. Looking into the eyes of his friend, Cade knows he's finally been told the truth. And for the moment, a lot of things are beginning to make more sense.

"Jesus Christ, man! Do you know what you're saying? The man we're going head-to-head with, the multibillionaire? He's your father? Man...what do we do now?"

Anderson sees the inner struggle now going on within his friend's emotions. He knows it is similar to the struggle he has dealt with all these years, since he was a kid. He also realizes it will be some time before his friend regains the confidence fostered by what Cade had thought was an honest relationship. "I'm not sure. I think he loves me, I'm just not sure there's enough there to overcome all of this."

"So, everything about you is a fake, your name, everything."

"No. Anderson is my name...legally. My father had it changed before I was old enough to know any different. I guess he knew back then of his plans...didn't want me associated with him in any way. Now a lot of things are beginning to make sense for me. Not that I like any of it."

"This is absolutely incredible! How'd you just turn your back on the billions of dollars your father has to be worth?"

"I know, hard to imagine. Here in America, it's almost unheard of. I guess it'd be hard for you to understand all his money means nothing to me. I'd trade it all, the wealth, the notoriety, everything he represents, for a family...something you take for granted."

Cade knew he probably couldn't argue that point. His friend was right about all of it.

"Japan's aggressions against America...America's retaliation during World War II, denied me of that simple pleasure in life. Since I've never known my mother, never really had a family, I chose to go on and start a new one. Now I guess that's all over too...all about to be taken away, such that it's been anyway. In some ways, I can understand my father's anger and lifelong quest for revenge...Yeah, I can understand his need for that, but the man's placed too devastating a condition on his satisfaction because of that anger. Too many people, innocent people, are going to be made to suffer, already have. This thing driving his life right now won't allow him to stop until he gains his own personal retribution. That's why I...we, have to do something to stop him."

"I'm just sorry I never knew all this before," Cade consoles his friend. "Now what're we gonna do?"

"The only thing we can do. Go to my father, lay all our cards on the table, and let him make his next move. Maybe he'll have the decency to make the right choice for a change. He and I have never agreed on much of anything. One, he still blames this country for what happened to his family and my mother. That's why I have no problem believing he's directing this plan Danny's uncovered. I just wish she hadn't, but now we know, we have to do something about it. We can't go to the authorities. How do we know who is involved and who isn't? "

"You really think that's the thing to do? I mean, what if...?"

"What? What if what? What if my father's as corrupt and ruthless as we all think he is? What if he'll stop at nothing to see this thing through? What if his only son gets in the way of his plans? Hell, what the fuck makes you think I have all the answers? I think we gotta be prepared for the worst. In old Japan, death is honor. He lives by that doctrine, but that's a chance I guess I'm gonna have to take. Don't see as I have any choice."

"I think we owe it to the girls to let them in on all this," Cade interjects. "Unfortunately, they're both as much a part of this as you and I, especially Danny. We owe them that much."

"Sandy already knows, but you're right. Danny will never trust me again, not now anyway, but we do owe her that much."

"We've still got a little time to play with. We can lay it all on the table tonight. Right now, I guess the best thing we got going for us is that Ankawa and his men may think Danny and I are dead. Even if they know we're alive, they'll probably play with us a little; I mean, what can two nobodies do in a city where all authorities appear to be bought off?"

Anderson glances at his watch, "Let's get some lunch, then I need to run by the studio. Got to check on a few things there, juggle some appointments; you know, the mundane things a poor business owner must do from time to time."

"OK, think I'll tag along."

"Don't think so. Think about it. If they're watching my studio, they see you, your cover and whereabouts are blown."

"I really don't give a shit! I'll take my chances. I need to get out. Cooped up in that hospital all this time; hell, I'm sick of lying around...doing nothing."

Minutes later, the two climb into the car, back out of the driveway and accelerate down the street. On their way out of the cove and the neighborhood, they pass a car parked on the street a little distance from his home.

As he hears them pass, Schuler raises up in his seat, watching the car disappear around the corner through the rearview mirror. "So, he's alive. If he's alive, Wilson probably is as well." He reaches for the key, turning the engine over till it starts, slides the gear into drive and slowly pulls it down the quiet street, up to Anderson's house, parking in front.

At the back door, Schuler jimmies the lock, forcing it open. Inside, he makes the decision to hit the desk where the computer sits idle. Finding little, with the exception of a picture he seems quite interested in, he moves to other areas of the house. In the spare bedroom, his failure to find anything of substance continues, going through the few private things Cade has left behind. He finds a piece of paper that also interests him, and stuffs it into his pocket, the same pocket now holding the picture he'd found moments earlier.

A lone car turns onto the cove, heading straight for Anderson's house. The sports car speeds toward the brown four-door sedan, sitting parked in front of the house, passing it, stopping in front of the driveway. Home early from her scheduled shoot, fatigued and feeling slightly ill, Sandy pulls herself from the car.

Inside, Schuler continues his search, carefully placing everything back the way he found it, thinking there is no hurry, looking for anything helpful in his crusade for information.

Sandy says her good-byes, thanking her friend for the ride home. She notices the car is gone, and figures she'll have some time to herself, to tend to some unfinished business. She also notices the brown sedan sitting in front of the house, shrugging it off as a visitor next door or across the street. Before she's able to make it inside, she vomits into her hand, figuring it to be because of what she knows and can't seem to tell Mark. Inserting the key into the front door lock, she opens it, quietly closing it behind her, as she always does.

Schuler continues unabated for the moment. Sandy lays a few of her things on a table, then walks upstairs, through the master bedroom into the bathroom in search of an antacid, Pepto, anything she can find to help her upset stomach. Leaving her bedroom to go to the hall bathroom, she passes one of the spare rooms, stopping quickly, thinking she's heard a noise from inside.

Taking a step back, she looks in. "Jason...is that you?" She's startled to find Schuler, as is he to see her. "What the hell are you doing in here?" she asks, immediately confronting him.

Instinctively grabbing for the gun nestled behind his back with her sudden appearance; he drops it back in its holster once he sees who it is. "Helping myself to whatever I can find that'll give me a clue to what your boyfriend and his friends are up to."

"Get out of my house! You have no business being here!"

Schuler pulls his badge, clipped to his belt, pushing it in front of her face, to a point where she will have no trouble seeing it. "This gives me every right."

"I told Ankawa I'd get him what he needs!" she counters.

"He's tired of waiting on you to deliver the goods and asked me to personally get involved. Now it's gone over your head, just like you're in over your head." Schuler pauses, glances at the dresser top, picks something up, folds it, and then shoves it into his pocket.

"That's OK; I've found what I need anyway. Ankawa will be glad to see what you've really been up to. Trying to buy a little insurance for yourself, missy?"

With that question, a tear finds its way down her left cheek.

"Ahhhh, poor baby. Don't tell me you do have feelings. I bet your boyfriend will be surprised to know that, especially after finding out he's living with someone he can't trust."

"You're a bastard! Get out of my house! Now! Take whatever you have and leave. Now!"

Schuler smiles as he walks past her, down the stairs, to the front door, stopping before passing through, turning for a parting shot. "No one knows about this, unless you want your man to know about you and all your little secrets. Understand?"

Sandy falls to her bed, sobbing, sicker now than she has ever been in her life.

Danny has a few things packed and continues copying the disks she now possesses, trying to make six complete sets. She pops the second, then the third into the drive slot as quickly as possible. In a few more minutes, she'll have everything she needs, and will leave to deliver them. Her additional insurance policies will finally be complete and in force

Sandy has some tough decisions to make, and she'll need to make them quickly. She sits with a glass of water, contemplating her next move. She knows she loves Mark. When she agreed to this job, she thought she'd be strong enough to handle it, free from any emotional attachments, and then get out, no regrets, no looking back. If she can convince him what he's doing is dangerous for her, maybe he will back off. If he ever finds out about her secret alliance, he will despise her for the rest of his life.

"I don't know yet how I'm gonna do it, Mark," she says, as though he were standing in the room with her, "but I'm gonna have you and get the job done at the same time. Then we'll be a happy family forever...you, me...and the baby."

CHAPTER 16

E vening arrives...Danny, Jason, and Mark converge on Anderson's home, all enjoying relatively quiet, uneventful days. Sandy's spent the afternoon successfully laying out a few plans of her own. She has also prepared a great dinner, a "last supper," so to speak...lasagna, salad, French bread, wine... the works. She will initiate her plan step by step. Everything she does from here on out will be an extension of her elaborate scheme, continuing from when she first met Mark.

At dinner, the conversation centers on everyone's day, the situation bringing all together, quickly floating to the surface as the topic of discussion. Anderson stands, lifting his glass of wine in a toast to the team. "My friends," he says, then turns to Sandy. "Honey...we are about to begin a journey for the masses. What we are about to undertake, may not be the smartest thing any of us have ever done, but one thing's for certain, it is definitely the right thing to do." They all nod in agreement, Sandy faking hers just for the sake of appearing to support the effort.

"So here's to the three of you," he turns to Sandy, touching his glass to hers. She forces a smile. He turns to Cade, "To my best friend with the exception of one." He glances back at Sandy. Finally, turning to Danny..."To the one person solely responsible for getting us all into this damn mess to begin with," his soured expression transforming quickly to a smile. "Thank you. What we are about to do, is totally the correct thing to do."

Three of the four now standing, hold their glasses together over the small, intimate table.

"Sandy?" Mark says, motioning her to stand, which she finally, reluctantly does.

"As a very wise man used to say, may Kami protect us all, be with us all throughout this mission."

"Thank you, 'Obi-Wan Kenobi.' Getting a little carried away with this, aren't you?" Cade jabs.

"Indulge me a little, man. I've always wanted to say something like this. No better time than now."

"This isn't some damned movie!" Sandy jumps in. "This is the real thing! We're talking real life and death situations, our lives, our deaths...yours, mine, all of us. Don't kid around about that."

"Hey, just having a little fun. What's wrong? I thought you'd be with us all the way on this," Anderson answers.

"No, Mark, she may have a point. You and she should consider staying out of this thing before we go any further," Danny interjects, appearing to side with Sandy.

Her sudden and unexpected alliance surprises, yet pleases Sandy.

"I know what I have to do," Mark continues.

"I don't believe you, Mark. You're willing to watch them zip me up in body bag, drop me into a gray casket, lower me six feet into the ground if this thing gets out of control? I know I'm not willing to watch that happen to you."

Momentarily in thought, Anderson replies sarcastically, "You're absolutely right. I've been so wrapped up in this thing; I didn't consider all the possible consequences."

"Hell, I'm already dead, and so far, my life hasn't changed a bit," Cade interjects.

Three laugh.

"You dumb ass," Anderson tells him.

"Excuse me, but you're all a bunch of dumb asses if you think that's even the least bit funny," Sandy throws it back at them.

"Look, honey, don't you have a shoot coming up in Europe?" Anderson quizzes.

"So?"

"When are you supposed to leave?"

"Day after tomorrow, but if you think I'm leaving you while you're planning this bizarre mission, you're crazier than I thought."

"That's exactly what you're gonna do. By the time you get back, this whole thing will be over."

Anderson turns to his two willing partners. "Let's get started. We need a complete set of plans, timetable...contingencies."

"After what I've said, you're still gonna go through with this?" Sandy attempts intervention one last time.

"Honey, my mind is made up."

She stands, storming out of the dining room, retreating upstairs, slamming the bedroom door for good measure and a little effect.

Dead silence prevails for the moment before Mark breaks it. "She'll be OK. She's had a lot on her mind lately. She'll come around."

"Yeah, well...maybe she shouldn't. Everything she says is true, potentially." Danny again sides with Sandy's point of view.

"My mind's made up," Anderson reaffirms staunchly.

"Mine too," Cade collaborates.

The three remain in the kitchen clearing the table, a very serious posture now penetrating the air around them. While putting things away, Danny grabs a bag of miniature marshmallows sitting idly in the cupboard. She opens it, grabbing a handful of the soft fluffy confections. Instead of eating, she zings a couple across the room, popping Cade in the face. She zings another at Anderson, then another.

"Hey, not fair, you got all the ammunition," Cade yells.

"No she doesn't," Anderson chimes in, grabbing a bag of the bigger ones from the pantry. He tosses a couple to Cade as both join forces to gang up on the one starting the whole thing. Cade quickly improvising in the midst of battle, pops one of the larger ones into his mouth, in seconds spitting it back out, his ammunition now a wet, sticky ball of sugar. He flings it across the room, like some kid flicking a booger off his finger. His new weapon finds its target, landing in the middle of Danny's face, temporarily stuck there before she reaches up to peel it off.

"Yuck! What is that?" she responds pulling it from her cheek. "What did you do?"

Additional white, wet, sticky globs fly across the room, Anderson quickly picking up on his partner's idea. Danny shoves a handful of minis into her mouth, spitting them back out, tossing the sticky mass at her enemies, reloading rapidly. The battle lasts as long as the ammo, until there's nothing left to throw, as

Danny and Mark watch Jason peel a wet glob off his shirt, then shove it into his mouth.

"Damn! You're sick. How do you know where that's been?" Mark asks.

That realization hits Cade, forcing him to spit it out on the floor. He grabs a glass at random from the table, swishing the liquid around inside his mouth before spitting it into the sink. Danny and Mark just look at each other smiling. Wet, white globs sticking far and wide, high and low, on clothing, faces, and walls...the mess is everywhere.

Sandy sits in the bedroom, pissed that Mark never followed to console her, offering to back out for her sake. Instead, hearing the laughter coming from the kitchen incenses her even more.

Taking a little time to clean their battleground delays the start of their strategic pow-wow. They needed this, the change of pace, the chance to laugh frivolously about nothing.

Danny speaks first. "We know what we have, kind of," looking at her two allies, sitting across the table from her, their faces producing uninformative, silent statements. "OK, OK. Maybe we don't know. Let's say we think we know what we've got."

The two nod in agreement to that revelation.

"The problem is, as I see it, we just don't know exactly what to do with it, or who can help us."

"One thing's for certain, we can't go to the Dallas Police, not with Schuler there," Cade offers up the obvious.

"No, his name's on the list. He and hard telling who else is a part of the Ankawa machine," Danny adds. "For all I know, you're probably related in some way," her comment in jest.

The two guys look at each other.

"What? What is it? You're not..."

"No, he's not," Cade jumps in, knowing she wouldn't be able to handle it right now.

"I've got it!" Cade adds, slamming his fists to the table, "My brother!"

"Who?" the other two ask in unison.

"My brother, Josh. He can help us."

Danny looks at Anderson. "What can your brother do?"

"He's in law enforcement. If he can't help us, he probably knows somebody who can."

"Isn't he in Memphis?" Anderson asks.

"Yeah...a deputy sheriff."

"Oh wow. Whoopee 'O Kiyaaa!" Danny's sarcasm mocks Cade's idea. "Nothing against your brother; I'm sure he's a nice guy and all, but what's a deputy sheriff gonna be able to do against the likes of Ankawa and his men? I mean, give me a break. This all has to be handled on a national level. I mean we need the likes of someone from government: CIA, FBI."

"Hell, with those guys involved, how we gonna know who the players are without a lineup, complete score card?" Cade responds.

"But a deputy sheriff, from Memphis, the home of Elvis no less? Come on, give me a break...no offense to your brother," Danny replies, Mark's chuckling irritating Cade.

"All right, smart asses, got someone else in mind? Someone you know we can trust? Let's have their names."

There's no answer from either.

"That's what I thought. We need to call him...tonight." Cade lays out his quick plan.

"We have to go there," Danny tells them both.

"Memphis?" Cade's surprise at her statement a little obvious.

"We can't deal with this long distance. No way we can explain the situation without the props to show him. He'll think we're all crazy."

Cade reaches for his back pocket, pulling a neatly folded piece of paper from his wallet...opening, unfolding it carefully. He looks at the numbers, and then stands to walk to the phone on the wall, punching the numbers into the touch-tone system, waiting for an answer from the other end.

"Uh, Josh...Jason. How you doin'? Yeah, Jason...Jason... Godamn it! Your brother, shithead!"

Cade looks at Anderson, rolling his eyes into the top of his head.

Danny sits, quietly wondering what the hell's going on, beginning to believe what she thought just moments ago when Cade first mentioned going to his brother for help.

"Little brother, I hate to be the bearer of bad news but I'm in big trouble!"

A few moments later, he hangs the phone up and turns to face them. "He's with us," Cade proclaims.

"Didn't sound like it," Anderson states. "Didn't sound like he even knew he had a brother."

After the phone call, the rest of the evening appears lost to four exhausted, worn-out friends. Lights out throughout the house, Cade has absolutely no trouble falling asleep on the large couch in the living room, having given up the spare bed to Danny. Almost into a deep sleep, he is awakened by two arguing. Barely able to make out what Mark and Sandy are fighting about, he strains to hear the words, to the point of almost not breathing.

"I know you think he's your best friend, but a best friend wouldn't bring you into what he's gotten himself involved in. And Wilson, she is not your best friend! She's a stranger, for God's sake! What she's gotten you two into, God only knows! I know one thing for sure; it's putting all of us in danger, including me."

"Sandy, I'm not about to turn my back on Jason now, and because he's involved with her, she's a part of it. Honestly though, right now, she's not even a part of the equation. This is me helping my best friend and my country, doing something that should be done. I can't let my father do what he's planning. I've looked away too often...until now."

"But...your father...you know he'll stop at nothing to get exactly what he wants," her voice rises in pleading.

"Shhhhhhhh! Their gonna hear us!" Mark whispers. "You're right about that, that's why I have to do this."

"But, what about me? Doesn't it concern you that if this thing blows up, gets violent, something could happen to me?"

"Yeah, of course it does. That's why I'm insisting you go to Europe early. You need to leave tomorrow. You've been looking forward to this trip, the shoot will pay some of the best money you've made in your career, and you get to see a country you've never seen before."

"I can't leave tomorrow. Not knowing you will be here, in trouble, in danger of dying. Don't ask me to do that."

"That's exactly what I'm asking you to do. You're going and that's final!"

"I wish those two had never shown up tonight, never entered our lives. We'd be better off if they'd actually been the ones killed in that accident!"

"I can't believe you really mean that."

"Yes, I do! If there's a chance of losing you because of this mess, I do mean it!"

The discussion stops, Cade presumes some making up now in progress. He's finally able to relax again...still unsure as to what all the fuss was about.

As things have quieted down, Sandy lies next to Mark, his slow breathing with a slight snore indicates he is asleep. She slowly, deliberately crawls from bed, careful not to awaken him. She goes to the dresser drawer, grabbing a cylindrical object from it.

Approximately one thirty-seven in the morning, a lone figure exits her bedroom, walking slowly, cautiously through the dark house, across the landing toward the stairway, down the stairs, her light frame taking the expected sound of wood creaking out of the quiet night air. Taking great care not to bump into anything, or warn Cade of her approach, the woman moves closer as he enjoys the subconsciousness of sleep he has searched for. He moves, turning in that sleep, a futile attempt at achieving additional comfort. She passes through a trace of moonlight filtering into the room through a window. As she does, the light bounces off a shiny, cylindrical object in her right hand. She carefully approaches the man lying on the couch, stopping at his side. Cade's back to her, she makes her next move. Leaning over his body, she raises her hand, tightly holding the metal object she's determined to use.

Half asleep, he rolls over, opening his eyes, startled, face-to-face, her flashlight shining in his eyes. She continues crawling onto the couch next to him, setting the small flashlight on the table next to it. "Mind if I join you?"

"You OK?"

"Can't sleep," she whispers. "You hear them arguing?"

"Yeah." He had, but the argument was the least of his concern at the moment, as he begins kissing her forehead, cheeks, mouth, caressing her softly. She responds, pressing her pale, slender body against his. He can feel her breasts against his bare chest. Her body warmth quickly transferred, his escalating excitement immediately detected.

His tongue works its way into her mouth...for the moment; she reciprocates, entangling hers with his. Then, as quickly as they have reached this latest crescendo, she withdraws. "I don't think we should take this any further tonight," she says softly. "I don't want to take it any further and make this all more complicated right now."

Cade continues his patient, methodical advance, initiating a light massage of her neck and upper back with his hands. Initially reminding her of the encounter with Robert, she experiences a low-level panic...her breathing quickens.

As did Robert, Cade misreads this as a growing passion, thrusting his tongue back into her mouth. Her response is as he had hoped, her kissing much more aggressive now. His breathing quickens, reaching a stage of intensity not felt by him in some time. As their tongues intertwine a second time, he can taste her, a taste very sweet...exactly as he had imagined. He slides his hand down her back, gently tugging at her negligee, pulling it upward, toward the middle of her back. With no resistance, he continues his quest, sliding his hand into the back of her panties, his breathing deepening, not yet out of control with every inch of movement. His hand moves into the narrow crevice leading to her warm softness, her buttocks tightening. His advancement slows, becoming deliberate...her initial reaction is to open her legs, accept what he has to offer. But then, without warning, she slams her legs tightly around Cade's arm, forcing his retreat. She has come to her senses, deciding this is as far as she can afford to let him go tonight. She reaches down, grabbing his arm, pulling his hand from where he had just worked so hard to get it.

"No...not now. Not tonight."

This sudden turn from what appeared to be a successful, final conquest frustrates him immensely. "Why? I mean, what's going on? I thought it was what you wanted. You think you can play games like this with a guy's emotions? They got a name for women like you."

She knew what he meant. "You're wrong. I could say the same about you. I'm very serious about everything I do, including tonight. I'm just not ready for a relationship yet. Please understand it has nothing to do with you."

"You initiated this thing. Hell, I was lying here minding my own business, trying to sleep. OK! I understand. No relationship is exactly where it will end!"

"You're not being fair. I want a relationship with you. I really do. We can have what we both want, we've just have to take it slow. It has to be on my terms this time."

"Yeah, I've been in one of those already. It ended in divorce. You can't always have everything your way. I have terms as well.

This has to be a two-way street. I have terms and conditions, needs of my own."

"Not now, not this time. I'm tired of men trying to claim me as their property, have their way with me. If we're to have anything, you'll have to meet my terms, or not at all."

"Then it's a dead issue."

"If that's what you want."

Silence prevails, neither really wanting it the way they've just negotiated, but neither willing to budge from their current stance, as though world leaders at an impasse in their negotiations of an important peace treaty. Danny, deciding she needs more control in her life, had decided weeks before it would begin with the next relationship, no matter who's involved. She feels good about taking her life back, but she'd hoped Cade would be a little more understanding. She feels the disappointment, but she's determined.

Both now sitting up, a couple of feet distancing them in the dark, Danny finally says something that's been on her mind since meeting Sandy.

"I know Mark's your best friend and he seems OK. I'm having a little trouble with Sandy. She's acting very strange. It's obvious she's against what we're trying to do. That's understandable, but..."

"She's OK. She's just scared. Hell, I don't know about you, but I am too."

"I know, I know, but I'm keeping an eye on her. There's something going on, something about her...I just haven't been able to put my finger on it yet. Call it woman's intuition..."

"She'll be fine when this thing's over, so I'm calling the airlines. We've got to fly to Memphis, so my brother can help, so we can get away from Ankawa, Carrigan, and their goons. Then maybe we'll be able to get this thing behind us."

"And you think going to Memphis will take care of that?"

"Look, I know you don't think my brother can help us and I'm not sure he can, but right now, he's the best we got, the only one I know who will go the distance with us. I know he's the only one we can trust outside our little circle. You think of someone else, let me know."

"You're right. I'm sorry. I'm just worried. Right now, we can't afford to be too careful about anyone."

Cade silently asks himself how he could've lost control of the situation. How he allowed their moment of passion to transform into a serious conversation of strategies, arguing filled with innuendoes.

Under the protective darkness of the house, Sandy's listened to every word of the conversation. She slips back into her bedroom, once certain their midnight liaison is over. She knows what she must do tomorrow. She's convinced more now than ever it is the right thing to do. She knows Mark will thank her someday.

Mark, his back to her, is awake. He rolls over to face her as she climbs back into bed. "Can't sleep?"

"No, still have a headache," referring to her fake malady she'd already perpetrated earlier this evening. "Just took some aspirin. That should help."

"You're just tense with all that's happened. Let me give you a massage. Maybe it'll help you get rid of the thing. I guess we're all a little tense right now."

The warmth of the moment almost leads her to a full disclosure of those things she's been keeping from him, to tell him how much she loves him...what she'll do for him...sacrifice for their love, their relationship.

Danny's since left Cade's side and is back in bed. He can't even begin to sleep, the events of the last several minutes arousing him to the point of comfortless rest. He sits up, reaches for the remote, turning on the TV; spending the next twenty or thirty minutes channel surfing, until he's soundly asleep again. Cade's sleep is short, only to be awakened by the clanging of dishes and a low-level conversation going on in the kitchen.

The morning brings a slight cooling, both inside and out. Danny appears to have little to say, while Anderson and Sandy carry on with the usual morning conversation of normal appearances, with the exception of the continuing argument about Sandy's trip overseas.

As Danny walks into the kitchen, "I don't care!" Mark says. "You'll be safe in Europe. This thing is going to blow over by the time you get back."

"I don't wanna leave you, knowing what I do."

Danny's suspicions pull her into the argument, uninvited, unwanted. "What do you mean?"

"Stay out of this! This is none of your damn business! Oh, I forgot, you're the one who makes everything your business!" Sandy lashes out, her attitude resurfacing, exploding into view with each passing second.

"You think so?" Danny responds sarcastically, not about to let this woman get the best of her.

Cade steps in, "Let it go, Danny! She's right. It's none of your business!"

"Don't you realize what she's trying to do?"

"I don't have a clue to what you're talking about. All I see is someone showing some compassion and concern for someone she cares about. As hard as that may be for you to understand, there's nothing wrong with that! Now stay out of it and leave 'em alone!"

The cold silence persists mere seconds before Anderson jumps in again.

"Sandy, please do this one thing for me, just this once."

Sandy stomps from the room without a reply.

Danny asks if she can borrow the keys to the rental. Cade hands them to her, slightly reluctant, asking what plans she has. "You're not going back to your apartment? That could be the most stupid, idiotic thing..."

"Listen to you. I have a little work to do, something I wasn't able to complete yesterday. If we're leaving tomorrow, I need to finish packing. It won't take me long. I'll be back in a couple of hours." She leaves, pulling over a few blocks away, turning the engine off.

Sandy carries a small duffel bag to the car. Anderson follows with two others, throwing them into the trunk of the cab. He slams the lid shut and walks up to her, standing toe-to-toe.

"I know you're worried. My father's not gonna let anything happen to me, you know that. I'm the only son he's got, so don't worry about it."

"It's not your father I'm worried about." She stares into his eyes. "I love you regardless of what happens." Runaway tears slide down her face, their journey uncharted, with no wrinkles to guide them. Anderson uses his thumbs, starting at each side of her nose, quickly brushing them away. He steps into her, kissing her pouting, trembling lips.

"I love you too...more than you'll ever know."

She ducks her head to slide into the backseat. Mark pushes the door closed, and steps away to watch the cab back out of the driveway into the street. He continues his vigil until she disappears around the corner at the end of the block. As she flees from his sight, she enters the view of another who plans to follow just closely enough to keep her in range. She remains as close to the cab as she possibly can without the chance of risking detection. Not quite sure if she's right, she plans to prove her suspicions one way or the other this morning. So far, everything about the cab's route to the airport looks normal until it careens right at the Y on Interstate-35, heading north.

Traffic still heavy from the waning moments of rush hour, Danny experiences some difficulty staying up with the cab, losing it momentarily in the crush. Locked into one of the middle lanes and unable to catch the target she chases, she decides to take a chance on her hunch, eventually pulling to the far right lane, exiting.

Quickly transformed into a rude, aggressive "driver from hell," she rides bumpers, blowing her horn at everyone in her path, inviting retaliation of the same from most...more appropriate, less dignified gestures of the highway from others. On the exit ramp, she speeds to the traffic light, turning left to pass under the interstate. She pushes the car in front to make the changing light, to the point of nearly bumping it through. Entering the intersection, the light changes to yellow, stopping traffic, but she's determined. No one will keep her from making her next move, quickly steering the rental sharply to the left to avoid a rear-end collision. Screeching tires, a slide and a couple of pissed-off drivers later, she is able to stop. Sitting several cars back of the next intersection to the west of the overpass, Danny strains to find her targeted cab, believing it to be somewhere up ahead.

Reluctance overwhelming her, she settles back into her seat, resigned to waiting. She turns her head to the right, glancing at the cars around her, immediately recognizing Sandy and her cab in the next lane. Danny's disbelief turns to near panic as Sandy turns in her direction. Danny turns away quickly, throwing her hand in a cupped position to the right side of her face, trying to shield it from Sandy's view. She won't drop her hand again until the light changes and the traffic movement takes the white cab away. Just beyond the intersection, her target takes a sharp right, turning into Ankawa's. It seems Sandy has indeed made good on Danny's hunch.

Danny arrives at the Crescent after semi-confirming her suspicions on Sandy, parking in a stall other than her own, one tagged "visitor," closer to the elevator in the underground garage. Riding the elevator to the eighth, she continues speculation as to Sandy's reason for going to Ankawa's. There can only be one explanation as far as she's concerned. She arrives at her floor, then shortly thereafter, at the door of her apartment. Her first thought, call Cade, let him know what she's seen, what her suspicions are, the confirmation...those thoughts pushed back as she decides she'll have plenty of time later.

Inside her apartment, she straightens things a little; packing a bag she'd started days before, when she had another destination in mind. Finished, she walks to her computer, deciding to make yet another copy of the infamous disks she possesses...this time; in addition she'll print out certain excerpts. These, she will mail, along with a personal note to Ankawa. With this mailing and final stab at communicating with her new nemesis, she will take the opportunity to let the man know what she has, what she's prepared to do should anything happen to her or anyone else.

At her final destination, Sandy attempts a rendezvous with Ankawa. Redirected to Carrigan instead, he welcomes her to his office, apologizing for making her wait. "I'm sorry you won't be able to see Mr. Ankawa this morning. It seems he has decided to visit his homeland, but I am well informed of your continuing efforts on his behalf. I know everything you've done to help us to this point and I commend you for your work. I'm sure his son will see you in a much different light once he knows of your devotion to his protection and well-being."

"You know about my relationship with Mark?"

"I know everything," he says. "Ankawa trusts me explicitly. I'm aware of everything that has anything to do with the safe and successful operation of this company, including those activities you've been absorbed with involving his son. I might add, he's also very concerned about the safety and well-being of his son, especially in this particular situation, as aggravated as it has now become. I guess you could say I represent all that is good and important in the life of Asao Ankawa, like no other in this organization. I am well aware of young Ankawa's friends...what they've uncovered. We've kept our distance...watching, waiting, giving them time to do the right thing, hoping they'd soon decide on their own to return the disks." Providing a startling amount of information, Carrigan has decidedly begun pulling her into his trust and confidence.

"Unfortunately, they won't do that as long as Wilson's involved. That woman doesn't care who she hurts, as long as she gets her way," Sandy offers. He sits quietly, waiting for her to tell him something he doesn't already know. Unfortunately for him at the moment, she says nothing more.

"You are referring, of course, to Ms. Danny Wilson," playing her for a fool. "She still works for me. Let me handle her. Once we find her..."

"Then you know she wasn't killed in that accident last night."

"We know."

"But the paper, it said..."

"And like so many others in this city, the paper is a mere puppet to our desires and needs. It prints what we tell it to. We wanted our dynamic duo to think we thought they were dead, let them relax; let their guard down a little. You know where she is?" he continues, probing for additional information.

"She doesn't care who she hurts, as long as she gets what she wants," Sandy mumbles. "So why should I care what happens to her?"

Fully hearing her mumbled commentary, Carrigan responds in kind..."She has provided a great deal of trouble and problems for this firm. Again, do you know where they are?"

"Right now she's staying with us. Mark has taken her in because of a relationship between her and his best friend. At least that's where she was when I left this morning."

"And this young man, Jason Cade, I believe, do Miss Wilson and he appear close?"

"Very...especially after their little encounter in the middle of the night last night." She can tell this last statement bothers him considerably, pushing his possessive mechanism substantially before he wrestles it back under control.

Needing much more information now, Carrigan continues playing the role he is into very well. Sandy's nervous, apprehensive side struggles with her need to seek help. It could be too late by the time she reaches Ankawa with her information. "There's something else you should know. Something they're planning to do."

"You can trust me. I'll make sure all situations are handled in an appropriate manner. What is it?"

Hesitant, but feeling she has nowhere else to turn..."They're planning to leave Dallas...tonight I think...for Memphis, Tennessee. I'm not sure what time or airline..."

"Really, why Memphis?"

"Cade has a brother there. I think he's in law enforcement...a deputy sheriff."

Carrigan's obvious concern is not about what Cade's brother might do alone; it's what he could do should Wilson's information reach authorities outside their sphere of control. He hadn't planned for this. With the disks Danny possesses, he and his son will be implicated totally as key members of Ankawa's legion, masterminds of much of the planning. And not only would it delay Ankawa's progress, it could stop it completely, eliminating his strategy to carry his plans out fully.

Carrigan stands, ready to usher Sandy out of his office, possessing all that he needs from her this morning. "I appreciate your coming and sharing what you have. I'll pass the information along to Ankawa as quickly as possible. Be assured...everything will be just fine. Everything will work out. You've done the right thing. You'll see."

Relieved, feeling now more than ever she's made the right move, she responds with a smile before disappearing through the door, out into the hallway. "You know your way out?" As she replies in the affirmative, Carrigan slips his reassuring arm from her shoulders, returning to his desk, sitting, appearing to talk to himself.

"Hell, we'd better find Wilson and persuade her it's time to give up her little venture. The last thing I want to have happen is to be forced to totally abandon my plans. I've come too far to lose everything now. It's taken me five years to get to this point."

"Not to mention thousands of dollars," Kirk adds, stepping from the dark bathroom connecting his father's office. "Wha'dyuh want me to do?"

"Check out Wilson's apartment. See if she's gotten careless, left anything. In her haste, she may have just forgotten something important."

"What about her friends?" his thoughts primarily on Cade and a little revenge he is ready to deliver himself.

"Got plans for them...a little going-away party. I think we'll throw 'em a big one this time, complete with all the fireworks. Take care of what I asked you to, then get back to me. Get your boys ready. The big party's happening soon."

"If I happen to run into Wilson?"

Smiling, "She's all yours. Do whatever it takes to stop her. When you finish with her, when we finish with all of them, they shouldn't want anything more to do with this...if any of 'em manages to survive, if you know what I mean."

"You got it!" Before exiting the office, he turns one last time; "You givin' me free reign to do whatever?"

"You have my blessing. If you should happen to find her, make an honest woman out of her. God knows I've tried."

Sandy sits in her cab outside the building, while the cabby communicates his destination to headquarters and rearranges the paper on the seat beside him. Now maybe she and Mark can get this current crisis behind them and finally settle down. Tomorrow after this is all over; she'll let him in on her secret. She'll surprise him by returning home tonight, after spending the afternoon shopping for the new addition to their little family. Once she tells him her secret, it won't matter she didn't go to Europe.

Inside her apartment, Danny continues copying from the disks, writing the additional insurance policy she will send Ankawa, the letter that will travel with it. In it, she will warn him he cannot trust those in his employ and attach the bit of the information she has uncovered to prove it. She will mention the Carrigans specifically in the note, trusting Ankawa to be a man of honor, despite all she knows at this point.

Anderson and Cade sit quietly at Mark's, as relaxed as possible, despite all those things surrounding their lives at the moment.

"Old buddy, one thing I can truly say for you and your taste in women; you still can't pick 'em worth a crap."

"I know. My performance of late has been less than stellar. Looking at her though, can you blame me?"

"Naw, guess not. I'd probably do the same thing if it were Sandy."

"It's just that I'm having a tough time figuring her out," Cade admits.

"That part's never easy where a woman is concerned," Anderson adds.

"You know, I don't wanna push her, yet I do. I guess I'm falling hard. The longer she plays hard to get, the tougher it is. One thing's for sure, the game she seems to be playing is working... she's hooked my ass but good."

"Yeah, sounds like it. You told her how you feel?"

Before Cade can answer, Anderson's mind wanders in a different direction.

"Look, man, I've been giving this thing a lot of thought."

"About what...me and Danny?"

"Hell yeah...that's all I've been thinking about lately. Hell no, dipshit...This thing we're involved in. I think we could be in for more trouble than any of us could ever have imagined. I think we need a Plan B, a little added firepower."

He stands, walks to a cabinet across the room, pulls a key from his right back pocket, and unlocks the door. He reaches inside, pulling out a small duffel bag, a bag he had brought in from the garage earlier this morning while everyone else was still asleep. He opens it, reaches inside, his hand re-emerging with an automatic weapon. Popping the cartridge clip from its handle, he turns to Cade, yelling 'catch' as he tosses a Glock in his direction.

Cade snatches the flying weapon out of the air, nearly dropping it to the floor once he realizes what it is.

"What the hell's this for?"

"Know how to use one?"

"Yeah, sure...sort of."

"Well, do you or don't you?"

"I guess I do. Anyway, I took a few lessons in Chicago after I got the apartment downtown. Figured I needed to be able to defend myself. Never used anything like this though."

"Good, then I won't need to take you through crash training. These things are pretty easy to handle."

"...Didn't say I was good. After a couple of lessons, I tossed it in the back of a drawer...haven't touched it since. It's still in Chicago."

"How long ago?"

"Year or so I guess."

"Good enough."

"Think we're really gonna need these? I mean, shit! You really think it's gonna get that bad?"

"Not sure, but we can't leave anything to chance. When my father decides to go after something, he usually doesn't stop till he gets it. We need a way to protect ourselves, that is, unless you want to call our friends on the force."

"No thanks. I'd rather take my chances with these," Cade says reluctantly, holding the hard, cold weapon in his right hand, the gun finally sliding into the right position, his finger sliding over the trigger. "So this is Plan B. Hadn't counted on it getting this bad."

"Be careful with that thing...hair-trigger," forgetting he'd popped the clip out before throwing it at his friend.

Danny's finished with her letter, proofing her work. She checks the time, seeing it's getting late, dusk almost in control of the end of another day. She decides she needs to finish and get out.

Below her apartment, a red Corvette pulls into the parking garage. Kirk steps from the car, sauntering past the empty slot marked "Wilson 815," toward the elevator. "Well, damn! She's not home. Thought I might get lucky and get in a little extracurricular activity this evening."

Danny finishes reading her letter, makes a few corrections and lays it on top of the copied transcript from the disks. Unknowingly preparing to send information that'll mean virtually nothing to Ankawa, it's at this point when she hears a noise at the door. She quickly steps into the living room. She can see the door handle turning. She runs to the phone, grabbing the remote from its stand as she flies back toward the bedroom, dodging furniture on her way to a perceived safe haven. Passing through the room, past the front door, it opens, exposing her worse nightmare.

Surprised, though pleased to see her here, Kirk lunges for her, just missing—that not stopping him in his escalating pursuit.

She's able to make it to her bathroom, closing the door, locking it. She quickly punches nine...one...then stops, knowing she probably can't depend on them for help. Frantic, she dials information.

"What city? Shit! The one we live in...Dallas. Mark Anderson. Shit, I don't know what street...Uh, uh, Lake Cove, I think." Pushing the talk button disconnects the operator, provides a dial tone as she frantically punches in the number just given her.

Carrigan slams his massive body into the door; almost forcing it open with his first attempt.

"Anderson, Jason Cade speaking."

"Jason! Oh my God! Help me! It's Kirk...no, please, no!"

Cade can hear the crashing sound in the background as Carrigan slams through the frail door. Another scream, sound of a struggle...silence...

"Danny! Danny! Talk to me! You OK?"

Mark walks back into the room, curiosity pulling him toward the one-sided conversation. "Who is it?"

"Danny!" Cade can hear heavy, labored breathing on the other end. "Who's this?"

A deep, clearly masculine voice comes through from the other end. "Who's this?"

Cade responds with another question. "Who the hell is this? What the fuck's going on? Carrigan, is that you? Look, you sick son of a bitch. You hurt her in anyway, I'll kill you!"

"What? You ain't gonna do nothin'. Yer little friend's OK. Matter of fact, when I get through with her, she's gonna be one satisfied little bitch. I'll probably ruin her for you and any other man...that is, if she makes it through this alive. By the time I get through with her, no other man'll ever be able to satisfy her again."

"Jason! Please help me. God no!" Danny's frantic, slightly muffled screams are more than Cade can handle.

"Listen you fat fuck! I'm telling you..." The last sound he hears from the other end is "click."

"I gotta go!" he says as he moves quickly toward the front door.

"What's wrong?" Anderson asks his friend.

"It's Danny. I gotta get to her apartment! Now!" Cade grabs the clip, popping it into his weapon, slipping that between his belt and stomach.

346

Both men are quickly outside, moving toward the remaining vehicle, an old pickup Anderson works on in his spare time restoring it, the Volvo put in the shop yesterday dictating their choice of last-second transportation.

Kirk has Danny cornered in the bathroom. He moves toward her...she searches for anything she can use against his advance.

"What the hell do you think you're doing here, Kirk? If your father knew..."

"He knows," Kirk interrupts. "This is something I've been wantin' to do for a long time."

She looks at anything as a potential weapon, anything she can get her hands on. A bottle of cologne from the vanity hits his head, shattering. He backs off, slightly dazed, as angry as ever, wiping the aromatic liquid from his head. Pulling his hand down, he sees blood from a cut, feeling the sting of the cologne entering the wound.

The anger in his face horrifies her. "Your father'll eat you alive if you hurt me."

"He won't do shit! Get it through yer crazy little head, girl, he's through with yuh. He could care less about yuh, much less what I do to yuh."

Danny catches him and herself off guard by lunging at him, going for his eyes with the only true weapons she has left as she gouges the corner of his right eye with her fingernails. Her surprising, aggressive first attempt pays off. Kirk yells out in obvious pain, the surprise attack momentarily stunning him. She tries making the most of her opportunity, squeezing between him and the doorway. He can feel her brush by him, recovering enough to grab her by her shirt, reaching for her hair. By now the two have tussled into the bedroom. Danny almost breaks free for an escape into the living room. His grip holds. He literally throws her through the double doorway from the bedroom to the living room...onto and across the couch. During her fall, she hits her head on the edge of the coffee table; her body going completely limp as a result of the harsh and sudden blow.

Feeling more and more in control, Kirk calmly walks over to where she lies, more than slightly out of breath, still smarting from her first attempt at freedom. Blood around his right eye, splattered to his cheek, continuing to trickle from the wound, indicates he may have gotten the worst of the battle just prior to his last maneuver. Her blouse ripped open, he can see a partially exposed tit, as he'd call it. "I can see why my dad had his thing for yuh, girl." He bends to pick her up, carrying her across the room, back toward the bedroom, talking to her as though she could hear every word, stopping to lift her petite body closer to his face, touching his tongue to her exposed breast. "Yer gonna love every minute of this, darlin'. Hell, even if you don't, I will."

Laying her out on the bed carefully like a new suit, he continues telling her many things, carrying on a one-way conversation, detailing the plans he and his father have for Cade and Anderson, mentioning Sandy's visit. Thinking she's completely out, he continues pulling her clothing from her body until she's completely naked, her semi-debilitated body providing no resistance. He stands back to survey her naked, almost perfect body lying, sprawled across her own bed.

"You stupid bitch! You really think you'd pull this thing off? Ankawa's girl told us everything, even about the little trip ya'll are planning fer tonight," he chuckles, now disrobing himself completely. "Ya'll are in way over yer heads. Yer friends are both gonna meet their maker soon."

Awakened a few seconds ago, but still very groggy and not in any control to this point, she can feel the bed give under the weight of his huge body, as he climbs on top, lowering himself on her. She wants to fight as he pries her bare legs apart, preparing to enter her, but she has little strength and little control of movement. Very close to hyperventilation, she tries to scream, but nothing comes from her mouth. She's about to lose it totally. She can feel his naked body sliding over her, rubbing against her legs, stomach, and breasts...feel the increasing pressure of his weight pressing her into the mattress as he settles on top of her. He smothers her; she exhales, struggling to breath against his pressing weight. She can feel his tool pressed against her groin, not yet inside. The smell of his tobacco-enhanced breath, his unbrushed teeth, almost forces her to vomit into his open mouth.

He kisses her, prying her lips and teeth apart, forcefully burying his large swollen, crusty tongue deep inside. His flavor is about the most foul, bitter tasting of anything she's ever had in her mouth, his total smell nauseating. If she is to survive, she must endure all that is before her, one of her young life's most degrading experiences. As she feels the distinctive hardening between her groin and his body, the darkness she's artificially created by closing her eyes to this point, becomes a darkness of reality. Fortunately for her, she succumbs, passing into a more protective world.

Minutes have passed before Cade and Anderson arrive. They pull in front of the building, Cade jumping from the pickup before Anderson can grind it to a complete stop. His concern for Danny, his sense of urgency, sense of duty to her, helps him forget he and Kirk's last encounter. The blows exchanged in the club, the outcome, the time he spent in a hospital, almost losing his life—all those moments have all but faded from his memory. Anderson catches him at the elevator, barely squeezing between closing doors.

Kirk Carrigan rides another to the ground floor, standing next to an attractive woman, a resident of the building, he discovers. Their conversation flirtatious, he's feeling no remorse for his most recent aggressions, that behind him as just another of his many conquests, already embarking on a new triumph. She is unaware of the crime he's just committed, much less the kind of man he is, his back-wood rugged appearance provides a certain level of attractiveness to those unaware of the total absence of any moralistic virtue. At the ground floor, she walks out, Kirk telling her to have a nice day, walking away with her phone number.

Prior to arriving at the eighth, Cade and Anderson both pull the automatic pistols in readiness. The two exit together, making their way down the hall to her apartment, stopping cautiously before entering. Cade carefully turns the handle, checking to see if the door is unlocked. Confirming that, he lunges into the apartment, his friend close behind. Everything inside is a complete shambles, Carrigan making sure of that before departing.

Hearing the two inside her apartment, Danny thinks its Kirk, back for more of the same. She's managed to sit up on the bed, sounds from the outer room causing her to sob, plead for mercy.

Cade rushes into the bedroom, seeing her naked, not the way he had envisioned he would for the first time, looking at her now with extreme concern for her welfare and her immediate condition. He pulls the comforter from the floor at the foot of the bed, covering her. She looks at him, realizing who it is, burying her face in his shoulder, weeping uncontrollably.

"I'll kill the son of a bitch!" Cade yells out.

Anderson, in the room now after surveying the damage to the outer area, offers his assistance. "She OK?"

"Don't know! Think we need to get her to a hospital!"

"No! No hospital! No doctors! Please!" Danny manages.

"OK, OK, calm down. He hurt you?" Cade asks.

"He raped me! The son of a bitch raped me!"

Cade's rage reaches purity of content, with no boundary at the mere thought of—much less the confirmation of—his arch nemesis touching her anywhere. Anderson recognizes his friend's current inability to deal with the situation unfolding as he seethes with a level of anger never before attainable. He steps in, helping Danny to her feet, and into the bathroom. The sounds of shower water running, her continued crying, fill Cade's senses. He's sickened at the thought of Carrigan having his way with her and ashamed of his inability to step up and be there for her when she needed his help. Sickly enough, he's also jealous, silently hating himself for allowing those thoughts to enter his mind at a time like this.

Emerging from the bathroom, leaving Danny for a few seconds in solitude, Anderson goes to the aid of his friend, pointing him in the direction of emotional containment. "Now is not the time, nor is uncontrolled anger the answer. Remember what you said earlier. We have to get to Memphis. We must stay together from this point forward; at least until we know you and she are safe."

Cade doesn't like what he's feeling at the moment. His anger now directed at her, feeling resentment toward her for not putting up more of a fight. Could she not have kept this from happening? Selfish, self-centered thoughts trigger resentment toward her, more from his earlier desires of intimacy with her, knowing Kirk has had that one pleasure he may never experience.

Out of the shower and slowly drying off, Danny can hear the guys in the other room. When she walks from the bedroom, Anderson asks what she had here that Carrigan might have been looking for.

She goes into her thought process for a few seconds, not sure she'll ever remember anything before the attack again.

"What about the disks?" he asks.

"Shit! The disks!" She steps quickly across the room to where her copies had been placed earlier. "They're gone. Guess my letter will be hand delivered."

"What letter?" Cade asks. "To who?"

"I wrote one to Ankawa. I wrote it to try to negotiate our safety. I copied a portion of the disks to send him, let him know what I had. I also let him know the Carrigans were working against him and attached proof....Well, guess that will never get to him either." With that, exhaustion overtakes her. Landing on the sofa, she nearly passes out.

This time Cade is at her side immediately, feelings from moments before gone, pushed aside by a sincere, near-loving concern for her.

Anderson turns to look out the window, seeing the sun slowly disappearing behind the horizon to the west. "We've gotta go if we're gonna be ready for our flight. I think she's gonna be OK. She seems to be one tough cookie."

Before departing, Danny has the presence of mind to go to her closet, pulling another set of the disks she had hidden earlier in this adventure.

The three soon find themselves inside the pickup, Anderson driving, Danny between him and Cade, no one talking. Danny's hand quickly travels a path inside Jason's for the comfort of a friend. The silence becomes a stark reminder of how serious the situation has now become.

CHAPTER 17

A t approximately eight o'clock, Anderson turns his pickup onto the street heading to his home. He immediately senses something isn't right, as he slows to turn into his driveway. Looking in his rearview mirror, he unwittingly turns off the engine.

Cade reaches for the handle of the door.

"Don't get out!" Anderson whispers excitedly, cold chills just completing their run throughout his body. "We have company and major problems."

"What's wrong?" Cade asks as he and Danny both turn around to look through the back window.

"No! Don't turn around! I don't want them thinking we know. We act normal, move slowly; maybe they'll let us inside. Just get out of the truck and walk toward the front door. But just in case..." Anderson pulls his gun, placing it between his legs to muffle the sound as he cocks it for use. Cade pulls his doing the same. Still not over the events of her day, Danny shutters with the anticipation of yet another encounter, trembling, almost shaking uncontrollably until Cade wraps his arm around her shoulder confidently.

"I remember now!" Danny blurts out.

"Shhhhhhhh! Keep it down," Anderson whispers. "Remember what?"

She begins crying again. "I'm sorry, guys." She pauses, trying to regain a certain amount of composure. "Just before...before... you know. Carrigan said they knew we were still alive, Jason. They also know about our plans to leave tonight. Something about an insider, Ankawa's girl he called her. They don't plan to let us leave town alive."

"That's what they think," Anderson responds. "Come on. Let's try to make it to the house. I've got another idea. Try your best to act normal."

The three climb out of the pickup, walking, talking as though they aren't aware of their company, each quickly picking up on the other's lead..

Inside a van parked a few hundred feet down the street; Carrigan watches the movement, giving his men their final orders. "Let them get inside. They'll be back out soon. They have a flight to catch. When they try to back out of the driveway, we'll have them all confined in the truck."

"Yes, sir," his group leader responds over the two-way.

"One other thing, once you get 'em where we need 'em, save the bitch for me. I want one more shot at her. I got some unfinished business."

"Yes, sir."

Inside, the three prepare for the inevitable. Anderson turns to Danny, evidence he did hear all she had said in the truck. "Carrigan tell you who the 'plant' was?"

"No." She wanted to tell them both what she'd seen this morning, but had no real proof yet.

"Here's the new plan. If their spy knew everything as Danny says, then they think we're going by plane and are expecting us back outside shortly, complete with luggage. Right?"

"That would seem reasonable," Cade responds.

"Then, we'll give them what they expect."

"What the hell are you talking about? Why would we do that? "

"Don't ask questions, man. Grab those bags upstairs in my closet. I'll take them to the truck and throw 'em in the back just like we were planning to leave. While I'm doing that, you two will be heading to the garage out back. There are two duffel bags inside an old gym locker there. Here's what you'll need to open the locks." Anderson hands Jason a piece of paper he has just written the combination on. "This'll disengage the perimeter alarm system." He hands Cade a remote.

"This keyless entry will also get you access to the car there. I'll give you a few minutes, do what I told you, and then I start my charade. In approximately ten minutes, I'll join you. Whatever you do, don't start the car for at least ten minutes."

Conversation concluded, his plan laid out, plain and simple, Anderson checks his gun one last time, popping the clip, pushing it back in. He picks up the two bags, one in each hand and starts for the door leading outside. Before he opens it, he turns to his friend.

"One last thing...Anything happens and I don't make it there in ten minutes, or if things get too hot and heavy, you two go on."

"No fucking way. I'm not leaving you here."

"Man, listen to me. You don't have a choice. You two gotta get to Memphis and your brother. Think about it!"

Anderson reaches for the knob, smiles, and winks before pushing it open, disappearing to the outside. Cade and Danny depart the house immediately through the back door, cautious to the possibility someone could be in the back. The two reach the garage without incident, opening the lock and door, entering the dark building, Cade bumping into the car upon initial entry. He flips on a light switch immediately seeing a flashlight on a workbench, flipping the light off and grabbing it. As Danny holds it on the combination lock, Cade follows the numbers in sequence as written on the paper, moving the dial right, left, then right again, pulling down hard, nothing...through the number sequence again, popping it open this time. As he opens the door to the locker, one of the bags inside falls to the floor, muffled clanging of metal causing great interest and curiosity. With little time to spare, he grabs the bags as instructed, whirling around to pull a cover from the car awaiting its passengers.

In the dark, neither can make out the model, but Cade knows enough to know this one is special. He depresses the button on the keyless entry and the passenger doors automatically open, lifting upward toward the ceiling. Lights inside come on exposing the interior of a Lamborghini Diablo. With barely room enough for three; Cade searches for the luggage compartment button. Completed, they slide inside, Cade behind the steering wheel, nervous that he may not know enough to be able to drive this vehicle.

Anderson heaves the empty bags, tossing them into the back of his old pickup as though they were weighted heavily. "What the hell's in these things? We're only gonna be gone a couple of days."

As he walks back toward the house, he continues his act, placing himself in a position for an Oscar nomination. "Will you two hurry up? We're gonna miss our flight." He disappears momentarily, reappearing with two more bags, laughing as though carrying on a conversation with someone still inside. He checks his watch on his second and final approach to the house, seeing it's been nearly seven minutes since the three parted.

Impatient and failing to follow orders, the man in charge of the commandos feels something's not right, motioning to begin their assault early. Anderson hears the footsteps behind him, as he steps to just in front of the door. He turns quickly, pulling his gun out of his pants, raising it toward the street. He fires several rounds in rapid succession; one of which finds its intended target, piercing the side of the old truck, entering its fuel tank. The ensuing explosion rocks the evening silence of a quiet neighborhood. Men crossing the street to engage the enemy are knocked off their feet, some unable to rise again. Anderson quickly disappears into the house as gunfire continues, bullets penetrating the wood siding and windows.

A van screeches to a sliding stop in front, Carrigan jumping to the street before it completely stops. "Goddamn it! I told you to wait." Walking by his second-in-command, he unloads four rounds, a final punishment for his misdeed.

"Get your asses around to the back of the house! Now!" He looks at his group leader lying on the grass, dying from his wounds. "You dumb fuck! I won't tolerate insubordination or rogue actions by anyone on my team." With that he makes sure he's out, firing two additional rounds into his semi-lifeless body. "Pick this piece of shit up and dispose of it."

"Get some cars in the alley! Both ends!" he continues yelling orders while approaching the front door. "Don't let those three out alive! None of 'em! I'll teach 'em to fuck with me! I am sick of their shit!"

The sound of the explosion has startled Cade and Danny, neither quite sure what they should do at this point. Cade checks his watch. It's been ten, eleven minutes. He glances at Danny.

"He said ten minutes we go," she reminds him.

"I know, I know." He fidgets nervously before crawling from the car, then back in, turning the key and starting the engine. Synchronized to the ignition, the garage door automatically opens.

Anderson reaches the deck on the back of the house, retreating down the stairs. Two of Kirk's commandos have reached the back as well, running between houses, firing several rounds at him as they break into the openness of the back yard. He reverses his intended direction, making it safely back to the house, firing rapidly at his attackers, clipping one with a lucky shot, popping the cartridge on the run, pulling another from his pocket and reloading as though he does this kind of thing all the time.

Cade shifts into low gear, pulling the sleek Diablo out of the garage, turning left toward the north end of the alley. Upset about leaving Mark, he feels he's just betrayed his best friend.

Anderson decides to pull out all stops in his quest for the garage. On a dead run, down the steps, through the yard, he empties his gun as additional men enter the backyard. One of their shots appears to hit him, knocking him to the ground, just feet from the empty garage. He lies there motionless.

Cade and Wilson are almost at the end of the alley, when a car pulls into the same alley from the street, facing them, blocking their exit. Cade looks at Danny. "Hang on!"

Thrusting the gear into reverse, he backs the shiny sports car down the alley in the direction from which they had just come. The car at their front begins the chase. With smoke pouring from screeching tires, the two move quickly back down the alley, gaining speed rapidly. Another pulls in at the opposite end, lights on, beginning its move toward the rear of the retreating Diablo.

"We're screwed!" Cade yells as he is already turned viewing his path to the opposite end of the alley.

"What?" No answer necessary as she turns to see the headlights of the car to their rear.

"Crap!" Cade yells out, steering the car with one hand, peering out the rear window.

Danny notices the garage door opening back up as the built-in sensor alerts its opener to the car's approach.

The men responsible for putting him down are on top of Anderson. Carrigan walks through the back door to the house, still several feet from them.

"Finish the asshole off! Make sure he's good and dead!"

As the two raise their guns to empty them into the lifeless body lying at their feet, Anderson raises his arm slightly exposing the barrel of his automatic, taking both out with a multitude of shots. Carrigan crouches behind the patio furniture, making sure he isn't due the same fate.

About to pass the front of the opened garage, Cade brakes, sending the car into a slide. Fighting the wheel, steering into the slide, he yanks the wheel at the last second to the left, takes his foot off the brake, slamming it on the accelerator as if he does this sort of thing all the time. The car responds magnificently, shooting up the short drive into the garage, but not before clipping the driver's side, metal against wood, the sound of which neither heard in all the commotion. With a few quick minor steering adjustments, the car stops half inside the garage, half out. As Danny opens her eyes, one of the cars flies past them, smashing head-on into the other. The sound of crunching metal, shattering glass and the illumination of a second explosion finishes awakening those who were not already awake within a two-block radius.

Cade throws the gear into first, but before he can accelerate, there's a tap on the window. Surprised and without thinking, he opens it.

Anderson bends down to go face to face with his partner. "Nice parking job. You must have worked as a valet. Got room for a third?"

"Not if you're going to bad-mouth my driving."

Anderson crawls inside and the three begin their mission via new transportation. As Cade turns out of the alley onto the street, Anderson looks back at the glow of the burning cars. "Shit. An open fire's in violation of the covenants. I'm probably gonna be asked to move after tonight."

"Yeah, looks like this flight is taking off a little ahead of schedule," Cade responds as the two continue their spirited word play with each other.

Carrigan walks through the garage and out into the alley. He surveys the wreckage to his right, in total disbelief his targeted prey has once again appeared to navigate all roadblocks he and his men have thrown at them.

"Looks like you got lucky again this time, but you'll never make it to Memphis. I promise you on my life I will stop you shitheads if it's the last thing I do."

In front of the house, the pickup still on fire, a cab pulls up, stopping several yards from the burning wreckage. Her planned surprise return for Mark will be ruined tonight. She steps out, shock and disbelief invading her senses.

Kirk's made it back to Ankawa's and is sitting in his father's office trying to explain how he could have failed so miserably... once again. For him, it is now more a personal matter than ever before. The first thing on the agenda is a quick debriefing on the events of the night and developing next plans.

"If they get to Memphis, they will be outside our control. We must make sure they do not."

Kirk looks frazzled and frustrated.

"Do I need to get someone else to finish this?" Robert queries.

"Why would you say that?"

"Seems as though this Cade has been quite successful at getting the best of you on a regular basis.

The two suddenly face interruption by a visibly shaken woman.

"You assured me no one would be hurt!"

"Look, I told you we'd deal with them properly. Besides, your man wasn't hurt and he won't be if he decides to cooperate," the older Carrigan responds to Sandy's unexpected intrusion.

"You're an asshole! I should've known better. I should've known neither of you could be trusted! I'm going to Ankawa. I can't believe he really knows all about what's going on right now."

"Wouldn't do that if I were you," Robert tells her. "I know all about your condition, it would be a shame if it hit the papers that you'd committed suicide trying to kill an unwanted mixed-breed baby."

"What're you talking about? You son of a bitch...you're bluffing."

"Am I? Are you sure you want to take that chance? You forget; I own the police. Nobody's gonna do a thing to me. So, I'd suggest you keep your fucking mouth shut. Unless, of course, you'd like to have my son show you exactly what he did to our little Miss Wilson this evening."

Carrigan walks to a closet, reaches inside a small safe pulling out two bundles of bills, setting them on the end of his desk and sitting back down.

"What's that?" Sandy asks.

"Oh, about a quarter of a million dollars to be exact. Take that and disappear until this is over."

"If I don't?"

"You, your baby, and your man will all be dead before daylight."

She takes the money, stuffs it in her bag and walks out of the office.

"Put a couple of your best men on her. If she even looks like she's gonna do anything stupid, tell 'em to get rid of her."

"What about the others?

"As I said, they get outside our control, they could severely damage everything. Just make sure they don't arrive in Memphis. There are a couple of helicopters waiting at the Southlake hanger. They're both customized and fully armed. I've already called ahead and made the arrangements. The crews are on standby alert."

"I can't catch 'em now; even if I do, how will I be able tell if it's them?"

"Just get to Southlake. The crews will be at your full disposal."

Kirk's determination is growing as he walks from the office without saying another word, heading for the corporate hangers about twenty minutes away. Robert picks up the phone connecting him with the direct line to Ankawa.

"Good evening, everything is fine, sir. I have the situation under control...No, your son has not been harmed, nor will he be. We are in pursuit of them as we speak. We should be able to catch them and bring them all back. I assure you, everything within my power will be done to make sure your son is not harmed. Thank you, sir."

Once again, Carrigan hangs up, grinning, "I can't help it if there's an accident or two along the way."

Cade stays behind the wheel forty to forty-five minutes without thought of stopping. Reaching Greenville, Texas, he pulls off the interstate into a service station, gassing up for the longer trip ahead. Anderson and Cade change position, Anderson now behind the wheel. Back on the road, Cade finally decides he'll ask him what he'd been wanting to for several miles. "Where the hell did you get this jewel?"

"What, the car?"

"Yeah, the car. You're full of surprises lately."

"My dad. He thought it was a great way to buy my love and loyalty awhile back."

"Did it?"

"What do you think?"

"Don't know. You still got it."

"I tried to give it back. He wouldn't take it. So, I let it sit in the garage. I haven't driven it much since it was delivered. I had to take it out once just to see how it felt."

"You trying to tell me you had something like this sitting in your garage and you never had the urge to drive it?"

"I drove it. That's why I still have it. Not proud of that fact, but true."

"We need to stay around the limit," Danny breaks in on their conversation. "We don't need to get pulled over right now. Hard telling what the Dallas cops got out on us right now."

"She's probably right, Mark," Cade agrees, looking over at the speedometer, readily noticing Anderson's already well over the posted seventy.

"Got everything I need to take care of that," Anderson tells them. He reaches under the dash, flips a switch partially hidden from view. What looks like a radar detector lights up overhead.

"Never really trusted those things."

"Me neither," Danny adds to Cade's comment.

"Never had a stealth system built into your car before."

"You're shittin' me?" Cade responds.

"Nope. They'll never be able to clock us."

Back in Dallas, the cleanup around Anderson's is already underway. With the exception of a few stains on the bricked street, it'll look as though nothing happened tonight. The neighbor's calls to police have already fallen on deaf ears.

By now, the three on their way to Memphis pass through New Boston, just a few miles from Texarkana and the Arkansas/Texas border. Their conversation to this point has been nonexistent, each reflecting on the past events of the evening and wondering where it's going to lead them next.

"I guess now's as good a time as any to tell you, Danny," Mark says.

Cade looks at his friend, fully aware of what he refers.

"What're you talking about?" Danny asks.

"Ankawa...my father..." silence, with the exception of the wind outside rushing past, in, and around the Diablo's smooth design.

"I could've sworn you just said something about Ankawa being your father. Please tell me my mind is playing with me."

"You heard right."

"You've got to be kidding me. No wonder they've known what we had planned all along."

"Hold on, Danny," Cade interjects. "Give him a chance to explain. There's no way Mark would've done something like that. I'd stake my life on it."

She chuckles sarcastically. "I think you just did."

"Look. I don't blame you at all for feeling the way you do. But trust me; I'm as much against what he stands for as you or anyone else with the balls to go against him."

"Pull the damn car over now! Now, damn it! Did you hear me?"

Anderson brakes, downshifting quickly, bringing the car to a complete stop. Anderson's move at humoring Danny's latest command may or may not be successful.

"Cade...Outside! Now!" Danny nudges him forcefully.

The two engage in a heated discussion. Anderson watches, unable to hear most of their conversation, fully aware of the subject matter. Soon, back inside, Danny is a little more subdued than when she left. "OK, for the sake of discussion, let's say I do believe Cade and I'm willing to place my trust in you. Why should I?"

"My father's ideals and way of life have never mirrored my own. I've not lived with him since before college. I've barely had a conversation with the man. He and I absolutely, unequivocally do not see eye to eye on any subject. What Jason is telling you is true."

"What about Sandy?"

"What do you mean?" Anderson responds.

"I didn't want to tell you this, but you know that Ankawa plant I was talking about earlier...?

"No fucking way! You'll never convince me she's the plant. There's no way!"

"How do you know?" Cade jumps in, directing his question at Danny. "What makes you think she's the one?"

"This morning, she was asking an awful lot of questions, strange questions. You two were too wrapped up planning our escape from Dallas to notice, I guess. I sensed something was wrong, so I followed her."

"You did what? What the hell gives you the right?" Mark asks, incensed at her unfounded mistrust.

"Just a minute…I have every right! Piss on you! Piss on your thinking I have no rights either! I followed her and you want to know where she went?"

Silence…

"I'll tell you. She didn't go out of town today. She went to Ankawa's. Now why would she go there?"

Silence continuing.

"How would they have known what our plans were? Either of you tell 'em?"

More silence.

"I know I didn't."

Instead of a verbal response, Anderson immediately shifts the car into first, slamming the accelerator to the floor, pulling off the shoulder, onto the highway in front of an oncoming eighteen-wheeler. In a matter of seconds, he's ripped through two additional gears, taking the car and its passengers to eighty-five. His belligerence toward Danny, her latest statements, the possibility she could be right, is transferred to an aggression against those traveling Interstate 30 near midnight.

"Goddamn! These fucking truckers are a pain in the ass!"

In the left lane, Anderson flies past those intelligent enough to stay out of his way.

"Yeah, it's bad, but killing us now isn't gonna solve anything, man," Cade tells him.

Anderson slams on the brakes, barely avoiding another of the huge trucks pulling into the lane directly in front of them, nearly forcing them onto the median. Cade, by virtue of not having the time to put his seatbelt on yet, slides off his seat into the dash.

"Shit! What the hell you trying to do, Mark?"

"These fucking truckers! They all drive like they think they own the fucking highway!" With his latest statement barely out of his mouth, he blows the Diablo's horn. He follows the truck in front of them closely, tailgating, flashing lights, flipping the guy off as he passes, blowing the horn again. He continues accelerating the sports car until they are beyond the line of five trucks convoying along the busy highway. Danny glances over at the speedometer, watching it register ninety, ninety-five, approaching one hundred.

"Come on, Mark. You're gonna kill all three of us. Pull this crap on your own time, when I'm not around!" she admonishes.

"Screw you! I'll drive my damn car any way I want!"

"Hey!" Cade jumps in again, "You two need to calm down. Come on, Mark, there's no sense in this."

Texarkana, quickly in view, Anderson finally slows the car to a manageable speed, actually flirting with the posted speed limit. He glances at the gas gauge, deciding to pull in for a fill-up. He guns it into a Roadrunner, pulls up next to a pump, bringing the car to a complete stop. The style and make of the car has everyone's attention at the station. Anderson pops the gas spout cover from the inside, then jumps out to pump the gas. Danny and Cade remain in the car initially, just glad to have gotten this far alive.

"God. We need to get him from behind the wheel."

"Aw, he's just a little frustrated and pissed off. Can't say I blame him."

"So am I, but you don't see me trying to kill all of us."

"You don't know the complete story, Danny. He's got a lot to deal with right now, on top of all this. More than you'll ever know."

She accepts it for now. All three out of the car, Anderson finishes wiping off the windshield, the nozzle remaining in the spout, running unattended; clicking off once the sensors are splashed with fuel from the fully loaded tank. Cade grabs the hose, pulling it from the opening, placing it back on the stand.

Five eastbound semis have since pulled into the truck stop, one of the drivers recognizing the Diablo. The drivers all still inside their trucks, one picks up his CB mouthpiece.

"There's our god damned speed demon."

"Let's pay him a little visit," another replies.

By now, Cade and Danny have made the necessary pit stops while Anderson pays his bill, and then disappears inside the restroom. Danny and Cade walk toward the door.

"Shit!" Cade says, stopping just short of reentering the night air. He grabs Danny's arm to make sure she doesn't walk outside.

"What's wrong?"

"Looks like we got trouble."

The two look through the window as the five truckers look over the Diablo, one opening the door, crawling inside.

Kirk arrives at Corporate Hanger No. 3. Sitting in front are three new RAH-66's, fully loaded, fully armed. These futuristic experimental beauties have been fully customized to meet the needs and standards as set forth by Ankawa when Uncle Sam delivered them as partial payment for the programs Danny helped design. His ability to acquire such powerful airships is one more example of his influence and power in North America. Carrigan pulls his car into the hanger. Three full crews stand ready while he makes a final phone call with his remote. A few minutes later, he slowly crawls from the polished Vette, appearing to the others to be in a little pain.

"Any idea where we're headed tonight, boys?"

Captain of the fleet Sam Connors approaches, shaking the hand of this evening's superior. "Yes, sir. We've already programmed the coordinates and all three ships are fully fueled and cleared for departure."

"Any idea what we're lookin' for...what our mission is?"

"Yes, sir. We're looking for a late model Lamborghini Diablo. Our mission...seek it out, destroy it and the occupants. We've already dispatched a scout and they should be on the target soon."

"Good. Let's go."

As Carrigan straps himself into what will be the lead ship, the three RAH-66's lift into the air with their quiet 1350 shp engines revving to maximum thrust for departure.

"We gonna be able to catch 'em soon?"

"Sir, these beauties can do 170 knots. That's 196 miles per hour in layman's terms. We'll be on top of 'em before they know we're coming."

"Good. The necessity for secrecy on this mission...how's that being handled?"

"Sir, ships like these, once ships like these are finally produced for the government, won't have near the features these babies have. Each one of these ships is outfitted with Longbow radar and stealth properties, making it nearly impossible for detection by conventional radar systems. Anyway, we'll be flying too low for any radar system. Let's say we make a mistake and we gain excessive altitude, the radar jamming system should kick in nicely."

"Appears my boss has thought of just about everything."

"Yes, sir...including the armament load on each ship."

"Yeah?"

"Yes, sir. Each ship has a 20 mm, three-barrel Gatling cannon, and eight air-to-ground Hellfire's. Those babies have Lock on Radar capabilities with an Imaging Infrared seeker guidance package. We're capable of knocking a moving target out at night with no problem. Hell, like I said, our little three-ship armada is more advanced than anything the government has right now."

"How we gonna find 'em on the highway at night?"

"We're also equipped with Target Acquisition and Designation Sight/Pilot's Night Vision Sensor. The system's linked to these Helmet and Display Sight Systems. Here, try one on."

Carrigan slips the futuristic, somewhat stylish helmet over his head, amazed at what he's capable of seeing through the darkness. The Integrated Infrared System literally turns night into day. As they fly over Dallas, heading east, his vision, aided by the advanced system, penetrates the walls of the Hilton Tower. He readily notices body movement within several rooms at this late hour to be quite erotic in nature.

"I'm gonna have to get me one of these when we get back."

At the truck stop, Anderson prepares himself for battle, Cade refusing to let him out of the building. "Let me handle this. You've gotten us in enough trouble already."

"OK, OK, but I'll be right here if you need me."

"That's comforting to know."

Cade walks through the door and out toward the assembled group awaiting the arrival of the Diablo's driver. "Can I help you guys?" Cade asks, plenty nervous at this point.

"You the asshole behind the wheel of this thing?" asks the one called Doc, who steps up as spokesman for the group.

Anderson and Danny watch the group surround Cade. Anderson tries to exit the building, but Danny grabs his arm, halting his progress, asking him to give his friend a few more seconds. "Those guys look at all like they're gonna get physical, I'll be right there with you."

Within seconds, Cade is shaking their hands as they all walk away smiling. He turns, motioning to his traveling companions to join him as he slips behind the wheel.

"What the hell'd you tell 'em?" Anderson inquires.

"I convinced 'em I was the one driving, just having a little fun. I apologized, told 'em I used to drive trucks on the open road, just like my dad and his father before him. Just convinced 'em I was one of them. Seemed to satisfy 'em for now. But I'm not taking any more chances. I'm driving the rest of the way."

Cade starts the engine, pulling the Lamborghini away from the truck stop. In minutes, Texarkana is just another small glow in the car's ever-darkening rearview mirror.

Truck traffic remains extremely heavy into the night and into the journey, as Cade continues struggling to make any kind of time at all. The constant shifting to change speeds takes its toll on his arm. His left leg begins to cramp after depressing the clutch with every change. For as many truckers in a hurry to make their destinations, there are just as many in no hurry whatsoever. Cade can now fully appreciate his buddy's frustrations earlier tonight.

Approximately ninety minutes later, his two companions sound asleep; Cade pulls into the sleepy town of Arkadelphia. His initial challenge is to find somewhere he can pull over, sleep, and be safe. He doesn't believe he can go on any longer, but he doesn't want his buddy driving either.

The town is shut down completely. The clock on the dash tells him why. At one thirty-seven a.m., very little will be open. A few lights a couple of blocks away tug at his curiosity as he drives toward the luminescence. Reaching his destination, he discovers a twenty-four-hour coffee and donut shop, business surprisingly brisk at this hour of the morning. He pulls into its gravel parking lot, shutting down the powerful V-12.

Awakened by his turning off the interstate and pulling into the town, Danny and Mark find themselves in front of a donut shop in God Knows Where, USA.

"I'm buying," Cade announces. "What's your pleasure?"

"Get behind the wheel again," Anderson says.

The other two ignore his statement; Cade pulling the keys from the ignition, sliding out of the car to satisfy his need for food, coffee, and some stretching. Danny follows, Anderson left behind. Cade steps back to the car, "You want something?"

"Naw, I'll just sit here and snooze."

The two emerge from the shop to find Anderson firmly planted behind the wheel, unwilling to budge, supplied with another set of keys he'd grabbed on his way out the door in Dallas. He convinces them he's fine, in a better frame of mind, and ready to roll. As he steers the car back to the interstate, to the on-ramp and into traffic, their journey continues.

A very few miles into this next leg, their driver's aggressive posture stirs once again. He flashes his brights, blasts trucks as they pull in front of him to pass, and at one point, pulls to the right shoulder to pass two running side-by-side. That final maneuver clears them of trucks controlling the road. Driving the next several miles without incident, Cade and Danny feel like they can finally relax. Anderson, believing he has cleared the last group for a while, actually calms, slowing the car to within ten miles of the speed limit. Danny falls asleep, allowing her head passage to Cade's shoulder. He is about to nod off himself, when the Lamborghini hits the crest of a hill. Off in the distance, the two see taillights of another group rumbling along in the night.

Anderson begins his mental preparation for the next showdown. He approaches the rolling convoy ready to do whatever it takes to get past without slowing their momentum. Quickly at the rear of the convoy, his earlier tactics don't work this time. The trucks blocking their progress slow, forcing Anderson's downshift to third.

"Mark, don't push it. Let's just let them have their way and forget it. You're on their turf now."

"Fuck 'em!" is all he says before gunning the car to the far right shoulder, this time the truck in the right lane moving to the right in front of him to block passage.

By now, Danny's awake, taking to biting her fingernails. Something she hasn't done much of before. "Come on, Mark, give it a rest. Jesus!"

Another group of trucks hits the crest of the last hill to their rear, bearing down on their unsuspecting prey, four in number, two by two, side by side. By the time he does notice, it's too late. Three abreast in front of them, the four go to three abreast to the rear; one pulling to their left, another to their right, locking the sports car into a mobile prison he'll be unable to escape at this point, despite any fancy maneuvering.

Slowing to a crawl...synchronized like a team of swimmers, the convoy forces Anderson's downshift to second, then first. Tail lights in front them illuminate brightly, signaling a complete stop. The glare of headlights in the rearview mirror brightens as all behind them switch to their upper beams. Surrounded by headlights, tail lights, customized trailer lighting, gives those imprisoned the appearance of a close encounter with a UFO.

"Damn it, Mark! I told you not to push it!"

"Put that thing away!" Cade tells him, referring to the automatic Anderson produces from behind his seat.

"These assholes want a fight, I'm ready to give 'em one."

"You're dumber than I thought!" Danny tells him. "Jason, do something."

By now, the trucker contingent has climbed from their cabs, huddling together just a few feet away from the three sitting in the Diablo, traffic slowly building to the rear, backing up as other night travelers converge on the altercation.

Miles away, gaining rapidly, another group converges on the crowded situation currently taking place in middle America, apparently miles from nowhere.

Cade climbs out telling Danny and Mark to let him try to handle it one more time. The two waiting in the car hear Cade greet the group cordially, as he slams the door shut.

"Evening, gentlemen. Great night for a drive." He walks into the group, which quickly engulfs him, cutting any route for escape, cutting him off from sight of his two friends. Anderson reaches for the handle of his door with thoughts of coming to his friend's aid.

Danny doesn't try to stop him this time. She too fears for his well-being.

Outside, Anderson takes a couple of steps toward the group, prepared to expose his weapon, when he hears laughter. The laughter becomes loud and continuous as the group of men part and Cade emerges from the middle. As they all stroll toward Anderson, the sight of him creates additional, near hysterical laughter.

Cade walks past his friend, muttering under his breath. "Let's go! Now!"

Cade climbs into the driver's seat again, pushing his buddy out of the way. Anderson hesitates, but follows, climbing into the passenger side. Inside, with the doors closed, Mark initiates the questioning.

"What'd you tell 'em?"

Cade smiles. "You don't wanna know."

"Yeah, I do. What were they laughing at?"

"You."

"What do you mean? What did you tell 'em?" Anderson repeats his previous line of questioning.

"I'm telling you, you don't wanna know. Just leave it at that."

The Diablo, freed from its confinement, rolls through the eastside of Little Rock, passing quickly through Benton.

"I think there are a couple of all-nighters on the other side of Little Rock. We'll get gas there and call Josh. I wanna let him know we're just a couple of hours away. I'm sure he'll be real excited."

To the west, three armed gunships continue racing to catch them. The lead scout ship is almost upon them.

In Memphis, Josh Cade sleeps soundly. He expected his brother on the flight from Dallas last night. When he didn't come off the plane, he had no number to call in Dallas and no way to check on him.

The Diablo passes through Little Rock, covering that stretch of highway quickly. In minutes, one of the truck stops alluded to earlier, moves within sight. Cade pulls off the road, into the station, up to and next to a row of pumps.

The clock on the dash tells them it's around four. "If you'll fill her up, I'll call Josh and let him know. He's gonna love this wake-up call.

CHAPTER 18

ay phones at this truck stop are inside, unlike most. Cade leaves his friends to make his call.

The scout ship bears down on East Little Rock and quickly passes overhead, "whisper" mode engaged. Maneuvering a few miles east, it circles back toward an open field behind the truck stop. Anderson finishes pumping fuel, then pulls the car into a slot at the front of the building. He joins Danny inside at a booth, ordering coffee.

"Jason still on the phone?" Anderson inquires.

"Yeah," she pauses, "I need to ask you something."

"Shoot."

"Bad choice of words considering everything."

Anderson finds room for a smile.

"Why didn't you guys tell me about your father before? How long has Jason known?"

"First of all, it was my decision not to tell either of you. Jason just found out right before all this happened tonight. He wanted to tell you as soon as he found out. I wouldn't let him. I had to be sure."

"Sure about what? Whether you could trust me?"

"That and whether I was sure this was the route I wanted to take."

"I guess I can understand that."

"What you said about Sandy, I know you're wrong...has to be some kind of explanation."

"Hope so, Mark. All I know is what I saw. There could be a reasonable explanation," stating that which she does not really believe.

The phone rings on the other end. Cade waits for his brother to pick up and finally he does, groggy from a deep sleep.

"Yeah, who the hell is this? You realize what time it is?"

"Josh. Jason...Your brother, you ass."

"Where the hell were you tonight? I waited at the airport for at least an hour. Gave up a date and everything."

"Had a change of plans. Couldn't fly."

"Why not? What's going on?"

"Had to make the trip by car. It was our only option left."

"No shit? Where're you now?"

"Some truck stop just east of Little Rock. We should be there in a couple of hours."

"Good for you," his response a little cold. "Making pretty good time sounds like."

Neither says much for several seconds.

"Remember how to get around Memphis?" Josh asks.

"It's been awhile, but yeah. Don't have any idea where you're living now, though."

"Harbor Town...on Mud Island. Forty-three ten Riverview Drive. Think you can find it?"

"Yeah. I'll find it." Cade looks at his watch. "It's about two-thirty. Probably be there around five."

"By the way, don't knock or ring the doorbell. I've been pulling some weird hours lately and I'm trying to catch up on a little sleep. I'll leave the front door unlocked. Come on in and find somewhere to land. I'll see you all in the morning."

"OK. Sounds like a deal. See you later."

They end their conversation and hang up...Josh to go back to sleep...Cade to rejoin his friends. Walking toward the booth, he can tell there's some serious conversation going on between his two traveling companions. He sits next to Danny, pushing her over as he slides in.

Anderson's look is one of bewilderment, rolling his eyes into the top of his head.

"What's going on?" Cade asks, a question he would soon be sorry for asking.

"You guys didn't think you could trust me. That's what's wrong."

"What's she talking about?"

"I tried to tell her. Thought you were OK with this, Danny."

"This about his father, what?"

"That and several other things...We've got to keep this thing open and honest between us...can't trust anyone except each other now."

"I agree," Cade responds, Anderson nodding.

"That all you're gonna say?" Danny asks both.

"Uh, yeah, guess so. What did you want us to say?" Jason asks.

"I wanna know why neither of you thought you could fill me in about his father?"

Jason is a little uncomfortable with her questioning. "We were going to."

"When? After this is all over?"

"No, nothing like that."

Anderson knows his friend's in trouble. "It's all my fault. Told you I asked Jason not to tell you. OK? Let's just leave it at that for now."

"Naw, Mark, we're both in this thing together," he says, turning to Danny. "OK, we made...No, I made a huge mistake. I should've told you the second I found out. I'm sorry."

"That explains it," Danny jumps in.

"Explains what?" Anderson asks.

"She knew, didn't she?"

"She knew," Anderson acknowledges.

"That explains her little side trip to your father's corporate offices yesterday morning."

"Maybe she was just trying to help us," Cade jumps in trying to add a more positive spin to Danny's comments.

"I'm sure," Danny responds.

"What time was this, did you say?" Anderson inquires.

"Must have been around eight-thirty, quarter of nine...I don't know the exact time."

Anderson tries to add two and two in his head. *Her flight was around nine. If she stopped at my father's, she couldn't have made her flight. She barely had enough time to do that when she left the house. I remember her saying something as she left about possibly being late. If she missed her flight, what'd she do? Where'd she go?*

"Let's go," Cade tells the others. "I'm growing weary from all this. There's a couch at my brother's with my name on it." The three stand to leave, Cade reaching into his pocket to pull out the money needed to pay their bill and leave a tip.

"I'll get it," Anderson tells him.

Cade and Danny disappear outside ahead of him, as he stands in line to pay the bill. A couple of truckers ahead of him slow the usual progress, flirting with the cashier. Outside, two men have intercepted Danny and Cade.

When he finally emerges outside, he walks to the car fully expecting to see them both, but they are nowhere in sight, the passenger side door left up and open.

He surveys the vicinity, asking another traveler if he'd seen the two.

"Yeah, I may've saw 'em…some guy and a good-lookin' woman kinda were hangin' around that sports car there?"

"You see where they went?"

"Yeah, I guess."

"Look…can you tell me where they went?" his frustration growing and showing.

"Yeah. Sure I can. They walked around the building. Around that side over there," he says, pointing to the south side.

"Thanks." Anderson turns away to catch up with his traveling companions, on the way trying to figure out why they'd come around here.

"But it wasn't just the two of 'em." The guy tells him before he can get out of hearing range.

"What do you mean?"

"There was three other guys with 'em. Looked a little peculiar to me, them havin' suits on and all."

Anderson knows they're in trouble now, wheeling quickly, running toward the corner of the building. He rounds it, coming face-to-face with the sight of a large helicopter sitting in the field behind the truck stop. He dashes back to the Diablo, opening the baggage compartment, pulling out one of the duffel bags. "I knew this stuff would come in handy," he mumbles.

Cade and Wilson stand a few feet from the ship, its blades continuing to whirl. The flurry of activity increases as the men and the ship's pilot prepare for departure, "Ankawa" painted boldly on its side. Both know if they step onto the helicopter it's over. Cade's about to make a move he hopes will free his traveling companions, as Anderson opens fire with his automatic to get their attention. They return fire and the pilot quickly engages his turbo. Anderson shoves a shell into his flare gun, firing a warning shot over the sitting ship. As the flare fired from Anderson's gun flies overhead and lands in a field of dried stubble it ignites a small fire that quickly begins to grow. The pilot, a little concerned and nervous, motions to everyone they need to go. Loading a second shell, Anderson takes aim. A second flies toward the ship, landing in front, just missing it by a few feet. By now, the men in suits have turned their attention toward the building.

Cade tries to seize the moment, breaking free, slamming his body into their personal bodyguard for a takedown. Recovering quickly, the guy aims his weapon at Cade lying on the ground at his feet.

Anderson drops to his knees, grabbing another pellet, cramming it into the open barrel, snapping it shut in quick preparation for his next shot. He pulls the trigger, sending the next flare toward Cade's attacker, igniting the man's clothing, turning him into a human torch. Cade grabs the gun dropped to his side, taking down the man now firing at Anderson.

The pilot gooses his heavy machine into the air as the field fire surrounds him, growing out of control. His escape to safety becomes paramount over all other priorities at the moment. Cade rolls over, facing up, firing several rounds toward the departing ship, hitting its fuel tank. As he does, fuel begins falling toward the ground, creating puddles still linked to the rising aircraft. Within seconds, growing ground fire has spread toward the accumulating fuel, igniting it; sending flames streaking upward like a lit fuse on a keg of dynamite.

Anderson, forty-five in hand, continues firing several rounds, providing cover as Danny and Cade run toward the building. His target practice continues to pay off. The half-full tank of the ship about to depart ignites. The ensuing explosion rocks the truck stop, many joining the three travelers, few witnessing all that has happened prior to that moment. Knocked unconscious, its pilot falls forward onto the control stick, pushing the remaining hull into a left list toward the two scrambling for safety on the ground. The impact of the burning ship as it slams to the ground produces a second massive explosion, throwing liquid fire and smoke high into the air. Another explosion throws the blade from atop the crumbling ship, its rotation unimpeded as it hits the ground behind Cade and Wilson. The uninterrupted momentum drives it toward the two, as they move to a running position. The large, spinning rotor blade gains on them, closing from behind. Diving for Anderson, Danny is pulled to safety. It looks as though Cade will lose his legs and more, when suddenly the slicing, spinning blade hits an area of recent construction, digging itself into are area of softened earth and abruptly making its final rotation deep into the ground, stopping no more than two feet from Cade's outstretched torso.

Anderson slides behind the wheel of the car, starting the engine as Cade and Wilson quickly make it inside. In the distance, sirens can be heard as the local fire department and sheriff have been alerted. Tromping the accelerator, he takes the Diablo out across the intersection adjacent to the truck stop. He hasn't turned his lights on yet, to aid their departure and clean escape. With darkness surrounding them, the deputy sheriff doesn't see the black car gaining speed up the on-ramp into interstate traffic.

"Shit! They don't give up, do they? How the hell did they know?" Cade wonders out loud.

"Didn't figure they would," Anderson answers.

Reunited, the three move out on the highway, speed capabilities of the Diablo a definite benefit.

Fifteen to twenty minutes have passed. The fire of the downed ship still rages in the field behind the truck stop. In the distance, to the west, a single light above the horizon brightens, and then separates into three distinctive sets as Kirk and his men continue closing the gap on their renegade fugitives. The trailing gunship's close on the truck stop. Reaching the area of the burning ship, flying overhead, Kirk's lead ship circles back to check out the damage, while the others continue on with their pursuit due east. As soon as semi-charred remains are identified as the scout through infrared sensors, the hovering ship turns east, racing to catch the others.

Anderson reaches under the dash, flipping the car's stealth system on. "We're gonna need this baby now." He shifts the car into fifth, pushing it, headlights now on, past one hundred miles per hour. They pass every vehicle in sight as though objects standing still. The Lamborghini approaches other cars and trucks so quickly; Anderson must use the best path available to make it around them, a couple of times taking a shoulder on either side.

The Diablo clears Brinkley, midpoint between Memphis and Little Rock, the machine's stealth system still fully engaged. Just a few minutes later, three warships fly over the same little east Arkansas town, the gap continuing to close.

Thirty-two miles west of Memphis, Kirk and his armada finally catch their prey. The ship's five-blade bearing less main rotor with its high-hinge offset, greatly aids maneuverability...its shark like airframe slices through the night air with little effort or sound. The captain maneuvers his ship, his right-handed stick controller generating easy and simple "yaw" control, changing direction with the slightest touch. Each ship's numerous automatic modes create pure pleasure for any pilot lucky enough to be at its controls. Undetected by radar, their infrared signature suppression will not be a factor tonight. Although this particular warship will not be available to the government until the early twenty-first century, Ankawa's billions, his contacts, and his power have all produced relative easy access to some of the first prototypes. As far as the government is concerned, not one of these ships exists, the UFO theory clearly in practice.

Infrared scanner on, the gunnery mate looks for the image of the Diablo...the car's design plugged into the computer system for simplified recognition. Once infrared sensors lock on, the process and dissemination of information within the ship's onboard computer will begin, within seconds allowing unquestionable detection of their target. With little chance of another car of this styling on the road tonight, the lead ship's navigator quickly announces his find. "Locked in on our target, sir. Looks like we got her."

A chance to finally put the Helmet and Display Sight System to real use, Kirk slips it back over his head, locking visual onto the suspected car traveling at a high rate of speed below. "Looks like there's three inside...I agree with your man; it appears we've finally caught their asses."

Within seconds and on top of them, Captain Lawrence orders the other ships to semi-stationary positions several hundred feet above the moving target; telling Carrigan they are about to conduct a class in the art of elementary seek and destroy.

"Wake up...not sure, but think we got company!" Anderson yells at his passengers.

Cade comes out of his light sleep, Danny raising her head from his shoulder, following his actions slightly delayed.

"What're you talking about?" Cade asks, turning to look back down the road, seeing only the normal headlights in the distance, tail lights from those driving west. He checks his watch, looks back ahead; seeing the lights of Memphis glowing against the low partial cloud cover hovering over the city.

"What're you talking about? I don't see anything."

Anderson points to the car's roof.

"...You getting religious on us all of a sudden?"

"We may all need a little of that right now. Hear the hum?'

"Now that you mention it," Cade answers.

"Not the car."

Cade lowers his window, sticking his head out to look above, immediately seeing lights reflecting off the base of the gunships. Anderson's already thinking survival, glancing down the stretch of highway ahead. His acceleration tells the others the chase is on.

"How far we from Memphis?" Danny asks.

"Not more than twenty miles," Anderson tells her.

The Diablo reaches a speed of one hundred ten on the straightaways, little match for the machines flying just a few hundred feet above.

"Whatever we do now, we can't stop," Danny states the obvious.

"Don't intend to," Anderson replies.

"What the fuck you waitin' on?" Kirk asks Lawrence.

"They're about to pass a convoy of trucks. Can't chance more collateral damage than is necessary. This has to be a clean takeout. We'll fly ahead; wait to clear, meet 'em head on."

"Lights comin' at us on the horizon. Must be Memphis. We gotta take 'em out soon," Kirk states unequivocally.

No reply to Carrigan's latest statement, the captain knowing fully what he must do.

"Black Knight to support ships...On my command, initiate a flyby, proceed five kilometers forward, return with open fire. Acknowledge."

"Knight Commander, this is Lancelot I...acknowledged."

"Knight Commander, Lancelot II...acknowledged."

Inside the Diablo, the three sit in silence, feelings distinctively different, as are curiosity levels as to what will happen next, one experiencing heart palpitations of extreme nature. Anderson hasn't let up on his speed, or desire to catch the caravan now seconds from impregnation, quickly entering the moving motor fortress.

Captain Lawrence gives his command. "Lancelot I and II, initiate sortie."

"Roger that, Knight Commander."

The two attack ships drop from the sky to within a couple hundred feet of the ground, slamming past the car and its caravan on both sides.

"There's more than one! Could be in some real deep shit here, folks," Cade says, observing the obvious.

The attack ships shoot down the interstate, leaving the caravan behind.

"Look, they're leaving," Danny observes, relaxing slightly.

Before those last words leave her mouth, the two ships separate, flying an outward loop away from each other, away from the highway, out of sight of those in the Diablo. Within seconds, their lights bear down on the convoy as they join each other in attack formation. Their pass will be at approximately 500 feet, the initial flyby warning initiated.

"Shit! They're coming back!" Cade yells.

"What do you think they're doing?" Danny asks.

"Don't know," Anderson replies. "Brace yourselves. Make sure your belts are on. I'm gonna try to react to their moves. Don't have any idea where things are going from here."

Within a few thousand feet and closing fast, the gunners aboard each ship grip their triggers tightly. Almost upon them, Lancelot I and II simultaneously fire the initial warning shots from their Gatling canons, strafing rice fields to the left and right of the caravan. Each shot rips through soil and irrigation water like tiny explosions from a grenade launcher. This likely to be the most exciting thing to happen to these truckers in some time, waking some who were most likely driving half asleep, they are all now on a heightened alert. One thing is clear, all are unsure of just what the hell is going on.

"Shiiiiiiiiiit!" the three in the Diablo yell simultaneously.

Truckers in and around the target jump on their CBs.

"What the hell's goin' on, fellas?"

"Not a clue, pardner. Sure as hell woke my ass up."

"Either the city of Memphis sent out a welcome party, or somebody's trying to stop us from gettin' there. For what damn reason, I ain't got a clue."

"Guys, this is Country Flash, ya'all noticed the little sports car's been ride'n under our skirts? You think those guys could be after 'em?"

"Don't know, Flash. Only one way to find out."

Anderson notices the rigs surrounding him beginning to maneuver into some sort of position slowing, exactly the way it had happened back down the road earlier in the trip.

"Shit! You sons a bitches are not gonna do that again."

Looking for an opening, he sees one, but it's also closing fast.

"Hang on!" he yells, slamming the accelerator to the floor, shifting into third, then quickly to fourth as the Diablo shoots out of its improvised cover, into the open.

Carrigan sees their latest maneuver as a reaction and an answer to the warning. "No more games. Take 'em out!"

"Yes, sir. Lancelot I and II, this is your captain. Eliminate target."

The two attacking ships begin their final run, dropping to attack altitude, arming Hellfire's while in the process. Missile rails, fully loaded, fully armed, drop from the stowed position inside the ships' bellies. Using their Imaging Infrared system, their missiles will seek out the exhaust of a very hot-running Diablo.

"Man, I need a phone!" Cade announces.

"What the hell's a phone gonna do for you now? You gonna call 911?"

"No asshole, my brother."

"In the glove compartment," Anderson tells him.

Cade opens it, seeing the phone, pulling it out, flipping it open and dialing. Once again, a groggy voice...

"Josh! Jason!"

"What the hell you want now?" Josh looks at his LCD on the nightstand next to him. "Man, why are you calling me at this hour?"

"Just shut up and listen to me! I'm in big trouble! Outside Memphis! They've caught us!"

"Who's caught you...what the hell you talking about?"

"Ankawa! They're on our asses right now and they aren't playing games!"

Josh sits up in bed. "Where are you?"

Cade searches for any sign to give his brother their exact location. "I know we're just west of Memphis. There! Just passed Shell Lake."

"OK. Doesn't give me much time. Can you make it to Memphis?"

"Don't know. We're trying like hell!"

Deep in conversation, Cade takes his mind off the war ships as they prepare to stick a couple of Hellfire's up the Diablo's exhaust.

From the command ship..."Lancelot I and II, fire at will."

Missiles explode from their mounted tubes, streaking toward the speeding car, passing to its right and left. As they do, their pass is so close; the three in the Lamborghini can see the trail of burnt fuel from each. Unknown to Mark, his father's fully customized gift includes the same infrared suppressers as those on a RAH-66.

"What the hell! Man, they're firing missiles at our asses!" Cade yells into the phone.

The two wayward missiles fly up the exhausts of two tractor trailer rigs moving east and a couple of thousand feet in front of them; the ensuing explosion demolishing both completely. Contents of the two trucks explode from their trailers, one carrying a load of food products, the other furniture.

"Watch the shit!" Cade yells as something white, wet, and slimy, sprinkled with glass slivers slams across the windshield, temporarily blinding their vision. Wood splinters from furniture on board the other creates a hazardous obstacle course.

"Lancelot, this is Knight Commander. Switch off infrared, go to Laser."

"What the hell?" Josh asks after hearing the explosion over the phone.

"I told you, man. They're shooting at us!"

"Get your ass to Memphis! Take the northern route to the lighted bridge...the big M. You know what I'm talking about?"

"Yeah, no problem."

"After crossing the bridge, take the first exit...Riverside Drive. The Pyramid's on the left. Can't miss it. I'll be waiting."

Cade finishes relaying his brother's directions to Anderson who acknowledges receipt. He drops the phone to the seat between him and Danny.

Anderson continues his maneuvering, as he attempts outwitting the war ships dogging their tails. Each time he pulls into the protection of a small convoy, the gun ships blow the trucks clear off the road. Watching from a distance, Carrigan becomes more pissed at each unsuccessful passing second.

Before anything more can be said, the two attack copters pass them on each side, low to the ground. Taking the same approach as before, about five kilometers out, the ships make their loops and are on their way back once again. The three occupants' emotions have risen to a level of complete and unadulterated fear, triggered by the sight of those same lights elevated in the air now coming toward them again. Anderson floors the accelerator, speeding beyond one hundred ten, his instinctively devised plan to reach three semis slowing ahead. The Diablo completes zipping through the smoking rubble spread across the two lanes before them. Danny grabs Cade's arm, burying her face in his shoulder. Any other time, he would have been ecstatic with her recent move.

Reaching the trucks, Anderson quickly downshifts, slamming on his brakes at the same time, easing into the perceived protection of the big rigs. The two ships slam past their intended target, unable to fire on them this pass as planned. Watching from a distance, Carrigian is getting more pissed by the second. "What happened? What the hell's goin' on? I thought you guys were supposed to be able to handle this!"

"Look, Mr. Carrigan. My men are preparing to take out the target. Our desire is not to take out any more innocents than necessary."

"I don't give a fuck about any of that! Just take that damned Diablo out and do it now, or Ankawa's gonna know you guys can't perform as advertised. They make it to Memphis; every one of you'll be in the tank! I can promise you that! I should've known you couldn't handle the assignment."

"Lancelot I and II, this is Knight Commander. Disregard protection of innocents...collateral casualties no longer a concern. Take target out, whatever the cost."

"What the hell do you make of it?" one trucker asks another over his CB.

"Can't say as I can tell. That looked like Bobby's and Luther's rigs they just blew up!"

The three Diablo passengers perspire profusely. "Boy, we're all going to need a bath when this is over," Danny observes.

"May not matter after tonight," Cade responds.

The guys both lower their windows for some fresh air. As Cade does, one of the copters appears to the right, a few feet above ground, progressing alongside the caravan.

"Shit!" Cade yells.

Seeing what has distressed his partner so, Anderson jerks the car left, pulling it into the passing lane, just in front of another truck trying to pass. Anderson pulls even with the truck he was following, using it as a shield to his right. To their left, the other ship appears.

Both engage their Gatling canons, a couple of shots barely missing the car, but damaging their cover. Anderson has since accelerated beyond his right shield. Gatling fire rips through the trailer of the big rig and its contents...explosives. The larger than expected explosion forces both ships to yaw from their immediate positions, dangerously close to elimination. The Diablo shakes violently as explosives continue detonating behind them, but the car survives each blast and resulting shock wave.

"Man, that was too close for comfort," one of the pilots tells his gunner.

For the next couple of miles, the cat-and-mouse game continues, Anderson actually appearing to get the better of his two hunters, his defensive driving skills improving with each passing second.

Unable to manage a clear shot at the speeding sports car, Ankawa's air force continues its pursuit, maneuvering for the best angle. The entourage rounds a curve heading into the town of West Memphis, Arkansas, on the west banks of the Mississippi. Six miles from Memphis and the lighted bridge spanning the river, the small convoy should begin breaking up, trucks pulling to safety as they ease into the twenty-four-hour weigh station, but for some reason, instead of pulling off, those in the convoy stay the course. Intrigued, maybe a little excited about the action developing on an otherwise dull night, the truckers have made a pact to stay with the sports car to Memphis, the convoy now beginning to grow in size as word appears to be getting out.

At the weigh station, Arkansas patrol cars sit, the occupying troopers standing outside their cars visiting with one another. As the early morning convoy passes, complete with flying war ship escorts; they react.

"What the hell's going on?"

"Let's go. I'll get on the radio. We may need help!"

Truckers again maneuver their rigs into a mobile fortress.

The trooper to the rear of the convoy radios a dispatcher for help. "This is Trooper Riley, car one eighty-five."

"Go ahead one eighty-five."

"You better get some backup...got a bad situation developing."

"What's your location one eighty-five?"

"I'm about a mile outside West Memphis, heading due east. You better patch me into Memphis. Looks like that's where they're headed."

Kirk slices through the technical chatter transferring from one ship to the other. "Take 'em out! If you have to blow every fuckin' truck off the road to do it, do it!"

As the moving fortress reaches the city limits, both airships fire one round each, missiles flying from their nest. One hits its intended target, blowing a trailer to pieces. The other misses, striking a restaurant on the side of the road. The resulting explosions send flames and smoke high into the air, rocking those trucks still churning along the interstate, waking those living in this small east Arkansas community. Anderson keeps the Diablo on course, looking for an opportune time to catapult from his cover.

Sitting across the river; pulling into position, waiting for his brother and friends, Josh Cade can see the explosions in the distance, muffled sound delayed by distance, hitting him seconds after each occurrence. "What the...naw...couldn't be."

The Memphis skyline, the lighted bridge spanning the Mississippi, the ultramodern Pyramid...each offers a stark contrast to this region's Civil War heritage. Directly to his rear, lights from the Pyramid and other buildings illuminate the immediate area. Peering through a set of binoculars, he looks for the sports car as described by his brother in their last conversation. He picks up his car phone, punching in a number he knows by heart.

East of West Memphis, past the greyhound racing track, the truck stops...the chase continues. Another Hellfire slams into an eighteen-wheeler carrying steel beams slightly exceeding the length of its trailer. A direct hit and ensuing explosion lifts the trailer from its cab, snapping cables holding steel girders in place, sending those beams into trailing trucks. Cade turns just in time to see one on its way toward the Diablo. He has no time to speak; or yell out a warning as a twenty-foot piece of metal slices across the top of the car, creasing it with a quarter-inch gash. Sparks from that contact; fly off to all sides. Anderson can feel the tug from the beam as it almost pulls the Diablo off the road with it. The piece clears in seconds, landing on the highway in the westbound lanes, forcing traffic to a complete stop. The dwindling caravan rounds its final curve. The sight before them has an enormous emotional effect on all three. The well-lit skyline ahead, the bridge, the Pyramid... are welcome sights.

"There it is!" Cade blurts out. "He said he'd be there waiting for us!"

Appreciative of their protection the last few miles, Anderson knows he'll need to leave it and make his move now. As he does, the action resembles the birthing of a newborn leaving its protective womb, cutting the umbilical, into the protective arms of an awaiting doctor. His quick and unannounced maneuver surprises the attack ships' pilots, giving him an advantage of precious seconds. In the space just previously occupied by the Diablo, rockets slam to the pavement, creating massive explosions, producing craters in the blacktop. That explosion forces those trucks and the troopers following too closely, off the road, down the embankment and into adjacent fields.

The phone sitting between Cade and Danny rings. Once, twice, three, four times...

"You gonna answer it?" Danny asks.

Cade reaches between them, pulling it out. "Hel...hello."

"Jason! That you guys causing all the racket?"

"Josh?"

"You weren't pulling my leg."

Cade listens intently as Anderson quickly approaches the bridge ahead of the pack, climbing the highway to a perceived safety.

The two airships have their target in sight. A clear shot this time will end the chase, allowing them to head back to Dallas, mission accomplished. Gunners reach for their controls, depressing the triggers to unload their rails. At the same time Anderson slams his foot, already on the accelerator, decisively to the floor, ripping through final gears. More of the same: numerous explosions, all shaking the speeding Diablo, missed opportunities by incompetent, ill-trained gunners.

Josh watches a speeding car fly across the bridge. Already in his Mitsubishi 3000, he turns it away from the Pyramid, toward the bridge, driving under it toward the intersection of Jefferson and Riverside Drive and the expected point of rendezvous. The black Diablo flies past the turnoff he had communicated his brother needed to take.

"Shit! You missed the damned turn!" Jason yells.

"Hell, I didn't know! I don't know the area! You didn't say a damned thing!" Anderson yells back.

Cade's memory engages. "Take Danny Thomas! We'll double back! Have to do a little adlibbing from here!"

The gun ships catch them once again, tracking the car's route flying slightly above the city's skyline. Kirk and his ship continue lagging behind, surveying the faltering progress of the chase.

Josh passes through the intersection where they were to meet, pulling his car up Riverside to Front. He stops, spotting the helicopters flying to the far eastside of the immediate downtown area. He shifts before flooring the accelerator.

"Turn here! Right!" Jason directs.

"This is a one-way street!" Danny yells, offering her only navigational contribution to this point.

"You see anyone out driving this hour besides us?" Cade responds.

Trying to outguess their next turn, Josh continues his search through downtown Memphis, reaching a speed of over sixty, traveling north on Front. Anderson, with his navigator's directions now has the Diablo at sixty to sixty-five, traveling back to the west on Poplar, approaching the Poplar and Front Street intersection. The speeding Mitsubishi approaches from the south. Within seconds, both cars hit the intersection, missing each other by inches, both slamming their brakes, spinning out to a complete stop a few feet from one another.

"What the hell?" Anderson yells as the Diablo comes to complete and decisive stop, pointed south. The Mitsubishi completes its three-sixty, Josh pulling it up alongside, the window on the passenger's side of the Mitsubishi down. Anderson releases his from its locked position.

"I ought to arrest your ass for reckless driving!" Josh yells.

"I had the green light! You didn't," Anderson answers.

Lights from the helicopters illuminate the intersection. Gunfire erupts from the Gatling's, hitting the ground around them, hitting the bumper of the Mitsubishi, knocking it completely off.

"Shit! Assholes!" Josh hollers, pulling a gun from the seat next to him, unloading the clip at his attackers. "Let's get the hell outta here! Whatever you do, whatever happens, stay on my ass till I stop! Got a little surprise for those shitheads."

Josh Cade pulls away, tires screeching, headlights off.

"Lights off!" Jason commands his pilot.

Anderson shifts, flooring the accelerator almost simultaneously, following Cade's brother down Front, right at Beale, left at Riverside. In the darkness of the early mid-South morning, Anderson's vision of the car to his front is aided by the glow of streetlights. Braking at the intersection of Beale and Riverside he realizes too late he will take the turn on two wheels. After a series of fishtails, both cars speed south on Riverside.

Danny glances to her right at the Mississippi, which she's never before seen in her life. She notices the lights of a tug slowly pushing several interlocked barges to the north.

This stretch is a good one to build speed. The attack ships drop to within a few hundred feet of the ground, immediately on top of the speeding cars. Gunners continue firing, missing by inches, another barely clipping the Mitsubishi again.

"You sons a bitches!" the younger Cade yells. Josh maneuvers his car from one lane to another, Anderson following his lead, doing the same.

Within seconds, the cars disappear around a curve between groves of trees on either side of the road, climbing out of the Mississippi River bottom to higher ground. As the road straightens, continuing their climb, the two drivers come face-to-face with a roadblock. Parked under an overhead walkway spanning the road, Memphis and Shelby County law enforcement officers stand ready, guns drawn.

"Shit! What's your brother gotten us into now?"

"Just do what he said! Follow him all the way!"

Just before smashing through, two cars in the middle of the roadblock part, allowing enough room for one. Anderson continues on course, right on his tail. Josh brakes instantly after clearing the mass of cruisers. His tail lights flashing to an extreme brightness without warning, Anderson is barely able to stop the speeding Diablo just short of ramming the back of his leader.

Gunfire explodes behind them, officers opening up on the two helicopters immediately on top of their position. The small caliber guns appear to be no match for the Gatlings or the survivability kits, including floor armor...bullets bouncing off the armored ships. The element of surprise is. Startled and initiating instinctive evasive maneuvering, the lead ship's pilot pulls back on his controls, lurching upward into the path of the trailing ship. The lead ship's eight-blade, fan-in-fin, anti-torque rotor catches the front of the other, slicing into its cockpit through the thick glass shield. The piercing sound of fan blade metal against metal, breaking glass, the ensuing explosion, sends debris in all directions, providing those living on the bluff a premature wake-up call. Many will believe they've just experienced at least a 7.0 magnitude earthquake of the New Madrid Fault. Remains of the trailing, mangled ship lists to a severe right, falling into the Mississippi. The remaining tangled mess falls to the pavement, erupting in several additional explosions, courtesy of the remaining armament onboard. Anderson, Danny, and Cade all sit in the car, out of breath, in total disbelief of their latest early morning episode.

Surveying the results of the chase from a distance, Kirk orders the ship's commander to head for Dallas. "You won this one, assholes, but I can guarantee all of you, it's not over."

CHAPTER 19

Out of his car and walking toward the Diablo, Josh notices Danny through its windshield before acknowledging anyone else. Despite the most recent harrowing experience, her beauty stands out in the semidarkness. Mark and Jason climb out to greet him, thanking him for his help as two of the ships once chasing them burn near the riverbanks.

"What the hell'd you do to piss 'em off?" Josh asks, looking beyond his brother and Mark, watching Danny finish her climb from the car.

"We can talk about that later. Right now I could sure use a bathroom, a beer, maybe somewhere to rest this weary body. It does have to be in that order," Jason responds.

"OK, but you guys are gonna have to give a statement about what's going on here. You can't just come into town, create a ruckus like you just did, and go to bed. I can probably persuade them to let you all sleep and talk tomorrow. Who's the babe?"

Jason turns to verify he's talking about Danny. "Her name's Danny Wilson. She's the reason for all this. Don't think you want to get involved."

"I'll be the judge of that." Josh walks up to the car and opens the door to help her out. "Hi. Josh...Josh Cade. Already know who you are. Maybe my older brother mentioned me," the younger Cade making a point to emphasize older.

"My pleasure," Danny greets him wearily.

The sibling rivalry has reemerged immediately between the two brothers who haven't seen each other for some time.

"You gotta be someone real special to get Jason to go through all this. After his divorce, he swore off women forever. Said they weren't worth the trouble. You OK?" he asks.

"...Doing fine now."

"Listen, you did the right thing, coming here, I mean. I've got friends and connections and I can protect you from whoever it is you're running from. I don't think anybody will be bothering you again." Their conversation diverts their attention away from the Memphis Fire Department's task at hand, extinguishing the last of the fires among the gun ship ruins. Kirk speeds westward, already deep into Arkansas airspace. "You must have uncovered something pretty important to this Ankawa—I mean, for him to take such an interest in you."

"How'd you know it was Ankawa?"

"Uh, you know my brother...can't keep anything to himself."

"I don't remember..." Jason begins.

"About that beer and shower...You three ready to go?"

"Lead the way," Anderson tells him climbing into the Diablo's passenger side. "You drive this time," he tells Jason.

"Danny...you coming?"

"She can ride with me," Josh jumps in.

The elder Cade climbs behind the wheel, kicking in the Diablo's powerful V-12, not yet cooled from their long trip. Danny climbs into the Mitsubishi, Josh closing the door once she's safely inside. Minutes later at Josh's apartment on Mud Island, the three guys drink beers while Danny showers not far from where they sit.

"So we gotta go talk with the FBI and the police tomorrow?" Jason asks his brother.

"Yeah. These guys stepped out on a limb for you three tonight. My ass is hanging somewhere out there too."

"I guess that'll be OK."

"They want all three of you in their offices no later than one."

"Speaking of time," Mark says.

"Five. Five in the morning," the younger Cade replies.

"I'm getting some sleep. I don't care who's after us," Mark tells the brothers.

"Man, the girl's hot," Josh repeats an earlier observation.

"Yeah, I guess. I'm not so sure she's worth all the trouble," Jason says smiling, unaware Danny has just entered the room.

"Look, nobody asked you to get involved."

"I didn't mean..."

"Danny, can I buy you a drink? Step into my bar. I make the best margaritas, daiquiris...you make the call."

As Josh and Danny disappear into the kitchen..."That son of a bitch..."

"What's wrong?"

"He's already making his play."

"Give me a break, he's just being hospitable."

"Josh could never let me date anyone without trying to take her away, usually with great success I might add. It's always been a game for him."

"Don't know about that, but you can't let this sibling rivalry get in the way of what's ahead of us."

"You're right, of course."

"Hey! What's with you? It's not like you've even gotten to first base with the woman. I haven't seen any major attraction either way and now you're worried about your brother moving in on you?"

In the kitchen, the conversation has a slight similarity to the one going on just a few feet away in the other room. "Memphis, what I had the opportunity to see anyway, is a pretty town, the skyline and all," Danny begins.

"Yeah, guess you weren't in much of a position to sight see on your way in tonight, huh?"

"You could say that."

"Where or how'd you and my older, and I stress older brother meet?"

She smiles. "We met on a plane a few weeks ago." She stops momentarily. "God, it seems like so long ago. Anyway we met on a plane. I was ending a relationship with another man; Jason kind of came into my life at a very inopportune time...for him anyway."

"You telling me you and my brother are in some kind of relationship right now?"

"No, not really. He's been great to help me with my crisis and all, but no, no relationship."

"You sound a little disappointed."

"Just tired…"

Outside, the sun is already beginning to rise in the east, slowly adding a low-level brightening to the early day. Traffic begins its daily ritual, normal people with normal lives beginning their daily trek to work. Along the Mississippi at Riverside, little evidence remains of the incidents from earlier this morning, with the exception of an area of charred ground. In the morning paper, late-night filming of a new movie will be the explanation given for all the early morning commotion.

"Danny, you take the spare," Josh tells her as they re-enter the living area, finding her two traveling companions asleep in a chair and on the couch. "I've gotta leave for a while, but I'll be back in time to make sure you get where you need to go. In the meantime, didn't you say you had a couple of disks with some information? Let me take 'em with me. I'll get someone at the lab to look 'em over this morning. We'll let them tell us what they make of your information."

Danny looks at Jason to see if he's awake, wanting to ask him for his approval.

His eyes closed: he speaks. "You can trust him. With all his faults, you can trust his integrity."

"Thanks for the vote of confidence, big brother. Appreciate the support."

Danny reaches into her small bag, pulling out the four disks. "Guard these with your life. They almost cost us ours." She hands him the disks, reluctantly, as though parting with her firstborn.

Josh drops them in his small briefcase after trying to unsuccessfully slide them inside his uniform's shirt pocket and leaves.

Within minutes, Danny has fallen asleep in the spare bedroom. Jason moves from the couch and lands on his brother's bed, asleep within seconds as well.

Josh spends the next couple of hours in his office, looking at the disks. The information could be very damaging to the efforts of Ankawa, if this is factual stuff. In the hands of the right public relations firm, it could also be made out to mean nothing. He reaches for his cell phone, making a long-distance call.

A few minutes later in Ankawa's private office, "I'm very thankful to you for your work. To know my son is safe is comforting. However, the fact they have made it to Memphis at the expense of some very good men and the millions of dollars lost in equipment is very disturbing. Our alliance in this matter is of the utmost importance to me right now...As I said when you contacted me earlier, you will profit greatly from your work...You must be very careful not to allow them to find out that someone so close to them, is in my employ...I am very confident you will complete your assignment in a timely matter. However, should you take longer than anticipated, I must eventually intervene. May the great Kami guide and protect you." Ankawa sets the receiver down.

Back in Memphis, Josh lays the phone on his desk.

Later, he returns to his apartment as promised. Upon his arrival, around noon, he finds no one awake. The noise he generates will take care of that. As Danny walks into the room, Josh sets their immediate agenda. "We gotta leave soon if we're gonna make those debriefings."

The bulk of their time is spent waiting, adding valuable time to their actual debriefings and time spent in the federal building. Josh seizes the opportunity to grab Danny for a personal tour. After the tour and in his office, he invites her to sit down. He then offers her a cup of coffee, or a Coke. She readily accepts the Coke.

"Danny, I've looked at your disks."

"And...?"

"And, looks like you may have something. I'm not sure how we go about exposing this mess, but if I have the time to dig into it, I think we can figure out the necessary next steps. Of course I've turned them over to the FBI, as promised. They may be able to help you. They'll get their analysts to look at them. However, by the very nature of what I saw this morning in those disks, there may already be a covert operation under way we normal citizens would know nothing about. I'll be able to tell by the response I get."

"How long do you think it'll take?"

"Could take a couple of weeks, could take six months. I asked them to get right on it. These are friends of mine and experts digging into stuff like this. They owe me. When they promise something, they usually deliver."

"If there is this 'covert' operation under way...?"

"If there is, it means they're already on it. Probably won't help us."

"In the meantime...?"

"In the meantime, we get to spend some time together, get to know each other. The three of you can relax under our protection, which is probably something you haven't been able to do for a while."

"You're right about that, but don't you think you're being a little presumptuous?"

"…About what?"

"What makes you think I have a desire to get to know you any better?"

"Hell, I can tell you're interested."

"Oh, and what gave you that idea?"

"You've tried to hide it since you first saw me, but I could feel it."

"Is that right? You don't lack for confidence, do you? Your brother warned me about you."

"You don't wanna believe everything he tells you. I could tell you a few things about him that'd curl your hair."

"I don't know if you noticed, my hair's already curled, thank you very much."

Although a little uneasy in his presence at times, she is nonetheless intrigued. She likes his looks. His strawberry blond hair, gray-blue eyes, his muscular physique…those features contribute to his rugged, boyish, mischievous persona. His confidence, over-abundant as it is, holds a certain amount of magnetism. A few days in Memphis might be just the thing she needs to help her forget all that's happened, including the horrible nightmare with Kirk. At least she'll be a long way from him.

There's a knock at the door. Jason and Mark push it open, walking into the office.

"Well I see you two finally found us," Josh digs. "I thought we'd hidden ourselves pretty well…gave Danny and me some time alone." He doesn't have to look at his brother to know his comments bother him. He knows him all too well. "Well, how'd it go?"

"OK, I guess. They really didn't seem too interested in what I had to say. I'm not sure what's going on but it looks like this whole thing could get swept under the carpet," Jason says.

"My friends are already at work," Josh tells them.

"What do you mean?" Jason asks.

"I turned the disks over to the FBI. They've probably acted immediately to cover it all up until they can get their bearings on the whole thing. Don't worry, everything's gonna be just fine."

Josh looks at his watch. "It's getting late...you all hungry?"

"Starved," Mark replies...the others in agreement.

"Then, let's go. How about a little barbecue, Memphis-style? The Rendezvous is just a little ways from here. You three go on. I'll meet you downstairs in the courtyard after I straighten up my office a little."

"Looks like the best thing for your office would be a torch," Jason tells his brother. "You haven't changed a bit. Once a slob... always a slob."

The three walk out into the hall, toward the elevators, down and out to the courtyard Josh had mentioned. Josh remains in his office, shuffling and reshuffling papers on his desk for what must have been the tenth time today...and as in each of the ten times before, no real progress made. Finished, he pulls one of his desk drawers open and throws a half-finished report about the early morning incident on top of the already partially covered set of disks given him by Danny earlier.

Outside, the three retrace some of their steps leading up to this evening.

"What do you make of what just happened?" Mark asks.

"What do you mean?" Danny asks.

"We just wasted our time here this afternoon. I don't know what's going on, but I'm not as comfortable with our decision to come here as I once was," he continues.

"I get the same feelings, my friend," Jason agrees.

"I really think you're both being a little paranoid. Jason, you were right about your brother. I really believe he's gonna help us any way he can. He proved that last night and today."

"I wasn't talking about him, Danny. I have no doubts where his loyalties lie. He's always been true to his ideals. He's not afraid to buck the system, no matter who's in charge. The one thing I'm worried about is his ability to keep his mind on the problem at hand."

"Why do you say that?"

"You telling me you can't see what's going on? Maybe what they say about blondes is true."

"You're an asshole! And I resent that! And I suppose you're gonna stand there and tell me you haven't been hitting on me since we met?"

"Well, not with the same intentions anyway."

"Bull! Your brother's a sweet person, offering his help, no strings attached, not to mention very good looking. How can you talk about him like that?"

"I can see I'm wasting my time with this."

"I really don't understand, Jason. Why are you attacking him? You forget; you're the one who suggested we come to him for help in the first place."

"Yeah, I know. Not the first mistake I've ever made."

Josh walks through the front doors of the building, acknowledging the three sitting on a bench under a tree, a tree beginning to lose some of its leaves due to the seasonal change. Walking up to them, he smiles, "Why so serious? Loosen up a little. You're safe. I guarantee you won't be bothered by your friends from Dallas anytime soon."

"What makes you so sure?" Mark asks.

"You forget; I have connections. Ankawa and I have an understanding," He pauses momentarily. "Just kidding."

"Shit, I need to do something to energize this group a little. Let's leave the cars here and ride the trolley to the restaurant... my treat."

On the short ride through downtown, Josh and Danny stand on the outside, holding on to the same rail, hands touching. Jason and Mark sit inside, Mark checking out each portion of downtown Memphis as they slowly move past, Jason starring at Josh and Danny. Jealousy had not been a problem with him where Danny was concerned, until now.

Mark's thoughts are miles away, in Dallas. He's concerned about Sandy; wondering what role she had in all of this, and if she's OK. He knows he will have to travel back there soon to face the music... to confront his father and Sandy. For now, he and Jason are on alert, watching each other's backs. Josh is a good man, but they may have already seen betrayal by those close to them

The food is great; the atmosphere better. Josh and Danny continue their indulgence with flirtation, appearing attracted to one another. They dance to a couple of country and western tunes as a local band plays one after another. At one point, the music works its way into a waltz; Danny looks across the table at Jason. Smiling, she asks him to dance. He declines. She stands, walking to his side, grabbing his hand. "Come on, dance with me."

"You wouldn't have to ask me twice, darlin'," Josh tells her.

That's enough to get Jason out of his chair, but the childish pouting continues. On the dance floor neither says much, Danny eventually resting her chin on his shoulder. She moves closer, he keeps a distance between them for good reason.

"What's wrong? I thought you liked me."

His only response is no response. He is about to tell her how much he does like her when she quickly pulls away, excusing herself to the ladies' room. He's alone for a just a few seconds before an attractive older woman walks up to him. "Need a partner, honey? I'd never leave you standing alone on any dance floor."

He doesn't acknowledge her presence or comment, walking back to the table.

"You ready to go?" Jason asks Mark. "You got an extra key?" He turns to Josh.

"Nope, but if you're leaving me and Danny alone, I'll give you the one off my key chain." He pulls it from the ring. "Here you go," he says, tossing it to his brother. "I'll make sure she gets home safe. No need to wait up."

Danny returns to the table as the two are walking away. Nothing is said, but they exchange glances. "Where're they going?" she asks Josh.

"Back to the apartment...Thought we might stay out and party awhile. I really want to show you Memphis, Beale Street, have some fun for a change."

Determined not to let Jason's childish behavior get the best of her, she accepts Josh's offer to extend the evening. If Jason isn't interested, there's not much more she can do.

The two arrive at the apartment, Jason excusing himself to make a phone call to his parents, in a southeast suburb of Memphis. He checks his watch and determines it's not too late. His dad will be up watching television. He dials, waiting for an answer.

"Mom? Jason...I'm doing fine. How are you and Dad? What are you doing up so late?" He laughs. "I'm in town...Yeah, I know. We didn't know we were coming until yesterday evening late. Yeah this trip was pretty much unexpected. Unplanned, I guess you'd say. Mark Anderson came with me...You know, my friend from college..." He turns to Mark who's relaxing with a late-night TV show. "Mom says hi."

"We're at Josh's...Yeah, I'll be out sometime tomorrow, if it's OK...Dinner would be great...I'll bring him. I may also have a third if it's OK...Her name's Danny Wilson...No, she's not the next Mrs. Cade. Well, maybe I shouldn't speak so quickly, the way she and Josh seem to have hit it off.

"...Dad there? OK, I love you too, Mom."

Jason awaits his dad's arrival at the phone. "Hey, Dad, how you doing? I'm doing pretty good. Naw, I told Mom she was just an acquaintance, nothing more...Yeah, sure. I'm looking forward to it...OK. We'll see you around five. Bye." He sits on the couch, taking the drink Mark had gotten him earlier, sipping it slowly.

Mark begins the conversation, "How're your folks?"

"They seem to be doing good."

"You gonna tell them what happened?"

"Don't think so. Mom would just worry. Dad would want to go after 'em."

"What's going on tomorrow night?"

"They want us to come to dinner. Feel up to it?"

"Sure, why not. I've always liked your folks."

Cade stands, walking to the window at the front of the apartment. He stops, standing in front of it like a sentinel.

Mark knows why he's there. "Come on, man. They'll be home soon. You want a relationship with that girl you're gonna have to show a little more interest. I mean she made a move tonight and you didn't flinch. I'm telling you right now, she's interested."

"Maybe...I just got fed up with the whole mess. I can't compete with Josh. Never could."

"I've never seen that defeatist attitude in you before. What's wrong?"

"Nothing. Let's just drop it. What about you?"

What do you mean?"

"What're you gonna do about Sandy?"

"Don't know. Guess I'm gonna have to get some answers from her first. I'll stay here with you guys a couple of days, and then head back to Dallas...see if I can get an audience with my father, straighten this relationship out. Hell, see if there still is a relationship."

"No sense in you staying around, I guess. Don't know what you can do here anyway."

"Think about it. As long as I'm around you two, I'm your insurance policy."

"Yeah, like last night when we almost got killed."

"I don't believe my dad had anything to do with that, as corrupt as I think he is. Nor do I believe he will approve of what happened. I gotta believe Carrigan is solely behind last night."

"You're probably right."

A car pulls into the adjoining lot, the GT sliding into a covered stall with Josh's apartment number painted above, the two inside waiting for Danny and Josh to walk through the door. When they don't, Jason stands again, walking to the window. He sees them walking slowly, side by side, down the road running along the Mississippi.

By the time Danny and Josh finish their walk, arriving back at the apartment around 1:00 a.m., they stop before entering the apartment, Josh tugging on her hand. As she turns to see what he needs, he attempts to kiss this beautiful woman, as he has tried to control himself, but can't any longer.

"Aren't you moving a little too fast?" Danny asks him as she puts her hand to his mouth to stop his advancement.

"Come on...I know you're interested."

"Oh, and what gave you that idea?"

"You've tried to hide it since you first saw me. I could feel it."

"Is that right? Your brother was right about you."

As the two finish their impasse and enter the apartment, Jason and Mark appear asleep; both camped out in the living room. No matter how quiet they try to be, the pair makes a fair amount of noise, Danny tripping over a pair of shoes left purposely in the middle of the dark room.

"You two have a good time?" Jason asks from his counterfeit sleep.

"We had a great time!" Josh says, placing his right arm around Danny's shoulder after turning on a light. She squirms a little but allows his arm to stay.

"It was nice. Why'd you leave so early?" Danny asks.

"I was tired; besides, I didn't think a third wheel would've been appropriate tonight."

"Maybe you ought to ask how other people feel on occasion instead of always taking matters into your own hands."

"...Looks to me like I made the right decision. Now if you don't mind, I'm tired and would like to go to sleep." He lies back down on the couch, rolling over with his back to the rest of the world.

In the other room, the conversational jabbing continues between the two. A genuine con artist at work, Josh Cade seems to be winning Danny over.

Perplexed with his indignation and apparent continued lack of interest, Danny soon retires for the evening.

Next morning, Jason awakens to the sound of laughter coming from the kitchen. He slides his feet to the floor, sitting on the edge of his makeshift bed, hair ruffled and totally out of place. His mouth tastes like some dog came along in the night and shit in it. Before he can stand to go and take care of any of that, the two in the kitchen burst into the living room. Danny's borrowed a pair of shorts and a tank top from Josh, performing some quick, temporary alterations so they fit snugly.

"Morning, Kramer," his brother greets him, poking fun at his appearance. "You look unusually radiant this morning."

"If there wasn't a lady present, I'd tell you what you could do with your 'good morning.'"

"You wanna go jogging with us?" Danny asks.

"Yeah, big brother, didn't you tell me awhile back you were a big health nut? I mean, as much as Danny's into it, I figured you'd be running every day."

"Screw you, As a matter of fact, I do run on a regular basis."

Lying there, half asleep, Anderson knows he hasn't seen his buddy running any since he'd come to Dallas.

"Let's go then," Danny says smiling. "I'll have two good-looking guys by my side this morning."

"Uh, you two go on. I'll catch up. I gotta get dressed; you know, put my shoes on, stretch, and everything."

"We gotta do the same thing. You aren't out by the time we're through we'll go on and catch you on the second, third, or fourth lap around the island. Need a pair of shoes, there's an old pair in my closet," Josh tells him.

"Thanks."

After the two leave the apartment, Anderson rises from the dead. "You're crazy. When was the last time you did any running?"

"That's not the point."

"No, the point is you can't let your brother get the best of you. Don't tell me you don't care about Danny. I know better."

Jason thought he could be ready before they finished stretching. He didn't want to give Josh any more of a head start or advantage. Shoes on, he glances out the window and as he arrives outside, his two would-be running companions are gone. Looking down the road, he can see them disappear around the bend. He quickly jumps into his stretching routine, spending just a few seconds before deciding what the hell and takes off. Rather than starting out in an easy jog, he kicks it into a near dead run, arriving at the bend of the road quickly and totally out of breath. "This feels pretty good...nothing to it." He says to himself gasping for air between every other word.

A tug pushing a line of barges up the river blows its horn as it chugs slowly past the island. Cade looks up, mostly unappreciative of the view before him. The churning, southern flow of the Mississippi makes sure the tug isn't having an easy time going against its current.

Before he can begin again, the two ahead of him disappear as they make the next turn, following the road at the perimeter of Mud Island. He begins again, determined to catch them, using a little more common sense on this second leg of his jog.

Little stretching and his beginning sprint have taken their toll. Unable to catch up, he must stop, limping slightly as he slows. Other residents of Mud Island continue waking, one in particular opening her front door, allowing a large Rottweiler access to the great outdoors. The huge black animal targets Cade immediately, obviously seeing him as a nice morning meal.

In front of the house and bent over to catch his breath, Cade doesn't see the dog until he hears the barking and growling. When he looks up, he has no problem quickly focusing on the source of his new problem. "Shit!" His first thought: run like hell! His next thought: run like hell! He turns to begin his retreat, slowly walking, limping, and trying not to draw the big dog into a chase, one he knows he cannot win. Glancing over his shoulder, he can see the dog stalking him, moving into what looks like an attack mode. The slow gate of the dog quickly transforms into a charge. Cade kicks it in as well; pain, limp, or whatever; he's not gonna be some huge animal's breakfast this morning.

Rounding the curve he has his brother's apartment in sight, and then he hears the pop before he feels the additional excruciating pain shoot through his hamstring. His dead run suddenly crumbles to a dead-limping crawl. The dog is no longer in pursuit, a buried electronic fence stopping him long ago at the edge of its owner's yard.

By the time he's reached the walkway leading up to his brother's apartment, Jason thinks he's pulled every muscle in his lower body. He looks down the road to see Josh and Danny turning the corner on their first lap of the island. He makes the best of the situation, stepping into a covered walkway, hiding as the duo passes by the apartment heading down the road, making the corner again, disappearing from sight.

His climb to the second-floor apartment is a difficult one. He reaches the front door, but the door will not budge. He has no key. "Why's this shit always seem to happen to me?" He turns slowly, moving to the top step to sit and wait on the inevitable, the return of Danny and his brother. Sweat glands kicking into overdrive, his T-shirt is soaked.

"What're you doing?" A welcomed voice from behind asks. "What the hell happen to you?"

"Am I glad to see you. Help me up."

Anderson bends over to help his pained friend, hearing the story, embellished slightly to cover obvious indignation and embarrassment. Danny and Josh complete their third, fourth, then the fifth and final turn around the island, going through the after-jog stretching, coming inside for a cool down.

"What happened, bro? Thought you were gonna join us."

"I decided to take a different course. I needed a little more strenuous workout than what the island has to offer."

"Where'd you go?" Danny asks.

Anderson sits across from his buddy grinning, waiting to see how he answers this one.

"Oh, I uh, went up Riverside, along the river, then into the downtown area. The hills gave me the workout I'm used to. It was great."

Josh looks at his brother, "That's a pretty tough workout. I run that every other day. You must've made it in record time."

"Maybe Josh and I could join you on that route tomorrow," Danny offers.

"I think that's a great idea." Josh jumps on this opportunity. "I look forward to it."

"Uh, yeah, that'd be great. Yeah, sure," Jason responds.

"Let's go get some breakfast," Josh suggests.

"You guys go ahead. I think I'll skip breakfast this morning."

"Too sore to move, big brother?"

"Did I say that?"

Josh winks at him.

"I've got a little problem, guys," Danny interjects. "I don't have anything to wear. I only brought the one outfit and I've been wearing it for two days."

"Yeah, we know," Anderson chides, holding his nose, playfully alluding to a fantasy stench. "I brought a little extra cash just in case. Let's go shopping. I think we all need to look into the clothing issue."

Plans are made to shower, and be ready to go in about an hour. Josh declines; saying he has to go to the office, unfinished work awaiting him. Jason informs everyone about the invitation to his parents for dinner tonight. Danny gives her regrets; telling him she's accepted a date with his brother for the evening.

Her announcement angers Jason immensely, prepared to concede to his brother and let the two have at each other.

Josh showers and leaves.

The threesome plan to hit a local mall, driving to one in east Memphis, just off Interstate 240. Before leaving the apartment, Mark retrieves one of the duffel bags from the Diablo, revealing an astonishing secret. After tossing it on the coffee table he tells one of them to open it. When Cade does, bundles of money, hundred dollar bills are exposed.

"There must be thousands in here. Where'd you get it?" Danny asks.

"There's approximately four-hundred to five-hundred thousand...came from my dad. He's sent it to me in much smaller amounts, but it's accumulated rather nicely over time."

Danny looks at Jason and he looks at her, before both look at Mark, responding simultaneously, "Five hundred thousand dollars?"

"Give or take a few thousand," Mark says. "And today we're gonna spend a little of it."

"What's the deal?" his friend asks.

"What do you mean?"

"You get all this money, the Diablo...thought you said you hadn't bought into the ways of your father."

"I sent the first cashier's checks back to him, torn to pieces, but I soon decided to keep and cash 'em in. Something told me to save it all for a rainy day...haven't spent a dime till now. Now maybe we will be able to use some of it against him. Besides, like I said before, I haven't always exercised the willpower like I should've." He peels off ten one-hundred-dollar bills three times, handing a thousand to each of them, pocketing a thousand for himself, stuffing the remaining money in the first bundle back into the pack, zipping it closed. "You think there's somewhere we can hide this?" Mark leaves the room with the bag in his hands, returning a few minutes later. "Let's go."

The day is most enjoyable. Jason can relax a little since Josh isn't there to compete with. After spending time at the mall and successfully hiding his muscle soreness, they move on to their next stop, the three strengthening their friendships as the day progresses. Jason continues managing his injury to a negligible limp, telling Danny he must have cramped up a little while shopping. Late in the day, Danny looks at her watch. "I've got to get back to the apartment. Josh will be wondering where I am."

Ending their day on a sour note, her statement sends Jason into another of his silent treatments. He'd all but forgotten she had promised her evening to his brother. She could have gone all day without reminding him of that. He'd actually thought after the enjoyable day they had spent together, she might look to cancel their date. Separated from Mark for some time now, the two find him on a park bench, sipping on a Coke, watching the merry-go-round loaded with small kids.

"You two OK?"

"Yeah, I guess. Are you OK?" Cade asks in return.

"Yeah, just thinking."

"Danny needs to go. Doesn't want to miss her big date tonight."

"Jason, you come up with a reason for me to cancel, I will. You want me to go with you to your parents'?" Danny asks, hoping to get a personal invitation to his parents', hoping he'll give her a good reason not to go out with his brother.

"No. Mark and I can make the trip. We'll be fine. You and Josh go out and have a great time. In fact, I better call my mom and let her know we may be a little late." He pulls the cellular Josh had lent them and dials.

While he is occupied, Mark asks Danny a question.

"What's with you two?"

"What do you mean?"

"I mean, what's going on between you guys?"

"Nothing as far as I know."

"This thing with you and his brother, I don't know if you noticed, but it's tearing Jason up."

"I don't believe that for a second. He's not even..."

Cade returns from the phone, interrupting the conversation before it can go any further.

"You ready? My mom said she's running late too."

"Sure," Anderson replies.

"Then let's go. I've had enough for one day," Cade tells him and with that, both leave the apartment. Cade figuring he is doing so, finally on his terms.

CHAPTER 20

DALLAS, TEXAS
END OF SEPTEMBER
6:35 PM

Stretch limousines pull up in front of the Ankawa building one by one extending back out of the long circle drive into the street. The motorcade of twelve has just completed its unescorted journey from Southlake where Ankawa's private airport now houses business jets used by those inside each limo. Security greets each, opening the passenger doors as well-dressed men step out into the early evening air, making their way to the front door of the Texas skyscraper, entering the building and proceeding through security check-points by displaying special-issue clearance cards.

As what appears to initially be the final car unloads, another rolls belatedly into the circle drive off the street, stopping before its lone occupant climbs out. All activity in front of the building ceases; coming to its total conclusion. The last man to arrive enters the designated elevator as those attending tonight's meeting will ascend to the top floor. A security guard in plainclothes leans inside, jamming a key into the slot, turning it, shutting all lights on the panel off with the exception of one. He steps back out of the way as the door closes, and the final participant speeds his way to the top floor and the facility specifically constructed for confidential meetings the likes of which is minutes away from beginning.

Two floors below that facility, in a semi-darkened room, Asao Ankawa sits alone, his eyes closed, his thoughts visiting a place he journeys to often...his subconscious. He sees himself as a child of eleven, going through a nightmare he has so many times since his family's deaths. His mother, father, his grandmother and grandfather...Yuan Mei, Massey—they all stand before him. As all visits to his reoccurring memorial subconscious before, they disappear before his eyes, human flesh and bones melting more graphically than ever previously, more graphic with each unplanned visit to a time he would just like to be able to forget. His inner vision darkened substantially; a light appears in the distance as he walks slowly toward it. Under the lone light hanging above a table, lies his beloved Miki. She can barely speak the words..."I love you." Then, as many times before, her body decomposes before him. As his sobbing begins, an earthquake awakens him. Waking in a sweat, he stands and walks to a window, gazing at the illuminated, well-defined Dallas skyline to the southeast, the skyline of Ft. Worth to the southwest.

"Asao...Asao. My friend, you are experiencing your bad dream once again," Yami awakens him from his apparent self-imposed nightmare. "It is almost time."

Minutes later, as he is now back to present day willfully. He remains standing, staring out a window at the illuminated, well-defined skylines. A phone to his ear, his conversation with an individual outside the confines of this building begins. This call comes from Memphis. Ankawa does not inform him their conversation is being recorded.

"No. Absolutely no one is to know of our working relationship. If anyone were to find out, it could be quite dangerous for you, and most importantly, my son. Yes, you will be rewarded handsomely, but as I have said before, only if my son is unharmed. I have taken the liberty to send a substantial payment showing good faith on my part. Yes, I know; they are all very strong willed, indeed, and as for my son, his heritage speaks for itself. I assure you however, he is a very trustworthy individual, with high ideals and good intentions. No, I do not believe it will serve any purpose for me to visit your city at this time. To do so would only complicate matters further. I would like to talk more, but I must go. I have a very important meeting about to begin...good night."

As Ankawa ends the conversation, Sandy walks into the room. "Was that Mark?"

"No. It was, however, someone very close to him at this moment."

"Then Mark still does not know about me, or the baby."

"Not at this moment, but the time will soon come for all disclosures. Only then will he learn of your condition."

His bodyguard and right-hand man returns. "Excuse me, Asao, everyone is assembled and enjoying their dinner. They await your arrival."

Turning to Sandy and respectfully bowing, "I must go now. We will continue this conversation at a later time."

The two friends proceed to their private elevator attached to the outside of the building, connecting the penthouse directly to the top floor. As doors close, all lighting extinguishes inside; a feature built in for Ankawa's personal pleasure. The loss of interior lighting opens as well as highlights a panoramic view of the city's lights before him. His companion presses the button marked Hiroshima, so named in honor of Ankawa's birthplace. The assembly he is about to address, representing a continuing rebirth of his commitment for retribution, is seconds away. The speed of the elevator, slow and deliberate, has been purposely calibrated so he may enjoy the view as he travels the exterior of his building, and so that he may have the time needed to collect all thoughts before entering the chamber.

Left alone, with the exception of a few servants working in other rooms, Sandy picks up the phone, dialing the building switchboard. "This is Ms. Greene, can you tell me about the call Mr. Ankawa just received, the one from Memphis, Tennessee, I believe? Yes, I must know its origination. I know it originated in Memphis! I just told you that! I want to know the number of the phone the call was placed from."

The operator reads the number to Sandy as she writes it on a piece of paper, then quickly hangs up without thanking her for her time and help. She pauses a few seconds, sighs deeply as if trying to gain a certain level of courage, picks the phone receiver back up, slowly, carefully dialing...stopping just prior to punching the last number to send her call on its way. A few seconds of reflection behind her, she presses the final digit, then sits back in her chair. It rings several times. About to hang up, a voice is heard from the other end, a man's voice, one she thinks sounds vaguely familiar.

"Hello."

"Hello," she replies nervously. "Who am I talking to?"

"Ma'am, this is Jacob Snyder."

"Who?"

"Jacob Snyder, ma'am...Who did you want to talk to?"

"The phone you're talking on. Where's it located?"

"Ma'am, this is the lobby of the Crowne Plaza in Memphis, Tennessee. It's a pay phone."

"Did you just say it was a pay phone?"

"Yes, ma'am, I sure did. The phone is stuck right here in the middle of downtown Memphis. Where you calling from, ma'am?"

No answer to the man's last question, as Sandy has since disconnected their line, hanging up and moving on.

In his car, finished for the day, Josh Cade pulls from the parking lot across from and in front of the hotel he has just visited, the Crowne Plaza. He steers through the necessary turns and points his GT in the direction of his home on Mud Island.

The gathering of men inside the Boardroom has grown quiet in anticipation of Ankawa's immediate arrival. These gatherings have been taking place approximately four times a year since 1987. The group meetings, although labeled as for the board of directors for the corporation, are meetings of Ankawa's hand-picked, bought-and-paid-for world leaders and high-powered executives. He has accumulated and convinced these men, one by one, of his desire to clean up corporate America, specifically the corporate conscience in general. They all agree it is spinning out of control and on a collision course with financial disaster, if not complete self-destruction. This gathering brotherhood believes in and is convinced Ankawa has the plan to bring this serious problem under control. As they band together to change the direction of American business, it doesn't hurt any of them to know Ankawa is also paying each of them obscene amounts of money to join him in this secret and highly confidential operation. They all laugh, calling it the Corporate Takeover of the Century.

The door to the private elevator opens as Ankawa steps out to a solid round of applause, complete with standing ovation. He stops, smiling and bowing to the room. Before the acknowledgment ends, he is already working his way around the huge solid wood conference table, inlaid with jade and marble and built in his homeland. The table is so large, in fact, it nearly fills up the entire room, a room built around it after it was shipped from Japan in sections, assembled in Dallas, and lifted by helicopter to the building top.

Not only is the room a meeting room, with its soundproof amenities, Ankawa has managed to cultivate species of plant life characteristic of his homeland, adding to that the appearance of a well-manicured Japanese garden, including a single mulberry bush. The glass enclosure resembles a large greenhouse, within a building designed to resemble a pagoda. The view any time of the day or night makes this one of his favorite places to spend hours in solitude. Additional amenities of the Boardroom include bulletproof glass with high-level insulating capabilities. The smoked glass textured with hand cut crystalloid designs, soften the glare of outside lighting or daylight, whichever the case may be.

Recurrently greeting each member of his elite board with a personal comment is one of several traits endearing the man to all. These personal greetings take some time as he moves completely around the table, delaying the start of the intended meeting. He greets J. J. Collier; one of three black CEOs of a Fortune 500 International conglomerate headquartered in the United States. With annual sales in excess of ninety billion, his company is one of the top ten in the world in total revenues.

The next man to greet him is Alexander Danning, chief executive officer of the largest automobile manufacturing company in the United States. A strange ally, indeed, in these times, considering the Japanese annual assault on the American marketplace with record auto sales. Next is the chairman of the International Bank of America, Jonathan Beech. With assets well into the billions, his bank is a world leader and financial market pacesetter.

Walking to the end of the table, Ankawa greets Texas Senator Jack Angstrom, member of three important Capitol Hill committees, including chairmanship of one. Considered one of the most influential and powerful members of Congress today, Angstrom brings national and world clout, as well as the innate ability to recruit other substantial, influential members of Congress. Next in line, as Ankawa works his way back down the other side of the table, is Senator Orin Smythe. Smythe chairs the Finance Committee, dealing with the regulation of banking and finance on a daily basis. Next is Alan Landers, head of the Federal Reserve, probably one of the three most important members of the group. With essentially final say on the nation's domestic and international financial situation merely through control of domestic interest rates, he can literally dictate the rise and fall of the Ankawa empire, not to mention American economic fortunes. Next to shake hands with their leader are recently retired General Ike Rosenthal, retired Admiral Nathan Brown, two additional corporate leaders, and a member of the United States Cabinet, secretary of finance, Jerry Clayton.

Approaching the end of his effort to work the room, and about to conclude his early meeting ritual, Ankawa extends his hand to probably one of the most unusual members of his team. Bobby Andrews, a member of the group for nearly two years, after a strenuous and exhaustive recruitment, adds an unprecedented level of energy to the group's efforts. Bobby, a very charismatic and popular television evangelist with an audience estimated into the millions and growing, has many devoted followers. His effervescent leadership of the masses aids his work convincing those masses to open their hearts, their souls, and most importantly their bank accounts to any cause he wishes.

What convinced Bobby to join this particular effort? Ankawa's promise to fund a crusade that would shake the rafters, crack the foundation of the American and international corporate communities. Convinced this crusade will drive the greed, deception, and dishonesty out of a corrupt business community, Bobby sees this as his opportunity to attack the feeding grounds of sin and expand his ministries and personal crusade around the world, an opportunity he could not afford to pass up.

Next, Dallas' chief of police, Archie Langston, and finally, Ankawa's right-hand man in the business for nearly fifteen years, Robert Carrigan. As Asao steps in front of him, Carrigan stands to greet his boss and mentor. The two friends and business partners forego the formalities of a handshake, breaking from tradition to embrace one another. This show of affection and mutual respect will enhance Robert's ability to achieve his ambition through the others. Before the night is over, he will have completed the initial phase of his grand plan.

Finally, Ankawa walks toward the one individual who has been with him, never leaving his side from the beginning. Above all others, Asao knows he can trust this man with his life and soul. The two old and dear friends bow respectfully, embracing. Yami and Asao have been through much together, since their days as children in Okayama and their first encounter just down the road from his uncle Tomoko's. Yami sits as his friend steps to the head of the table. He looks upon this man about to speak, as more than just a friend. Since those earlier days, Yami has grown to love and respect Asao as a brother. He would do anything for him, absolutely anything.

Ankawa finally faces the group before him. As they grow quiet, he smiles. "Gentlemen, once again, I welcome each of you to my humble home. As always, it is good to see every one of you. I trust your travels were comfortable."

Most nod their heads in silent reply, most also smiling in appreciation.

He hesitates, walking to one side of the room to enhance and build anticipation of what he is about to tell them. He is quite gifted in working an audience. "We are very close to the achievement of our goal. Each of you is to be commended for your individual accomplishments; however, there are still many hours, days, even months ahead before our brilliant plan will be complete. There remains much work to be done and for the sake of this great country, indeed the world, this mission must not fail!"

Loud applause follows his last statement.

"I have seen the many reports coming in from each of you, but as is customary, I ask you to present an abbreviated update, so that all may share in your success. After which, I will make a few additional comments." He sits, looking down the table, nodding his approval for the first to stand..."Senator Angstrom."

"Gentlemen, I regret to inform you, as my distinguished colleagues from Washington will attest, all is not well in the White House." A few seconds pass before a smile appears on his face. "Isn't that what we've all worked for?"

Around the table, laughter and applause punctuate his remarks.

"As you know, and as is most evident from our friends in the media, President Stephenson has his hands full. Believe me, there is much more to come. As my people continue to release documentation on schedule and in a most timely manner, the president will become more and more occupied with personal damage control." Angstrom drinks from his glass before continuing. "The president's popularity and approval ratings continue to decline. He continues to wrestle with domestic affairs, and, as you all know, he knows little of foreign. His wife continues to be a thorn in his side." Angstrom pauses. "The man is definitely in over his head.

"I've been quite successful exposing several pieces of legislation introduced by him and his staff, persuading many of my mindless colleagues, those in attendance here not included, to side with me as we continue our quest for control of the vitally influential committees. Continuing at this pace, the average taxpayer will be so disillusioned with the president, his policies, government, as well as big business, they will be willing to listen to anyone with a reasonable plan to bail this country out of trouble. As our plan continues to work, this country will move closer and closer to financial ruin. The market will experience its normal ups and downs, a final gain, and then a massive devastating plunge."

"Will we be on target to execute our strategy by the planned date?" Carrigan asks the senator.

Without hesitation, the senator replies. "Most definitely, Robert...By August of 2000, there will be little in the way to stop our machine, taking the American financial infrastructure to its knees just prior to the end of year one of the new millennium. Just before Election Day, our coalition will rush in to save the American people by stopping it just before total collapse. Unfortunately, there will be risks involved, as we all knew when we signed on. We cannot do what we are about to, without some level of risk."

"Has the mechanism we've put in place to stop it, should we find that avenue necessary at the last second, been proven to be successful?" Andrews asks.

"...Only on paper Bobby, only on paper."

A bit of squirming and a sense of uneasiness in the men seated around the table after that last statement raises the volume of chatter from around the table.

"What happens should we not be able to stop the collapse after the process has begun?" Andrews persists.

"We cannot allow that to happen. As you all know, our plan is simple. Our government, as we know it, will most definitely experience a complete and total collapse. Unemployment benefits will quickly dry up. Those out of work—and by that time there will be millions—will have to steal for their families to survive. The Social Security division will be bankrupt, primarily because our government will deem it necessary to borrow from it to handle day-to-day operations. Internally, the governmental process will become cannibalistic, totally consuming itself. The United States will suddenly find itself in the role of a Third World country, an impoverished nation in much worse shape than many of our neighbors to the south. We will, for all matters, become open prey for any military power with even the slightest of military might. Interest rates will crash to an all-time low, but it won't matter. No one will be able to borrow anything. There will be little to no gold reserves to back up our currency. We've all seen to that as we've slowly eliminated those reserves over the years. Our domestic banking access to international moneys will quickly dry up, as the world looking on will deem our financial situation to be at a point of no return, with little chance for survival. Many we have helped in the past will sit back and await our demise, then like economic vultures, try to swoop in to devour our remains. Foreign, as well as domestic investors will begin fire-selling in great magnitudes, to rid themselves of worthless properties." Angstrom pauses for very good effects. "There will be a mad rush by opportunists to buy up everything in sight.

"We will witness utter and complete chaos. We will then step in to save the day. As a friendly conglomerate with unlimited financial resources, those resources quite safe in foreign financial institutions and investments, we'll be able to buy anything we desire, gaining control, looking like white knights riding in on white stallions. Sort of a reverse bailout, if you will."

Out of breath, Angstrom completes his presentation. "We will, in effect, own the American people. Need I say more?"

In Memphis, Jason and Mark arrive in the small suburb just outside Memphis. The drive east provides a nostalgic trip for Cade. Josh and Danny arrive at a place in Memphis many believe you definitely take someone to impress, although Danny struggles to erase Jason from her mind completely this evening.

The updates continue in Dallas, Ankawa pleased with every account. It soon becomes Bobby Andrews' turn to stand and deliver.

"Gentlemen, the lord has quite obviously been very good to all those around this table!" he begins. His updates, continually resembling a sermon under the tent, have their dramatic moments. Carrigan despises this man's updates, as he thoroughly despises the man delivering them.

"Praise God!" Bobby continues. "My congregation continues to show their love and support through their pocketbooks! Their trust in me, their love for Jesus will soon be rewarded as we help this wonderful man save America." He opens his arms toward Ankawa in what he would term a divine gesture. "Glory will be God's as the millennium arrives." Upon saying that, he points to Ankawa again. "Thank you, sir! Praise Jesus!"

Robert sits patiently waiting his turn, wondering when this fake bastard will be shutting up and sitting down.

"I am very pleased to announce, my congregation is giving generously, at an incredible pace of nearly one million dollars a day! Glory Hallelujah! Praise God!"

Carrigan believes he is about to puke. His eyes find those of Rosenthal's, a staunch supporter, at the opposite end of the table. As Robert's eyes roll upward into his head, Rosenthal smiles, reading the gesture for its exact meaning.

"My private ledger shows we have in excess of ten billion dollars in various banks and investments worldwide, while my flock continues to believe we barely have enough to keep the ministry afloat," Andrews continues. "With growing interest and the continued funding by my congregation as they turn over their life savings, we should be able to add another three to three and a half billion before judgment day arrives. Our war against the wretched sins of greed will be won! Praise God!"

He sits to strong applause and a chorus of "Amen," many as bogus as each man's commitment to saving and improving America.

Carrigan is finally able to stand to give his update. His act begins. He appears troubled. "Gentlemen," he pauses, "it is true; we have made great strides to date. I would be the last to impose a sense of alarm within this respected group, but it seems there has been a breach of confidentiality within this organization."

Ankawa looks up from the script he should be hearing from Carrigan. A script he requires all who speak to supply him one week prior to all meetings of this nature.

"Please excuse my departure from the planned script, sir. As the man in charge of security for this mission, I must warn all of you not to bring additional and unwanted scrutiny unto our organization. I assure you, I do have the current problem under control; however, we must not have any other situations like this one surfacing. We are too close to the fruition of our goals."

Small conversations break out around the table. Carrigan knows Ankawa will be quite troubled by this recent disclosure;

unhappy he has not been made aware of his intentions to disclose them before now.

"I must warn each of you. Do not trust anyone outside our circle. As there can be no one else allowed in, there will be no current member, absolutely no one allowed out of this organization at this late date without very serious and dire consequences." Some sit uneasily as the statements are being made. He feels at the moment, his comments are accomplishing all he had hoped for.

"Gentlemen, gentlemen…! Please! There should be little cause for concern. As sure as I am standing here before you, I will return to our next meeting with the full disclosure of those involved. I am confident I will be able to tell you all at that time, the problem has also been eliminated," Carrigan finishes, sitting in his chair.

The room remains quiet, no one else apparently willing to stand after Carrigan. Ankawa slowly rises to his feet, standing momentarily, as though speechless, as if searching for the right words. "We must not…we will not allow this setback, however serious, to stop us from succeeding. We still have much to accomplish before everything is finally in place."

Forcing a smile, he wishes everyone a safe journey and tells them he has something special planned, a reward for the excellent work they have done to this point. "Keep in mind, in a matter of months, in a matter of just a very few years, everyone in this group will be recognized across America as true modern-day heroes. Your greatest reward will be the knowledge that each of you had a part in saving this great country. You will each walk among your peers as true examples of the prototype hero of the future, extremely wealthy heroes, but heroes nonetheless. America...the world, will be yours for the asking. You will be the true, I might add, the new corporate America! Thank you."

Ankawa applauds his group, as they do him in return. He shakes the hand of each departing man, satisfied he has turned the silent negativism driven into his meeting by Carrigan's revelations. Yami stands at the elevator doors, handing each man an envelope before he boards for the descent to the ground floor. Carrigan remains seated at the table. He is very pleased with himself and with what he has just accomplished. Phase one of his elaborate scheme has just been initiated and is now, in the books, so to speak. He will soon be able to make another announcement that will shock all those involved.

The next meeting of the board will be his first curtain call. At that time, phase two will be well on its way, moving him in place to grab all he deems rightfully his by the power vested in him by the man now approaching.

Ankawa walks to the table, sitting across from Carrigan. Everyone else has gone from the room, with the exception of Asao's most trusted friend, Yami. Ankawa and Carrigan sit in silence, neither ready to speak until one finally breaks that silence.

"Why did you bring the situation involving my son up to the group tonight? You are forcing me to make decisions I do not want to make."

"Asao, I will make sure your son is not implicated in any manner with this most recent issue. You must agree, however, we have to stop the others from whatever it is they are trying to do. We cannot withstand the kind of damage a disclosure of our plans would bring The media would have a field day. Our organization will crumble and your team will abandon you. As such, I felt it prudent to make my announcement to the group so anyone thinking of possibly doing anything similar, would at least have second thoughts."

Ankawa stands, walking to the end of the large glass enclosed room. He faces the view of the city to the north of Dallas, in the direction of Addison, then eastward toward Highland Park. "A decision will be made tonight before I retire. I will let you know of my final requirements tomorrow."

He slowly walks toward the elevator, stopping to tend to one of the many bonsai scattered about the room, turning to survey the empty room with one man still seated at the large table in the center. Yami awaits his friend, opening the door as he steps in front of him. The two board their private elevator just before the doors close. During its descent, Yami chooses to speak out, bringing his most recent concerns to light.

"I do not usually try to tell my good friend what he must do, but I feel I must now speak my mind."

"What is it, Yami? I truly value your thoughts and judgment above all others. You know that. Tell me what is on your mind."

"I do not trust that man. Never have."

"Carrigan…?"

Yami shakes his head in positive reply.

"Why do you say this? What is the origin for this distrust of someone whom I have worked side by side now for so many years?"

"I have this feeling. Inside my heart, I believe he cannot be trusted to carry out your wishes. Indeed, I believe the man has developed his own agenda, one I am certain contrasts that of your own."

"With the exception to you, he has been with me the longest. He has helped me mold and develop my company. I have taken great caution in allowing him access to my many plans for final retribution; to the point that he does not know of my exact plans, or why I am targeting the specific time to finalize those plans. I assure you, I have been very careful.

"No, Yami, I must stand firm, as I did many years ago where my best friend was concerned. He has done nothing to cause me alarm or concern. No, my friend. I appreciate your loyalty and friendship; as I did with you years ago, I will also stand with him. I believe him to be a staunch ally."

"Then I will say no more. I certainly understand your sense of loyalty. I pray to Kami that you are making the right decision."

Seeing his friend's disappointment, Ankawa feels he must reassure him. "I will be very cautious, I assure you. Your judgment has been most valuable in the past and I cannot afford to look away now. I will indeed heed your warning."

This appears to please Yami, settling his uneasiness for the moment.

"I have a favor to ask of you. I must request that you go to your godson and convince him to return to Dallas. He will listen to you. You may reassure him, neither of his friends will be harmed. His place now, I believe, is with me, his wife, and his unborn child."

Their conversation continues out of the elevator into the living quarters.

"You know I too love your son as though he were my own. I will go and do as you ask without hesitation. It would be good to have young Asao with us once again. Does he know of the impending arrival of his new son or daughter?"

"No, and you should not take the liberty to tell him, unless of course, it is the final option to convince him how important it will be for him to return," Ankawa finishes.

Carrigan leaves the building, pulling out of the garage, immediately on his car phone, dialing his son's number. There is no answer at his apartment or car. Robert ends his quest in disgust. "Damn it! Where is he when I need him? I can never depend on that kid!"

Robert knows the only course of action Ankawa can now take is to bring his son and Danny back to Dallas. He knows he must have Kirk involved in that extradition. Cade is expendable. He will choose the right moment to recommend Kirk's participation in the expedition to Memphis, an expedition that must happen soon. But since he cannot find his son, he will delay further searching until tomorrow. Tonight, he seeks relief from the stress of the day. He will visit Dickson. She'll know what he needs, as well as what to do.

In Memphis, Mark and Jason are ready to leave the company of Jason's parents. Mark climbs into the driver's seat while Jason thanks his mom and dad for the enjoyable, relaxing evening. Hugging his mother, he says, "Thanks for the great meal, Mom. I really appreciate your asking my friends out tomorrow night for the cookout."

Turning to his dad, he reaches out to shake his hand, hugging him instead.

"Good to see you, son." His dad places his arm around his oldest son's shoulders, nudging him toward the car. He leans a little closer, speaking so his wife cannot hear his next few comments. "I appreciate you being a good sport about tomorrow night. She's wanted to do this since Josh told us a last weekend you were coming into town."

That statement doesn't register until he's in the car backing out of the driveway. "How the hell did Josh know we were coming last week? Hell, we didn't know until a couple of days ago."

Arriving at his brother's apartment, Jason notices the Mitsubishi in the carport, and then looks at his watch. It's almost eleven. Relieved they are home, considering they may not have had such a great evening on their date after all, he isn't prepared for what he will soon encounter. He inserts the spare key his brother had given him earlier, he and Mark enter unannounced. What they find surprises them both. Locked in a passionate kiss, Danny simply tests her inner feelings for the younger of the two brothers. Josh indulges for other reasons. She believes she has found early in their embrace, there is little to go on, but allows the moment to flourish to completion just in case.

Her extreme and immediate embarrassment shows. Josh smiles broadly, knowing he's upset his older brother, who reacts by exiting abruptly.

Danny tries to rise and go after him, but Josh grabs her arm pulling her back onto the sofa. "Where you going? Won't do any good to go after him now. Give him time to cool off."

She pulls herself up and out of the couch anyway, following Jason out the door. On the balcony, she can see he is progressing down the street, walking along the river. She catches him, arriving at his side, slipping her hand in his. He immediately pulls himself from her affectionate, apologetic grasp.

"What's wrong?" she asks, fully knowing the answer.

"Nothing. Just need to be by myself for a while without your pity affection. You better go back. Don't want little brother getting the wrong idea about our relationship."

"What makes you think I care?"

Cade stops, turns, and looks her straight in the eye, the glow from the full moon adding to the streetlight's a few yards away. "What kind of game are you playing anyway? You having a good time? If you're trying to send me a message, it worked. I just got it loud and clear. You don't mind, I'd like to be left alone."

"You don't understand," Danny tries to explain.

"You're right, I really don't. You know something? I really don't want to either. Just leave me alone. I've got some things to think about."

Back at the apartment, Mark stands up for his best friend. "Come on, Josh. What the hell are you doing?"

"I don't see any rings. She's not promised to him, you saw that when you came in. As far as I'm concerned, she's fair game."

"You smug little shit! You know Jason's interested in her and you know exactly what you're doing. It's just like he told me."

"What're you talking about?"

"He told me all about you and him before. It's more than the girl thing though, isn't it? It's a big game with you. You can't stand to see him happy. How can you do something like that to your own brother? You really hate him that much?"

"I don't hate him!" He pauses, walking to the window, "I don't know why I do it. I guess it's the challenge. I don't know. I know I don't hate him." Before they can go any further, Danny enters the apartment through the front door.

"Where's Jason?" Mark asks.

"Out there somewhere. Walking," she replies.

She retreats to the spare bedroom, closing the door behind her without saying another word. Anderson exits the apartment to the outside. Josh moves to the spare bedroom door and knocks, the door opening after a short wait.

"What do you want?" Danny asks.

"We need to talk."

"I think we've done enough for one night."

"I don't know why you say that. We haven't done anything wrong. I haven't done anything wrong."

"It's not you. It's all me. I need some time alone to get my thoughts together. After that, we can talk all you want," Danny tells him.

Josh turns away and ventures outside to the balcony. He must tell Mark and Jason what he knows. His movement is halted as he watches a lone car drive past the apartments, lights out, passing Anderson, sliding to a stop where his brother walks alone.

"Hey, Mistah! Got a light?"

"Sorry. Don't smoke," Cade responds, continuing his walk without looking up.

"What the fuck you just say? You call me a nigger? That what I just heard you say?"

452

Cade stops, turning to address the voice from within the car..."S'cuse me? What the hell are you talking about?"

"Let's teach this piece o'white shit some manners. You fuckin' whities come from Dallas thinkin' you own the place."

"Wait a minute. What's going on here? How'd you know I was from Dallas?"

Five inside the car pile out onto the road, Cade preparing to defend himself against his would-be attackers.

The one doing all the talking steps into Cade going for the first blow. Cade surprises him, taking the first shot; rocking the man back into the car. Two grab his arms while the others take shots at his face, blood rushing from his nose after the second fist may have broken it . His is a valiant struggle, almost gaining his freedom at one point, but the five are definitely in control now, picking him off the ground after several additional shots to his stomach and face.

"Your friend in Dallas wants ya to back off. He wants his disks back. Next time, you get tossed in the river with a hole in yer head. I got yer attention now ass-wipe?"

The gang is about to toss his body into the river anyway, when Anderson joins in on the fracas. "I wouldn't do that if I were you!" he yells out, emerging from the shadows of the night.

"Who the fuck are you?" the gang's leader inquires.

"Just a friend...his friend."

"Mistah, you're a little late to help the man now. I suggest you turn around before we do the same to your Oriental ass."

"Don't think so," Anderson replies, pulling an automatic from his back, pointing it at the group and firing one round into the air before drawing down on the apparent leader's temple.

"The next one's aimed at your fuckin' head, asshole. Now lower my friend to the ground, climb back into that piece of junk, and go back to whatever hole you all crawled out of."

"Hey man, no problem. We wasn't gonna really hurt him too bad. We was just told to rough him up a bit. I ain't gettin' shot over this…wasn't paid enough money to get killed."

"What're you talking about? Someone paid you guys to do this?"

"Let's go, boys."

"No wait a minute!" Before Anderson can say more, the five are back in the beat-up Buick and on their way off Mud Island.

Josh watches from the balcony of his apartment, apparently satisfied of the outcome, no plans to offer any help as he re-enters his apartment.

"You OK, man?" Anderson asks his friend who is pushing himself up to a sitting position.

"Yeah, I'll be OK. Goddamn it! I'm getting fucking sick of being everybody's punching bag lately!"

"This was a setup. Those guys were hired by somebody to rough you up."

"I'm not sure it was gonna stop at that."

"Naw, if they'd wanted to kill you, I think you'd be dead." Anderson's glance back toward Josh's apartment signals the beginning of a new suspicion, one he can't afford to share with his friend just now.

"They knew I was from Dallas. How'd they know? This could be your father. We gotta make a move soon," Cade tells his friend.

"It may be too late."

CHAPTER 21

osh exits his apartment, descends the balcony to the lawn in front of the building, and then finds his way down the road toward Anderson and his brother sitting alongside the banks of the river. As he approaches, the two turn to face him. "Guys, we gotta talk...What the hell happened to you?" He acts surprised at Jason's facial cuts and bruises as less than adequate lighting makes it challenging to see Jason's swelling, bruised face. Those conditions continue to exacerbate themselves more readily each passing second.

"What do you mean?" Jason asks.

"What the hell happened?"

"Couple of guys mistook me for a punching bag...seems everybody's having that problem of late."

"You OK?"

"Yeah, I'm OK. Just a little pissed. What do you mean we need to talk...about what?"

"I gave those disks to the FBI and they refuse to do anything with them or the information. I'm sorry, but I guess this whole trip's been a waste of time...for all of us."

"They even look at the damn things?" Anderson asks.

"They say they have. I can't be certain. But if they tell me they have, I have to go with that. Don't have any other choice right now."

"Maybe Jason and I need to talk to 'em. Maybe we need to be on their doorsteps waiting in the morning," Anderson suggests.

"I'm with you, buddy," Jason agrees. "Those guys tonight were some of Ankawa's thugs. We need to get this thing under control before one of us loses our asses, primarily me."

"What're you talking about?" Anderson asks. "How do you know they were with Ankawa?"

"One of 'em told me as much."

"Yeah?" his brother says. "What'd they say to make you think that?"

"Something about his friend in Dallas wanting me to stop what we're doing...give the disks back."

"He mentioned the disks?" Anderson asks.

"Yeah. Think we better get in to see your friends first thing tomorrow, little brother."

"Don't think that's gonna be a wise move at this point. I didn't want to bring this up right now, but I guess now's as good a time as any," Josh answers.

"Bring what up?" Jason asks.

"Ankawa's threatening to press charges against all three of you."

"Yeah? For what?" Anderson asks.

"Theft and blackmail for beginners. He's so damned big and influential; he could put all three of you behind bars for a long time."

"He could never make something like that stick," Jason says. "He can't afford to have this looked at by the courts."

"Not only can he do that, his high-powered lawyers can quite probably see to it Danny is sent to a federal prison. If he's doing what those disks and the three of you imply, he'll probably be able to carry everything out without fear of intervention of any kind."

"Where the hell'd you ever get information like that? How do you know my father's..." He stops himself, pausing after stating what only one had known to this point. "...planning something like that?"

Josh doesn't flinch as though he already knows Anderson is Ankawa's son or he hadn't heard the gaffe, although he had. "You two gotta convince Danny to release the disks back to Ankawa before someone else is killed, or before they initiate the legal proceedings. After that's initiated, I doubt anyone can help any of you."

"This is damned ludicrous!" Jason yells. "I can't believe, after everything we've been through, the beatings, the shit back in Dallas, all the shit the other night. Hell, we were almost killed! I can't believe all that can be swept under the rug like it never happened."

"Believe me, it can, it will, and it probably already has," Mark affirms. "I've seen the man in action. When he wants something bad enough, he can move governments to work on his behalf. Why should the U.S. be any different? No, none of it surprises me."

"Well, I'm gonna leave you two to stew over this. You gonna be all right, big brother?"

"I'm OK. Once I get all this shit behind me, I'll be a whole lot better."

"I gotta get up early tomorrow. I hope you all can make the right decision. I figure you have a couple of days before your world begins caving in on you."

"You didn't answer my question," Mark reminds him.

"What? How did I know what Ankawa's planning? Easy...someone with the government called the local FBI office. One of my friends told me there's an extreme amount of pressure on 'em right now to turn the disks over. Sorry guys, there's not much more I can do now. Its outta my hands at this point."

Josh walks away from the two. Jason thinks to look at his watch...fifteen past midnight. He looks at Mark. "What do you think?"

"Initial thoughts are to give up...give the damn disks back to the man. Hell, I think my father has more far-reaching control on this thing than any of us ever imagined."

"That could be the biggest understatement yet."

"You noticed too."

"Noticed what?"

Mark's about to mention his suspicions about Jason's brother, those suspicions aroused greatly when he never flinched at the mention of Ankawa being his father. "Never mind, we can't give up now. We gotta get those disks back. We're gonna have to do it ourselves. We may need to think about excluding Josh from any further involvement though."

"Why do you say that? I don't think we got a legitimate shot unless he helps us. How you expect to get the disks back?" Jason asks.

"I don't think we can get 'em back without his help. I'd have no idea where to look for the things. I know I don't want to add breaking and entering a federal office to our credentials. We get caught there; we can forget our problems with my father. The shit with him will seem minor."

"Then it's settled. We go on," Jason reaffirms.

The next morning, it's late again before Jason and Mark stir. Jason remembers hearing his brother showering and leaving. It had to be the crack of dawn. Josh wasn't pleased when they told him of their decision last night. But he did tell them he'd support them no matter what.

Josh pulls into the parking lot across from the Crowne Plaza. He walks through the lobby as though looking for someone, arriving at the open-air restaurant on the ground floor, recognizing the person he's looking for. Walking up to the man seated at a table; he extends his hand. The man of obvious Japanese heritage stands to shake his. The two sit...the first thing out of Josh's mouth..."They're not backing off."

Back on Mud Island, Danny is up preparing herself for a midmorning jog. While getting dressed, she thinks through the chain of events that have brought her to this point in time. She finishes lacing the pair of shoes she bought on the shopping spree yesterday. The shopping trip was one of the few times since meeting him she'd been able to actually enjoy Cade's company. God! That flight from Chicago to Dallas seemed like years ago.

Jason is awake, the door closing contributing, as Danny ventures outside to run. He hurriedly throws on a T-shirt and tennis shoes, wearing the shorts he'd worn to bed last night, running out after her.

"Mind if I join you this morning?" he asks.

"What happened to you?" as she readily sees the damage done to his face late last night.

In Dallas, Ankawa meets Carrigan at his residence for brunch. The two sit eating; discussing the normal business of the corporation, a conversation sprinkled intermittently with idle conversation. After brunch, the real conversation begins.

"I've asked you here to tell you of my plans. I am sending Yami to pick up my son and Ms. Wilson. We know where they will be this evening and we have been assured of little interference. We will leave Mr. Cade alone. There is nothing he will be able to do to damage our plans after those two disappear."

"Asao, I think you are making a big mistake. By not dealing with Cade, you send the wrong message to others who may have the same ambitions at some future point."

"No. The decision has been made. My son will be back with me soon, willingly. When he is told of the upcoming birth of his child, he will happily return. I will then convince him my plans are for him and the future of his family."

"Then I must agree with your wishes and give you my total support. I do, however, ask one favor."

"You have only to ask."

"I would like my son to accompany Yami to Memphis. He can provide valuable assistance to him on this important journey."

"I see little need for him to go along. Yami is quite capable."

"Sir...Will Yami be able to carry out your plans to the letter? His emotional involvement with your son might push him to do otherwise." Despite Carrigan's repeated efforts to convince Asao otherwise, Ankawa will not relent. Carrigan is not through yet. Kirk will be on that helicopter one way or the other.

The day has been as pleasant for Jason and Danny as possible, all events progressing quite casually and uneventfully. Knowing more of what is in store for them potentially; Cade cannot find it in himself to tell her of the major setback they may be looking at. He can't until he knows for sure. They enjoy their run together, although Cade's muscle strain from a day ago makes it most difficult to keep pace.

Josh arrives at his apartment around three. The four prepare to leave for a cookout planned in Jason's honor.

Danny has plans to go with Josh in his GT. She realizes she's risking further alienation and quite possibly anger from Jason; however, she has a few things she wants to get straight with Cade's younger brother, including her real feelings for Jason. The two climb into the Mitsubishi and are on their way before Jason and Mark can finish getting ready. Approximately five minutes behind, the two friends finally begin their trip. Jason has convinced Mark to let him drive, on the premise he knows the way. But there are definitely additional motives compounding this move.

Josh has taken the northern route around Memphis. He flips his radar detector on.

"Hope you're not planning anything stupid. I've had enough high-speed driving to last a lifetime."

"Just a precaution. Hate to give any of my buddies a reason to stop me. I'd never live it down."

Jason drives up the ramp in the direction of the north I-240 bypass. He has already flipped the switch on the stealth system,

461

automatically engaging the radar detector. His speed quickly climbs to seventy-five, occasionally pushing eighty. A couple of miles ahead, Danny is about to ask Josh why he told Mark and Jason what he did last night, without discussing it with her. Josh slows to take the Walnut Grove exit. He drives under the overpass, around the cloverleaf, and is soon headed east. He makes it through the first stop light at Baptist Memorial, but has to stop at the next. He accelerates on the green. As he does, Jason slows to take the same Walnut Grove exit off 240, about a half a mile behind. Rounding the curve, heading due east, Josh quickly has the Mitsubishi to sixty-five in the fifty-five mile an hour speed zone through the Shelby Farms park area. His detector begins initiating its warning, but he doesn't slow.

Danny looks at the speedometer. "Don't you think you ought to take it easy?"

"It goes off here all the time. It's just all the signal towers around this area. We're OK."

The Diablo, with Jason at its controls, rounds the same curve heading into the straightaway. He's not sure, but he thinks he can see his brother's sports car a short distance ahead. In seconds, he has the Diablo at eighty-five, closing fast on the Mitsubishi. Josh glances in his rearview mirror, smiling. Unaware of what is about to happen, Danny begins a long lead-in to one of the topics she had planned to discuss. Before she can get many words out of her mouth, the Diablo blows by. "Oh no," she moans.

"All right, big brother!" Josh yells as though exhilarated by his brother's show of competitiveness. "Your ass is mine now!" He tromps the accelerator to the floor, shifting gears as he speeds through each one. In seconds, he has his car to ninety-five, and gaining.

On board the Lamborghini, Mark makes one comment. "I knew you two were a couple of dumb-asses, but now you're really pushing it beyond that."

"Hang on! I'm gonna beat him at something if it's the last thing I do!" Jason continues watching his rearview mirror as the smaller car gains on him, part of the game he's initiated. Almost to Germantown Parkway, the two cars have slowed as they catch a sizeable grouping of much slower moving traffic.

The cars still fly over the bridge spanning Germantown Parkway, Josh able to stay on his brother's tail due to the slower traffic in front of them, as they each maneuver in and out of three lanes provided for the next two or three miles. Jason knows if he can hit a clear straightaway, he'll lose him, his GT no match for the sheer power of the car he is in control of. Approaching a stoplight, both cars must slow. Jason's error in judgment has him blocked from making a swing from the far right to the left. Josh jerks his GT across two lanes speeding through the intersection, almost clipping the tail end of a car running the yellow light, crossing through to the south.

By the time Jason has freed the Diablo from its temporary confinement, the Mitsubishi has disappeared around the corners of what is now down to a winding two-lane road. Passing a small church on the right, a signal tower on the left, the Diablo emerges from the short two-lane stretch, into a straightaway about half a mile long. He can see the taillights of Josh's car disappear as he brakes for curves and slower traffic. For the next mile both will have to slow several times, managing the next and upcoming two-lane section of winding road with hills and sharp-angled turns. Finally opening up to a straightaway, Jason gooses it.

Josh slows his car at the dead-end intersection of Walnut Grove and Raleigh-La Grange, about a quarter of a mile ahead of his brother. His next turn will be a right. Jason completes the curve coming off the new bridge, and approaches the short line of cars stopping and starting at the intersection's three-way stop sign. Pulling in behind the line of cars, Jason sees his brother in the Mitsubishi making his right turn onto Raleigh-La Grange. Quickly glancing in both directions, Cade takes his chance and makes his move.

"You're not gonna...?" Mark begins to ask just before Cade steers the Diablo out and around the line of five to six cars, their drivers all patiently waiting their turn at the stop sign. The car hits the intersection, Cade turning the steering wheel ever so slightly. Quickly under control after taking the sharp turn, he catches his brother. Speeding to catch him, Jason pushes his younger brother from the rear. After an oncoming car passes, he slams the clutch to the floor, pushes the stick into third, and floors the accelerator, pulling to the left. Just about to pass as the next and sharpest curve yet approaches, a dump truck rounds the same curve heading in their direction.

"Look out!" Mark yells.

Jason slams down on the brake pedal hard, quickly maneuvering the car back to its original position.

"You two are absolutely, without any doubt in my mind...freaking crazy!" Danny yells.

"Ooooh, such language," Josh plays with her.

"We got Ankawa on our tails, probably gonna kill all of us, and you two are bound and determined to get the job done before he can! Don't ask me to ride with you again!"

"...Just a little friendly rivalry between brothers," Josh answers, maneuvering his car through the next series of sharp and twisting turns. He glances in his rearview mirror repeatedly to check out his brother's position...still hot on his ass. The cars pass through Mother Nature's natural tunnel, completely tree covered, winding road, hills, looking like foothills of a mountain range.

For the next half to three-quarters of a mile, the two are bumper to bumper...another curve and the road opens up to the expected straightaway, crossing a bridge about a quarter of a mile in length. Both drivers react simultaneously, pulling their cars to the left passing lane. Still bumper to bumper, Josh is clear of the single car they both need to get around. His normal move would be to pull into the right lane, but he doesn't, waiting for his brother's next move, knowing his only chance to win this one now will be to stay at his tail and wait for an opportunity. A car rounds the curve ahead, just feet away from a head-on collision. Josh, holding his position in the left lane as long as possible, yanks it to the right.

Jason, already guessing his brother's actions, holds to the left lane, forcing the oncoming car to the shoulder just before coming onto the bridge, where there will be no shoulder to bail to. Jason takes the curve in the passing lane, pulling in front of the Mitsubishi, cutting his brother off, forcing him to the shoulder, then a road veering off to the right. Josh slams on his brakes, sliding to a complete stop, resting sideways in the middle of the road. He slams his hands to the steering wheel, a smile across his face. "Excellent move, brother!"

Driving into the block-long street leading up to the cove, they see several cars lining the circle of the cove around the contour of the curb. Evidently, there is more to this cookout than originally known, and as they pull into the driveway, they can readily see a few of the guys playing basketball where Jason and his brother used to go one-on-one. Jason parks in a spot left at the end of the driveway. A few seconds behind, his brother and Danny pull up, Danny out, walking briskly toward Jason, "What the hell were you trying to do back there, kill all of us?"

Jason smiles, Josh acknowledges his brother's recent victory. "Great moves back there. You got me this time."

"Chill a little, Danny. You made it here. No one got hurt," Jason tells her. His flippant attitude is enough to set her off on a tyrannical ass chewing, but...Before she can reply, Mr. and Mrs. Cade are outside greeting their sons and their friends. It's approximately five fifteen.

The late afternoon turns to early evening, Mrs. Cade and Danny hitting it off from the beginning, becoming quick friends, allies against the men, if you will. She helps the Cades' mom finish preparing the food in the kitchen, their mom telling stories of their childhood through teens, finding out more about them than she could have imagined possible any other way. While the guys visit with Mr. Cade in front of the tube, a baseball game in progress, now in the middle innings, talk builds of the memories of pickup games on the driveway, who would beat who, and how badly. It was funny how neither's memories of a particular game's outcome matched the other.

During the early stages of the party, several old girlfriends greet Jason with hugs and kisses. These are some of the infamous high school flames, snatched from him by Josh, later dumped by Josh. Most of them ignore his brother's presence, apparently trying to make amends with Jason for what had happened years before. Thoroughly enjoying the attention, he doesn't notice Danny watching from a distance, never saying much, yet very interested in the proceedings.

"What do you think of the 'Boys'?" Mr. Cade asks. "They're gonna win it all this year."

Jason remembers his dad's consistent loyalty to his favorite pro teams, even through the bad years due to many years spent in Dallas when they were much younger. He can also remember him always being there for him as well, throughout the good and the bad. He remembers the years spent living in Dallas, going to baseball, basketball, and football games. He can remember how he hated to go to those games back then. How he wished he could turn back the clock now for do-overs. Those times would be treated differently now if he could go back.

"I don't know, Dad. You really think so? I mean, I know they're winning, but if I were a betting man..."

"That coach's gonna take 'em all the way this year, if that damned owner'll stay out of it. Count on it."

"OK, Dad. I believe you." He knows better than to argue with his dad when he has such strong convictions about something, specially the "Boys."

Josh leaves the room during the conversation between Jason and their dad. By virtue of still living in the area, he hears that stuff on a regular basis, so doesn't feel he needs any replays tonight. Through the front window he has noticed one of his folks' neighbors, Jack Grant, in his driveway. He also works for the sheriff's department and was instrumental in getting Josh his first job in the department. He and Josh have become close friends in the last couple of years.

"Jack!" Josh yells walking across the cove toward the Grants'. "What's going on?"

"Not much. How's the party going?"

"Pretty good, I guess. Think my brother's enjoying it anyway."

"Get a chance, bring him over. I'd like to see him. It's sure been awhile...about twenty years at least. "

"Why don't you and Susan come over and join us. My parents wouldn't mind."

"Uh, no, that's OK. I uh, I've got some errands to run. We're gonna be leaving the house in a few minutes anyway."

"Honey, oh hi, Josh." Grant's wife saunters down the driveway toward the two.

"Hi, Susan, how're you doing?"

"I'm doing real well. Honey, that call you've been waiting on just came in. He says it's important. Sounds like long distance."

"OK. Guess I better get it. See you later, Josh."

Minutes later, Ankawa is still on the phone. "Thank you for confirming their location. You should be receiving your payment soon."

Grant quickly finishes his phone conversation.

Upstairs in the bonus room, Josh completes his call, the phone still on the separate line as it was when the two brothers were teens living at home, thus providing the required privacy for this particular conversation. Retreating downstairs, he finds the group. The food's ready and everyone's filling their plates, then moving to different locations throughout the house, most of the guys planting themselves in front of the television, trying to catch the remainder of the game.

Dinner over, everyone sits; visiting, talking of old times until the next challenge is issued. The two brothers are designated captains and begin the task of choosing up sides for the next pickup game to be held on the driveway for old time's sake. Once outside, the players begin warming up. The painted free-throw lane still faintly remains from earlier years when their dad had painstakingly added it to the driveway. Everyone moves outside initially, which makes the game take on an even more competitive posture. The brothers decide to go one-on-one.

"Boy, that's a big mistake," Jim Cade comments.

"You're right about that," his wife agrees.

"What do you mean?" Danny asks.

"Those two are as competitive as you get. I remember one day when I got a call at the office, they were playing a pickup game with the neighbor kids and their mom was gone to the store. Jason separated his shoulder in a game just like this. Each covered for the other, but I knew the thing had gotten beyond the point it should've. Ouch!" Their dad winces as the first blow is struck on a driving lay-up.

The blow from Josh sends Jason sprawling to the ground. Adding insult to his brother's current position, Josh high-fives his teammates.

"Ooooo." Danny winces, putting her hand to her face not particularly wanting to see the blood suddenly drawn in battle at this point.

A couple of others join in on the fun, pushing and shoving, escalating the aggressive rough play as they fight for the ball. Jason picks himself off the ground and lifts his arm to survey the damage done to his elbow. He has given first blood. Retaliation is not far behind as the brothers' work for position under the basket. The pushing and shoving escalates as Jason pushes off Josh to get to a pass from a teammate. The aggressive move knocks Josh to the pavement. Scrambling, he is able to partially block his brother's three-point attempt. Problem is he also takes him out, landing on top of him as they fall into the neighbor's fence bordering the east side. The war is on! Everyone else eventually backs away, to the side and off the driveway court, deciding to let the brothers go one on one.

Their dad finally feels the necessity to step in, like he would've back when they were children. Placing two fingers in his mouth, he blows as hard as a man his age can, whistling loudly as the game's self-appointed ref. "You two need to calm down before someone really gets hurt." When they continue as though they haven't heard a word, he turns to walk into the house, passing Danny on his way, "I'm not gonna stay out here and watch anymore of this."

"Can't you stop 'em?" Danny asks, almost pleading.

"They're grown men. They can't handle a little competition and keep it within the proper boundaries, I'm gonna let 'em go at each other all night long. Unfortunately, one or both may end up in the hospital before it's done."

Disgusted with the display of aggressiveness and total disregard for each other's physical well-being, Danny follows Mr. Cade inside.

470

The body bashing continues. Josh takes his brother out again on a rebound, turning to do a little trash talking, "Had enough yet, big boy? There's no way you can take me. This is my game. I own your ass on a basketball court."

Jason walks by him to get the ball lying in the grass just off the driveway. As he does, he quickly raises his arm, driving a solid forearm to his brother's face forcing blood from his nose.

"You son of a...Your ass is mine," the younger Cade announces, wiping blood on his shirt.

Josh pushes back and the two have to be pulled apart by the group of guys still watching and enjoying the blood sport. Mark makes an attempt to stop the spectacle, now totally out of control. Suddenly, the answer to everyone's prayers arrives in the form of an approaching storm. The wind begins blowing, gusting, and swirling in and around the trees. Lightning appears to have suddenly and very quickly escalated out of nowhere, but this is an unusual storm. Within seconds, the winds are as strong as any hurricane.

Mark knows immediately this is no storm. Looking to the sky above the cove, he sees the landing lights of a large helicopter. The jet-powered ship is so quiet; only the whirl of its blades cutting through air can be heard and as just experienced by all on the driveway, strong winds generated by its power.

The brothers continue their battle as the rest of the group turns their attention toward the darkness above the cove, venturing toward the street, stopping short of the curb. Soon, Danny and Mr. and Mrs. Cade are outside watching the machine land. Emblazoned on the side, the large corporate logo announces the ship's owner..."Ankawa Corporation."

"Jason!" Mark yells above the wind in the trees.

The two brothers conclude their battle, noticing everyone's gone to the street, why they've gone. Jason yells to his folks..."Call 911!"

All unaware of its meaning are frozen in their spots, awed by the landing of a ship like this one in the middle of their cove, disturbing the events of the evening in this sleepy little Tennessee suburb.

"Dad...Call 911! Now!" Jason yells again.

This time his father hears his command, moving quickly inside the house.

Inside the helicopter, bodies can be seen moving around. The large door on the side facing the Cade's house slides open as the ship lands in the middle of the cove. Two men are immediately outside, brandishing automatic weapons, appearing to be machine guns, or some type of assault rifle.

Josh mutters, "This is not supposed to be happening this way."

Standing beside him, Jason turns toward his brother. "What'd you just say?"

"I can't believe this is happening."

Stepping from the ship to the pavement behind the two men, a familiar and friendly face to Mark anyway, appears. Yami walks up to Mark, extending his hand in friendship. "Your father wishes to see you. He would also like Ms. Wilson to accompany you back to Dallas. He promises no harm."

"What if I refuse?" Mark responds.

"We have orders to do whatever it takes. They'll demolish the neighborhood." As he says it, he motions to the men brandishing arms outside the ship. Practically on cue, the fully loaded escort

RAH-66 drops from the dark sky above, into full view of everyone still standing in awe as though experiencing a wild Fourth of July fireworks show. The second ship is now low enough for all to see the Hellfire's mounted to its undercarriage.

"You do not come willingly, I will have no choice. I will be forced to take you both against your will. If we have to do that, a lot of innocent people, your friends, may be hurt. Come with us now, you have my promise no one will be hurt," Yami concludes, looking around at the many gathered at a distance.

Mark looks at his friend now standing at his side. "I must go with them," he yells above the sound of wind swirling about. "They won't hurt us. Danny!" Mark yells back toward the house. He motions her to join him.

She walks to where he stands with Cade. As she passes him, Jason grabs her arm. "What're you doing? You don't have to go with 'em."

She pulls away. "This has already gone too far. I should've done this a long time ago. I should never have involved you or your family in this."

"Jason, it'll be OK. Yami's promised neither of us will be hurt. I think its best we go back. One person I can trust is Yami."

"If you don't…?" Jason asks.

"We could be jeopardizing the lives of everyone standing here," Mark tells him. "One thing I do know. Yami's word is as good as the friendship you and I enjoy. He has promised Danny will not be harmed in any way."

"I'll go," Danny tells Mark. "Jason, it's best if you back off and stay out of this." As she says that, another body inside the helicopter moves to climb out of the machine, growing tired of the obvious and willful delay. Sensing things are about to unravel, he has pulled his gun, drawing down on the group of three. She recognizes him immediately; the sight of him sending chills throughout her body. She knows immediately she does not want to go along on this trip. He points his gun directly at Mark. "Both of you...Get in the goddamned helicopter! Now!"

Yami turns toward the large man, "Our agreement was for you to stay on board. Everything is off. They will not accompany us back to Dallas."

"Like hell they won't!" Kirk shouts, motioning to the two men with guns. "Get 'em both and put 'em on the ship."

To Yami's surprise, the two obey. He moves to intervene. Gunfire erupts, Carrigan gunning him down before he can make any further move.

Mark rushes to his fallen friend's aid, kneeling at his side. Yami looks up at him. "Don't let them take the girl. Your father..." He dies in his arms. Before Mark can stand, he feels a sharp pain in the back of the head, the blow from behind taking him out. One of the men picks him up, dragging him to the helicopter, two other's load Yami's body onto the cargo area to the rear of the large ship. In the background, sirens grow loud as the locals approach the cove.

Before she can move, another man grabs Danny. She knows there is no way out. She looks at Jason, mouthing the words, "Please, let this go."

At that moment, guns make little difference to him. He runs after Danny and the men forcing his friends' early departures. Josh bolts for his brother, knowing his death may be eminent if he continues. As Jason approaches Danny and the man pulling her into the ship, Kirk takes steady aim, drawing a bead on his forehead. His finger, itching to pull the trigger, nears the point of no return.

Josh catches his brother before he can get to Danny and her attacker. The man whirls around to deal with him, stepping into Kirk's line of fire as the gun discharges; Jason drops to the pavement. The man holding Danny stops momentarily to look around toward the helicopter. Kirk motions to him to board immediately. Josh throws both hands into the air in a gesture of surrender. "Let it go! You got what you wanted!"

Kirk lowers his gun, motioning to the pilot to take it up. Once everyone's on board, the pilot increases blade rotation for immediate takeoff.

Sirens wail, as the locals turn the corner at the end of the cove. Just before their arrival, the large ship rises into the air. In a matter of seconds, both ships are engulfed by darkness, traveling well into the night. As quickly as they have arrived, as quickly as Danny had entered Jason's life mere weeks before, they are all gone.

CHAPTER 22

Paramedics work on Jason; this particular scene becoming a regular thing it seems; reviving him minutes after the locals arrive. Josh is busy explaining his most recent actions to his father and he'll have more explaining to do when his brother's senses are more in line with the present.

"You don't understand, Dad. By taking Jason out in the middle of this mess, I probably saved his life and all the rest of you. I wasn't sure what he was going to try to do, but that woman has his attention in more ways than one. I believe he was about to become one of the most irresponsible dead men on earth tonight and I was afraid his actions might cause several here to make the same extreme sacrifice. You see their firepower? Not only were the men on that thing extremely armed, the other ship was a flying fortress. I had to take him out, otherwise the big man was gonna do it, and hard telling who else in the process."

"You may be right. Guess I didn't think of it that way."

Now standing behind the conversation in progress, a little wobbly from the blow delivered by his brother, Jason's ready to confront him. "I should've known not to come to you for help! ...you working with these guys, asshole?"

"It's not that I didn't want to help. It's just that, the more I become involved, the more I'm beginning to understand the extreme danger this whole thing is placing everybody in. But guess you don't care about anyone else in this thing as long as you get your piece of Wilson! Right? Am I right?"

Jason throws the best punch he can generate on short notice, considering his state of mind and his diminished physical competence at the moment. He connects with a glancing blow as Josh leans away, just not far away enough to miss a connection entirely. On the ground, Jason is quickly on top, his brother not putting up a fight. Friends still gathered around them, pull them apart, their father among them.

"Guys, guys…! Come on. What's this going to solve?" their father tries to intervene. Their mother begins sobbing and then, Jim Cade clutches at his chest, going down quickly. Paramedics still there, they quickly move to his aid, loading him onto a stretcher, before being able to revive him.

He looks up at them, "I'm OK. Haven't had my nitro yet tonight. Should have taken it before now," he says, as he reaches inside his pocket, popping one into his mouth. Things progressing back to normalcy, the paramedics attending him concur, as conditions with their latest patient seem to be quickly rolling back toward the status quo.

"You didn't show the disks to anyone did you?" Jason continues confronting his brother.

"Not true, man. I consulted with a friend of mine from the local FBI branch. He didn't see anything worth pursuing. There wasn't enough information to do anything. You can go to hell! You want the guy's name…I'll give it to you. Be my guest. Call him," Josh says, walking toward his car. "Thanks for the evening, Mom; see you later, Dad." He climbs in and drives down the street, disappearing quickly around the corner.

Local police finish taking statements on the events just completed. They ask Jason not to leave town for a few days, saying they may need additional information soon, but he knows he won't be staying long, can't possibly with this sudden turn of events.

"You guys mind if I spend the night with you?"

"Sure, honey. You can sleep in your old room," his mother tells him.

"You know you're always welcome, son," his father adds.

"I just don't think I can deal with Josh anymore tonight."

"Don't be too hard on him. Otherwise, they would probably be hauling you off to a morgue tonight. Hard telling how many of the rest of us might've been in the same boat," his father reasons.

"Yeah, I know. Josh comes out the hero once again. You're right. I'm sorry. I should be more understanding. I just need to think through what my next move's gonna be and I can't do it at his apartment."

"Son, I think you need to fill us in on what's going on. It's obvious you can't take on someone with the kind of power this Ankawa seems to have. You need to think about backing off whatever it is you've gotten yourself involved in."

"Can't...Besides, don't really want to talk about it anymore tonight. For now, I just need to get rid of this damned headache. I'll be thinking more clearly tomorrow. I'll decide my next course of action then."

The next day Cade is up early. Unable to sleep, he sits on the deck drinking coffee with his dad.

"Want part of the paper?" his father asks.

"Naw. Anything in there worth reading? Anything about last night?"

"Nothing, nothing at all. Guess it was too late to make it."

"Don't buy that. That's the way it's been during this whole ordeal. I'm betting you won't see a thing in the paper about tonight."

"What do you mean?"

"Oh there was a situation back before this whole mess got started. I was beaten up pretty bad. Almost died."

His dad drops the paper in his lap. "What? Why the hell weren't your mom and I told about this?"

"Didn't want either of you involved, much less worrying. Besides, I came out of it OK. But you know, I was told the paramedics about gave up on me. Mark and Danny made them keep working on me. I owe 'em. I owe the both of 'em big. That's why I gotta help them now."

"Guess you've made your decision."

"Yeah, before I went to bed last night."

"What're you gonna do? How you gonna help 'em now?"

"Don't know yet, but I gotta go back to Dallas."

"Anyway, getting back to what we were talking about. There were several incidents that should've made the papers," his dad continues, "but didn't?"

"Right, that's about the gist of it."

"This guy Ankawa...looks like he's got enormous clout. I think I've read a few articles about him," Mr. Cade adds.

"Like you always taught me, you gotta size up the enemy before you try to take them on. I know there's a weakness. I may already know what it is, but I got to figure it out for sure."

"Do me a favor?" his dad asks.

"Sure. If I can."

"Don't tell your mother about any of this. She won't be able to handle it. She's upset enough as it is right now without you stirring her up more. I almost wish I didn't know what I do."

"OK. I'm sorry Dad...didn't want to involve either of you."

"Do me another favor."

"Wait a minute. I'm not sure I can do more than one at a time."

"Well, this one's easy. Ask your brother for some help."

"I don't know, Dad, that won't be as easy as you think...already gotten my family into more than I should have. Frankly, I'm just not sure how far I can trust him anymore. Anyway, think I'll shower. Think I'll take it easy today, get up early and head for Dallas tomorrow."

"How's your head?"

"Still hurts a little. It'll be OK."

While he's in the shower, his father makes a phone call.

"Son, it's your dad. He's doing pretty well actually. No. He's planning on leaving first thing tomorrow. That's why I called. He needs your help. Yeah, I know how stubborn you both can be. You got that from your mother. No, he didn't say that directly... Don't be that way, son. He needs your help and I'm asking you to help him. With all your connections, I know you can. Come out and talk to him. You offer to help, I'm pretty sure he'll accept. No, not in so many words, but he doesn't have anyone to turn to and he certainly can't take all of this on himself. OK, see you later."

Mr. Cade hangs the phone up and turns to see his wife standing behind him. She's worried. How much she heard, he hasn't a clue.

"Honey, it's something they have to do. We gotta be proud of 'em both for wanting to help their friends and get involved. We have to support them, no matter what." Apparently deep in thought right after he says it, the elder Cade's mind process contradicts his actual statements.

The day goes smoothly. About three in the afternoon, Josh pulls into the driveway at his folks' home. He enters, as he always does, without knocking and finds his mom in the kitchen baking. She bakes when she's nervous or upset about something.

"What's going on? How's my favorite lady?" he asks coming up from behind, hugging her and kissing her on the neck. He begins to pull away, but she grabs his arms, holding him there longer than planned.

"You gonna help your brother?"

"What do you know about all this?"

"I know a lot more than anyone thinks, including your father. I love him to death, but he makes me so damned mad sometimes! He's always trying to protect me. When he does, he ends up shutting me out completely."

"He's just trying to take care of you the only way he knows how."

"I know. But I'm sixty-nine years old...almost seventy. I'm also a grown woman. I need to know what my sons are up to. I don't want you two doing anything like I know you two are getting ready to, but I'm proud of the both of you for wanting to help Danny and Mark. I resigned myself a long time ago after you decided to be a deputy there were always gonna be times like this. I knew sometimes you'd have to live with a little danger and excitement in your life; besides, I've always liked Mark. And that young lady; she's someone special, I could tell. Have I ever given you any grief about your chosen profession, or the decisions you've had to make?"

"All the time."

"Well then, there you go."

"Where are they?"

"They went down to the square. Dad thought you ought to join 'em there. He thought it'd be better. You know that bunch your dad always meets down there to play dominos and drink beer with..."

Josh thought a second. "I think I understand." He pauses a moment again. "Guess I'll see you later."

"Your dad and I were both kind of hoping you'd say that." She leans toward him, hugs him, and kisses him on the cheek. "I love you, honey."

"Love you too, Mom."

Josh arrives at the downtown square shortly after that. Nothing much happening as usual, or changed from the picture of the square hanging on his mom and dad's wall in the hallway, except for the year and model of the cars now parked around the square. He walks into the old tavern frequented by many men and women alike, but mostly old-timers. Playing ancient games of chance—poker, dominos...competing with each other the only way their age will now allow, and looking for an excuse to drink a cold one with friends. He sees his dad and brother sitting at a table full of men his father's age, all friends his dad, he, and Jason have known for years. He walks up, grabbing a chair along the way, pushing between the two, playfully nudging both with his elbows. His dad smiles, welcoming him, as do the others around the table. His brother's reaction is slightly delayed, but a smile soon graces his face, before delivering a retaliatory nudge, knocking his brother's ass to the floor.

The three spend the rest of the afternoon together, shooting pool, drinking beer, telling stories from days now well behind all of them. Losing track of time, the Verdin clock standing on the square's northeast corner just across the street, rings loudly, proclaiming the new hour, except the clock on the square has not told the correct time in years, the new hour having passed several minutes ago. The religious hymn it's designed to play in the mid-South town rings out loud and clear, "Rock of Ages." It was loud enough to get Jim Cade's attention, reminding him it is dinner-time, something he had not missed too often in forty-plus years of being married to Betty. "Your mom will be waitin'. We better go. You both know how she gets when you're late for dinner."

As the three walk outside the small pool hall, Jason sees the square and all the trimmings surrounding it in a much different light. The beauty, the quaintness, the serenity expounded by the quiet air and the laid-back visual effects sobers him quickly, and almost completely.

Dinner is great; baked buttermilk chicken, mashed potatoes, saw-mill gravy, home-made biscuits, fresh cob corn...the works. It all brings both boys back to times in their lives much easier and much simpler than now. They say their good-byes around ten and both depart for Josh's apartment. They've decided to leave from there, very early, Josh agreeing to go with his brother, Jason agreeing to let him.

Jack Grant comes out of his house as they pull out of the driveway. Both Jason and Josh wave. He waves back. In his rearview mirror, Jason can see Grant walking across the cove.

"Your boy going home?" Grant asks.

"Yeah. Going back to Dallas in the morning."

"Well, getting late. Guess I better hit it. Gotta be up early in the morning."

"G'night, Jack."

Cade walks into his house, going immediately upstairs to join his wife, but she's not in bed. He can't find her anywhere, until he looks out back on the deck. He hears her crying. Walking up to her, he wraps his arms around her. "I know. I felt the same thing, but we gotta be strong. They're not boys anymore."

"Wasn't tonight wonderful," she tells him. "Just like when they were kids."

"The whole day was great! I had a blast!" the elder Cade replies, his eyes now swelling with tears.

Grant finishes locking up after walking into his house. Instead of going straight to bed, he detours momentarily to the phone in his study. He picks it up and dials long distance...a number in the Dallas, Texas, area.

CADE'S MUD ISLAND APARTMENT
EARLY MORNING

An early morning alarm signals the beginning to the day and the start of their journey, their second in recent days into the impending bowels of deception. Awakening slowly, both feel as though they just went to bed. Dressing quickly, no breakfast, and having spent a few minutes loading but a few things, neither is really ready to depart Memphis, leave its comfort or safety via such extreme distance for what may lie ahead.

The decision was made to take the Diablo back to Dallas because of its progressively apparent customization, its speed capabilities, and because it is simply fun to drive. Outside all that, it just looks good on the road. Prior to sliding into the car, Josh Cade excuses himself momentarily. "I forgot something I think we're probably gonna need."

He unlocks his door and steps back into the deserted apartment to retrieve the object he carefully made sure he left moments ago to provide his much-needed excuse, an immediate justification for privacy. He locks the door to stop any unannounced, chance entry by his brother. Picking up the phone; he dials long distance, a number locked in his memory since this whole thing began, one he'd called many times in the last several weeks, a number also in the Dallas, Texas, area. After six or seven rings, there is finally an answer on the other end.

"It's me, Cade. We're ready to roll. Yeah, I'm bringing the only copy they had. You're absolutely sure the other two haven't been hurt yet? I mean, they are OK? By the way, my brother's coming with me. Naw, there's no other way...didn't have a choice. Tried, but couldn't think of a reason to keep him outta this. He's in too deep emotionally and knows too much already. No, he doesn't know about my involvement, yet. Yeah, I know. I want this thing over as much as you. Yeah, I suppose you're right. We gotta do whatever it takes to end it soon. Look, I'll call as soon as we arrive, when I can get away. OK." Josh places the receiver back on its cradle, about to join his brother waiting impatiently in the car, almost forgetting the item he used as an excuse to come back in and make his call a private one. He retreats momentarily, picks the cellular up in his left hand and stops to look around one more time, realizing he could be seeing this place, his apartment of three years, for the last time...another realization entering his thoughts, one not totally new to him.

OUTSKIRTS OF TOWN
DALLAS, TEXAS
7 HOURS AND 53 MINUTES LATER.

The Diablo, its body molded protectively around the brothers, tops the rise at the southeastern edge of Rockwall, Texas. Their travel and progress to this point has been most uneventful, a great deal unlike Jason's most recent travels in the other direction just days ago...that trip to Memphis seemed like months, years ago. Now his friends are gone and he doesn't know their fate. Before him and his brother lies the two-mile long series of bridges crossing one of the northernmost arms of Ray Hubbard Lake, to the north and east of the huge Dallas-Ft Worth metroplex, and Dallas city proper. In the distance and laid out before them, the skyline juts from earth like a mirage in the middle of a desert. Late afternoon heat continues as temperatures escape the Texas horizon, rising from the pavement before them, creating a rippling, visionary illusionism of that skyline. Still daylight, late afternoon, that sight chills Jason who reaches up to close off the air-conditioning vents in front of him. It hasn't been that long since he left, running for his life. His return, much less pronounced, this entire trip, has him wondering, worrying what might have happened to his friends. For most of the journey, he's maintained an apparition of Danny in his mind, the words she mouthed to him just before her forced boarding of the helicopter running through it as though he'd heard them spoken loud and clear.

He looks over at Josh, sitting next to him in Mark's customized Diablo, as they approach LBJ Expressway and prepare to enter Dallas. Still pissed a little that Josh saw fit to make a game of it, vying with him for her affections, he is his brother and he does care for him, regardless of what happens now. Looking at him again, he knows Josh is the one person he can count on to "watch his back" and step up in any time of need. His brother, now most likely a former deputy with all that's happened, is certainly a little more equipped and trained to handle something like this. For that reason alone, he is very happy his brother has decided to support him in his journey back.

Traveling across LBJ, remnants of rush hour continue. Jason at the wheel this final leg; he heads directly for west Dallas, Ankawa headquarters eventually coming into view. He wonders if Mark and Danny are there. Where's that fuckin' Carrigan? Is he with Danny? Has he...? The memory of what the redneck asshole did to her just a few days ago: the rape! "Fuck!" He yells out, pounding the steering wheel, gripping the seat to the right of his leg. The mere thought there is any possibility Carrigan's even near Danny at this moment makes his blood boil, fear of any future encounter with the big man, the son of Danny's former lover no longer any concern. Regaining some emotional control, he's convinced himself he is looking forward to the next encounter with the redneck.

"Shit! What the hell you doing? You OK?" Josh asks, grabbing the steering wheel to get them off the shoulder, hoping to get his brother back to his immediate senses and to the lane that'll take them where they need to be going. Passing cars blast their horns...unsure what's transpiring inside the sleek black car, much less sure of the driver's next, more immediate intentions.

Saying nothing, almost at full restoration of his inner feelings, to a point of some inner control, Jason steers the car onto an exit ramp about half a mile south of the incident, three-quarters south of the building. He pulls the recently well-traveled sports car into the Anatole's parking lot, up to the canopy covering the unloading and registration area. Seeing the shiny, expensive car coming up the drive, valet workers fight for position, figuring a large tip inevitable. The winner, an aggressive, very attractive young female, beats the others to the driver's side, greeting Jason with a beautiful smile. The door opens and he steps out. Seeing her, forgetting for a fraction of a moment the events bringing him and his brother here in the first place, he immediately surmises she would have won regardless who got to his door first.

"Welcome to the Anatole," the perky blonde greets them.

Jason hands her the keys. "Be careful. She's something special; she's been through a lot." His comments of growing fondness for the inanimate object on wheels a precursor to a potential emotional breakdown, his continuing, deepening involvement "I can see that, sir. No problem."

Bags unloaded and placed on the cart; Jason grabs the one with the money repacked neatly inside. Josh grabs the bag with the weapons; a cache of which has dwindled considerably. As they walk toward the front door, the sound of screeching tires startles both. They do an abrupt three-sixty; Josh quickly reaching inside the bag he carries, groping for a weapon. Seeing it is the valet pulling away in the Diablo; the two take a deep breath, simultaneously grinning and shaking their heads.

She parks away from the building, making sure she's blocked herself and the car from anyone's immediate view. She turns the engine off, but before crawling from inside, she quickly glances around and pulls a set of mini-power tools from her pocket. A small battery-powered saw, the aid of a screwdriver, helps her gain quick and relatively easy access into the passenger-side door panel. She finds the set of wires she's looking for, based on the diagram she's studied, and begins clipping through the exact wires she knows will do the trick. The sound of a second car approaching, she hurriedly completes her task, not slicing completely through the specified wiring, attaching something resembling a miniature plastic explosive. Closing the panel, repairing the small opening, screwing everything back to its original tightness, she quickly sticks the pocket tools back in her pant pocket before exiting the car. The young woman walks to another, climbs in and drives away, leaving in her past the job she'd held for only a couple of days.

Inside, the brothers register under their real names, thinking little of doing so amid meager defiance in the face of those who could be watching for their arrival on the scene. The cheapest thing available without reservations is a six hundred-dollar a night, two-bedroom suite. They decide to take it, as money is no object on this trip. Jason digs into his pocket, pulling out a wad of hundred-dollar bills, peeling off twelve. Handing them to the cashier, he tells them they may need to stay longer, although not sure at the moment. They both know there's plenty more where that came from. It's only fitting the two stay in Dallas at the expense of Ankawa, particularly after all he'd put them through.

"Oh, no problem, sir...If there's anything I can do to make your stay more enjoyable, just let me know," the desk clerk tells him after Jason hands him an extra hundred.

Inside the suite minutes later, the attendant finishes placing the last bag in the front room of their temporary living quarters as Jason peels off another hundred from his quickly dwindling pocket stash and hands it to him.

"Yes, sir! Thank you, sir! If there's anything...anything at all..." his sudden enthusiasm as obvious as the hundred-dollar bill he stuffs in his pocket.

"Yeah, I know. I'll call you. Thanks."

"Don't you think your throwing' those around a little too freely?" Josh asks after the door closes.

"Shit, man, I'm enjoying this. I like spending Ankawa's money. Don't see anything wrong with it. Why should you?"

"Suit yourself."

Josh relaxes on a couch while Jason relieves himself. Coming out of one of the bathrooms, he announces he's going to get a newspaper, not disclosing his intentions fully.

Before he can completely exit, "Why don't you call your friend? I'm sure he'd jump at the chance to earn another hundred. Hell, they're probably all sitting right outside the room... probably do anything you want."

"Yeah, screw you too!" he answers smiling. "Need to stretch my legs, besides; this place holds a few memories, good and bad. Think I'll walk around a little. I'll be back in a few minutes."

While his brother is out of the room, Josh is able to accomplish what he had planned upon arrival, completing a local call. As he waits for it to go through, he continuously eyes the door for any sign of his brother's return. Someone on the other end finally answers.

Jason exits the elevator at lobby level, walking into one of two connected atriums, ceilings appearing to him to be some fifteen, twenty stories from ground level. Funny how he had never noticed any of this before. A combination of the many smells drifting throughout the hotel hits him like the solid punches thrown at him several months ago in his second encounter with the big man. His knees and legs weaken as he approaches the club where he and Danny enjoyed their first drink together, where he was wheeled out on a stretcher almost dead. Doors open, he sticks his head in, the crowd beginning to build with sporadic arrival of the after-five pack. Legs still slightly shaky, his adrenaline streams throughout his body, filling his muscles, his mind, his senses with the frantic, agitated excitement he knew he had to experience once just to get this thing over with...sweat it out of his system.

"Can I help you, sir?" asks the little waitress, slight concern on her face with his ashen appearance becoming more and more pronounced as well as noticeable even within the darkening confines and interior of the club.

"No. No, I'm fine." Jason turns, walking from the club with so many bad memories left behind; memories of the closest thing to death he'd ever experienced. His entire body perspiring profusely, he has to stop to catch his breath, sitting on the edge of a park bench momentarily. As he does, Kirk Carrigan walks through the entrance to the hotel with a couple of his buddies. Jason glances up to see the three of 'em coming his way, his initial thought, to face them all down, confront Carrigan immediately. Then, feelings he had experienced just moments earlier, inside the club, invade his mind and body once more, to the point of severe hyperventilation. He stands quickly, turning to walk in the other direction, fear mounting with each quickening step. Near a point of expelling his last meal, a false attempt to expurgate his system of those feelings and notions of all previous encounters with this man, he almost passes out. Not as willing to confront Carrigan as he thought he would be when he and Josh passed Ankawa's corporate headquarters earlier, Jason battles with as severe an attack of fear and hatred as he has ever felt before.

"Hey! Well how 'bout that shit, fellas, look who's decided to show his fuckin' face, after all we've been through."

The voice, unmistakable...Jason would recognize it anywhere. Cade stops. Turning slowly, he sees Carrigan in the distance, walking toward another man, grabbing his hand and shaking it vigorously. Ashamed of his cowardice at the moment of potential opportunity, the moment of confrontation he thought he was prepared for, Jason can do nothing more than head toward the elevator and his perceived sanctity of refuge.

"We're here...The Anatole...Yeah, it's time to tell him. We'll be there...Pappacito's? Yeah. Eight o'clock sharp...He'll be there too. We'll tell him then, together. I know. No, I don't think we have any choice now. We have to deal with him and his continued involvement; might as well be now. Don't know if he will or not. Guess we'll soon find out."

Josh hears the key as it's inserted in the lock, the door opening. "Gotta go!"

He walks from his bedroom, into the living area. "Feel like some Tex-Mex tonight. What do you say we take a drive to Pappacito's?"

Jason's preoccupation with his most recent "close encounter," he hasn't heard a word his brother's said.

"Man, what happened to you? You look as though you've seen a ghost."

"Huh?"

"What happened?"

"Aw nothing. Just thinking about...What was it you were saying?"

"I said, how 'bout some Mexican...Pappacito's OK? I've been there before and it was great."

Not really in the mood for much of any kind of food, he answers in the positive anyway. "Uh, yeah. Sounds good to me. Who were you talking to?"

"What're you talking about?"

"The phone...You were hanging up when I walked in."

"No one. I thought about calling a friend...decided it might not be the best time to do it. The fewer people know we're here, the better."

"Yeah, my thoughts exactly, at the moment anyway," the second half of his statement trailing off to a low mumble. "When we gonna finalize all our plans? I want to get this thing over, before I lose what little nerve I still have left."

"Soon. We can begin over dinner. After tonight, the plans... everything will be a lot clearer. I promise."

"Can't afford to wait around much longer. Hard telling what Ankawa or Carrigan might do to Danny or Mark," afraid he's beginning to lose his desire for a renewed encounter as well.

"Believe me, they're gonna be OK. I know what I'm talking about. Ankawa can't afford to hurt her and you know he isn't gonna hurt his only son. We got some time, I'm sure of that. With what we may have to do in the next few days, we need to move cautiously. We're not up against a bunch of amateurs."

"Right as usual. OK. I feel a little better, I guess. I got time for a quick shower? Need something to liven me up a little."

Josh looks at his watch. "Yeah, go ahead."

Before his brother can get into the shower, there's a knock at their door. Josh steps to open it, his hand on the handle, about to turn it...but as a thoughtful precaution, he stops his progress to peep through the hole. "Yeah, who is it?"

"Room service, sir."

"Jason, you order room service?" he yells to his naked brother who is just stepping into the shower and can barely hear over the running water.

"No. What is it?"

"No idea," he says, turning toward the door. "Didn't order any room service," he yells back, searching for his gun, eyeing it on the table, several steps away.

The deliveryman looks at the ticket. "It says on the ticket, four-eleven. Must be a gift from someone, sir."

Weapon retrieved, Josh grabs the top of the fully loaded automatic, sliding its chamber back into a cocked position, his right index finger a fraction of an inch from tripping the trigger if needed. "Just leave it outside. I'll slide a couple of dollars under the door." He delivers with the money as promised and the guy follows his orders. After a few seconds, Cade slowly, carefully opens the door to a large fruit basket, chocolates sprinkled around and on top of a bottle of Japanese plum wine lying diagonally across the basket, the tip money still on the floor, untouched. He can see the wine is of a nineteen sixty-four vintage, from the Akuno Vineyards of Japan. Before picking it up, he quickly but carefully glances up and down the hallway, then carries it back inside.

Assured he's made the delivery, the bogus hotel employee discards the tray in a trash bin, and moves quickly toward ground floor, out the front door into a waiting car.

Josh pulls the card off the top of the basket, opening it to read the note.

"Welcome back to Dallas. Your continuing energetic spirit is most admirable. I salute your extended strong will and the unflagging challenge your arrival proclaims. I most assuredly look forward to our next encounter soon, very soon."
Respectfully,
Asao Ankawa.

Josh crumples the card, throwing it in the trash, tossing the basket and its contents in a closet where it will remain out of sight for now. Wondering why Ankawa would have sent that to the room, knowing what he does, and risk exposure of everything to this point. Rethinking an earlier move, he reaches inside the trash can, retrieves the note, smoothing it out before sliding it into his back pocket. His brother comes out of the bathroom a few minutes later, dressed and ready to go.

"What did we get?"

"What do you mean?"

"Where's the room service?"

"Wrong room."

Downstairs they hand the valet a claim ticket. He runs to get the car, no sight of the good-looking blonde. The increasingly familiar sound of screeching tires can be heard from the lot.

Josh climbs behind the wheel this time. Knowing exactly where they're going, he pulls out onto Interstate 35 heading north. Passing Ankawa once again, Jason won't take his eyes off the building until his peripheral vision can no longer function appropriately. He is still trying desperately to conceal his escalating fear by not staring outright. Reaching LBJ Expressway in just a couple of minutes; Josh Cade steers right, exiting I-35 and heading east on the four-lane eastbound side. Both brothers appear externally in as relaxed a state as possible under the circumstances. Josh spends a few moments contemplating the upcoming encounter; how it will be handled and what he will say to his brother, knowing Jason will be disappointed, angry, betrayed, but hoping he'll understand why he is taking this tact. His hand brushes across the pocket holding the disks he is about to hand over to the other side. He's suddenly becoming very uneasy about the whole thing, although he doesn't show it outwardly. This is the right thing to do, to end this thing once and for all, potentially saving several lives.

As they travel LBJ, west to east, fragments of rush hour continue; although in Dallas, there never seems to be a letup on the loops. Heavy traffic forces them to slow occasionally to between forty and forty-five. A car quickly works its way toward them from behind, weaving in and out of traffic, decidedly gaining ground on the Diablo. Tinted windows beyond the legal limit prohibit anyone from seeing inside, especially now, as the other side of dusk gives up its hold on Texas, soon giving way to nightfall. Within seconds, a customized, totally restored '74 Catalina rolls alongside the Cades, the driver's window lowering slowly.

The driver, a young Hispanic male, approximately in his late twenties, motions to Jason to lower his window, which he does, thinking there could be something wrong with the car. The electric window stops momentarily, something apparently wrong with the switch. Cade jiggles it and the window continues in the opening mode.

"What's wrong?"

"Don't know. Haven't had problems with anything on this baby before. Could be a short, especially after all she's been through," Josh answers.

"Know how she feels."

Inside the door panel, electronic impulses jump from the partially cut wiring, intercepting the open wire a fraction of an inch away. The Diablo's continuing movement shakes those wires closer to the point of total separation. Jason thinks nothing more of the window's apparent temporary malfunction. The small piece attached to those wires; set to trigger upon complete separation, waits for the moment to occur like an animate object with a mind of its own.

"Hey, homes. Nice car, man," the kid yells, then smiles, nodding his head.

"Thanks, man," Jason yells back, turning to look at his brother.

"You wanna see what she can do, man? My car's pretty hot," the kid yells back.

Jason looks at Josh, both smile.

"Not tonight, my friend. No offense," Jason replies.

The driver smiles while nodding, glancing to his right. He looks back in the direction of the two brothers.

Another car approaches from the rear, this one a black, late-model sedan. It pulls even with the Catalina, along the right side, the Catalina now acting as a buffer and shield between it and the Diablo. Three other late-model vehicles, on a mission through traffic as well, speed to catch the three already involved in the apparent escalating encounter.

The young man glances to his right once more, then back toward the Cades. He smiles again, nodding his head. Everything happening in this instant suddenly begins to seem powerfully strange. The driver checks to his right one last time.

"What in the world is he doing?" Josh asks.

"Maybe he wants to try to run us," Jason responds smiling.

He looks back at the two brothers approaching the turn they're planning to take to the north, the direction they will need to travel to make their next planned rendezvous. As though knowing the exact route in their plan, the driver must make his next move now.

"Adios mother-fuckerrrrrrrs!" the kid yells.

The window rises on the Catalina, closing completely. The Cades look at each other curiously. "What did he just say?" Josh asks.

Before Jason can turn his head back toward the Catalina; the kid floors his accelerator, pulling ahead quickly, apparently making room for the car to its right. The void to their right exposes the second car two lanes from the Diablo, but merging left quickly into the lane closest to them. At this point, nothing really seems too unusual, but the kid driving the Catalina pulls in front of the Diablo; brake lights indicating an immediate slowdown, although there is no traffic in front of it. As Josh brakes and slows to avoid rear-ending him, the car next to them follows suit, although nothing directly in front impedes its normal speed or progress either.

"What the hell's going on?" Jason asks.

Both sets of eyes focusing on the Catalina, neither pays much attention to the car to their right as Josh is forced to brake again to avoid rear-ending the car. The tinted windows of the sedan drop...front and back. Without warning, gunfire erupts from within, multiple bullets finding their way through the closing window on the passenger side of the Diablo. Josh feels a sharp pain in his arm; wetness following as his own blood soaks his right shirtsleeve. He gropes for his gun, pulling it to return fire, but notices his brother slumped in the seat next to him. His left hand fumbles for the control panel and the right button to push. The passenger-side bulletproof window moves again after the weight of an injured man stopped its progress momentarily, closing just enough to shield his brother from further injury. Bullets from the sedan hit the window, instead of shattering it, leaving only blemishes where the bullets attempt entry. The electric window continues malfunctioning, Josh pushing the button, releasing it, pushing it, releasing; doing that while he steers the car to the shoulder attempting an illegal pass to the left of the Catalina. Inside the right door panel, electronic impulses continue to jump from one wire to the next. Finally Josh is able to shove the window completely closed; the explosive device installed earlier failing to perform its intended function. Unaware something is actually going in their favor at this particular moment; Josh Cade continues his efforts to escape whatever it is they are now involved in.

Josh methodically searches for the right move, flooring the accelerator, shifting in pain as he does with his injured right arm, pushing the Diablo to the shoulder on the left, past the Catalina, away from the sedan, around the curve to the left, heading north on Central Expressway. Before completely escaping the left side of the Catalina, its driver slams the car into the side of the Diablo, that jolt forcing the Cades off road, in the direct path of an oncoming triangle of safety impact-barrels, scraping cement lane barricades to his left. Slamming through those initial orange and white-striped devices designed to warn them of a more serious consequence should they proceed further by stopping them from reaching the solid concrete bridge supports, Cade begins his most recent maneuver. In a split-second, almost completely through the barrels, he's able to steer to the right, clipping the rear of the Catalina. The left side of the Diablo scrapes the concrete support, passing with no room to spare, its powerful V-12 helping the Cades accelerate to a dangerous speed and momentary safety. Slower traffic forces them to the shoulder, passing unwary travelers on this northbound side of the freeway, weaving in and out of the steady evening traffic. The cars in pursuit, now joined by three others, run those in their path to interception and completion of their assigned task, off the road. The Catalina continues its fight to regain its former position at the front of the Diablo, its driver's uncanny anticipation able to match every move almost before Josh makes it, his souped-up V-8 quickly allowing the successful completion of his immediate goal. In front again, the driver continues braking every few seconds as Josh slams into its rear-end several times before shooting to the outside once again, then around it for the open space he'd been looking for.

"You assholes! Jason, you OK?" No answer..."Shit! What the hell's going on? This shit's not supposed to be happening! Fucking Ankawa! What have I gotten us into now," his remorse apparently a bit late for his brother.

Josh frantically searches for the right exit he will need to reach some form of safety. In seconds, he sees the restaurant to the right where the planned rendezvous was to have taken place tonight. Already past it, he realizes he is about to miss the exit and slams the brakes to the floor, beginning a slide sideways across two lanes. As he fights to regain control, he slams his foot down hard on the accelerator, shifting, running through each gear as quickly as his semi-coordinated, slightly impaired reflexes will allow. The pain in his arm increases with each movement, the additional loss of blood pushing him closer to a lethargic state, near passing out.

Outside the restaurant, waiting on the covered patio, Detective Schuler awaits their planned arrival, but has heard the commotion...the screeching tires, horns blaring, gun shots. In a few short moments, he has run from there, to the front of the building to witness the Diablo flying toward the exit, instincts as a police officer kicking in.

One of the cars giving chase; accelerates toward the Diablo; smashing it from the rear, another ramming it from the left side. A third accelerates to the right, those three now in control, directing the Cades to the only possible course left to take, pushing the brothers in the direction with the most potentially damaging outcome. Their subsequent impact forces uncontrolled acceleration as Josh makes one last futile attempt to brake before it's too late, his foot slipping to the accelerator after a sizeable jolt from the rear, sending the car into a temporary construction embankment.

The high-powered engine responds as it was built, delivering acceleration in an untimely instant. The car's inadvertent and forced speed climbs quickly as it hits the embankment. Cade's momentary loss of control, their speed and momentum, lift the heavy Diablo into the air. Josh instantly sees their doom before them just before passing out, flying through the evening air, off the exit ramp, out into the middle of the clover leaf where construction crews have parked a fuel tanker for the night. Any other car might have had a chance of clearing the parked truck, hang time for the Diablo shortened due to the weight of the armor plating. The car slices into the tanker, rupturing its steel casing, the resulting friction and sparks from metal against metal igniting a horrific flash from the pocket of fuel contained inside, that fuel instantly covering the yet uncrumpled sports car while also shooting well into the night air. Their impact creates a tremendous initial explosion, many more following in sub sequential delivery, blowing windows out of nearby businesses, those in a tight perimeter and closest to the explosion. The display of pyrotechnics is an unfortunate outcome of the collision, but an awesome spectacle to those within view.

Schuler is already running down the access road, not taking time to find his car. Almost there, the force of another explosion caused by the breach of a second pocket of fuel within the tanker knocks him off his feet to the ground. He rolls over on his stomach and slowly pushes himself to his knees, wobbly, unable to stand.

Windows in surrounding buildings explode inward, injuring some of the many patrons in other restaurants as glass flies, penetrating clothing and skin. Glasses at the bar and on the tables shatter with the reverberation of shock waves traveling across the grid of surrounding land. Schuler's back to the fiery hell the two brothers are now consumed in, he is about to turn around, when another explosion, followed by a series of smaller ones, erupts. Minutes after, he's finally able to complete his three-sixty and sits on the ground, resting his head in his hands. Blood trickles from his right ear, his closeness during the second explosion, bursting his eardrum, the pain and instant loss of equilibrium keeping him from standing, the severe ringing notwithstanding.

Much of the evening traffic on the north- and southbound sides of the parkway has stopped along the expressway as debris litters the eight-lane road. Those in the immediate area stare in disbelief, no movement being made toward the tanker. Emergency vehicles now en route, sirens grow louder as they approach from all directions; those inside the fire trucks, ambulances, and police cars unsure of the level of catastrophic event they believe must have just taken place. Those involved in the chase have stopped half a mile down the road, surveying their work one last time, only to pull away; assured in their own minds no one could have possibly survived the crash. Black smoke from burning rubber billows high into the night sky, quickly disappearing, blending with the evening's increasing darkness; luminous flames lighting the immediate area surrounding the crash.

As quickly as this latest episode in the Cade's lives began, it is as quickly and most decidedly over.

CHAPTER 23

Unusually cool fall days appear to have little effect on kudzu still clinging for life to those trees and natural southern indigenous growth lining the many streets, back roads, and highways in this mid-South community and area. A successful invasion in progress for decades from the Asian mainland, the plant's ability to overtake its prey, smothering, eliminating any hope of survival, helps it by nature to create a green topiary effect deep into autumn and long after most plant life begins winter hibernation. Statuesque unconstrained monuments of the broadleaf plant across the South pay tribute to its ability to overcome all who oppose its out-of-control spreading. Few in the world have been able to enjoy the success this simple plant displays against all attacks on its mere existence. Unfortunately and unlike the resilient green plant, there are two who have finally succumbed to an attack on their existence, coming home to a final resting place as friends and family mourn their passing in the wake of a recent battle hundreds of miles away. As their young lives have ended, the kudzu continues its unimpeded quest for survival. Trees surrounding the old cemetery on the southeast side of this suburban community are especially beautiful at this time of year, not yet overcome by the kudzu plant's advancement.

Local residents have turned out in numbers today, as evidenced by the long procession following near-matching gray hearses. The slow-moving line of cars in controlled procession, enter the old cemetery through its northern entrance, flanked on either side by aging stone pillars. The solid iron gates are open and swung back against the four-foot, gray native stone wall surrounding the entire cemetery.

The hearses come to a complete stop seconds before any of the vehicles following, just beyond the path most followers will take to reach two freshly dug graves awaiting the plain, yet moderately elegant coffins about to be unloaded. Family cars, three in number, one carrying two teenage boys and their mother, stop just behind them as men climb from each driver's side. Those men step quickly to the back doors, opening them so grieving family members may join their friends for one last tribute to their fallen loved-ones.

Red-eyed from several days of crying, Mrs. Cade is helped from the same car her former daughter-in-law and grandsons have just departed, each step aided by her husband, Jim. They will follow the pallbearers as they carry their sons' remains to a final resting place under a single sprawling magnolia, in a family plot surrounded by healthy azalea bushes, this late in the year devoid of the colorful flowering next spring will surely bring.

A somber, distinctive crowd estimated to be in the area of one hundred, quickly converges on the site where one last eulogy and prayer will be delivered before everyone departs with only memories of their local native sons and longtime mutual residents. Lives shortened by many years; accomplishments of little magnitude in relationship to world events, Jason and Josh Cade may have been on the verge of notoriety brought about by heroic deeds in the act of saving one's country. Accomplishments dramatically limited within the real scope of what used to be two normal lives; there had been little evidence of normalcy the last several weeks.

Already eulogized and remembered by many in a very long ceremony, the young Cades would have been in awe of their own tributes. The ceremony, closed casket, due to the severe nature of their injuries, took nearly an hour...the crowd so large; not everyone could fit into the small Methodist church on the square. The size of the crowd also comes to the aid of two men who are strangers and unknown in this area, standing in the background observing all events taking place. They will leave only after making sure both caskets have been lowered into the ground.

Silence falls over the standing gathering, many settling in behind the gray awning in place primarily for those immediate family members, others closing in from other sides. The minister begins, about to deliver a shorter version of his service at the church, one he most always plans for graveside starting with a short scripture reading. Mrs. Cade sits quietly, her sons only a couple of feet away. She has nearly cried all she can. Now she can only stare through the cool, fall air, envisioning her boys in their youthful past, as her subconscious takes her beyond the tragic reality of the moment. Mr. Cade's stoic expression may hide his true feelings for only a matter of time. Raised like so many men in his time to never show emotion outside the privacy of solitude, he will certainly succumb after these last few days are finally behind him and he can retreat to privacy.

Jason's former wife, Janice, sits with his parents, more emotion displayed than one would expect, considering her and Jason's estrangement of these past few years. His teenage sons, Bobby and Jeff, sit sandwiched between their grandparents, Jeff holding his granddad's hand, Bobby his grandmother's. Anguish of the last few days amply displayed across each face, they will have years ahead to try to make sense of their father's early death. Tears continue their slow progress down Bobby's cheeks, wiping them dry with his coat sleeve. Jeff, the eldest son, holds back for his mother; struggling to remain strong. Dad would have expected him to be a man, show little emotion, he believes. Like his grandfather, he also believes there would be enough time later for that.

This wasn't the kind of reunion Jason had hoped to pull off with his boys, but he hadn't found the time to see them since leaving his job in Chicago. Everything leading up to the current realities had snowballed almost overnight...happened so fast he couldn't have met with them to at least apologize for so many of his past transgressions. As the events leading up to the brothers' deaths had escalated with a horrifying savagery, there had been little time for anything resembling normalcy.

The final prayer ends and the minister shuffles slowly past the family, offering each remaining member seated his sincere condolences while cupping their hands inside his. His gesture of divine comfort and sympathy is gratefully received by the Cades, with many in the crowd falling in behind to offer a clasp of mutual bereavement and continuing friendship. Off in the distance, chimes from the clock on the square hit the melodic "Amazing Grace" as though set and timed to do just that for this moment of concluding grief. Winds pick up slightly, rushing in and around the many still working their way to console the Cade family. Those winds offer a cooling reminder of those wintry days ahead, offering a soothing, yet chilling backdrop of whistling, rushing sound while falling leaves gain ample momentum toward the already liberally covered ground, possibly nature's way of acknowledging her most recent surrender of youth.

Departing their son's gravesides, the elder Cades stop momentarily a few feet away to turn and watch as Jason and Josh's caskets are slowly lowered, one then the other, interred within the good earth, both finally out of sight.

The crowd dispersing shortly after and vacating the cemetery, two men begin pushing dirt on top of the caskets, one with a shovel, the other climbing aboard a tractor front-loader. Working to complete the final burial nearly seven feet below ground level, the two will step up their laborious duty in seconds in preparation for another burial just a couple of hours from now. Two men dressed in suits, the same two in distant observation on the town square, approach.

"Excuse me, we're with the United States Internal Revenue Service," one begins, pulling his wallet from inside his coat, opening it, closing it quickly. The undereducated men are duped into believing what he says is true.

"Yes, suh," Bo answers. "What was it you wanted?"

"Need to see inside those coffins. Need to make sure there's nothin' funny goin' on. Your government has a lot at stake in these situations."

"And, what situation would that be, sir?" Bo's intelligence, seasoned by the many years of hard work and due diligence in providing for his family, slides to the surface.

"We have lot at stake when paying off our government-funded insurance policies. You did know these gentlemen were working for the government?"

"Don' know nothin' 'bout that, sir. We just dig graves for po' folk like these when they die. We don' know nothing about any government policies, or whatever."

"Let me assure you, everything is on the up-and-up here. We just need you to let us view the bodies, make some sort of official identification, then we'll leave you to finish your work."

"Well, uh, I don't know about that, sir. You see, we just bury 'em 'n all. Yuh know, we don' have much else to do with this stuff. I don' know if that'd be proper 'n all."

"Can I help you gentlemen?" Jackson Davis, proprietor of the funeral home in charge of the most recent proceedings, asks as he approaches the small gathering.

"Uh, Mr. Davis, these gentlemens wants to look inside the coffins."

"That true?" Davis asks.

"I know this may be highly irregular, but I do need to see the bodies. I know this is not a request you're probably used to granting, but I do believe Uncle Sam would look kindly on you at tax time should we be allowed this slight impropriety."

"Uh, Mr. Davis...they sez they with the Internal Revenue."

"Is that right?"

"Yes, sir, we are. I showed your friend here a badge. If you need to see it..."

Standing, looking down as though weighing his options, thinking through clearly the man's comments, he says, "Boys, bring 'em back up. Let em look inside. Doesn't matter ta' me who sees 'em. They won't be able to tell much anyway." Looking back at the two government imposters, "I gotta warn you, it's pretty gruesome. I tried working with the bodies, but every time

I lifted a limb, it'd separate from the body, you know, kinda like a well-done turkey at Thanksgiving."

As the first casket rises above ground, Davis breaks the seal, pulling the lid open. A lump of remains, the two assuming a human carcass, can be seen through the specially lined, thick plastic bag used to keep the stench of rotting flesh from penetrating the casket, at least during the service. Upon sight of the body bag, the two look at each other. Once the bag is open, the smell of charred, rotting flesh is more than anyone standing within a hundred-feet can handle.

"Whew! I shore had no idea it's this bad, Mr. Davis," Bo offers.

One quick look at the inside, one of the bogus IRS men quickly removes himself from close proximity, purging his stomach of nearly everything he's eaten previously this day.

The second rises above ground and as Davis moves to open it..."That's OK. I've seen enough. I don't need any more convincing."

"I told you it was pretty bad."

By then, the two men are on their way to the car parked off in the distance.

"Go ahead, boys," Davis tells the two doing all the physical work. "Let 'em back down and cover 'em up. Those poor boys need to be able to rest. Don't think anyone else will be wanting to see inside again anytime soon."

Hours later and after everyone has finally left their home, the silence of the moment seems much more final for Jim and Betty Cade than when their sons had decided to leave the nest to go into the world on their own years ago...and of course it is.

Tomorrow will bring another day. Jim Cade knows that. The reality of all that has happened has not set in at this point. He climbs the stairs to check on his wife, who has finally fallen asleep, with some medical assistance. The sounds of two boys playing a video game off in their father's room, seeing Janice asleep in the other, all pointing to a feeling of self-assurance that no one will be aware of his next act, he retreats back downstairs, grabbing the cellular on his way to the sunroom. The phone he now holds in his hand will be one he'll use privately and exclusively in the future. This phone, designed to restrict monitoring by outside surveillance, a gift from Josh before his final departure that fateful day, will continuously scramble its signal. He walks through the living room, into the sunroom without turning on a single light. Ginger, the family pet, follows, sitting close by. Cade looks at his watch as though checking to see if the time is right for his next action. Instead of making a call, he activates the power and sets the portable on a small table next to the lounge chair he plops his weary torso in. Ginger moves to a standing position beside him, looking for the scratch on the back, "nub rub" as Mrs. Cade calls it, she knows will soon come, always does in these moments with her master. She raises her right leg, landing a paw on his to beg for the affection she's so used to.

"Come on, girl," he tells her, patting his leg. On cue, she jumps up, draping herself across his lap, where he begins stroking her. "You know, don't you, girl? You know something's not right." Glancing up, her panting quickening, Ginger is satisfied just to be close to the one person in her life she knows she can always depend on. "You're a good old girl," he tells his springer, talking to her as he has always done since buying her as a puppy.

He glances over at the cellular again, as if waiting for a call. In actuality he's checking to make sure the power is still on, the small blinking green light affirming that. Waiting several minutes, almost asleep...Cade stares out into the darkness now engulfing his neighborhood and home.

Many more minutes later, the quiet darkness is intruded upon by the sudden ringing of the phone, on time and on cue. Jim Cade takes a deep breath, picks it up, and answers. The number of this phone is known by few.

"Hello? Yeah. It's done. No, she nor anyone else has a clue. I really don't like this one bit. This thing could really get dangerous, but I guess you know that better than anyone. You sure you know what you're doing? OK. Yeah. OK, I gotcha. Be careful. I love you too, son."

Cade closes the flip phone, ending the signal and the call. He turns it off, expecting no other calls tonight, for some time for that matter. He looks through the glass ceiling into the darkened sky. The stars emerge through the darkness of night, in their simple splendor, to a brilliance he has never noticed before. Ginger pushes her cold, wet nose through his hand. She can always sense when there is something wrong. He strokes the hair of the fourteen-year old springer. A tear begins its formation in his right eye, then the left. Though brought up not to show it, his emotional side is about to kick in. When death would have at least brought finality to it all, he can only know there is more yet to come, quite probably a repeat of today's events, the next time possibly a decisive reality. The days' events have brought with them the validity of life, past, present, and future to this sleepy little town, to the doorsteps of the Cade family. Jim Cade looks to the starlit sky again. The last few days have physically and emotionally drained him. He will have little trouble falling asleep tonight.

Sitting in his comfortable chair, before he closes his eyes, he speaks as though visiting with someone in the room. "What the hell have you gone and done this time, Josh? God, I hope you know what you're doing." Ginger nudges his arm. He hugs her like he would a child because at the moment, it's the closest thing to that he could hope for.

EPILOGUE

DALLAS, TEXAS

As mentioned earlier in the book, the Diablo, a gift from Mark's father, was a specially constructed vehicle with armor plating and bulletproof windows. As the Cades have deprived death of two more victims in the latest horrific crash and explosion at the end of the book, they will move forward in their effort to help Danny and Mark against Ankawa, the Carrigans, and others who plan to take the country to the brink of financial collapse. As they find the courage to once again go up against the odds before them, they will most assuredly meet with many dangerous obstacles, and unfortunately, one will be lost. As one man continues his quest to achieve revenge, many more will succumb to the loss of life, hope, and the future.

There are those who are not as they seem, nor owe an allegiance to any side. One will show his true colors at the opportune time and more will be settled once and for all in *Revenge Factor: Final Retribution.*

Made in the USA
Columbia, SC
11 September 2020

19162955R00287